ime seemed suspended as St. Bryce loomed slowly toward her. A shudder of endlessly suppressed desire passed between their bodies and then his long, lean forearms and hands were gathering her near.

His tongue burned the delicate outline of her ear, memorizing it as she shivered, then traced her cheekbone, brow, nose, chin, and finally the silky curve of her throat.

Then his warm, leisurely mouth was at her breast. The sensation was astonishing. Slowly, he explored the sweet bud that seemed to swell with each touch of his tongue, waiting until she was on the brink of sobbing before he finally began to tug and suck on her nipple.

She gasped, unprepared for the storm of sparks that flickered downward to intensify the ache between her thighs. He is cruel! she thought wildly, yet prayed he'd never stop.

She longed for him to press her back into the pillows— now!—and thrust so deeply inside her that her very heart would be jolted....

You, And No Other

CYNTHIA WRIGHT

BALLANTINE BOOKS • NEW YORK

Library of Congress Catalog Card Number: 84-90849

ISBN 0-345-30807-7

Manufactured in the United States of America

First Edition: August 1984

FOR KAY DULEY

*Whose wondrous friendship makes every day
a journey through that low door in the wall....*

*"The king is handsome, dark-complexioned . . .
    and as much at his ease as any gentleman
    of the world . . .
He dresses magnificently. A man of inexhaustible
    endurance,
        he is ever chasing now stags, now women."*

The Venetian envoy to the court
of King François I.   1520

PROLOGUE

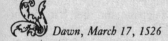 *Dawn, March 17, 1526*

Rippling water reflected a fiery coral sunrise as the boat carrying two young hostage-princes, their governesses, and the escorting officer, Marshal Lautrec, moved toward a floating platform in the middle of the Biadossa River that divided France from Spain. Another craft approached from the Spanish side. It held Lannoy, Viceroy of Naples, and a tense King François I.

Nearly a thousand noblemen, archers, and Swiss Guards waited on the edge of French soil to greet their king, who had been imprisoned in Italy and Spain for more than a year. Thomas Mardouet, seigneur de St. Briac, stood in front, a wry smile flickering at the corners of his mouth; he wondered whether François would be surprised to see him there. The court had always teemed with men jockeying for the powerful positions that were granted at the king's discretion, but St. Briac had never courted François's favor. Since their youth, he had given only friendship and asked the same in return. He'd made the arduous journey to be here today as a friend and because he yearned to view the bold countenance of his dashing king.

Across the Biadossa, François spoke quietly to Lannoy, whom he had learned to trust. "I am filled with melancholy at the prospect of my sons being imprisoned as I have been. They are only children," he told the viceroy.

"The princes will become stronger men as a result of this experience. And as you know, it is most important that you return to rule France. As soon as you fulfill the terms of our emperor's treaty, your sons will be returned to you."

The king nodded, repressing a sigh, and stared across the water. The terms of the treaty, he thought. Impossible! Turning over Burgundy to Charles V, Holy Roman Emperor and King of Spain, was out of the question. For years François and Charles had coveted each other's lands. It had been a delicate game, with the balance shifting back and forth often according to the cards played by a third monarch, Henry VIII of England, who supported François one year and Charles the next. In 1515, France had won the duchy of Milan in the famous battle of Melegano and then had all but lost it during more fighting in 1522. Finally, all-out war began after the treason of Charles of Bourbon, the constable of France. In July 1524, Bourbon led a mixed army into France; he was beaten at Marseilles and driven back into Milan. It was there, during the ill-fated battle of Pavia, that King François I was captured by the emperor's army. For more than a year, he had endured captivity and even a life-threatening illness. Finally, for the sake of France and his own freedom, a desperate François had forfeited his knightly code of honor for the first time in his life by promising to sign a treaty that would give the duchy of Burgundy to Charles. François had no intention of keeping his word, and his sons might have to pay the price.

The oarsmen were drawing alongside the pontoon. Moments later the king was embracing young François, the dauphin, who was eight, and his seven-year-old brother, Henri, duc d'Orleans.

"We are going to Spain to help you, Papa," declared a stoic little François.

"To help France, dear son." Tears filled the king's hazel eyes.

Henri clung to his tall, broad-shouldered father. "I have missed you so very much, Papa."

"As princes of France, you two young men must show your strength and bravery to Spain—and the world," he managed to say. "Look after yourselves. Eat well. I . . . I promise to bring you home very soon."

One son wiped tears away from the king's strong cheeks while the other held fast to his arm. Gently, François disengaged himself. "We must say *adieu*. Be well. I will see you both soon." Sadly, he made the sign of the cross over each small head and then turned toward the boat that would take him to France.

Before long, the crowd on the far shore became visible, and the king's excitement began to replace his melancholy. *France!* His home, his land, his people. It seemed that he had been locked for an eternity in Charles V's tower rooms, but now he was free once more. *King* again! For the moment even the dark hours of the battle of Pavia, which had led to his own capture and the grisly deaths of so many of his brave knights, receded in his memory.

François recognized one figure on land before any other— St. Briac! Taller and more powerfully built than any man around him, St. Briac was a joy to behold. Even his turquoise eyes, gleaming with fond amusement, seemed visible across the water.

François had grown up at the chateau of Amboise, which perched above the wide, lazy Loire River. Not far to the west, the village of St. Briac huddled against the dark forest of Chinon. Thomas, who was just a year older than François, had been sent to Amboise for periods of time as one of the companions to the future king. His parents were independent thinkers; they told Thomas that he need not stay unless the experience was enjoyable and fruitful. The two, along with other friends such as Robert de la Marck, now seigneur de Florange, practiced archery and hunting, played Italian games, wrestled and fought mock battles. Louise de Savoy, François's strong-willed mother, saw to it that her son received an extensive education, and his friends benefited as well.

Thomas had never felt subservient to François. When he was homesick or bored, he'd return to St. Briac and his own family. Now his parents were dead, and he was the lord of the village. His life was his own, and his friendship with the king was only one important aspect of it. François loved and respected St. Briac for his independence and integrity. Their camaraderie transcended boundaries of class and court etiquette.

As the boat drew near the soil of France, the king thought that what he loved best about St. Briac was the fact that he never hovered about like so many leeches at the court yet always turned up when needed. Thomas professed no interest in affairs of state, and many called him lazy for not seizing the opportunities afforded at court. But François was well aware of the many times when St. Briac's clear mind, wit, and strength had helped him through trials, including the death of his dear Leonardo da Vinci at Amboise in 1519, the meeting with Henry VIII on the Field of the Cloth-of-Gold in 1520, and especially the horrendous battle of Pavia, when St. Briac had risked his own life to save his friend from death though unfortunately not from capture.

The crowd on the beach was cheering. Tears welled again in François's eyes as Lannoy helped him from the boat. As his feet touched French soil, joyous faces filled his vision. Finally, after acknowledging a seemingly endless stream of greetings, the king found St. Briac, who was waiting with a patient smile.

"Mon ami!" François hugged his comrade with unashamed affection. "How good it is to see you!"

"I share your sentiments, sire. Welcome home." St. Briac couldn't help wondering whether life in France could ever be the same again for the king. Shortly before François had left for battle, he had received word of the death of his greatest knight, Bayard, the *chevalier sans peur et sans reproche*. Then, soon after his departure from France, Queen Claude had died at age twenty-five, after giving birth to seven children in eight years. Now the king's two oldest sons were bound for imprisonment in Spain. It seemed that life could not go on as before, and yet St. Briac knew that Louise de Savoy was waiting to greet her son only a few miles north in Bayonne, along with his sister, the adoring Marguerite, and undoubtedly the latest royal mistress, Anne d'Heilly.

"It was good of you to journey so far to welcome me," the king said.

"I've missed you." St. Briac's neatly trimmed beard concealed dimples when he smiled, but the warm sparkle in his eyes was unmistakable. "I suppose that I speak for all of France."

"Since you've come this far, won't you consent to spend a few weeks with us? I yearn to ride and hunt and eat and drink and—"

"Cavort?" St. Briac supplied merrily.

"An apt word." The king laughed. "One that embraces all manner of pastimes."

"All of which you certainly deserve to indulge in, sire."

François was in the process of mounting a splendid Turkish horse. "I agree!" Glancing back over one shoulder, he added, "Are you coming?"

"I wouldn't miss it for the world." St. Briac swung onto his black stallion Sebastien and quickly matched the king's pace.

"By the way, Thomas, where is that insolent manservant of yours?"

"Gaspard? I left him in St. Jean de Luz two hours ago, snoring heartily."

"Are you saying that he couldn't be roused to witness the return of his king?"

"Astonishing, isn't it?" St. Briac laughed as they galloped away from the crowd, northward into France. "However, unless you are planning to shackle him and have him thrown into the Conciergerie, I have to say that I did promise we would pause at the auberge to fetch him. I only hope he will be dressed and finished eating by the time we arrive."

"I must say that both of you display excessive insolence in your treatment of your king."

Somehow St. Briac managed to keep a straight face. "I am forced to plead guilty."

After a moment of silence, François said, "I suppose you have heard that I am to be married." His tone was flat.

"To the sister of Charles V? Yes, I'd heard . . . but wasn't certain whether to believe the rumors." He measured the set of the king's profile. "Is there no love at all between you?"

"No, but I hardly know the woman." The corners of his mouth twitched irrepressibly. "I vow, my friend, that I would have pledged to marry the emperor's mule to escape Spain's protective custody."

The two men laughed together. Then, lifting his proud head, François breathed deeply of the crisp early spring breeze and exclaimed, "*Ah, mon Dieu*, how wonderful it is to be home!"

PART I

A chip of chance more than a pound of wit;
*   This maketh me at home to hunt and hawk,*
And in foul weather at my book to sit.
In frost and snow then with my bow to stalk.
*   No man doth mark where I ride or go:*
In lusty leas at liberty I walk.

SIR THOMAS WYATT
(c. 1503–1542)

CHAPTER I

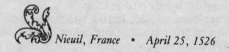

Nieuil, France • *April 25, 1526*

"*Aimée, you must* come home with me now. Maman insists!"

"I will not go unless you give me a reason." Aimée de Fleurance settled herself more comfortably against a birch tree. She was seated in a bed of new grass and moss sprinkled with tiny violets and yellow primroses. Overhead, budding spring leaves made a bright, lacy canopy pierced by delicate shafts of sunlight. The woods were at spring's sweetest peak.

"It's a surprise. I promised not to tell you." Honorine was all of seventeen and much more proper than her eighteen-year-old sister. She pointed her perfect nose skyward.

"In that case, I intend to finish my cheese and wine . . . and my poetry."

"Certainly I will not remain here to soil my gown even one more minute, *ma soeur*." Honorine glanced disdainfully at Aimée's crumpled blue frock. The bodice was more richly colored than the skirt, with close-fitting sleeves that puffed out gently at the shoulders and a low, square neckline that emphasized the girl's lovely bosom. Honorine was still waiting for her own body to assume the charming curves of Aimée's. "It obvious that you have no such considerations for your appearance."

"That's true," Aimée admitted with a grin. "I do save my

9

silks and satins for more formal occasions than afternoons alone in the woods. I apologize if such vulgarity offends you."

"I'll thank you not to ridicule me." Honorine sniffed and tossed her carefully coiffed golden curls. "And I will leave you to your grass and poetry, both of which are far too rustic for my taste."

"If you insist." Smothering a giggle, Aimée added, "Tell Maman that I will be home soon."

Honorine disappeared into the April foliage while Aimée broke off a chunk of crusty bread to go with the cheese she had been eating. Bending her head once again toward the sheaf of poems scattered across her lap, she concentrated on translating the English words into French.

Less than a quarter hour passed, during which the only sounds were her bites of crisp bread. Thus, when other distant noises reached Aimée's ears, she paused to listen. From deep in the woods the crashing and crunching drew nearer, until suddenly a magnificent stag vaulted in a high arc across the clearing. Pieces of parchment and cheese scattered as Aimée scrambled to her feet, alarmed, just in time to avoid being run down by a half dozen barking hounds that thundered through in pursuit of the stag. Horrified to realize that someone meant to kill one of the most splendid creatures in her woods, she didn't hesitate for a moment when the two hunters galloped into the clearing.

"*Monsieurs. Arrêtez!* I beg you to halt."

Somehow the men were able to rein in their horses quickly. The nearer hunter turned in his saddle and bowed from the waist, sweeping off a soft velvet cap with a frothy plume.

"We are at your service, mademoiselle. How may we assist you?"

Aimée had been appraising the situation. Obviously, the men were not of noble birth, since they rode without the usual accompaniment of grooms, huntsmen, and pages. Still, the man who spoke was richly garbed in a doublet and haut-de-chausses of forest green velvet, both slashed to reveal puffs of blue satin. His blue jerkin was trimmed with sable and set with emeralds. The eyes that regarded her with a mixture of concern and impatience were hazel, slanting upward slightly at the corners as though prone to laughter. The man's face was hardly handsome yet arresting all the same. Aimée thought she had never seen a nose quite so large; it grew like a pale zucchini nearly down to the poor fellow's mouth. All the same, he gave off an air of bold confidence and pride.

"Did you understand me, mademoiselle?" the hunter prompted. Glancing over at his companion, he touched a finger to the side of his neatly bearded chin and sighed.

"Yes, m'sieur, I understood. I was just waiting to reply until I was certain the stag was safely away. Pray forgive me for spoiling your sport, but I couldn't allow you to kill him."

The green-garbed hunter stared thunderstruck. "*You* couldn't allow *me?*" He swiveled in his saddle to address the other man. "Did you hear that? Did you? This, this, *girl* couldn't allow *me* to kill a stag!"

"My friend, do not lose sight of your sense of humor. After all, this could have been an ordinary day like any other, but instead we have encountered a lovely wood sprite who bravely protects the creatures in her forest." St. Briac gave François a dazzling grin.

"Hmm." The king glanced back at Aimée. A burnished sunbeam poured over her gleaming ebony curls, thick-lashed green eyes, rosy lips, and softly curving young body. "I see your point, St. Briac. No doubt such a compassionate maiden would offer comfort to disappointed hunters as well?"

Aimée was flooded with relief. "Oh, yes. If only you will not be angry with me."

The men exchanged grins and swung down from their horses. Watching them approach, Aimée experienced a tiny pang of apprehension. The man with the large nose was very tall, with a strong body, yet his companion was even taller and stronger. She regarded him closely and could scarcely believe what she saw. He was astonishingly handsome, with crisply curling chestnut hair and rakish beard, dark turquoise eyes that crinkled with humor, sculpted cheekbones, a slightly aquiline nose, and a whimsical smile that was indecently white against his sun-bronzed face. He wore a simple yet rich doublet and snug breeches of gray velvet set off by ivory linen revealed through the slashings. His hunting boots were of the finest black leather.

Suddenly Aimée realized that she had been staring, and she looked quickly toward the other man. "I will be glad to provide what comfort I can, m'sieur, but I fear that all I have to offer is some wine, bread, and cheese ... and the soft green grass upon which you may relax."

The king stared fixedly at St. Briac. "My friend, I put this situation in your hands," he murmured evenly.

"You are too kind," came the ironic reply. For a long moment he regarded the enchantingly lovely girl, wondering what her game might be. It was obvious that she was of simple birth and surely old enough to have mated, probably married. Was it for gold that she teased them? "I suggest that we sample the wine and cheese and explore this matter further."

Uneasily, Aimée wondered at the man's air of mischief. She watched the two men settle themselves in the grove of birch and then brought them her basket. When she bent over, two pairs of male eyes burned the creamy swell of her bosom, sending a hot flush through Aimée's cheeks. Something was wrong.

"I apologize for the simplicity of these refreshments," she murmured. "I hope you will not object to sharing a cup."

François could barely conceal his distaste. Watching her fill the pewter cup with what was doubtless some sour peasant wine, he thought longingly of the elaborate repast that waited for him at his hunting lodge. St. Briac appeared to be amused by this ridiculous farce, yet the girl hardly seemed on the verge of shedding her dress so that the three of them might frolic together, and he would never resort to rape.

Aimée had reluctantly taken the place indicated by the handsome man and now found herself bracketed by wide shoulders. By the time the food and wine were gone, she was feeling anxious.

"You seem nervous, my sweet," the long-nosed man remarked with what sounded like impatience. "Don't you like men?"

"I—" She swallowed. "I suppose that some men are rather agreeable."

The king raised his eyes to meet St. Briac's over her head. Thomas realized that bolder measures were called for. "What about the king? Surely you have heard that he is delivered from his captivity in Spain? What would you think were your path to cross his?"

At last a topic of conversation that Aimée could sink her teeth into! "I have no use for the king! I understand that his charm is great, but I have seen so many poor, suffering people that I can feel only disdain for a monarch who could waste so much time on extravagant, frivolous pursuits."

St. Briac had gone pale under his tan, and François could only gape. Fearing for the foolish girl's life, St. Briac made a valiant attempt to smooth things over. "Are you not aware that our king has spent many years at war? His courage is legendary. In fact, he was in the thick of battle at Pavia when taken prisoner."

Aimée rolled her eyes and made a gesture of dismissal with one pretty hand. "His involvement of France in these silly wars is proof of our king's childish male vanity. Why does he not concentrate on improving the lot of his own country instead of always attempting to take someone else's away? The poor man's character is obviously hopelessly shallow."

François had begun to cough and then choke, and Aimée turned worried eyes on him. "Oh, dear. Are you all right?"

When he could breathe again, the king said hoarsely, "That will teach me to eat the stale bread of a peasant wench!"

She straightened slim shoulders. "I *beg* your pardon, sir."

St. Briac was torn between amusement at this scene and concern for what it might lead to. Fortunately, he was spared further involvement by the far-off sound of his huntsman's horn. "There's Perot, my friend! Let's be away to join the others."

The king was already rising. "No, no, St. Briac. I insist that you remain and accept all the comfort from this charming wood sprite. I for one have had my fill." He gave them both a terse bow, mounted his horse, and galloped off through the woods.

Cringing, Thomas lay back in the lush grass, closed his eyes, and then let the laughter rise irrepressibly in his chest.

"Your friend's behavior was quite odd," Aimée observed. She reached for the basket and began to replace flask, cup, and linen serviette. "Has he some special regard for the king?"

"You might say that." The smile that curved St. Briac's mouth was at once that of a devil and that of a little boy. Slowly he began to laugh, remembering all that had happened.

Aimée looked on in consternation. Obviously both men had been lost in the woods for too long. Still, she couldn't deny that this tall fellow stirred confusing feelings within her, feelings she had believed to exist only in poetry or in her sister's romantic fantasies. She stared at him. The thick gray velvet of his doublet was tailored so that it stretched taut across his broad shoulders, strong tapering chest, and flat belly as he continued to lie back in the grass, helpless with laughter. Finally he raised one hand to brush tears from his sparkling eyes and sought to regain some composure. Aimée noticed that his fingers were long, clean, and aristocratic yet sun-darkened like those of a peasant who had no use for gloves. Glancing over, she discovered that he was watching her. Curiosity mixed with humor in his gaze.

"I apologize, mademoiselle," St. Briac said softly. "You must think that my friend and I are quite mad."

"The idea has occurred to me," she admitted. When he chuckled again, she couldn't help smiling in response. The man exuded something much more potent than charm. "Why were you laughing so? Don't you share the regard your large-nosed companion feels for our monarch?"

St. Briac stared in delight and then put a hand over his eyes and shook his head in an effort to contain his mirth. "Large-nosed companion?" he echoed. "My little wood sprite, you are wonderful. Tell me your name."

"I am Aimée de Fleurance, m'sieur."

"It is a great pleasure to make your acquaintance, Aimée. To answer your question, I do in truth feel real affection and respect for King François, but at the same time I see the truth in much of what you said." He found himself fascinated by this piquant, outrageous girl and couldn't help wondering whether he had fallen from his horse and was dreaming this entire episode. Never had St. Briac seen eyes as green as the spring leaves or such thick, feathery black lashes. Her eyebrows arched delicately, betraying a quick intelligence, yet the minx was spellbindingly feminine. Flushed cheeks and lips the color of rosebuds bespoke her awareness of him as a man.

Aimée dropped her eyes under St. Briac's open regard. When he lifted her chin with a long finger, she shivered.

"You are very lovely, mademoiselle," he murmured. He was seized with a longing to hold her in his arms in the fragrant grass, to taste her sweet mouth and creamy skin.

Aimée felt chilled and then burningly hot. Frightened, she drew back, her eyes wide as a fawn's. "I, I—" In horror, she realized that the peaks of her breasts were outlined against

her thin bodice and that St. Briac's eyes were on them like
a brand. "I have to be getting home. I'm late as it is."

He realized then that Aimée was completely innocent;
they had misjudged her. Sighing, St. Briac tried to forget the
hard throb in his groin as he helped her rise. She turned
away, unable to meet his gaze, and hastily began to collect
sheets of parchment that now were scattered about the clearing. He joined her and puzzled briefly over the poems, written in English, that covered the pages.

"*Merci*," Aimée whispered, assembling all the papers and
placing them in the rush basket. "Again, I am sorry about
the stag, at least I am sorry if I spoiled the afternoon for
you and your companion. Also, I would appreciate it if you
would convey my regrets to him. I did not realize that my
opinion of our king would upset the poor man so."

St. Briac grinned again, his eyes crinkling, and Aimée
saw the dimples through his trim beard. "Think nothing of
it. My large-nosed friend is oversensitive."

"Well, *adieu*," she said primly, and extended delicate fingers. They were lost in his strong, dark hand.

"Mademoiselle de Fleurance, I beg you to grant me one
favor before you leave." St. Briac's eyes were soft, melting
her resistance. "I never met a wood sprite before today, and
I crave a kiss to remember her by."

She opened her mouth but could summon neither words
nor breath. Gently, the man was drawing her into his embrace. For a moment he held her against his chest, one hand
caressing her small back as if to soothe her fears. Aimée was
conscious of steely muscles against her cheek but also of
warmth. A faint, pleasantly masculine scent assailed her
senses from the velvet doublet, and she heard the slow thump
of his heart.

"Fear not, *miette*," St. Briac whispered, tilting her chin
up so that he could search her wide leaf-green eyes. When
his lips touched her own, Aimée thought wonderingly that
they too were hard yet warm, but then she forgot all else as
his arms tightened, crushing her breasts against him, and his
mouth slanted over hers. A wave of intense sensations broke
over her body. His lips had parted, demanding that she reply,
and she tasted his tongue. She was shocked yet exhilarated.
One of his arms encircled her waist like a steely band, while
his free hand slid into her glossy curls. Through her simple

frock and petticoat she was suddenly aware of something rigid pressing against the unfamiliar ache between her thighs.

A horse whinnied and stamped behind them, followed by an exasperated voice. *"Bon Dieu!* It would seem that I cannot leave you alone for a moment."

Aimée broke free and whirled around to glimpse a small, thin man with white hair. He was clad all in black and sat astride a restless dappled horse. Humiliated and confused, she instantly scrambled across the clearing to snatch up her basket; then she lifted her skirts and disappeared into the woods without a backward glance.

St. Briac stared after her and then pivoted to face his manservant, who had dismounted. "Gaspard, you fat wit! When will you learn some manners? Have you no sense at all?"

"More than you, I think," Gaspard LeFait replied calmly. "The king will have your head for consorting with a treasonous female if you are not at the hunting lodge in time to dress for tonight's festivities."

St. Briac grimaced. "The maiden is no traitor. She didn't realize she spoke to the king himself." Remembering, he tried to repress a smile. "Has the king told everyone what happened?"

"No, he's far too embarrassed. He related the story of your lost stag to the rest of the hunting party, but only I heard of the insults that chit heaped upon his royal head." Gaspard's lips twitched. "When you didn't follow him immediately, he bade me save you from the madwoman."

Swinging into his saddle, St. Briac gave a snort of wry laughter. "More likely he was imagining what he was missing."

Before turning Sèbastien in the direction of the hunting lodge, he glanced once more at the empty clearing and felt a surprising pang of regret.

CHAPTER 2

 *April 25, 1526*

Twilight was gathering swiftly as Aimée ran for home. How long had it been since Honorine had told her she must come immediately? Crossing the meadow, Aimée passed the dovecote and drew near her family's small stone chateau. It had seen better days, when her grandfather was seigneur and before he fell out of favor with Louis XII, but the two machicolated towers with pepperpot roofs that flanked the dwelling were still imposing, and the name of de Fleurance was respected in the village. Now, to support his family, her father raised cattle and collected rents for the current seigneur. He never seemed satisfied with his lot and dreamed of the day when his beautiful daughters would marry noblemen and make them all wealthy.

Breathless, Aimée dashed into the tiny courtyard and threw open the massive oaken door. She came face to face with her mother.

"In the name of heaven, where have you been?" cried Éloise de Fleurance. "I sent Honorine to fetch you hours ago."

"Oh, now, Maman, it hasn't been quite so long. I know I am late, but I beg your indulgence just this once," coaxed Aimée. "You see—"

"Just this once?" Two spots of color appeared on Éloise's

usually pale cheeks. "You are habitually late, almost as if to antagonize your poor father and me. I am at my wits' end trying to deal with you. Our patience is exhausted."

"But if you would just let me explain—"

"And look at you. If I didn't know better, I would swear you were a milkmaid, the daughter of a peasant."

"Maman, please."

"There is not time for me to suffer another of your elaborate excuses. Come along. There is a bath prepared for you, and if it is cold by now, that will serve you right."

Aimée had no choice but to follow Éloise up the darkened stone steps to her bedchamber. She noticed that her mother was clad in her best burgundy satin gown, her faded blond hair arranged carefully in two rolls that curved into a jeweled caul. Diamonds and sapphires sparkled on her fingers.

"Turn around. I will unfasten you. There is not a moment to waste."

Aimée obeyed wordlessly. She was in no hurry to discover what was afoot since it was unlikely to hold any pleasure for her. Moments later, naked, she stepped into the tub of lukewarm water and accepted the bar of violet-scented soap that her mother handed her. It was reserved for special occasions.

"Suzette is helping Honorine dress her hair, but she had laid out your costume on the bed and will be in to speed you along. Wash your hair, child, and scrub your face well. When you are ready, join us in the hall." Éloise sighed again in exasperation. "Your father and I had hoped to share an unhurried conversation with you, but your irresponsible behavior has made that impossible."

When the door closed sharply and Aimée was alone in the cool, firelit chamber, a chill crept down to the pit of her stomach. Already she dreaded the meeting with her parents.

Gilles de Fleurance steeled himself with a long drink of wine when he heard his daughter approach the hall. Éloise was seated beside him in front of the massive stone fireplace, apparently studying one of the two tapestries that flanked it.

"Just remember," she whispered firmly without looking into his eyes, "that you are her father. Aimée must obey you, and you cannot allow her to change your mind a second time."

"Yes, yes, I know. Her situation must be resolved once and for all." Still, he stroked his black beard nervously.

"Papa, Maman, I am ready." She spoke softly from the doorway as though hesitant to cross the threshold.

"Sit with us for a few minutes, *ma fille*," bade her father, indicating the chair across from them. "There is something we would discuss with you, though time is short."

Gilles barely recognized his daughter as she approached. She was a vision in crimson velvet, pearls, and gold, her ebony hair agleam in the firelight. Éloise was right; the girl was a woman in spite of her free-spirited ways. The time had come to tame her.

"You are beautiful, child."

"*Merci*, Papa. It is kind of you to say so, but I do not feel very beautiful with all these heavy skirts and this silly wire shakefold to push them out. Also, my corset pinches."

"Stop complaining, Aimée. You must accept these things with womanly grace," Éloise said sharply. "Have you not realized that the gown is new? Are you not curious?"

Aimée sat down uneasily. "I suppose."

"Armand Rovicette brought it and two others as a gift for you. He just arrived today from Angoulême."

She didn't want to hear what was coming. "Speaking of new people in the area, I met two more today. That's why I was late. I encountered two hunters about to kill a stag, and I stopped them. They forgave my interference and shared the food and wine I had with me."

"Cease your prattling," Éloise scolded. "Your father has something important to tell you, and then we must depart. From now on you must not socialize alone with strangers in the woods."

Gilles de Fleurance shifted in his hard chair. "The fact is, dear child, Armand Rovicette was not dissuaded by your refusal to marry him last year. As you will recall, I agreed reluctantly to give you another year of freedom, but that time and more has passed. We have no choice in the matter. As your *chère maman* points out, it seems that you would be content to languish here, cavorting in the woods indefinitely. No other man more to your taste has offered for you, and so I have accepted Rovicette." The sight of Aimée's eyes, wide with shock and pain, made him avert his own gaze. "You will have a good life in Angoulême. The man has become quite rich as a merchant."

"What your papa is trying to say, Aimée, is that we have fed, clothed, and cared for you long past the time most parents keep their daughters. M'sieur Rovicette has generously offered to . . . help us all in many ways. You must face the fact that your childhood is over." Éloise stood. "Now we must be going. In all the confusion, we have forgotten to tell you the reason for our excursion tonight. King François has graced Nieuil with a visit to his hunting lodge and has graciously invited all of us to join in tonight's festivities." She paused beside the chair to touch her daughter's cold cheek. "Armand Rovicette will also be in attendance. No doubt he will take pleasure in the sight of you looking so beautiful in the gown he chose."

Gilles patted Aimée's curls as he followed his wife to the vestibule. They were calling for Honorine, but Aimée could neither move nor think. She was numb, and she hoped that feeling and comprehension would spare her their bitter return.

François straightened the ruffled fraise of his shirt collar so that it showed evenly above his blue and silver doublet; then he turned to face his friend.

"I'm in an intolerable mood tonight. If you're wise, you won't speak of that peasant wench."

Lounging in a chair near the window, St. Briac drank from his goblet of Burgundy wine and tried not to smile. "Nonsense, sir. You are famous for your high spirits. I cannot believe that you would allow them to be crushed by a simple maiden."

"Maiden? More likely whore! Never, in all my life, have I endured such incredible insolence. Even in Spain I was granted more respect." The king stared out the window over the purple-shaded garden below.

"The girl did not know your true identity. Can you not see the humor in the situation?" St. Briac's turquoise eyes sparkled, although he managed to keep his mouth still.

"Obviously *you* can!" Lifting his silver goblet, François drank deeply. "I suppose you had your way with the wench after I departed. No wonder you show such charity toward her."

"I wish that were the case." St. Briac smiled. "However, I fear that we misjudged the girl, for all her rudely expressed opinions. She was innocent and as skittish as a colt."

The king's mouth hardened. "At this moment I would that I had frightened her into silence and sought my own satisfaction. She deserved worse!"

Knowing that his friend was far too gallant ever to do such a thing, St. Briac held his tongue. "I shall not mention the maid again, sire, except to convey to you her apologies for any offense she might have given."

"You told her?"

"Nay. Without knowing your identity, she expressed regret for speaking hastily. She was sorry for upsetting you, a man she thought to be like any other, who simply held his king in high esteem."

François stroked his carefully groomed beard, considering. "I suggest that we both forget the entire incident. Suddenly I find that I have a monstrous appetite, my friend. Shall we grace the gathering downstairs with our presence?"

St. Briac rose lithely, unaccountably relieved by his king's dismissal of the events in the woods. He only wished he could dismiss Aimée de Fleurance so easily from his own mind.

Chateau de Nieuil was charming, quite small by the king's standards but well suited to the favored limited group with whom he chose to steal away to hunt in these woods which were not far from his birthplace at Angoulême.

The curving white marble stairway swept down to an entry hall two stories high and built of white stone with a black diamond pattern inlaid on the white marble floor. Beeswax candles were all about, and tapers burned in sconces set into the walls. Looking down from the upper level, St. Briac let his gaze rest on the finely garbed guests, the mounted heads of wild boar and stag that lined the entry, the handsomely carved chests and buffets, and the superb paintings carefully selected by François himself. Tantalizing fragrances drifted upward from the rooms below, promising an evening of pleasure.

The king glanced back over one broad shoulder. "Anne waits in the dining hall with my mother and sister. Shall we join them?"

St. Briac nodded, but before he could take a step, the sight of a new group of people entering below made him freeze. He blinked, leaning forward over the carved marble railing. *Impossible!* Obviously the maiden in the woods had

had a stronger effect on him than he'd realized, for the young lady who was handing over her cape to a servant looked exactly like Aimée de Fleurance. Exquisitely beautiful, she wore a gown of crimson velvet with a square neckline cut low to reveal a generous swell of ivory-hued breasts. A golden girdle set with emeralds rode just below her tiny waist, accentuating the curves of her hips, and from it hung a thin gold cordelière and its small attached mirror.

St. Briac's eyes slid down to the maiden's pearl and gold embroidered hem and then back to her face. The candles lent an indistinct haze to her features, but he felt certain that he could not mistake the mouth that now looked strangely sad, her retroussé nose, or especially those luminous springgreen eyes with their thick fringe of black lashes. The girl's hair was shining ebony, as Aimée's had been, but instead of the flowing, rebellious curls he had admired in the woods, St. Briac now viewed locks that were parted carefully and drawn smoothly back into a lovely crispenette of golden net sprinkled with pearls and rubies that brushed her soft shoulders. She wore just one necklace, a single sapphire that dangled daintily from a gold chain.

"*Mon ami*, are you unwell?" François touched St. Briac's arm, and a tiny smile curved his royal mouth. "Perhaps that peasant wench put something in your wine?"

"No, I'm fine." Thomas managed a laugh. "I was just admiring the beauty of one of the ladies below."

"I should have suspected as much." François's own hazel eyes scanned the assembled females.

Realizing what might happen if the king saw Aimée—if she was Aimée—St. Briac hastily pointed out a blond maiden nearer the stairway. Her loveliness was genuine but the sort that aroused no more than indifferent admiration from St. Briac.

"Ah, yes, I see what you mean. I wonder who she may be."

"I suggest, sire, that we descend and find out."

In the dining hall, Aimée looked around in search of the king. "Is he here?" she whispered at length to her mother.

"Not yet, thank heaven. It would have been most impolite of us to arrive after his entrance, and we nearly did, as well you know."

Honorine stood at her other side, looking more elegant

and confident than Aimée could ever hope to be. Both of them had met the king before at this same chateau, but it had been so long ago—before the war with Italy and Charles V—and Aimée's blurred memories of that evening did not include the face of François I.

Armand Rovicette also was not yet present, and so it was with a certain elation that Aimée accompanied her sister to the long table replete with the kind of food they usually only dreamed about. The dining hall was spectacular. Every window told a story in stained glass that Aimée longed to view in the full light of morning. The ceiling and walls were panels of carved oak, but the centerpiece of the room was the magnificent fireplace of white stone that boasted sculptures of a salamander and an ermine, the emblems of François and his late queen, Claude.

"I don't know where to start," Aimée exclaimed, staring at the array of food. She remembered that she had eaten only a few bites of bread and cheese all day. Before her now were arranged platters of roast beef, pheasant, lamb, hazel grouse, ortolans, green oysters, herring, strawberries, melon, pineapple, artichokes, peas, potatoes, spinach, cheeses from Picardy, Brie, Auvergne, whole sugar loaves, sweetmeats, sugared almonds, and several types of wine as well as cider and even beer.

"Try to remember that you are a lady, Aimée," said her mother, "not a pig."

Dish in hand, Aimée glanced up to reply, but her eyes traveled instead to a figure entering the room. "Oh, my! Do you see that man in the doorway with the tremendous nose? He is the same one I met in the woods today. I fear he didn't like me very well after I voiced some less than favorable opinions about King François." Her green eyes twinkled with mischief at the memory.

Éloise had gone white as a ghost, while behind them Gilles began to cough and choke on the oyster he'd been in the midst of swallowing. Alarmed, Aimée thumped on his back with her palm.

"Papa, what is it?"

Finally, breath restored, he lifted wild eyes to meet her confused gaze. "You *idiot*! That 'man with the tremendous nose' *is* King François! Do you have any idea what you have done?"

Aimée was speechless with horror as she tried to absorb

her father's words. Instinctively she pressed one pale hand to her bosom and took a step backward, only to bump into another person. Whirling around, Aimée confronted a wide chest covered with amber velvet and gold; she looked up to meet the dancing turquoise eyes of Thomas Mardouet, seigneur de St. Briac.

CHAPTER 3

 *April 25, 1526*

"*Mademoiselle de Fleurance,* I believe? What a delightful surprise!" exclaimed St. Briac, his tone laced with mockery.

Aimée could only gape, all too aware of her family's presence as the man bowed gracefully and lifted her hand to his lips. The kiss he pressed to her tender palm was insolently sensuous.

Gilles, caught off guard by the sudden appearance of this stranger, asked him, "M'sieur? Are we acquainted?"

St. Briac straightened as Aimée snatched her hand away. He looked down at the man who must be her father. "I am Thomas Mardouet, seigneur de St. Briac."

"Oh!" Collecting his wits, Gilles bowed before the taller man. "It is a great pleasure, monseigneur. Your fine reputation precedes you. I am Gilles de Fleurance. May I also present my wife Éloise and daughter Honorine . . ." His voice trailed off as he realized that somehow Aimée already knew this dashing comrade of the king.

After exchanging amenities with the rest of Aimée's family, St. Briac took pity on her confused father. "No doubt you are wondering about my friendship with your charming Aimée," he said smoothly, enjoying the color that stained her cheeks at his choice of words. "His Majesty and I had

25

the pleasure of encountering her in the woods today, and she was gracious enough to share her basket of food with us."

Gilles gasped. "*Mon Dieu*! Then you know of my daughter's foolish behavior. I am humiliated to learn that my own flesh and blood could insult our noble king." He wrung his hands, thinking that François would surely ruin them all.

St. Briac's smile was merry. "Fear not, M'sieur de Fleurance. The king did not learn Aimée's name. He believes that the girl was a..." He paused to glance in her direction, obviously greatly amused. "...peasant. I'll allow that she did look very different just a few hours ago. I have convinced him that the girl spoke innocently, for of course she was unaware that she was addressing the king, and I believe that his heart has softened. Still, I would advise Mademoiselle de Fleurance not to tempt fate by engaging in another conversation with His Majesty here tonight. My instincts suggest that he will not recognize her if she strives to remain inconspicuous."

"But, but," Gilles sputtered, "I must present my family to the king. What can we—that is—how—"

"If I may offer a suggestion—"

"Oh, yes, monseigneur," Gilles exclaimed anxiously.

"His Majesty's tastes these days run to blondes, if you will pardon my honesty. He has already commented on the loveliness of your daughter Honorine. I would advise you to introduce only her to the king and keep Aimée out of the way. I doubt that he will notice her at all."

Aimée glared at him, seething. How dare he? First the rogue had called her a peasant, and now he implied that her looks were so plain as to render her virtually invisible!

Honorine meanwhile was glowing under this lavish praise and fluttering her eyelashes at the tall, handsome, and charming seigneur de St. Briac. The man must have been created in heaven.

"We do appreciate your kind assistance, monseigneur," Éloise was telling Thomas with a warm smile. "Perhaps you might be generous enough to stand with Aimée while we speak to the king. She might appear conspicuous were we to leave her alone."

St. Briac nearly choked with laughter as he cast a sidelong glance at Aimée's smoldering countenance. "I would not mind in the least, Madame de Fleurance. I am at your service."

To Aimée's consternation, her mother blushed like a maiden before turning to deliver a few parting words to her. "Do try to behave yourself this once, child."

As the trio swept off toward the king, who already was surrounded by an adoring crowd, Aimée clenched her fists and indulged in a barely audible growl.

"What's that I hear?" St. Briac teased lightly. "Next I'll be treated to the sight of smoke escaping your flared nostrils."

"Why don't you close that intemperate mouth of yours for a change?" Momentarily, Aimée was stunned by her own insolence, but she continued giddily. "First you play me for a fool in the woods, letting me go on the way I did about the king, laughing at me while you enjoyed your smug little secret. Then you had the audacity to force your intimate attentions on me even though I had made it clear that I was thoroughly repelled by you! *Not* the behavior of a gentleman, monseigneur!" She paused to catch her breath, further infuriated by St. Briac's obvious delight in her tirade.

"Please, don't stop," he begged with a grin.

"I assure you that I am not finished. As a matter of fact, I could go on all night!"

"I'm not certain I care to hear that much, but I'm willing to give it a try," St. Briac responded, smiling agreeably.

She wanted to shriek with frustration. The man was infuriating. "As if your behavior in the woods today was not bad enough, you have certainly added insult to injury tonight. Obviously, my looks are so repulsive that I am surprised you can bear to look upon me!"

"I try to be charitable about the physical appearances of the people I meet," he murmured humbly. "I have even gone so far as to offer companionship for a fellow afflicted with one of the largest noses in France."

Aimée gritted her teeth. She felt a nearly uncontrollable yearning to smash the nearest pitcher of wine over the head of this complacent jackass. St. Briac meanwhile sensed that the game had gone on long enough.

"Mademoiselle, before you do me physical injury, allow me to beg your pardon. I have only meant to tease, not insult you. In truth, you are such a pleasure to talk to in comparison to most of the ladies of the court with whom I must associate that I fear I've indulged in that delight overmuch."

Once again he had caught her unawares, neatly deflating her anger. "I, well, that does not excuse your rudeness," she replied lamely.

St. Briac's turquoise gaze held Aimée captive as he told her softly, "I am contrite. Can I make amends by insisting that in truth you are the most exquisite lady here tonight?"

Torn between shyness and outrage at what she felt must be a lie, Aimée replied clearly, "I have no need for compliments born of pity, monseigneur."

Tanned fingers lifted her chin. "Mademoiselle, you must believe that pity is one emotion that stirs not at all within me when I am near you."

Aimée saw more in the gleaming depths of his eyes than she could comprehend. She considered the revelation that he was the seigneur de St. Briac, lord of one of the most charming villages in the Loire valley. Only a year ago, en route to visit an aunt in Brittany, she and her family had passed through St. Briac, and Aimée could recall clearly the enchanting chateau perched above the town. She remembered wondering what sort of person might inhabit its artful white towers.

A hand slid around Aimée's waist, rousing her. "Let us call a truce by sharing a plate of food," St. Briac was saying gently. "I will find a bench where we can sit out of François's sight."

She looked up, and her heart melted. What power did the man possess? "I don't know," Aimée murmured doubtfully. "I suspect that you've caused me to lose my appetite." In an effort to repress a smile, she averted her eyes and glimpsed Armand Rovicette across the room. The man was older than her father, with thinning gray hair and a belly that bespoke his affluence. Shuddering inwardly at the thought of enduring his company, Aimée gave St. Briac a vivacious smile. "On second thought, perhaps I *am* ready for some of that delicious food . . . and a truce between us."

After arranging a dish of fruit, asparagus, ortolan, cheese, and chunks of lamb, they took refuge on a cozy bench built into the far corner of the room.

"Ah, *miette*, alone at last."

Aimée nibbled at a plump strawberry and surveyed St. Briac with what she hoped was casual detachment. Again she thought that his looks were impossibly wonderful, his beauty thoroughly masculine. Seated so close to his tall, broad-shouldered body that she could feel the muscles of his thigh through her velvet skirt, Aimée realized that he made two of her. His doublet of amber velvet, slashed to reveal puffs of gold, was rich yet cleanly cut. Matching haut-de-chausses snugly outlined long, hard thighs and met plain gold garters below St. Briac's knees. Most of the men present wore fancy striped hose, but his were a soft, simple brown. Apparently disdaining the current fashion of copious jewelry, he wore a single gold chain around his neck from which hung a square-cut emerald, and only two rings: a gold one engraved with his crest on one hand and a round sapphire on the other. Slowly Aimée raised her eyes to the snowy pleated fraise that emphasized the bronzed strength of St. Briac's neck; then she looked higher to find him staring at her.

"You have a way with a strawberry." His smile was at once lazy and wicked.

Nervously, Aimée licked the juice from her lips and reached for a piece of lamb—safer fare, she hoped. "I am wondering how someone like you came to know our illustrious monarch."

Amused by her implied derision toward both François and himself, St. Briac bit back a grin. "I grew up with the king. I spent large periods of my youth as one of his companions at Amboise. He is like a brother to me."

Aimée arched a delicate brow. "I have heard of you men who profess to love King François better than your own lives. You defer to his every whim, follow him like trained dogs, and reinforce his already considerable vanity with incessant flattery."

Momentarily speechless, St. Briac thought that this was the most outrageous female he had ever met. "Mademoiselle, you wound me. Do you imagine that I am such a man?"

"Well, the conclusion is obvious. If you possessed a character of strength and independence, you would have better things to do than languish here at the beck and call of the king."

He bent his head, pressing long fingers to closed eyes, and his shoulders shook with laughter. At length he looked up and managed to whisper, "Aimée, I find your unguarded tongue a source of great delight, but I must advise you to sheath it in the presence of other members of the court. If you do not, the consequences could be painful for you."

She tossed her head, ebony hair and golden crispenette sparkling in the candlelight.

"As for your observation about the king's *gentilhommes de la chambre*," he went on, "I must agree to some extent. But you see, I am not part of that exclusive group. I do not live to win the favor of François. He is my friend; that is the extent of my obligation to him."

"And I suppose that if he chose to appoint you an admiral or governor or to reward your devotion with a duchy, you would refuse?" Aimée asked with sweet sarcasm.

"I already have, *miette*," came St. Briac's even reply.

She blinked. "Why?"

"You would have to know me better to understand, but suffice it to say that I am satisfied with my life as it is. I have more than enough to occupy my time and talents, such as they are, looking after my chateau and the people of my village. I cannot neglect them." He paused to select a piece of melon. "Also, I don't care to be encumbered by such heavy debts to the king. Our friendship is easier without those complications. He knows that my reasons for sharing his company have nothing to do with his crown."

Watching as St. Briac's even white teeth bit into the melon, Aimée sensed his tension. Obviously this was not a topic of conversation he was fond of, and she wondered why he had not turned her question aside with a laugh and a jest. Unable to help herself, she pressed further, inquiring softly, "Would you have me believe that you do not enjoy your life at court?"

His smile was ironic, even a trifle sad, Aimée thought. "Minimally, mademoiselle. In my opinion there is so much glitter and pageantry that there is little left for life's simpler pleasures. Intricate affairs of state and court intrigue hold no allure for me."

"And what of all the beautiful ladies?"

St. Briac flashed a grin. "I did not say that I disliked all aspects of court life, mademoiselle. Fortunately, my friendship with the king is not the only redeeming feature."

Conscious of an unfamiliar sharp sensation in her breast, Aimée gestured toward a woman who stood across the room beside François. Her own sister appeared to be vying for attention at his other elbow. "Is she one of the redeeming features?"

St. Briac glanced over at Anne de Pisselieu d'Heilly. "For the king, perhaps." He smiled. "Not for me."

Aimée stared wonderingly at François's mistress. She was slim and blue-eyed, with curly blond hair and a proud bearing. Her countenance hinted at intelligence, which was not surprising, but the lady was certainly no more beautiful than many others present, Honorine for example. What made her first in the king's heart?

A moment later Aimée repeated the question aloud.

St. Briac laughed softly. "You may as well ask me the reason why your own parents are married, *miette*. I can assure you that the king is quite human. No doubt the same mixture of intangibles drew him to Anne that causes any of us to fall in love." Regarding a wedge of cheese, his eyes were averted as he added, "Anne d'Heilly may not appeal to any man but François, but then you obviously would not strike his fancy at all. *C'est la vie*. How wise was God to give each of us different tastes and points of view."

Aimée tried to decide whether she had been insulted, but St. Briac's study of the cheese made it impossible to read his eyes. "Hmm. Well, some say that the king loves his mother and sister better than any other woman."

"What a scholar of gossip you are, mademoiselle. Are you acquainted with Louise and Marguerite?"

"No."

"Then pay attention. The king's mother is seated on that bench to the right of her son. Do you see? She is slicing a pear. Marguerite, who is a particular friend of mine, is beside her mother. Observe as she lifts the goblet of wine to her lips. The lady is not only graceful but compassionate and intelligent as well. The devotion François feels for both of them is only the sort that we all strive to attain within a family. Because he has become king and they are proud of him and have missed him this past year, Louise and Marguerite display a love for him that is easy to understand. I understand his for them as well."

Aimée pondered this, piecing together clues from St. Briac's conversation. If it was true that the king respected independence and undemanding affection in his friends, it made sense that he would cherish those qualities in all those close to him. How many could refrain from constantly agreeing with the king and deferring to his ideas? How many cared for him as a person rather than a king? The answer was obviously Louise de Savoy and Marguerite d'Angoulême plus, apparently, Thomas Mardouet, seigneur de St. Briac, and Anne de Pisselieu d'Heilly.

"I see what you mean," Aimée whispered.

St. Briac's eyes rested on the king's mother and sister. Louise, now fifty, was sorely afflicted with gout and had undergone great suffering to travel south to meet her son upon his return from captivity. She was an intelligent, passionate, shrewd, wise woman of action. A widow at age nineteen, she had lavished all her attention on her children, particularly the son she was certain would become king of France one day. Marguerite, two years older than her brother, had adored him from the beginning. Through the years of her first marriage, unhappy and childless, she had found comfort in François, who fairly exuded a zest for life, and in her religion. Now there was talk that the king would have his sister wed Henri de Navarre, who had become a hero after his escape from the castle at Pavia. St. Briac hoped that Marguerite would find the fulfillment she deserved if that marriage took place.

"It was thoughts of Louise and Marguerite that sustained the king during his captivity," he remarked to Aimée. "And, of course, his determination to see France again. Louise, as you probably know, served her son's interests very competently as regent in his absence, and Marguerite displayed enormous courage by journeying to her brother's side in Spain. She arrived at a time when he was near death from a fever caused by an abscess in his head. He swears to me that her prayers were his salvation."

Touched by this story, Aimée gazed at her king with softer eyes. Perhaps she had been hasty in forming her opinion of the man.

"Your sister would appear to be making the most of her evening." St. Briac leaned back with a smile and sipped his wine.

"That is not surprising, knowing Honorine." Indeed, the girl was staring in rapt fascination as François spoke to her. No sooner had Anne d'Heilly turned away to answer a nobleman's friendly greeting than Honorine was laying her hand lightly on the king's forearm. "Wealth and power intoxicate her."

"But not you?"

"Need you ask?" Aimée retorted disdainfully.

St. Briac admired her proud, exquisite profile. All too well he remembered the sweet warmth of the mouth she now set so firmly, the violet essence of her abundant curls that now were tamed by the formal crispinette. Slowly, Aimée turned her head, and wide leaf-green eyes locked with gleaming turquoise ones.

"Excusez-moi."

A shadow darkened the bench. Startled, Aimée gasped and looked up to discover Armand Rovicette regarding her with hot, nervous eyes.

"M'sieur Rovicette." She was swept by a wave of revulsion. "May I present Thomas Mardouet, seigneur de St. Briac."

"My pleasure, monseigneur," Armand muttered coldly. "I am certain that you will forgive my intrusion when I explain that I simply was unable to allow another man to enjoy the considerable pleasure of my fiancée's company for another moment."

CHAPTER 4

 *April 25, 1526*

Aimée watched St. Briac laugh with the woman who leaned toward his cheek. She was beautiful, honey-haired and garbed in sumptuous pink satin. Meanwhile, Aimée endured the proximity of Armand Rovicette. The pungent fumes from his mouth told her that he had imbibed extensively before summoning the nerve to confront her and the seigneur de St. Briac. Now the man prattled on about their wedding and all the possessions he planned to lavish on her afterward. Aimée pretended to be polite, but she was certain of one thing: Their marriage would never take place.

Thomas meanwhile was keeping an eye on Aimée de Fleurance in his own nonchalant manner. It astounded and saddened him to think that a girl of such quality should be forced to marry a man who resembled one of the boars mounted in the entry hall.

"St. Briac," a voice exclaimed beside him. "How good it is to see you."

He turned to discover the face of an old friend. "Teverant! It had been far too long, *mon ami*."

The two men embraced heartily. Georges Teverant barely reached St. Briac's shoulders, but his body was solid and muscular, crowned by a profusion of short brown hair and a face that boasted even features and clear blue eyes.

They had been friends since childhood. Teverant came from Brittany but had visited his grandparents in the village of St. Briac frequently. As a young man he had courted Thomas's younger sister, Nicole, but the romance collapsed when she met, fell in love with, and then married an impoverished Parisian artist. Now twenty-five, Nicole was still radiantly happy with her choice, but the friendship between Teverant and St. Briac endured. They'd met often at court functions after Georges won the position of assistant to Jacques de Beaune, baron de Semblançay, who served as the king's master financier.

The old man was a wizard who had the skill to balance the crown's private and public funds. In 1522, however, Semblançay had managed not only to make an enemy of the king's mother, Louise de Savoy, but also to find himself hounded by questions about his handling of the king's finances. The following year he had been forced into retirement. Teverant had remained to work for the man who held the new post of treasurer of the national savings and who was also an enemy of Semblançay's. Although much time had passed, Louise continued to nurse her grudge against the old baron, particularly after he refused to lend the king more money for his Italian campaign. It already had occurred to St. Briac that Louise might turn her attention once more to the Semblançay affair now that her regency was at an end.

"I trust that all is well with you?" he inquired of Teverant.

"I fear not, my friend; in truth I am frightened. That is why I have come here to be with my king and reassure him of my loyalty. I have heard rumors that Louise de Savoy, unable to take revenge on Semblançay, may have set her sights on me instead."

St. Briac's brows went up. "Indeed?"

"You must think me mad, but I assure you that my reason is intact. After all, it was I who carried out much of Semblançay's dealings. I did so with many doubts at times, but he was so powerful! What was I to say?" His blue eyes wandered toward the king's mother. "Do you see how she watches me and whispers in the ear of that devil Chauvergé?"

St. Briac glanced at Louise, and then his gaze fell on the weasellike countenance of Louis Arçet, chevalier de Chauvergé. "If Chauvergé is encouraging her to plot against anyone, it is more likely me than you, my friend." His voice was cold. The chevalier was one of the few people for whom the affable St. Briac had no use.

Teverant considered mentioning that Chauvergé's sourness toward him might stem from George's long-standing friendship with Thomas, but this seemed tactless. "Everyone knows that Chauvergé only hates you because he is consumed by jealousy. You have attained with ease all the goals he struggles in vain to reach."

"The man is warped." St. Briac shook his head. He knew that Teverant spoke the truth, however. Even in their youth, when Chauvergé had been invited to Amboise out of kindness, the boy would lavish insincere praise on François, only to be rewarded with wary, polite nods from the future king and the galling sight of Thomas effortlessly winning François's honest affection. Now, even though he had attained the position of *gentilhomme de la chambre*, Chauvergé's attempts to gain the respect, friendship, and ear of the king remained ineffective. Bitter frustration fed his grudge against the merrily nonchalant seigneur de St. Briac. "But Georges, putting Chauvergé aside for the moment, I really don't think you should be so alarmed. The king is fair. He won't allow you to be made a scapegoat for Semblançay. You were only doing what you were told. You had no choice."

"There's a bit more to it than that. The king became angry with me four years ago, and I sometimes worry that he's never gotten over it."

"What do you mean?"

"Do you remember when France all but lost Milan in the battle of la Bicoque?"

"Of course. François had set aside 400,000 crowns to pay Swiss mercenary soldiers, but his mother convinced Semblançay to give the money to her instead. When the Swiss didn't arrive and François blamed Semblançay, he told the king what had happened, and Louise felt betrayed. That was the beginning of her grudge against Semblançay, wasn't it?"

"That's correct, but what you don't know is that I acted as the intermediary between Louise and Semblançay! When all the trouble began, I was blamed not only by the king but by his mother as well. She thought I should have persuaded Semblançay not to tell the king where those 400,000 crowns went." Teverant sighed and then strove to sound cheerful. "Let us speak of something more pleasant. How fares your family?"

"Tante Fanchette is just the same." The thought of his strong-willed aunt helped St. Briac replace concern over Teverant's disclosure with a smile. "Her presence at the chateau almost fills the void of our parents for Christophe. He is fourteen now—can you believe it? Before I left last month, he was showing me what he is convinced are the beginnings of his beard."

Georges Teverant laughed, but his blue eyes were soft as he murmured, "And Nicole? She is well?"

"A mother again. This time I have a nephew. Michel has actually sold some paintings, so they are living quite comfortably these days."

"I'm glad."

"And what of you? Is there a lady in your life?"

"Not the sort I'd like, though I admit that the company tonight is giving me ideas. That reminds me. Who was that beautiful maiden you were staring at in the corner?"

St. Briac's eyes belied his light tone. "Just an acquaintance, I assure you. I've neither the time nor the inclination for romance at the moment, and if I did, I would certainly not choose that lady." He paused and couldn't help turning his head to look toward Aimée and the obviously enamoured Rovicette. "Besides, she is betrothed to that swine whom you may observe pressing wet kisses to her hand."

"Oh, well." Teverant stared at the face of his friend and then hastily sought to avert the conversation from the ebony-haired beauty who apparently was affecting him so strongly. "There are many ladies we can pick and choose from, St. Briac. I prefer a fairer type, at any rate." He nodded toward Honorine, who continued to converse brightly with the king. "Now there's a female worthy of our admiration. Fit for a king, one might say."

Aimée had never been so happy to see her mother's face. Éloise had pasted on her best charming smile, and upon reaching the bench, she exclaimed, "What a lovely couple you two make! I do hope you have enjoyed yourself this evening, M'sieur Rovicette."

He had risen and bowed and was kissing her hand with moist lips. "Most assuredly, Madame de Fleurance! I anticipate the time when I may enjoy your daughter's... ah...charms on a permanent basis."

Aimée shuddered, only to be rewarded by a piercing glare from her mother.

"I know that my dear Aimée is equally eager for that day, m'sieur. Now, however, I fear that we must steal her away. My husband is waiting to bid you good evening."

Rovicette made an elaborate parting from his betrothed. When he had crossed the room to approach Gilles, Éloise turned to her and hissed, "Go outside and wait for us while we say good night to the king. Honorine has made a particular impression on him, and I'll not have that ruined if he discovers that *you* are a member of our family."

"Maman, really. You speak as though I were a leper."

"Don't argue with me; just do as I say."

Fuming, Aimée stalked across the salon, through the hall, past servants, and out the front door. A moat curved in a wide shimmering arc around the gardens behind the hunting lodge, but here there was only a sweep of lawn brushing the distant woods. The air was crisp, the sky blue-black and showered with stars. Aimée took deep breaths, blinking back tears as she thought of the terrible tangle of her life.

"*Miette*, could you be so cruel as to leave me without a parting word?"

St. Briac's soft voice startled her so that she jumped a little. Shakily, she turned, one hand against her thudding heart. "Oh! You should have announced your presence, monseigneur."

"I thought I just did." He smiled. Moonlight accentuated the gleam of white teeth against tanned skin.

Aimée was dizzily conscious of strong hands reaching out to steady her shoulders. In that moment reality spun away to be replaced by enchantment. She leaned against St. Briac's broad chest, wishing she could stay there forever, memorizing the texture of his velvet doublet, its warm stirring scent, the slow sound of his breathing, and even the square emerald that chilled her brow.

"We'll not meet again, Aimée," said St. Briac almost ruefully. "The court departs for Blois two days hence."

She tried not to think, luxuriating instead in the sensation of his arms surrounding her back. How safe and fragile she felt within his embrace.

This time, instead of bending down, St. Briac lifted Aimée off the ground, and she welcomed his kiss. Her own arms twined about his neck, her fingers caressing his crisply curling hair. Their mouths joined and tasted with an urgency beyond passion. She yearned to lose herself in him.

When the muffled sound of voices reached their ears, Aimée's feet returned to earth with a jolt. St. Briac had to unlock her clinging arms and hold her away from him.

"Your family," he whispered harshly. The eyes that gazed up at him were as fresh and innocent as new spring leaves. "Aimée, this must be *au revoir* for us." St. Briac's tone had softened along with his heart. "Promise me that you will hold fast to your courage and your principles. You have the spirit to win if you will only fight."

Hot, confused tears filled Aimée's eyes as she caught a glint of turquoise in the shadows before his head bent and his warm lips grazed the back of her hand. In the next instant, St. Briac was melting gracefully into the night and the door to the hunting lodge had opened to reveal her family.

"Au revoir," Aimée whispered to the stars.

It was long past midnight before Aimée was able to shed her velvet gown, free her curls of the golden crispenette, and crawl naked into bed. She could hear Honorine chattering in the passageway with Suzette, the family's serving girl; she was still awake when the door to her chamber swung open.

"Surely you must be far too excited to sleep, dear sister. Don't you want to hear about my conversation with the king?"

"Not particularly. If you'll recall, I have conversed with him myself and found the experience less than inspiring."

Honorine giggled, lit a taper with a bit of candle she held, and perched on the bed. "That is only because you didn't know who he was and were so inexcusably rude to poor François. How could you expect to glimpse his charm under those circumstances? And, oh, Aimée, he is so very charming. One could swoon!"

"He probably swoons himself under the weight of that great nose," she muttered under her breath.

"I heard that! How can you be so disrespectful of the most magnificent king France has ever had? Everyone agrees that he is a hero, that he fought alongside his men at Pavia and displayed astonishing courage during his captivity."

Since her discussion with St. Briac that evening, Aimée had come to agree with much of what her sister was saying, but certainly she would never admit that to Honorine. "Everyone also says that the king is a trifler, my dear, and if I were you, I would not be particularly proud to be added to the long list of those he's trifled with."

Honorine gasped and tossed her blond curls. "You are just jealous because he couldn't bear *your* company. You are pouting because you had to sit in the corner all night while I was being complimented and admired by the king of France!"

An odd pain spread over Aimée's heart as she thought of the man whose company she had found so stimulating for most of the evening, and the pain deepened when she remembered Armand Rovicette, who would be remaining in her life now that St. Briac was disappearing. "I'm tired, Honorine." She pulled the covers higher.

"Then you must stop interrupting, dear sister," Honorine said sweetly. "Lie back, and I will tell you my story."

Aimée hadn't the energy to protest. Eyelids drooping, she endured a detailed account of the king's descriptions of court life, Paris and the Loire valley, and especially the chateaus he had built òr added to.

"He began a new one at Chambord before that nasty war with Charles V, and now he says that he means to devote himself to finishing it. It will be the grandest palace in all the world." Honorine sighed expressively. "In fact, François told me that this will be his last visit to Nieuil for a very long time—possibly forever—because he has exchanged this hunting lodge for more land at Chambord."

"I am surprised that you are not desolate over the prospect of never seeing the king again," Aimée murmured sleepily.

Honorine stood and leaned for a moment against the bed hangings, savoring her next words. "But *ma soeur,* that is the best part. When I said that I dreamed of experiencing life at court and that I longed to view Chambord and his other magnificent chateaus, François winked at me and whispered, 'Well, mademoiselle, perhaps that might be arranged!'"

For all her protestations of fatigue, Aimée discovered that she could not fall asleep once Honorine left her. The day's events crowded her mind in a chaotic swirl. François, St. Briac, Rovicette, her parents, Honorine—one by one their faces and voices haunted her. Ironically, in spite of her frustration over the marriage that was being forced on her, Aimée found herself thinking of St. Briac more than anything else. It bothered her that the feelings he aroused within her, ranging from violent dislike to inexplicable passion, seemed to be beyond her control or understanding. Part of her never wanted to see him again, but another part despaired at that prospect.

The manor house was dark and quiet when Aimée finally thrust back the covers and got out of bed. She lit a fresh candle in the embers of her fireplace, donned a soft shift, and wandered restlessly down to the great hall. She shifted from chair to window, unaware of the passage of time. The arranged wedding to Armand Rovicette was not something Aimée cared to think about, yet it was impossible not to. Was it possible that she might learn to accept an existence as his wife, share his bed, bear his children, and live with him until death?

Swept by chills and nausea, Aimée tried to redirect her thoughts to the light banter she had exchanged with St. Briac, but the gloom would not be dispelled. Recalling the seigneur's parting words of encouragement, she began to weep. "Fight," he had said, but how? All the power belonged to her parents, and it was obvious that Éloise would never allow Gilles to be swayed by any plea his daughter might make.

Dawn was breaking, gray and drizzly in contrast to the previous day, when Aimée sank down in a chair padded with dark red leather. "Dear Lord," she sobbed, "I beg you to show me some escape from my predicament. Do I not deserve a life of happiness and love?"

It was only moments later that a quiet knock at the door roused her from her misery. Not even the servants were astir yet, and so she crossed the stone hall and opened the door. There stood a page, richly garbed in green satin.

"I've a message for Mademoiselle de Fleurance."

"I am she," Aimée murmured dazedly.

She had just begun to break the seal when the boy added, "It's from King François. He asks you to reply immediately."

The fog cleared from Aimée's brain as she realized that the note was meant for Honorine, not her. Yet instinct caused her to smile at the page and open the sheet of parchment.

Your wish to see Chambord is granted, if you will be generous enough to grace my court with your lovely presence. I apologize for not asking you, and your parents, in person, but I beg you to understand that time is short. We leave for Blois tomorrow morning, little more than one day from now, and I would have you with us. You shall want for nothing in your future life; neither shall your family. I beg you to be kind to your king. I shall be desolate if I cannot look upon you, a perfect rose among the simpler flowers of my court ladies.

F.

Aimée's thoughts turned fleetingly to her sister, who seemed to possess every skill necessary to succeed in the world they inhabited while Aimée herself was invariably out of place and out of step. Was this God's answer to her prayer?

She looked up at the page and gave him a dazzling grin. "You may tell the king that Mademoiselle de Fleurance accepts his invitation with great pleasure."

"I'll be back to fetch you tomorrow at this same time, mademoiselle. You can bring everything you own if you care to. The court does not travel light."

After the page bade her good day and Aimée closed the door, a storm of doubts assailed her. What about the king's contempt for her? What about Honorine? Quickly she convinced herself that somehow she could manage to avoid François long enough to make good her escape. And once he realized what had happened, it was likely that he would send for Honorine after all. They would both win in the end.

And what of her parents? She brushed away her feelings of guilt; her mother had been cruel to force her, and wasn't their main objective to get her out of the house and thrust her into adulthood? They would have their wish sooner than any of them had anticipated.

Suddenly Aimée began to yawn. She climbed the stone stairway just as the servants began to open doors below. Dropping her shift on the floor, she snuggled back under the covers. But before falling into a deep, peaceful sleep, one last thought made her smile mischievously.

Thomas Mardouet, seigneur de St. Briac, had not seen the last of her after all.

CHAPTER 5

 *April 27, 1526*

In the hours before she departed her family home, Aimée was too worried about what might go wrong to spare a thought for later problems. She became convinced that someone in the manor would awaken and discover her before she could leave with the page. During her few hours of fitful sleep Aimée dreamed that François himself had arrived to fetch his beautiful new mistress; a nightmare ensued as he woke everyone, raging over the trick a peasant wench was trying to play on him.

In the end, though, all went smoothly. Aimée and her two trunks of possessions—including the gowns from Armand Rovicette, which she had packed with a grin—departed with the young page while the entire household slept.

Aimée was aware of the size of the court that traveled with the king, having witnessed his entry into Lyons in July 1515, just before his first, more successful invasion of Italy. She had been only eight at the time, but her memories of that occasion were still vivid. François's approach had been greeted by a ship towed across the Saône by a white stag, a reminder of the legend of King Clovis, who had learned from a stag of a ford by which he might overtake his enemies.

The gateway to Lyons was decorated with a salamander and a tree of Jesse. The processional route had been decorated with the king's colors, and along the way girls were perched on columns, each holding a letter of his name. Best of all, Aimée remembered the many *tableaux vivants* that had been performed by leading citizens. In her favorite, François had defended the peace against the duke of Milan and the Swiss bear, but Honorine preferred the one that showed him as Hercules gathering fruit in the garden of the Hesperides. The high point of the day, aside from their glimpse of the proud young king, had been the performance of a mechanical lion designed by Leonardo da Vinci for his friend François.

What Aimée remembered now, though, was the feeling that one could become lost easily in such a court. Thousands of people and thousands more horses traveled with the king, apart from the enormous baggage train that carried furniture, tapestries, and all sorts of precious ornamental objects. The ladies of the court traveled together in a procession of coaches. Aimée found herself being handed into one of these by the young page. There was no sign yet from the hunting lodge of either the king or St. Briac, and she settled back against the leather upholstery with a relieved sigh.

No sooner was Aimée's mind at ease, however, than the boy was opening the door and announcing, "Someone here to see you, mademoiselle, from your home."

She sat up with a gasp, her heart pounding so that she thought it might burst. She was certain of doom until Suzette's familiar face appeared in the rectangular opening.

"Suzette, what are you doing here?"

"Only my duty, mam'selle. You could not go to the court without a proper servant." The girl giggled then, her rosy cheeks and bouncing dark curls aglow in the sunrise.

"Did you say that you wished to be free of my family?" Aimée asked sarcastically.

Suzette put her head farther into the coach. "That's part of it, but to be honest, I've grown quite fond of one of His Majesty's squires."

"You'll be faithful to me through all of this?"

"Did I make a sound when I heard you leave before dawn?"

"I appreciate that, Suzette, but I do believe your motives were partly selfish. You really must give me your word."

"You have it, mademoiselle. I've always loved you best and hoped that you'd find a better place in life. I'll do whatever I can to help you."

Aimée laughed. "*Merci*! And in return, I shall help you, within reason."

"Can I ride with you then?" Receiving a nod from her mistress, Suzette climbed in and took the opposite seat. "You know, mam'selle, you're quite a sight. I almost didn't recognize you!"

Aimée wore a headdress belonging to her mother. Gable-hooded, with long lappets folded back from her cheeks, it concealed her black hair completely. Her gown was a stylish rose taffeta, but it too was nearly concealed by a voluminous dark blue cloak. "I couldn't take a chance on anyone knowing that the king's newest lady is supposed to be blond," she murmured absently. She drew the window curtain back a bit to observe the busy crowd readying the court train for departure.

"Suzette, was everyone still asleep when you left?"

"*Oui*. Don't fret. Even if they are awake now, they'll never guess that you've run off. Just as likely, you'd be out for an early stroll in the woods."

"What if someone discovers that all my things are gone? Your absence is another problem. When my mother finds both of us gone, she may suspect—"

"Suspect something perhaps, but not that you would escape to the French court. It does not sound like an adventure to which you would be suited, mam'selle. Your sister, perhaps."

Aimée scarcely heard her. Her eyes were fixed anxiously on the open door to the hunting lodge as she scanned each person who came out. Most of the court, she knew, had found lodgings in the village or with noble families in the area. Only those closest to the king had been assigned one of the few chambers within the chateau itself. Now she watched Marguerite d'Angoulême emerge, holding the arm of her slow-moving mother. Louise paused en route to their sumptuous coach to greet a man with a weasel's face whom Aimée recognized from the night before. They whispered; she nodded and then smiled as he bent to kiss her hand.

A moment later Aimée's breath caught at the sight of St. Briac. Nearly tall and broad enough to fill the great door, he wore his sage-green doublet, tan breeches, and boots with casual grace. Even from a distance Aimée imagined that she could see his eyes twinkle in the early morning sunshine as he turned back to speak to the manservant who had interrupted them in the woods. The little man shook a reproving finger at his master as the two of them walked toward a familiar horse. St. Briac took the reins from the groom, swung onto the stallion's back, and then laughingly reached down to tweak the valet's button nose.

"Now there's a man," sighed Suzette dreamily. "Paul, my squire friend, says every woman at court is secretly in love with the seigneur de St. Briac."

"I cannot imagine why," Aimée replied as frostily as she was able.

"*Mon dieu*, are you blind?"

"I certainly am not, and I'll thank you, Suzette, to show me the respect befitting our present situation."

The girl stared at her usually fun-loving, informal mistress and then shrugged. "As you say, mam'selle. I apologize."

"Ah," Aimée exclaimed with relief, "there's the king. We'll be leaving soon." She was further relieved to see Anne d'Heilly walking by his side. The king's favorite gazed up at him with possessive fondness; it seemed to Aimée that she would not allow him to stray far.

There was a moment of panic when François paused to speak to the page who had brought Aimée. The boy pointed toward the coach with its curtains closed except for one tiny slit. Aimée was able to breathe easier only after she saw the king smile with satisfaction, slip the page a coin, and continue toward his own coach with Anne.

Soon the entire court train began to move slowly down the drive to the road that would take them all away from Nieuil. Aimée sank back against the cushion, suddenly exhausted, and laughed.

"So, Suzette, we are safely away, and the adventure begins!"

The first night of their five-day journey was spent in the village of Gençay. The next day François and his court would enjoy the festivities of a royal entry into Poitiers, but now they would rest and make their preparations. Gençay offered only a roomy, clean auberge and a few homes to accommodate the court. Only the lesser members of the train were forced to pitch tents for shelter.

Aimée was assigned a large chamber at the auberge, sparsely furnished but dominated by a huge, comfortable bed with red velvet draperies. The strain of avoiding François all day had nearly done her in, and she retreated into this soft shelter with relish.

"Suzette, if anyone comes, just say I am indisposed." With that, Aimée drew the curtains and snuggled into feather pillows. She was instantly asleep. There would be time enough tomorrow to think of a way to get through the ceremonies at Poitiers.

Downstairs, François had finished a light supper and was seated before the fire with St. Briac and his other trusted friends, the seigneurs of Florange and Bonnivet.

"I wish we were at Blois now," the king sighed. "I am finding that this travel tries my patience."

"You are still exhausted from your captivity, sire. I think that after tomorrow's festivities at Poitiers, we should not pause for any longer than necessary until we reach Blois. You need the comfort of your home," advised Florange. Blond, blue eyed, and possessed of an ironic manner and cool energy, Robert de la Marck had been devoted to his king since childhood. His bravery in battle was legendary, and he well deserved the title "the Young Adventurer."

"Florange is right," St. Briac murmured.

Standing to refill their goblets, Guillaume Gouffier, seigneur de Bonnivet, only smiled. He preferred as much jollity as possible if he was going to travel with the court. Bonnivet was another childhood friend whom everyone liked. It had been said that he made love like war and made war like love, and for all his bravery and affectionate devotion to the king, he could not claim an excess of intelligence.

"It's that cursed treaty with Charles V that has me so on edge," the king exclaimed. "My own sons are being used as pawns, and I know full well that I can never turn over Burgundy, even though I gave the emperor my word—"

François broke off as a tall, thin shadow fell over the trio. "Ah, *bon soir*, Chauvergé," he greeted the chevalier smoothly.

"I do hope I am not intruding."

"No, no. My lovely Anne is feeling unwell tonight, so I am forced to substitute the company of these men. Alas," he added, sighing dramatically, "'tis not the same."

Everyone laughed at this, easing the tension that Chauvergé's appearance had injected into the mood of relaxed camaraderie.

"May I join you?" the chevalier inquired silkily.

"I beg you to take my chair, Chauvergé. I suddenly find that I am far too fatigued to remain another moment." To prove his point, St. Briac produced an elaborate yawn that was as loud as it was false. Rising, he let his twinkling eyes meet only for an instant the mirth-filled gaze of the king. Then he made a low, mocking bow to Chauvergé. "Do enjoy yourselves, my friends. I shall fall asleep imagining the riveting conversation I'll be missing."

François caught the edge of a sage-green sleeve as St. Briac passed his chair. "Not so fast, Thomas. I've a craving for even more entertaining company than this, hard as that may be to believe. My thoughts run to our new lady, the exquisite Mademoiselle de Fleurance. Would you be so kind, my friend, to pause at her door on your way to your own chamber and inform her that I shall visit her in, say, a quarter hour to inquire after her comfort?" His hazel eyes slanted merrily upward.

"You always were a conscientious host, sire," St. Briac muttered dryly. "*D'accord.* I shall inform the unsuspecting Mademoiselle de Fleurance."

Walking away, he heard Chauvergé whine, "But Your Majesty, there are matters I would discuss with you that are surely more important than a mere maid."

François's reply was muffled, and at any rate, St. Briac's thoughts had turned to Honorine de Fleurance. It seemed a poignant bit of irony that Aimée, whom he found uniquely lovely and whimsically intelligent, had been left behind in the country to marry an oaf while her pretty but unremarkable sister enjoyed the extravagant existence of a court lady. But Aimée would never have been able to conform to a lifestyle that always would make one unswerving demand: François I above all else, including oneself.

Pausing outside Honorine's chamber door, St. Briac felt a twinge of pity for the girl. If she was still a maiden tonight, tomorrow she would be a mistress. However, obviously she had accepted this fate or she would not have chosen to join the court train. He knocked and then lifted both brows at the sound of a great bustling commotion within the chamber. Two different high-pitched whispers could be heard, and one of them struck an unnerving chord in his memory. After a long minute during which his curiosity mounted, the door opened a bit, revealing a flustered, rosy face.

"Who are you?" he demanded.

"Suzette, monseigneur. Mademoiselle de Fleurance's maid."

"I must speak with her."

"*C'est impossible*, monseigneur. Mam'selle is very ill."

"Indeed? I am desolated to hear that, Suzette, but still I would speak to your mistress. I must take my personal account of her condition to the king."

Valiantly, Suzette tried to resist his pressure against the door, "I cannot allow it."

"*Vraiment?*" Amusement and impatience mingled under the surface of St. Briac's cool façade. "Pray explain."

"She can't talk!" The girl pointed excitedly to her own neck. "*Mal à la gorge.*"

"No!" Dark turquoise eyes widened in mock horror. "Suzette, I promise not to inflict any further injury on your mistress's throat if you will only be so kind as to open the door."

"No, no, monseigneur, you must leave. She's asleep."

"I heard her speaking to you after I knocked, and I doubt that Mademoiselle de Fleurance has dozed off since. Now, my girl, I must insist that you either stand aside or prepare to be moved."

Suzette's loyalty stopped short at the risk of physical injury. Sighing, she backed away from the door. You are a hard man, monseigneur," she said mournfully.

"A beast, no doubt about it." St. Briac went straight to the bed, where red velvet curtains were drawn tightly all around. "I almost hate to look," he muttered, and then slowly parted the draperies. The occupant of the bed was huddled in a ball, completely obscured by covers.

"I am desperately ill, m'sieur," came a muffled, pitiful voice from the depths of the bedclothes. "I beg you to leave me to suffer in solitude."

"I'll be happy to, mademoiselle, just as soon as you show me your face so that I can more accurately describe your condition to the king. He would insist were he here."

"I—I am too ashamed to let you view me. I am positively haggard!" The voice that emanated from the mound of covers sounded more irritated than pitiful.

St. Briac was sorely tempted to turn his back on the entire situation, yet for some incomprehensible reason he could not. It was with acute dread that he grasped the edges of the bedclothes and drew them back. The girl remained curled up, her shapely bottom in the air, her face pressed into the mattress. It was unusual for someone to go to bed clothed, but she wore a clinging silk shift. St. Briac didn't need to see the maiden's face; her abundant ebony curls confirmed his worst fears.

"Damn, I knew it! In the name of God, what do you think you are doing here, Aimée?"

CHAPTER 6

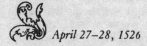 *April 27–28, 1526*

Aimée turned and sat up. It was her turn to be filled with dread. The tone of St. Briac's greeting had not been cordial.

"Monseigneur, what a surprise! Although I suppose I shouldn't find it surprising that you are in the habit of bursting into bedchambers uninvited and then attacking the innocent female occupants."

St. Briac blinked incredulously. Tendons stood out in his strong neck as anger and a sudden urge to laugh warred within him. "Child, you lend new meaning to the word audacious," he told her at last. "Have you no shame?"

Aimée, slightly relieved by his response, hugged silk-covered knees to her chest and gave him a winsome smile. "I realize that my presence here must come as quite a shock," she ventured, "but—"

"A shock? You must be mad. In truth, I'm certain of it. Do you long for an early grave? I can think of no other reason for you to tempt fate this way. What do you think the king will do when he discovers you, the only female he despises in all the world, as his bed partner tonight?"

She swallowed and echoed, "Bed partner?"

Can it be that the brazen Aimée de Fleurance is at a loss for words?" St. Briac exclaimed sarcastically. His massive body towered over Aimée and caused her to shrink uncertainly against the pillows. "You foolish girl. What did you think François wanted Honorine for, dinner conversation? He bade me stop here to inform her that he would join her shortly, only there is no Honorine." He paused, leaned closer, and said evenly, "Only you, *miette*."

Aimée shivered. "You are cruel. How can you attack me this way after advising me just two nights ago that I must be strong and fight back against the fate my parents were thrusting upon me? When I received the king's invitation to Honorine by mistake, it seemed an act of God. Deliverance! I could only think of escape, but even if I had imagined that I might have to share the king's bed, I still would have gone. At least he would be preferable to Armand Rovicette."

The corners of St. Briac's mouth twitched. "No doubt such an extravagant compliment would warm François's heart, but the fact remains that even if he did not hate you, you are not his type. The lady he invited was adoring and golden-haired. You are neither. In truth, the most pleasure the king could take from you would doubtless be the entertainment of watching you tortured creatively."

Aimée gasped. "How can you say such a thing? Have you no sympathy at all for my plight?"

Sighing, Thomas sat down on the edge of the bed and ran a hand through his crisp, dark hair. "Any sympathy I might feel, mademoiselle, is lost under a tide of aggravation. Tell me, does Honorine know you have come to the king in her place?"

"No," Aimée admitted in a small voice.

"And what plan did you make for the moment of your inevitable encounter with François?"

"None," she whispered, looking away from his penetrating eyes. "I could hardly believe that I would be able to get away at all. If that much succeeded, I just assumed that I would think of another plan. Really, I suppose I've hoped that the king would be so preoccupied with Anne d'Heilly that I could stay in the background, at least until we were far enough from Nieuil that I could leave the court train and take up a new life."

She was so pitifully desperate that it made St. Briac's head ache. He could feel himself being drawn in to the girl's chaotic scheme, but he was determined to resist. "A new life. What sort of a new life?"

"I don't know," Aimée answered plainly.

He had been distractedly rubbing his brow, but now he turned his splendid head and looked at her for a long minute. Her heart quickened.

"This adventure you have made for yourself is quite serious, Aimée. It could turn out to be worse than marriage to Armand Rovicette."

"But I had to take that chance." Suddenly her green eyes swam with tears. "I had to fight, just as you told me."

Suzette had whiled away the past few minutes folding and then refolding the contents of Aimée's trunks, listening curiously yet attempting to appear invisible. Now a soft knock at the door made her jump.

"Mademoiselle de Fleurance?" It was the charming voice of François I. "Will you grant me a few moments of your time?"

"*Hélas!*" Panic-stricken, Suzette rushed over to the bed. "Hide, m'sieur. Hurry!"

Caught off guard, St. Briac found himself being pushed on one side and pulled from the other into the bed. The curtains were closed hastily behind him, and in the next instant he heard the door to the chamber being opened. Suzette was greeting the king, but St. Briac was more concerned with the amusing activities within Aimée's bed.

"Get in," she whispered against his ear. "Get down!"

He obeyed without argument. Aimée held the covers back, draped them over St. Briac, and pushed him downward next to her. He wondered briefly whether she realized that this would hide his large body even less effectively than it had hers should François decide to investigate, but her warm nearness obliterated all thoughts.

They lay there together, not daring to move, as Suzette informed the king of her mistress's illness. In the confusion Aimée's small foot had become trapped between St. Briac's hard-muscled thighs, and her silk shift had ridden up so that he discovered a smooth bare leg under his hand. The curve of her hip, he realized, was just inches away, not to mention other tantalizingly uncharted territory. Best of all, her hands were in his hair, holding him close as if to ensure his stillness. Her creamy breasts, nearly exposed by the shift's deep, square neckline, brushed the side of his face. St. Briac could hear the anxious thump of her heart as he inhaled her clean violet scent.

Dimly, the two of them heard Suzette suggesting that she and the king should continue their conversation in the corridor to avoid waking Mademoiselle de Fleurance. He assented, and the door closed behind them. Aimée stirred, abruptly flooded with embarrassment as she became fully conscious of St. Briac's intimate proximity.

"Shh," he cautioned. "They could come back."

The sensation of his face turning against her breasts sent a stunning jolt of desire through her body. Ever so softly, St. Briac's parted lips grazed her skin. His breath was warm, tantalizing her with the soft tickling of his beard and mustache. She lay rigid, barely stifling an urge to whimper aloud and crush him against her aching breasts. Totally conscious of his chiseled male lips, Aimée finally did sob with pleasure when his mouth caressed a taut nipple through the silk of her shift. Then she felt the heat of his tongue through the thin fabric and began to tremble. Reflexively, her leg drew up and came in contact with something hard—a long vertical ridge between St. Briac's hips.

"Oh, *mon Dieu*," she breathed, realizing what this thing must be and why it was so drastically altered.

"Aimée." St. Briac moved to free himself of the covers, to take her in his arms and kiss her delicious lips. The girl was simmering with desires and passions she didn't even comprehend.

Suddenly the bed curtains were thrown open. "You can come out now, monseigneur," Suzette exclaimed. "It must have been very hot for you under those blankets. The king is gone. He prays for the return of your health, mam'selle, and to that end is having a cup of brandy sent to banish your fever."

St. Briac pressed tanned fingers to his eyes and smothered an expletive. He couldn't get out of bed and face that dimwitted maid until his obvious desire subsided, but fortunately Aimée had moved away to sit on the edge of the mattress. Although her profile was averted, he could see clearly that her cheeks were flaming.

"You're right, Suzette, I was very hot under those covers, and my suffering was to no purpose. You ladies forgot that the king himself sent me to this chamber, and so it would not have surprised him at all to find me here. In truth, he probably wonders why I did not return to inform him myself of 'Honorine's' illness. I'll wager that he's gone to my rooms to pursue the matter further and cannot understand what has become of me."

Aimée was burning with shame over her wanton behavior. When St. Briac swung long booted legs over the side of the bed and stood up to go, her desperation surfaced.

"Wait, please!"

He glanced up from straightening his doublet and arched an amused brow. "I am at your command, mademoiselle." Blue-green eyes flicked toward the bed as if to taunt her.

Aimée blushed anew but would not be silenced. "I beg you, monseigneur, to have mercy and help me. There is no one else."

"No. You have brought nothing but trouble to my life since the moment we met, mademoiselle, and I would be a fool to allow myself to become further entangled in your affairs. *Au revoir*." He nodded at Aimée and Suzette in turn and then forced himself to turn away and leave the chamber.

Gaspard LeFait waited in the corridor, his gray eyes narrowed suspiciously. "What have you been up to now? Cuckolding your own king? You are shameless, monseigneur!" The little man clucked his tongue several times for emphasis.

"François has yet to sleep with the lady himself, Gaspard, you meddling windbag, so I fail to see how it would be possible to cuckold him." He strode past the manservant, adding, "The situation was quite different at any rate."

"Different?"

St. Briac whirled on him, his eyes blazing from high above. "I am exhausted. You are wrong. It is none of your affair, anyway. Now leave me in peace! I have enough aggravation without further contributions from you."

The little man was stunned. Such a rude outburst was completely out of character for his merry master, who usually could manage to jest under the most trying circumstances.

He watched the tall, wide-shouldered figure stalk down the hall, and then he heard a door slam as St. Briac disappeared into his chamber.

"A perplexing turn of events to be sure," Gaspard mumbled under his breath. He stared for a moment at the door of the mysterious Mademoiselle de Fleurance before turning to descend the stairway, bound for his own bed in another part of the village.

* * *

Moonbeams slanted through the window at the end of the corridor. They were the only source of light as Aimée crept barefoot through the cool, dark silence that occurs between midnight and dawn. It had taken a great deal of coaxing and finally harsh warnings to persuade Suzette to venture forth and investigate until she learned which chamber had been assigned to St. Briac. Now Aimée felt each door, counting her way toward the one she sought. The latch in question lifted noiselessly, and in a moment she found herself in St. Briac's chamber. Spangles of moonlight and the embers of a dying fire barely penetrated the darkness.

Torn between determination and the urge to flee, Aimée finally made her way over to the massive bed. Heavy curtains were tied back at the posts, granting her a view of the bed's occupant. Aimée didn't need a candle to identify St. Briac. His sculpted head and torso, bronzed against the white bedclothes were unmistakable. For a long minute she indulged in the luxury of staring, her eyes lingering on his broad chest with its mat of dark hair, the strong column of his neck, the smudge of lashes against the curve of his taut cheekbones, his gleaming, sleep-ruffled hair. Finally Aimée leaned forward to touch St. Briac's long, hard forearm.

"Monseigneur?" she whispered.

Instantly he bolted upright, reaching for the sword that was propped against the bedpost. Terror-stricken, Aimée was certain he would run her through and ask questions later. She turned to flee, but St. Briac was quicker. What felt like iron hands caught her wrists; she found herself sprawled across his lap, with only a thin sheet between herself and his nakedness.

"*Dieu me sauve*, it's you! Aimée, will you never cease plaguing me?" There was an undercurrent of keen relief in his exasperated voice that made her wonder who he had expected a surprise night visitor to be. Someone who needed fending off with a sword, apparently.

"I had to talk to you, monseigneur," she whispered urgently.

His grip relaxed only slightly. "In the dead of night? Can I find no peace even in sleep?"

"I feared there would be no other opportunity to plead my cause to you."

"So you stealthily entered my room? Foolish child. You are fortunate I did not kill you. Aside from that, what if I had been awake?"

"It seemed unlikely at this hour."

"I might have been enjoying the company of a *jeune fille* or two from the village." His dark turquoise eyes sparkled in the shadows.

"You have the manners of a pig!" Cheeks aflame, she struggled to free herself, but he held her effortlessly. In her battle for escape, Aimée felt her face pressing St. Briac's chest; its warmth shocked her so that she sat instantly upright and silent.

"It is not my manners that are in question but yours," he said tersely. "Tell me what you want so that I can go back to sleep."

This scene was not going the way she had hoped it would, but Aimée plunged bravely ahead. "I had to beg you to reconsider your refusal to help me, monseigneur. Tonight's events and all that you told me have made me realize how very foolish I was to think that I could avoid the king. Will you not consent to aid me at least in small ways?"

St. Briac sighed. The ache of unsatisfied desire had fueled his temper earlier that evening; it had not taken long for his heart to soften a bit toward the girl, but she'd be the last to know that. "This predicament is one that you have made entirely, Aimée, and I am not obligated to assist you in any way."

"I know that, monseigneur. I appeal only to your charity, to your gallantry, to your—"

"*Assez!*" He put a hand over her lips and for an instant was keenly aware of their soft, moist contours.

Aimée meanwhile shivered as she inhaled the wonderful scent of his skin, felt its warm texture, and was seized by a craving to taste him. Then the hand was drawn away abruptly; she saw that St. Briac was looking out the window.

"Why should I do this for you, mademoiselle? Unfortunately for you, I am not one of those knights of old, ruled by the code of chivalry."

For a moment Aimée was silent, marshaling her courage. She had to remind herself of the way his body had responded to hers, of his growing passion and clear frustration when they had been interrupted. Taking a deep breath, she murmured, "This is all I have to offer, monseigneur."

Alert, St. Briac turned his head and looked hard at her.

She was a vision in the moonlight, glossy black curls spilling down and framing her piquant face, but his gaze was drawn to the neckline of her robe. With delicate hands she was drawing it open until he could glimpse the pale, perfect swell of her breasts and then the crests, fresh and pink as spring rosebuds. Inexplicably, rage welled up inside St. Briac from deep in his belly, and he reached out to pull the edges of her robe together.

"What do you take me for? Some degenerate animal, totally lacking scruples? Do you actually imagine that I would demand your body in return for my protection? *Incroyable!*" He broke off at the sight of tears spilling from Aimée's stricken eyes. "Now what is wrong?"

"You despise me. I have shamed myself forever."

Against his better judgment, St. Briac gathered her into his embrace and patted the silky curls he longed to kiss. "*Mais non, miette.* I do not despise you, but what you have just done was an insult to us both."

She wept into his chest. New and confusing emotions swirled within her. "You find me disgusting."

"Not quite." His voice was soft with amusement.

"I only thought that after what happened before, this might be the only thing that would convince you. I have heard of men who even use women against their wills or who employ all manner of tricks to—"

"Spare me the details," St. Briac interrupted dryly. "Suffice it to say that I am not one of those men."

"What about the *jeunes filles* you spoke of earlier? You would have used them both at once without even becoming acquainted with them?"

"Do you see any village maidens in my chamber?" he inquired a trifle testily. "I was not serious, Aimée."

"Oh." Her tears had stopped, and she knew that the time had come to sit up, but the sensation of snuggling within the strength of his embrace, listening to his breathing, was too delicious.

At length, St. Briac could bear no more; his powers of resistance were strained to the breaking point. Gently, he lifted Aimée away, and immediately a breeze chilled his chest. "*Miette*, you must go, before we . . . fall asleep. As for your offer, I believe I do understand what prompted you. I can only tell you that if one day we ever *should* make love, your motivations must be drastically different."

She nodded and stood, fresh tears stinging her eyes. This had been a singularly humiliating experience from which nothing had been gained except St. Briac's contempt. At the doorway she whispered, *"Bonne nuit*, monseigneur. I apologize again for disturbing you."

"Don't fret, Aimée." He paused, regarding the forlorn figure that waited in the shadows for his farewell. "Just to prove that I don't despise you, I'll agree to help with your charade."

Suddenly she was whirling back into his arms, kissing his face all over and sobbing, *"Merci, merci, merci!"*

St. Briac forced himself to be stern, holding her away from him. "Don't be too grateful yet. I haven't earned it, and there are conditions."

"Anything," Aimée cried joyfully.

"I will help to steer François clear of you if I happen to be nearby at the appropriate moment, and I will try to warn you if you are in danger of discovery, but I will never tell the king a lie for your sake. Is that clear?"

"Mais oui, perfectly clear. Oh, monseigneur, I owe you my life!" She sank to her knees beside the bed and attempted to kiss his hand, but he snatched it away.

"Get up! Return to your own bed and try to sleep. You'll need a clear head tomorrow for the entry into Poitiers."

"As you say, monseigneur!" she sang as, beaming, she backed up all the way to the door.

It was all he could do to smother the laughter Aimée so effortlessly evoked. "Before you collide with that portal, there is one more request I would make."

"Name it, and it shall be done, monseigneur!"

"Kindly cease constantly using that term of address. You wear it out."

"But then, by what name shall I address you?"

"My own will do." He settled down into the pillows and closed his eyes. "Thomas."

CHAPTER 7

 *April 30, 1526*

On the fourth day of her journey, Aimée found herself enjoying a midday meal in the village of Chenonceau. Suzette had brought it to her in the carriage. François, Anne, and the small group closest to him had been lured by an enthusiastic innkeeper to dine in one of his private rooms. Aimée had delighted in the conspiratorial wink St. Briac gave her as he passed through the inn's arched doorway.

Now she nibbled the last of her chicken and smiled at Suzette. "It's almost over, if I can just stay out of the king's sight until we arrive at Blois tomorrow."

Suzette nodded, but privately she wondered exactly what her mistress planned to do when this journey was concluded. She had spoken of traveling on to her aunt in Brittany, but Suzette knew this would require money they didn't have. Besides, the aunt was a loyal sister to Éloise de Fleurance. So far Aimée's tactic of crossing each bridge as they came to it had worked, but Suzette feared that only disaster would greet them when they crossed the final bridge to Blois.

They were now truly in the Loire valley, the garden of France. Already Aimée was under its spell. Mild breezes, a dazzling blue sky, shimmering poplars, and an atmosphere that seemed golden with luminous lights filled her with peace and pleasure. Chenonceaux was nestled along the banks of the Cher River, a tributary of the Loire, among enchanted woodlands and rich rolling pastures of vivid green. Tonight the court would rest at the nearby chateau, which Aimée had heard was a rare jewel in the necklace of castles that lent added glory to an already magical region.

"It's been a wonderful journey, hasn't it?" she murmured to the younger girl. "If nothing else, we've had that much."

Suzette thought back to the hours of celebration that had accompanied the court's entry into each village or town where they planned to stay for the night. Liveried citizens, trumpeters, and other musicians escorted them into town, and François received the town keys and offered his pledge of protection to the citizens. Gifts were bestowed, and then the king rode along a procession under a rich canopy and over a surface covered with sand or rushes. Suzette had never seen anything like it; color and laughter and festivity saturated the air. Even the façades of the narrow houses were hung with tapestries. A service of thanksgiving was offered at the main church, followed by a banquet and merrymaking that lasted long past midnight. Suzette was usually able to join Paul, her squire, for some fun of her own, but it made her sad to see that Aimée's only pleasure came from peeking from around the curtains in her coach or watching from her bedchamber window. Still, it would appear that her mistress preferred such pastimes to life in Nieuil.

"How is Paul these days?" Aimée asked, her green eyes slanting upward with mischief. "I saw you two kissing yesterday as you watched the procession. Tsk-tsk." She was leaning indolently against the cushions, basking in the fragrant sunlight that spilled in through the coach windows. Slowly she peeled a grape with her teeth.

Suzette's fifteen-year-old cheeks burned. "Oh, mam'selle, I hope you won't think me a harlot. I just couldn't help it. You are older than me, after all; you must know that kissing is *magnifique!*"

It was Aimée's turn to blush. "Why, who would I have been kissing? M'sieur le Pig from Angoulême?"

Suzette considered this. "You are so old, there must have been *someone*. You look as though you know about kissing, mam'selle." Suddenly the girl's blue eyes were alight. "I have it. What about the seigneur de St. Briac? What did you two do all that time in your bed while I was speaking to the king? I wondered about that later, especially after you had me discover his room. Didn't he even kiss you then, when you came to him in his bed?"

"Suzette, I bid you to cease," Aimée warned in a low voice.

"Well, if I were you and it were true, I'd be proud." Suzette pretended to swoon, tipping the basket over in the process. "He is absolutely—"

"Bonjour, mes filles!" The door swept open, and there was St. Briac. The interior of the coach was suddenly in turmoil as the two girls scrambled to compose themselves and Suzette clumsily recovered the basket and its lost contents. He proceeded to make polite conversation about his meal, inquired after theirs, and then informed Suzette that she would be riding his manservant's horse the rest of the way.

"Paul is waiting for you with the horse," he explained. "Gaspard will ride mine. He isn't at all pleased with the scenario, but I did feel it necessary to steal a few minutes of conversation with your mistress." St. Briac's light gaze had been on Aimée the entire time he was addressing Suzette.

"Mais oui, monseigneur! Naturellement!" She grinned knowingly at Aimée and then bade them both a hasty goodbye and ran off to join her squire, lunch basket in hand.

"Is this safe?" Aimée asked anxiously as he settled not into Suzette's seat but next to her. The two of them filled the small space.

His eyes twinkled in the sunlight. "I have the king's blessing, *miette*. Do you mind?"

"N-no!" Aimée found that her mouth was suddenly dry. "But, do explain, mon—I mean, Thomas."

"Well, the fact is that François did not come to speak to me that night at Gençay as I had expected; apparently he found other diversions. Since then he has been so busy and Anne has stayed so near that he has spared you—or should I say Honorine—barely a thought. However, today at the table, Anne and Marguerite moved away to chat together, and the king asked me if I had any idea how Honorine fared. I, he said, was the only person who had spoken to you since Nieuil."

Remembering St. Briac's vow never to lie for her, Aimée turned panic-stricken eyes up to him. "What did you say? What does he think? Does he know?"

He laughed at her excessive terror. "Never fear; your secret is still safe, mademoiselle. As I told you, I did not lie. He asked if you could still be so ill; I replied that I thought not. The king then wondered, logically I think, why you continued to hide from everyone."

Aimée's chest hurt from holding her breath. "And?"

"I offered the theory that you were shy about being thrust into the court, and especially about facing the king alone. I felt that explanation remained within the bounds of truth. Don't you agree?"

"I have no interest in your truth and lies, monseigneur!" she cried impatiently. "My only concern is remaining undetected."

"Well, you may not realize it yet, but François exhibits uncommon gallantry and compassion—and respect—for the ladies of his court. That is not to say that any of them comes before the king himself." He gave her an ironic smile. "However, his softer side is easily appealed to. I actually think that he was quite touched by my tale of your maidenly shyness."

"Don't you take that tone with me. I may not be very shy with you, but at least I am maidenly."

"Through no fault of your own," he couldn't resist murmuring. Catching the little hand that flew up to slap him, St. Briac continued. "At any rate, the conclusion of this tale is that the king decided, after a few suggestive comments from me, that it might be best to allow you a chance to settle in at Blois before confronting you." A chestnut brow arched. "You are safe, for today at least."

Aimée was irritated by his arrogance and sarcasm, but gratitude won out. "Oh, *mille mercis*, monseigneur! You have been truly wonderful. If there is ever anything I can do to repay you, please do not hesitate to tell me." Impulsively, she threw her arms about his neck and found herself looking into turquoise eyes that crinkled with laughter at the corners.

"Aimée, haven't we been over this before? I have asked you to call me Thomas." He saw her face soften into a relieved smile, and his heart seemed to melt. "Besides, your happiness is repayment enough."

Aimée held fast to his wide shoulders, tingling with the anticipation of his kiss. She willed St. Briac's mouth to crush her own . . . hungered for it.

"*Miette*, you must open your eyes and loose me. We arrive at the chateau momentarily."

She slid back onto the seat and stared out the window, blinking with surprise. She hadn't even realized when the coach began to move, and minutes must have passed. Her eyes skimmed the long avenue of plane trees.

"You'll find the origins of Chateau de Chenonceau interesting, Aimée," St. Briac was saying lightly, kindly filling the silence. "You see, it was built for Thomas Bohier, a man who was the financier for three kings. A dozen years ago, he obtained the property, had the previous manor razed, and constructed a chateau on the foundation of the old mill, on the granite bed in the middle of the Cher River. It's quite remarkable and breathtaking."

"Will we meet M'sieur Bohier?"

"I'm afraid not. He died two years ago, and his wife followed only recently. After looking at his debts, the Bohier offspring had no choice but to turn the chateau over to the king. This is his first visit as owner."

"That's the most ridiculous thing I've ever heard," cried Aimée. "Why in heaven's name should François want another chateau? I'll wager he couldn't even count the ones he owned before this, and it will probably be years before he returns to Chenonceau again. It's indecent!"

"What would you have him do with it?"

"Why, he should have allowed the Bohiers to have kept or at least given it to someone needy!"

"Like you?" Thomas suggested, hands raised to protect himself from her ferocity. Still, the merry sparkle of his eyes was visible between his fingertips. "Are you going to carry on this way about each indulgence you find the king guilty of enjoying? That could become quite tiresome, *miette*, not to mention life-threatening for you. I fear you'll have to adjust to the idea that François is the king. He's certainly not the first monarch who believed that God himself has elevated royalty to a higher plane than the rest of us. François takes it for granted that he will be pampered, spoiled, and catered to by everyone."

"Do you expect me to just smile as though I were witless and get in line to grovel at his feet?"

"Look here," St. Briac replied more sharply. "Neither the king nor any member of his court invited you to be here today. I would only suggest that you give François a chance, taking into account the circumstances of his birth and current position. Underneath the trappings and ceremony, our king is a very good man." His square chin went down a few inches, and he stared at her evenly. "I wouldn't be here if that were not the case."

Properly chastened, Aimée turned hot cheeks toward the window and looked out as the coach drew near the chateau. Stone sphinxes marked the entrance to the forecourt. Gardens were laid out on either side, carefully tended in the newest Italian style. A moment later, the coach crossed a bridge and came to a halt on a rectangular terrace surrounded by moats filled with water from the river. St. Briac pointed toward the large keep that stood to the right of them.

"That's the Tour de Marques, all that remains of the original chateau that once stood on this spot. And there"—he gestured out the window—"ahead of us on the river is Bohier's marvelous new creation. Do you blame the king for accepting it?"

Aimée drew a surprised breath, staring. Never in her life had she seen a structure of greater elegance, charm, and beauty. The very sight was intoxicating.

"Architecture is changing at long last," Thomas remarked, looking briefly out the door to see how long it would be before the entire line of coaches could gather on the terrace. He wanted to wait until the two of them could melt into a crowd before leaving their own vehicle. "You'll see it more and more at these chateaux where the rich have been able to afford alterations, and people like the king can simply build anew."

It was perfectly clear what he meant. In the past, when her own family home had been built, fortification dictated building styles. Now, obviously, beauty and grace were the ruling factors. The Chateau de Chenonceau loomed up between fields and woods in the midst of a lazy bend in the Cher River, its airy white spires and towers awash with golden sunlight.

"I would swear that I am having a vision," Aimée managed to breathe at last.

"It's quite real, and at this moment so is our need to get you out of this coach undetected." Seeing that she still stared dreamily at the chateau, St. Briac gently slapped one flushed cheek. "Aimée!"

She scowled but swallowed sharp words at the sight of

his bemused smile. "You have my full attention, monseigneur," she told him primly.

"Good! The king has just stepped from his coach, and I will go to join him. You wait here until we are inside. Do not open the door until Suzette or Gaspard comes to fetch you. I will keep François occupied in the meantime."

He shook his head and gazed upward for a moment as though unable to believe that he was saying these things. "Thank God this nonsense will be at an end tomorrow." Opening the door, St. Briac paused and looked back at Aimée with narrowed eyes. "Be careful. And just remember—if you are caught, I will deny all knowledge of you and this mad plot!"

CHAPTER 8

 *April 31, 1526*

Although it was past midnight, Thomas was wide
awake in the kitchen of the Chateau de Chenonceau. The
conversation at supper had spoiled his appetite. Louise, the
king's mother, had ranted on about Semblançay and his assistant in deceit, Teverant, who had slipped away from the
court train on the third day. Chauvergé had looked more
than ever like a weasel as he egged her on, agreeing that
someone must be punished for Semblançay's treason while
signaling for her glass to be replenished with wine. The king
himself seemed to hear little of this, even when St. Briac
spoke up to defend Teverant. His mind was on his sons and
the treaty with Charles V that he must confront very soon.
Finally, after a huge amount of wine was consumed and the
chatter grew unbearably loud, St. Briac left for his chamber
on the first floor, across from the one shared by François
and Anne d'Heilly.

For two hours Thomas attempted to sleep. He tried to
ignore the boisterous shouts from the dining hall; he tried
not to think of his friend Georges Teverant, who had certainly left their party out of a fear that would seem entirely
justified; he tried to dismiss the worries of the king from his
mind. However, it was the insistent reappearance of one
face, one voice, in his thoughts that kept St. Briac from

slumber. Finally, after the chateau had grown quiet, he cursed Aimée and his rumbling stomach and then threw back the covers and put on a soft white shirt, gray breeches, and hunting boots.

The kitchen was located deep in the chateau, so close to the pillared foundation of the one-time mill that at times the river swirled about its windows. Although the nobility had long since departed for their beds to prepare for tomorrow's journey into Blois, St. Briac discovered that the kitchen fairly brimmed with high-spirited servants. The enormous room was lined with polished dressers, cupboards, and shelves. In the middle stood a long oak table, paneled and set on trestles. A barrel of pungent red wine had been opened; the cups had been filled again and again from the look of the assembled crowd.

St. Briac was on the verge of turning back toward the stairway when Suzette called out, "Monseigneur, can't we help you?" The other girls giggled suggestively, but she went on with no more than a blush. "Are you hungry? There's fondue and toast and—"

"Rabbit with prunes," exclaimed an old woman with the authority of the head cook. Before he could reply, she was reaching for one of the copper pots that gleamed against every available space of white wall.

Suzette's young squire was pressing a large cup of wine into St. Briac's hands. Moments later, he found himself eating heartily of the delicious rabbit that had been stewed with prunes and drinking several cups of wine. Finally, some of the crowd showed signs of tiring. The high-pitched voices quieted, and St. Briac turned to Suzette.

"I hope that your mistress was completely safe from anyone who might be awake before you left her alone," he murmured in a tone that was far from light.

"*Bien sûr*, monseigneur! She was fast asleep, and I made certain that His Majesty had retired as well before I left to join Paul and our friends."

St. Briac believed her. He knew well enough that the stone corridors of the chateau were dark and quiet, yet uneasiness stole over him. François had been unusually dispirited and restless tonight, and Anne had been complaining of malaise once again. There was no guarantee that the king was as fast asleep as Mademoiselle de Fleurance. A little voice told him that the entire matter was no affair of his;

Aimée had leaped headfirst into this dangerous undertaking without the slightest push from him. There was no reason for him to interrupt his pleasure in the food, wine, and unpretentious company. Yet...

"I find that my hunger and thirst have been pleasantly satisfied," he told those in the crowd who paused to listen. "I am grateful."

Everyone bade him good night, and moments later he was climbing the staircase back to his room. A high vaulted hallway of white stone divided the ground-floor chambers. Even in the dim light, it was possible to pick out of the motifs of the enameled tiles on the floor the Bohiers' motto, written in cartouches: "If it comes right, I'll be remembered."

St. Briac was aware of a careless warmth imparted by the wine. He could give way to sleep if he chose, and yet... He was just a few steps from his own room when the door across the hallway swung slowly open.

"Thomas," a familiar voice hissed in relief. "What are you doing up at this hour?"

Somehow he was not surprised. "I might ask you the same question, sire. I've been down to the kitchen for a late meal. Was that your intent?"

"No." François gave a sly grin and eased the heavy portal shut before crossing over to his friend. "I've grown bored with this tiresome malaise of Anne's and have decided that the time is ripe to have a friendly little chat with Mademoiselle de Fleurance. A man can endure only so much when it comes to women and their moods."

St. Briac's common sense told him to turn his back and go to bed, but some other maddening instinct interfered. "Pardon me for saying so, Your Majesty, but don't you think it is a trifle late for a social call? The young lady has surely been long abed."

"I hope so." The king laughed softly. "You needn't look at me that way, Thomas; it was only a jest. I don't intend to steal into the maiden's bed unless she invites me." He was already starting toward the stairway and found St. Briac keeping pace. "I'll simply have that servant of hers wake her, and perhaps we can share a goblet of wine. I simply wish to soothe the poor girls anxieties about what lies ahead...you know, life at court and all." He winked gently at his friend, who managed a wan smile.

Halfway up the stairs, St. Briac realized that he could not

accompany the king to Aimée's chamber without looking like a fool. There seemed to be no recourse except to say good night and leave François to continue on alone. He knew he should be glad that the matter would be resolved, the lie exposed, and his involvement ended at last. But standing there on the stone step as François disappeared around the corner to the upper hallway, Thomas was troubled by an unnerving concern for Aimée's welfare. What would happen to her? He had just turned to descend, when Suzette appeared on the landing below.

"Monseigneur, are you still about?" The wine emboldened her to give him a flirtatious smile. Was it possible that he might be interested in a serving girl like herself? Oh, how the others would drool with envy if she could tell tales of being held in the arms of the seigneur de St. Briac, being kissed by his warm hard mouth, being—

"Suzette!" His whisper was harsh. "The king has gone to visit your mistress. It is up to you to intervene. Hurry now!" His steely hand gripped her arm and thrust her up the stairs.

Only a moment later, the voices of François and Suzette drifted back to him, frustratingly unintelligible. Then, to his surprise, the king reappeared on the stairway.

"Are you still here, St. Briac?" he murmured distractedly. "'Twould seem the shy little bird has flown her cage. The maid surmises that she must have gone outside for a stroll."

"Oh, well, you'll see her tomorrow at Blois. A good night's sleep will do you good, sire."

"Nonsense!" François tossed a light, spirited laugh over one shoulder as he passed his friend. "I mean to join Mademoiselle de Fleurance. What better place for us to become acquainted than under the stars here at Chenonceau? I'll need a jerkin to ward off the night's chill." With that, he disappeared around the corner, caught up in thoughts of the elusive golden angel who waited outside.

St. Briac reclined against the stone wall and let out a groan. *"Dieu me sauve!* What next?"

"Monseigneur!" It was little Suzette, flying down the stairs toward him in a panic. "Has he gone after her?"

"He will as soon as he's fetched a jerkin," Thomas told her wearily.

"In that case, you must hurry. Now! Run to warn her. Hide her!"

"No! If she was foolish enough to leave her room, she

deserves the consequences. I don't want to get involved in this for another moment! I refuse."

"How can you be so cold-blooded? Have you no sense of gallantry at all? Would you make no move to rescue a sweet, innocent maiden in her time of need?"

St. Briac raised strong hands to his face and shook his head from side to side. "Why can't someone else extricate Aimée from these predicaments she is so expert at making for herself? If she truly were sweet and innocent, she'd have remained at Nieuil and we'd all be better off."

"We have no one to turn to but you, monseigneur! I beg you to hurry before the king appears again."

Expelling a harsh sigh, he clenched his fists and turned away from the serving girl. "*D'accord*, I am going!" St. Briac spared her one last murderous glance. "But this is absolutely the *last* time."

The night was magnificent. A snowy, translucent crescent moon hung against a starlit sky that was as rich as deep-blue velvet. Gentle spring breezes rippled over the river, whispered through the budding trees, and caressed St. Briac's cheeks as he traversed the drawbridge.

Reminding himself that it would do no good to find Aimée if the king spotted either of them first, he stretched his long legs into an easy sprint. After passing the Tour de Marques, he paused to cup palms around his mouth and whisper loudly, "Aimée! Aimée, can you hear me?"

There was no reply, but his sharp turquoise eyes caught a movement in the distant gardens laid out in the forecourt. A person? St. Briac ran across the next bridge, through the pathways that separated flower beds, and discovered Aimée hiding in a row of yew and box trees. She wore only a simple gown of periwinkle-blue wool, cut low to disclose the curves of pale breasts partially obscured by tumbled curls blacker than the sky.

"You must be utterly insane!" His whisper cut the air like a knife. "Why in the name of God would you be so foolish as to wander about on the last night before the court reaches Blois?"

"Because I was trying to avoid insanity!" She whirled on him, her green eyes ablaze as she tried to pull free of his iron grip. "If I had remained one more moment in that chamber—*any* chamber—I would have begun screaming. I wanted to run in the fresh air, smell flowers, bask in the moonlight, gaze at this wondrous chateau without having to sneak about! So, after everyone had gone to bed and Suzette tiptoed off to join her friends, I dressed and bolted for the door."

St. Briac did not relax his hold on her delicate arms, but his spirit softened toward Aimée. "Yes, I see." He found that he had to swallow before he could continue. "All the same, you've risked much and put others in jeopardy: Suzette and, of paramount importance, *me*! The king knows that you are out here, and so I came to offer a warning, against my better judgment—"

"That goes without saying!" Aimée couldn't stifle a soft ripple of laughter.

"That's right, laugh at me in a moment when I am risking the friendship I value most to come to the aid of a demented, impulsive female. I'll tell you what goes without saying, mademoiselle, and that is that this is absolutely the *last* time I will turn up to help you in your inevitable hour of need. I am *finished*! *Comprends-tu?*"

"*Mais oui. Absolument,*" Aimée retorted in her frostiest tone. "Don't let me keep you, monseigneur."

In the starlight her beauty was quite mesmerizing. St. Briac told himself that it was only the creamy glow of Aimée's skin, the gleam of her ebony hair, the flash of her eyes, the sight of her breasts straining against the periwinkle-blue bodice that caused him to linger . . . for one more instant only.

"Mademoiselle de Fleurance?" It was the king, calling from the distant drawbridge. "Honorine? It is I, François."

Muttering a string of French epithets in a tone all too familiar to Aimée, St. Briac unceremoniously pushed her to the ground. "*Silence,*" he hissed when she opened her mouth to protest. In the next instant, they were lying face to face against the yew and box trees. A hand covered her lips roughly; she yearned to bite it, but the harsh glare St. Briac bent on her gave her pause.

"Honorine, my little rabbit, show yourself. There is no reason to be shy of me." François's coaxing voice came closer. They could hear his footsteps on the gravel that covered the forecourt bridge.

The king's entreaties made Aimée suddenly want to giggle, and she caught a glimpse of St. Briac rolling his eyes for an instant before his visage hardened again. "*Damn,*" he whispered, barely audible. He pulled her against the length of his body, realizing that their only chance was for François not to recognize him and to mistake Aimée for an adventurous servant. Thank God for the difference between Honorine's and Aimée's hair. Reaching over, he spread abundant, sweet-smelling black curls over his shoulder to obscure the king's view of his face. He whispered, "Put your arms around me. Pretend to be kissing me."

St. Briac's whispered commands tickled her ear, and Aimée gasped. "Why, how dare—"

"Is that you, my precious one?" François exclaimed, pausing to listen. "Did you call me?"

"Bitch!" St. Briac hissed the word, and then Aimée felt a large hand cup her buttocks, pulling her hard against his manhood while his other hand caught the back of her head to still it for the angry assault of his kiss. Heart pounding, Aimée realized that she would be a fool to attract François's attention by struggling. Instead, she suffered the hot pressure of St. Briac's mouth and swallowed another gasp when his tongue forced her lips apart. All at once, she was achingly aware of the male strength of his big body against her own delicate form.

When François came within a few paces of them, paused, and muttered an apology before turning away, Aimée was only slightly relieved. Afraid that St. Briac might release her, she twined eager arms about his neck and returned his kiss with fervor.

A delicious fire had begun to rage within her. St. Briac was equally aroused; Aimée remembered the giant thing she had accidentally touched that night in the bed at Gençay. It had grown again. She felt it now through his breeches, pressing her belly. She rubbed her own ache against his steely ridge instinctively, as though seeking relief for an exquisite, consuming urge.

They kissed on and on, voraciously. Aimée could not get enough of the taste of Thomas's mouth, the texture of his tongue and lips, could not get close enough to his strong body even though it seemed crushed against her. She wanted to feel his skin, to have him touch her own.

When St. Briac realized that she was pulling at his shirt and that small hands were in the hair that covered his chest, a measure of sanity returned. "Aimée—"

"Please!" The word was a sob. She rubbed hungrily against

him, and then there was no turning back, only urgency as his long fingers opened the bodice of her gown. He tasted the sweet, satiny curves of Aimée's throat, shoulders, and nape, and finally, with a groan, caressed the fullness of her breasts. They were taut and eager. Thomas trailed lightning kisses over pale flesh, avoiding the deep-rose crests until she begged him, clutching at his crisp hair. The sensation of his mouth on her nipple was almost too exquisite for Aimée. He kissed it, tugging gently and then sucking, and she pressed him closer. Eventually her hands stole back inside his shirt as he lingered over her breasts, and she explored the muscular contours of his chest and broad back. It tapered down to a lean waist and flat belly that she touched over the tightness of his breeches. Then, finally, teasing him as he had her, Aimée let her fingers slide around the exciting evidence of his manhood.

St. Briac let out a moan and turned her back into the rich grass. "This is your last chance," he warned, one brown hand on the hem of her gown.

Her smile was like starfire. "Hurry."

A nagging voice in his mind told him that this would be a mistake, just one more in the long list of those he'd made since happening upon Aimée de Fleurance in the Nieuil woods. It wasn't difficult, however, to dismiss common sense entirely. The sight of Aimée's slim, pale legs, the knowledge of what would follow, and the raging throb in his groin left him no choice. She wanted this as much as he; she'd made that clear.

Bliss welled up within Aimée as she watched St. Briac quickly strip off his boots and breeches. Curiously, she studied his long, hard-muscled limbs, so masculine, so different from her own. The same crisp hair that covered his chest glinted over his legs in the moonlight. Although the hem of Thomas's shirt obscured his manhood, it was still tantalizingly evident. Aimée blushed with a fresh wave of fever. She wanted to see him completely naked and wanted him to remove all her clothing, but this was not the time or place. Even what they were doing now was more abandoned than anything she had ever imagined.

St. Briac was bending over her, kissing her again, sweetly this time. He caressed her glossy hair, brushed warm lips over temples, chin, brow, and nose. Finally, as Aimée was arching instinctively upward, seized by a desire she'd never dreamed possible, Thomas found her hand and kissed first the pulse at her wrist and then each slender finger. His turquoise eyes burned her face, and she returned his stare. Slowly he moved her hand down his torso, until she touched the hard, waiting shaft below his hips.

"*Parbleu!*" Aimée forgot to whisper in her wonderment, and St. Briac could only chuckle at the enchanting freshness of each new moment with her. His hand drifted away from her exploring fingers to lift the periwinkle-blue skirt. Thighs like satin parted in welcome. Her arousal was clearly evident, but still St. Briac touched and teased, gathering more pleasure for them both as his fingers evoked flinches and gasps from the unsuspecting Aimée. At some point her teeth sank into his shoulder, and he allowed eager little hands to press him home. His conscience had warned that she might be a virgin, but tonight Aimée's passion had been far from maidenly. Now, almost moaning aloud with the keen sensation of entering this female who was incredibly taut, warm, and wet all at once, feeling her body straining upward, Thomas encountered the dreaded barrier that confirmed his worst suspicions. *Merciful Lord!* He was taking the maidenhood of a girl whose very presence had complicated his life right from the moment of their meeting, whom he had prayed never to see again after arriving at Blois.

Aimée squirmed with pleasure, loving the feeling of St. Briac's hard manhood filling her. But why had he stopped? She was ravenous to have all of him inside her. She impatiently pushed her hips forward. There was a sharp, burning pain, and then, with a groan, St. Briac shut his eyes and began to move back and forth, in and out, slowly, the torment and ecstasy on his face mirroring her emotions.

Soon her pain was forgotten, as was his torment, and they clung together, his mouth fastening over hers again as their bodies fused in a timeless, accelerating rhythm. For Aimée it was like being caught in the vortex of a cyclone; all she knew was the storm of their union, the urgency of their mouths, loins, and limbs. His strong fingers were in her hair, savoring its texture, conscious of each minute detail. The sensation of the splendid muscles of his back moving under her clasping hands would be imprinted forever in her memory.

When her climax began, Aimée couldn't have been more astonished. Fiery contractions spread out in waves, causing her thighs to tremble, the peaks of her breasts to tingle and harden almost painfully. He molded her buttocks in two hands and held her fast so that it seemed he would penetrate to her very heart before he let out a harsh gasp and relaxed slowly. In the starlight she crazily memorized the sight of his corded brown neck and wide shoulders. After he had lowered his face into the cloud of her hair, they lay sated, hearts pounding, for long minutes. Aimée gloried in their entwined legs that were so utterly dissimilar yet complementary. Never had she imagined such total fulfillment for both body and spirit.

"Damn."

It seemed to Aimée that St. Briac's curse was more deadly uttered quietly than shouted in anger or frustration. He was withdrawing from her, and she wanted to sob and hold him there. Her body, singing with warmth and elation just moments before, was now hollow. Night breezes showered her with gooseflesh as she watched him yank on clothes and boots.

"I'm sorry!" Her tone was defiant, but tears swelled in her throat.

St. Briac looked back over one shoulder; Aimée was fumbling with her bodice. Remembering the skirt that bared her legs, she paused to yank it back to her toes; then she returned her attention to the fastenings that refused to close over her shaking breasts. An unwelcome pain grew within St. Briac's chest.

He sighed heavily. "Oh, stop it. Don't make me feel any more guilty than I already am." Moving to her side, he deftly closed the bodice and tried to ignore Aimée's quavering fingers. "It's my own damn fault; I accept the responsibility. I just wish to hell that you hadn't been a virgin."

"Oh, *excusez-moi!*" Outrage dispelled her tears. "Obviously your conscience would be clear if I were a wanton woman who gives herself to every—"

"Stop!" St. Briac turned his head and raked a hand through moon-silvered hair. "I don't mean anything personal. It's just that it wasn't fair for me to have taken advantage of you in this situation, to have robbed you of the gift that should have been saved for the man you love, for your husband."

She wanted to scream. "Since you put it that way, monseigneur, I absolve you of all guilt and responsibility. I gave myself willingly. I chose to become a woman tonight. I was ready." She wanted to add that it had been an act of love, but such words were impossible between them. "And I enjoyed myself."

St. Briac stared. He wanted to believe her, yet how could he be guiltless when just a few days before the girl had been a sheltered, innocent wood sprite who didn't even know how a man kissed a woman? Now she was speaking of their passionate coupling as if it had been just another frivolous adventure. Would her life have altered so radically without his presence? He smothered another groan. Certainly it had been a contrary fate that had allowed their paths to cross at all. "*Miette.*"

Aimée pretended not to hear him. She scrambled to her feet when his long fingers grazed her cheek. "I know that you think I am a foolish child who doesn't know what she wants, but that is not the case at all, Thomas. I am an adult, just as you are, and I am grateful to you for making that transition complete for me tonight."

Slowly, almost painfully, he rose and stared down at her. "I just cannot help wondering—"

"Shh." Somehow she gave him an enchanting smile and lifted a hand to his mouth. "Don't be so serious; it's out of character for you. We've had a fine time tonight. Leave it at that."

St. Briac stared up at the stars. "I cannot dismiss this so easily."

"Whyever not? *Parbleu!* You are known for dismissing nearly all of life with a laugh and a jest. I had a marvelous time tonight and will always look back on our interlude in the gardens of Chenonceau with a smile. Would you crush me by saying that you enjoyed yourself any less?"

His mouth did curve up at last, for it was impossible to resist Aimée's charm, yet a sigh lingered within. "If it had not been wonderful, I would not worry so, *miette.*"

"Let us put the matter behind us then and return to the chateau. I suddenly find that I am quite fatigued, and tomorrow promises to be an eventful day."

St. Briac put an arm around her slim shoulders as they started back across the forecourt. "I regret that fatigue did not overtake you earlier and prevent you from leaving your room."

"Do you mean that?" Aimée couldn't make the words sound lighthearted when she ached so inside.

The sigh escaped from St. Briac, and an ironic smile played over his hard mouth. "I don't know," he answered at length.

CHAPTER 9

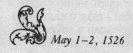

May 1–2, 1526

"*Monseigneur!*" *exclaimed Gaspard LeFait* as he threw open the bed hangings to admit a brilliant shower of sunlight. "How is such slothful inertia possible?"

St. Briac lay facedown in the pillows, his sinewy arms encircling his head to obliterate reality further. "What's the time?" he finally mumbled. Only Gaspard could have deciphered words spoken into bedclothes rather than in his direction.

"Nearly nine o'clock," the little man said crisply. "I'll not even ask the reason for this condition of yours. *Naturellement*, it is none of my affair; I am but a servant, after all. Never mind that the king has been looking for you, that he hoped you might join him and his family in chapel, and heaven forbid that I might disturb your peace with the news that His Majesty was here in this very chamber in search of you last night, well past midnight, I gather."

Gaspard's pause was expert, but still Thomas's head did not emerge from the protection of arms and bed. "I realize that your personal...ah...activities are no concern of mine, but you might at least have the common consideration to force yourself out of bed at an hour that would not cause inconvenience to others. I have only just gathered your clothing from last night, which I must now tend to in a shockingly short space of time. Also, there is a scent about them that is not popular among men—violet." His voice rose subtly but triumphantly. "I could not help remembering, when I smelled the violets in your shirt, that the king muttered something about seeing someone who resembled you, monseigneur, among the flower beds and box trees late last night."

Finally, unable to bear the sound of one more smug insinuation from his manservant, St. Briac hoisted himself onto his elbows and turned slightly, one brow arched in a sharp, unfriendly manner. "Not another word, *comprends-tu*?"

"As you say, monseigneur." Gaspard glanced away, looking offended. "I was only trying to help."

"At this moment you can help me most by procuring a *cuvé*, soap, and lots of hot water so that I may bathe. Food, too, and my clothes." He gave the little man a severe look. "I did not employ you for your expertise at meddling and dispensing unsolicited advice."

The manservant nodded woodenly, bowed, and exited. Only then could St. Briac let a smile steal over his face. Both of them were well aware that Gaspard's nosiness and loyalty were traits that his master found endearing despite the occasional irritation they stirred up. God forbid that he should ever mind his own business! Now, however, Thomas's thoughts flew off in a different direction. The violet scent that Gaspard had mentioned so pointedly clung to his skin, tantalizing and tormenting him with memories of the night before. *Aimée!* How could he have been so irresponsible, so blind, so lacking in strength as to allow such a thing to happen? With a groan, he buried his head in his arms again and wished that he could forget not only the act itself but the sheer, blinding magic of Aimée's lovemaking.

Two kitchen maids were carrying in a silver *cuvé*, followed by several more with buckets of steaming water. St. Briac forced himself to sit up, his brown legs swinging over the side of the bed. He ran both hands through his touseled hair and glanced over to see the clutch of servants staring in anticipation.

"*Merci*," he murmured wryly. "I think that I can find my own way to the bath."

They departed in a flurry of blushes, giggles, and curtsies. St. Briac smiled and walked naked through the morning sunlight to the *cuvé*. Then he realized that it was the memory of Aimée's laughter, rosy blush, sparkling green eyes, and so very much more that was making him smile. Settling into the hot water, St. Briac shook his head once more and asked God why He had been so vexing as to thrust Aimée de Fleurance into his previously well-ordered existence.

It was not yet ten o'clock when François glanced up to see his friend Thomas entering the guardroom. The king was looking particularly splendid this morning in black and gold silk, a fur-trimmed cape, and a soft black velvet hat with a white plume and jewels, yet the sight of St. Briac was never less than arresting. The guardroom, with its elaborately painted beamed ceiling, Flemish tapestries, and floor of majolica tile, served as a perfect backdrop to the seigneur's magnificence. He was taller, more masculinely chiseled, and somehow richer of spirit than any man François had ever known except Bayard, his dear, dead friend and best knight. Today St. Briac was clad simply in blue-gray velvet slashed to reveal puffs of darker blue satin, all of which should have accentuated the turquoise of his eyes. Those eyes, however, looked unusually muted; there were fine lines of exhaustion or strain at the corners and at his mouth as well.

"*Mon ami*," François murmured in greeting, "you look tired. I do hope you're not ill."

"Not at all, sire. In truth, I may have slept too long. Gaspard was scolding me for missing chapel. Did you desire my presence?"

The king selected a perfect pear from a nearby dish and smiled vaguely. "The matter is not serious, but I find myself puzzled by some of last night's events."

"Indeed?" St. Briac examined the sleeve of his doublet and then managed to meet his friend's curious hazel eyes. "Were you unable to locate the elusive Mademoiselle de Fleurance?"

He snorted derisively. "I begin to think that the girl does not exist at all."

"Well, the mystery will soon be solved, for Blois awaits us," Thomas interjected, hoping that would end the conversation.

"There is another mystery that I would solve, my friend. Do you remember our encounter on the stairway last night when I informed you of my plans to look for Honorine outside? I went to fetch a jerkin and then looked everywhere for her, in the gardens, calling into the woods, until I heard a noise in a row of trees off to one side of the forecourt. To my embarrassment, I glimpsed a couple lying in the grass, locked in a passionate embrace. The female was brunette, so I knew it could not be Honorine, and I turned away with haste."

"Your tact is legendary, sire." St. Briac wished there were a sorcerer present who could make him disappear.

François would not be deterred. "The man—though I caught but a glance in the moonlight—seemed to be you! I told myself that it could not be possible, that you were inside the chateau just moments earlier, and that I was certain you were bound for bed. So I went to your chamber to discuss these curious events, but you were not to be found." He paused for a significant moment, took another bite of the pear, and then continued. "*Voyons*, I realize that I have no right to pry into your affairs, but I have been so puzzled, and I thought you might know something about Honorine."

Unable to lie, Thomas rubbed his brow and said tersely, "It was I in the garden last night. When you returned to your chamber for the jerkin, I was already on my way. It was an interlude that I am not proud of, however, and would prefer to forget."

"But why?" the king demanded with a mischievous wink. "The maid appeared quite fetching, not unlike that girl we encountered in the Nieuil woods. Was she a servant from the chateau or part of the court train?"

"I would rather it hadn't happened because the passion came out of nowhere, like a summer storm. Conversation was all I'd intended, and then"—St. Briac blinked, reminding himself that this was one problem he shouldn't talk over with his friend—"then lust got the better of me. The girl was no common slut who lifts her skirt for every man she meets, and I'm concerned that—"

"Never mind. I understand." François inclined his head toward the chapel entrance to indicate that they would not be alone for long. Any further private words must be spoken quickly. "Put it out of your mind. Before dawn breaks again, you will be with Ghislaine at Blois, and I'll wager that she will make you forget that comely kitchen wench. Would you like me to invent a royal errand that would take Ghislaine's husband to Paris for a few days?"

St. Briac tried without much success to smile at this men-

tion of his lover, a stunning, shrewd, yet kind duchess who
had never been so far from his thoughts as during this past
week. He'd almost forgotten that she waited for him at Blois.
Perhaps her presence there would help him forget Aimée.
"I will leave any possible diversions for the duke entirely in
your hands, sire," he replied.

The king was looking toward the chapel, which opened
off the guardroom's eastern wall. Jutting out from a pier
head, its triagonal stained-glass apse faced upstream and was
awash with sunshine at this hour. Louise, Marguerite, Anne,
and Chauvergé were emerging from the vaulted entry. Behind them were Florange and Bonnivet in the company of
several other *gentilhommes de la chambre.*

"Be kind enough to tell me one more thing, won't you,
Thomas?" said the king in a deceptively light voice.

"Gladly." St. Briac thanked God for sending this crowd
to rescue him from the intimacy of their conversation. Just
one more question...

"Did you see Honorine last night? Could it be that she
was hiding from me? I would not have her afraid."

He drew a sharp breath. "Honorine? No, sire, I saw no
sign of that lady in the garden last night."

"Eh bien, mon ami." François smiled, whispering as the
group drew nearer. "I find myself very anxious to hold Mademoiselle de Fleurance in my arms once we reach Blois. I
need just such a diversion from the problems of the treaty
and Charles V. Semblançay and Teverant, and the fate of
my hostage sons."

"Your list of trials is endless," St. Briac murmured in
ironic agreement as he watched Chauvergé lean down to
murmur something in Louise de Savoy's ear. "I only hope
for your sake that Mademoiselle de Fleurance will not add
to it."

The king thought of the lovely golden maiden who had
gazed at him so adoringly the night at the hunting lodge.
"Impossible!" He laughed and then put out a hand in welcome to his family and mistress.

Aimée stood on the barge and gazed dreamily over the
wide, alluring Loire River. It shimmered, aquamarine bordered by banks of golden sand. A mellow breeze stirred the
gable-hooded headdress that so effectively concealed

Aimée's ebony curls, and she sighed, at peace if only for that instant.

She wished it were possible to put St. Briac completely from her thoughts, and François as well. She was tired of worrying, of starting anxiously at every noise, even this afternoon, when she knew that he and his comrades were sharing a leisurely meal in the cabin of this great royal boat. It had been a long day. Twilight was approaching, yet Blois was still far away. The court train had traveled over land to a point between Amboise and Chaumont and then surprised Aimée by boarding this tremendous barge. The Loire was a dreamy river, and gliding over it made her feel as if she were dreaming too, that the soreness between her legs wasn't real, that there was nothing to worry about, that only happiness and love waited for her at the king's chateau at Blois.

"Mam'selle!" It was Suzette, her cheeks glowing in the spring sunshine. She held a baguette and wedge of cheese aloft triumphantly, drawing a grin from Aimée. How hungry they both had been, yet neither dared venture toward the food being consumed by François's party. Obviously, Paul the squire had provided these emergency rations. Now Aimée ran to join her maid in a little nook toward the back of the barge that they had claimed immediately upon boarding. It was shadowed, yet it offered a sweeping view of the river and the chateaux, villages, vineyards, mills, fisheries, and hunting lodges that perched amid budding trees on the chalky banks of the Loire.

The two girls ate with relish and savored the unfolding panorama. From time to time Suzette stole a glance in Aimée's direction. Her mistress looked more drawn than at any time since their abrupt departure from Nieuil. It had been a trying ordeal as well as an adventure, and Aimée deserved to appear pale; she had earned the mauve smudges under her lovely eyes. Still, there was something about those eyes and the way her pretty mouth turned down at the corners that alerted Suzette to more complex problems. She sensed that they shared a common source: the man called St. Briac.

"Isn't there something I can do to help, mam'selle?"

Aimée blinked in surprise. "Help? I am fine. You have helped enough for one day by seeing that the way was clear when I left Chenonceau."

"That was easy enough since all of them were in chapel or the guardroom!"

"And by obtaining this feast for us," Aimée continued blithely, as though she hadn't heard the maid's words. "You must not be concerned about me. I am only fatigued and, I admit, a trifle worried about what tomorrow will bring."

At length, her hunger appeased, she leaned against the side of the shadowed, swaying nook and closed her eyes. Sleep came within moments.

Suzette continued to fret until a loud "Hsst!" reached her ears from the far side of the barge. She peered around the corner and saw the distant but unmistakable figure of the seigneur de St. Briac outlined against the azure sky. When he beckoned, the serving girl forgot her sleeping mistress and scurried across the deck to his side.

"Suzette, why don't you take a stroll and look for Paul so that I may have a private word with Mademoiselle de Fleurance. There are . . . ah . . . certain things she should know about Blois before we dock."

"But monseigneur, she is asleep."

"I will wait, then, for her to waken," he said with a note of finality.

Suzette turned her head to watch him stride toward the rear of the barge, thinking that she had never seen such a tall, broad-shouldered man move with such grace. She wondered once more what was going on between St. Briac and Aimée. What had happened last night when he went to the garden to warn her about the king? It had been a long time before her mistress had appeared in her upstairs chamber, looking flushed and disheveled, with bits of grass and leaves tangled in her curls. Was it possible? Suzette sighed heavily at the notion and set off to search for Paul.

St. Briac also was sighing as he stood above the sleeping girl. In spite of the ridiculous headdress, there was a lushness about her that betrayed last night's interlude. Her lips, pouting slightly in repose, were a darker rose and seemed fuller, as though bruised from so much unaccustomed kissing. Was it conceivable that such an experience could actually impart an aura of womanliness to a girl, that she somehow could change overnight? Even Aimée's breasts looked riper within the bodice of her simple sea-green gown.

Stirring in her sleep, she turned her head, and a downy black curl freed itself from her hairline and escaped the headdress to caress Aimée's brow. Shadows played over the elegant line of her throat, but St. Briac's eyes were drawn to a small lilac-hued mark that was now visible near her nape. He had left it there, branding her in the blaze of passion she'd aroused in him. A bittersweet mixture of emotions rose in St. Briac. Reaching out with one long, dark finger, he brushed the baby curl on her forehead and then traced the velvety line of Aimée's face down to the smudge of lilac.

Briefly, a smile touched her mouth, and she made a soft, contented sound before awareness dawned and her eyes flew open. Even as Aimée straightened and stiffened, St. Briac deliberately let his fingertips continue to rest near the nape of her neck.

"You," she whispered. Shadow and sunlight combined to etch his body against the blue sky. *Quel splendeur!* Wide shoulders tapered down to a trim waist under his doublet of blue-gray velvet, while snug haut-de-chausses outlined the long muscles of his legs. Aimée almost could feel the taut, warm, golden-brown skin under her fingers. "What do you want?"

Her hand reached to pull his away from her neck, but then his fingers were holding fast to hers, and suddenly she felt chilled and then flushed.

"I only want to discover how you fare today, mademoiselle," St. Briac told her softly.

"Very well, of course. I hope that your conscience is not still plaguing you."

"*Miette*, would you truly have me lighthearted and uncaring?"

Aimée tried to avoid his penetrating turquoise gaze. "Well, there is no reason for you to be other than lighthearted. *I* certainly am not in mourning for my lost innocence. On the contrary, I feel reborn! You have relieved me of a tremendous burden, monseigneur."

"*Burden? Reborn?*" St. Briac shook his head. "You baffle me, Aimée."

"Perhaps I flatter you!" She strove for a bright smile and tried to ignore the deafening thud of her heart when he settled onto the bench beside her. His expression was masked by the shadows.

"Perhaps," he said finally after staring pensively into space for an interminable minute, "I am not able to be so casual about lovemaking, particularly when I engage in it with a virgin."

Aimée looked over at his profile; he seemed intent on the

village that the barge was passing. Surreptitiously, she scanned his thick, curving eyebrows, the almost angelic sweep of his lashes above narrowed eyes, the aquiline nose that bent so attractively at its bridge, and finally the mouth that seemed made for kissing. Surprisingly, she realized that she had touched him long and well enough even to know the shape of the hard, square jaw and the appealing dimples hidden by his beard. Resisting the husky tone of his voice seemed impossible.

Still, Aimée made an effort. "Monseigneur, I have told you that I feel no guilt for what happened between us, so I would appreciate it if you would stop speaking of it in a way that makes me feel as if I *should* feel guilty."

He blinked and looked over at her. "All right. I will not belabor the point."

Aimée could not repress a smile. Could any woman regret losing her virginity to such a man? Yet he would not understand this, and it was not a sentiment she could voice. "I implore you, Thomas, to forget last night if it upsets you so. For myself"—she grinned enchantingly—"I shall remember every moment, always, with a smile."

"You may feel differently when you meet the man you love, Aimée. That is what worries me."

"Well, you needn't worry. I can take care of myself. I have a free will, which I exercised last night. Just because I am a female doesn't mean I was at your mercy, monseigneur. You take care of yourself, and I will do likewise."

"Fine!" Suddenly he was almost shouting. "You do that, Mademoiselle de Fleurance, from now on!"

St. Briac stood up, glared at her, and then strode away. For several minutes Aimée found it difficult to breathe; then the sight of a town on the horizon distracted her slightly. It had to be Blois. Houses and buildings clustered together over hillsides above the Loire in a charming scramble, while the chateau itself perched on a promontory, checkered in white stone and red brick, like a crown for the village. It was a huge dwelling, with at least three wings that looked as though they'd been built years or even centuries apart.

Aimée stared up at the chateau, barely conscious of the sun that beat down on the barge as it veered northward toward the golden sands that bordered the town of Blois.

CHAPTER 10

 *May 5, 1526*

The moment was at hand. Somehow Aimée knew that she and François would be meeting face to face very soon. She stood at her window and watched the scene unfolding in the magnificent courtyard below. After two more days of waiting and wondering, it was almost a relief to think that her fate would be settled before the morning's end.

Other, subtler emotions made Aimée's chest ache. It seemed that an eternity rather than only three nights had passed since the court's arrival at Blois and her own installation into a spacious room in the Louis XII wing. It adjoined the Estates General meeting hall that connected the more recently constructed wing that held the apartments of the king and those closest to him. Aimée's chamber boasted a handsomely carved pillared bed set on the loveliest tiled floor she had ever seen. Tapestries hung on white walls; there were benches, a secretaire, a prie-dieu, and a charming balcony. There was even a private cabinet for Suzette.

It hadn't been difficult to avoid the king's notice upon their arrival at Blois. He had been far too occupied with the festivities and his own excitement to spare a thought for "Honorine" de Fleurance. St. Briac had also been preoccupied with a matter obviously more important than her welfare: an intimate exchange of greetings with a toffee-haired beauty who seemed unable to keep her hands off him. That first night, Aimée's emotions had fluctuated from panic at the prospect of finally confronting François to a sick rage as she watched St. Briac kissing the other woman in the torchlit courtyard.

But the night had passed without the appearance of François. Next morning, he and several of his *gentilhommes de chambre* left the chateau on horseback. Suzette learned that they were making an impromptu visit to Chambord since the king craved a glimpse of the castle that had filled his dreams during the long months of captivity. St. Briac stayed behind, ignoring Aimée just as she had insisted he should. She had no choice but to remain in her chamber, pacing and occasionally stealing onto the balcony, only to be rewarded with the sight of St. Briac and his mistress strolling arm in arm in the courtyard or gardens.

Suzette volunteered information gleaned from the servants at Blois. The toffee-haired woman was named Ghislaine Pepin, and she was the duchesse de Roanne. Her husband, Marcel, loved court life and hunting better than a beautiful woman, and so he did not begrudge her her own amusements, the principal one being St. Briac. Suzette whispered that Ghislaine was over thirty but that St. Briac continued to choose her over young, eager maidens because of her intelligence, wit, and generosity of spirit. One of the duchess's own servants had told Suzette that the woman never berated him for his absences, never questioned him about how or with whom he spent his time, and never talked of the future. It seemed that Ghislaine had learned to enjoy each moment by St. Briac's side and coveted nothing more.

Aimée pretended a lack of interest in Suzette's gossip, but inwardly she was conscious of a growing animosity toward the duchesse de Roanne. Obviously, the woman was very shrewd, and St. Briac was too densely male to realize how she had trapped him in her silken web. Men could be so obtuse!

Even now, as she watched the king crossing the courtyard, Aimée's eyes strayed back to the figure of St. Briac and his married lover. It was positively decadent that the woman was so lacking in conscience as to carry on this way right under her husband's nose. How could she laugh with St. Briac with such a total absence of guilt? They were standing close together on the second balcony of the magnificent

spiral staircase that was the centerpiece of the François I
wing's façade. Built of white stone in an open octagonal
tower, five sides of which projected from the wall, it boasted
lavish decorative panels carved with the king's salamander
emblem. Aimée seethed as she noted the light touch of the
duchess's fingertips on St. Briac's cheek. Morning sunlight
streamed through the open stairwells and struck sparks off
her burnished-gold hair, causing Aimée to think that her own
curls were the gloomiest color possible.

She forced her gaze away from St. Briac, who was looking
splendid in a plain fitted doublet of cocoa-brown velvet, and
sought the figure of the king again. Members of the court
seemed to stop him at every turn, but he was working his
way gradually toward her wing, and she knew with unerring
instinct that she, or rather Honorine, was his goal. Heart
pounding and palms perspiring, Aimée crossed the chamber
and climbed back into bed. There wasn't time to dress properly, and perhaps a sweet, half-asleep appearance would
blunt François's inevitable rage.

Out in the courtyard, a pair of tiny gray eyes in a wizened
face also were following the progress of the king. After
watching him reach the entrance to the Louis XII wing,
Gaspard LeFait made haste toward the great stairway.

"Monseigneur," he called, his foot on the first stone step.
"Monseigneur, I crave a word with you!"

St. Briac lifted his head with a grimace. He and Ghislaine
had been deep in a discussion of what they would pack
for their luncheon in the woods. Already he could taste
the Chinon wine, the succulent oranges and strawberries,
cheeses, cold salmon and pheasant, sweetmeats. . . .

"Gaspard, you meddler, speak your mind." Something
told him that the subject would be one he would prefer not
to consider, yet when the little manservant bade him descend
the stairs for a word in private, St. Briac apologized to Ghislaine and went to hear the news.

When the knock sounded at her door, Aimée thought
fleetingly that it was a good thing Suzette was exploring the
town today. Humiliation would be easier to bear alone.

"Mademoiselle de Fleurance?" The soft, imploring voice
was familiar by now. "Will you be gracious enough to admit
me?"

Aimée sat up in bed, pressing the coverlet to her bosom, and steeled herself. "Of course, sire. *Entrez, s'il vous plaît.*"

The heavy paneled door swung open, but she could not summon the courage to look in his direction.

"Chérie," François was murmuring gently as he came around the side of the bed, "you cannot imagine how many times I have wished to see you, to share your enchanting company since that night in Nieuil. You have been ever in my thoughts, and I confess that I had begun to fear that you were but an illusion after so many days without even a glimpse of your beautiful—"

The sound of his gasp made Aimée wince. What would he do? Murder her? Was such a punishment allowed, even for the king?

"Nom de Dieu," he managed to whisper harshly. *"You! Impossible!* Who would practice so shocking a deception at my expense? Where is Honorine? Answer me! *Answer me now!"*

Somehow Aimée managed to turn her head and meet his fiery hazel eyes. She had never seen such an expression on the king's usually merry face. Shrinking back against the pillows, she breathed, "Honorine is in Nieuil, Your Majesty."

"Nieuil? Nieuil? Sacré bleu!" He stared at her incredulously and then paced across the room and around the massive bed. "How has this happened? What devil sent you in her place?"

It was obvious that François had not forgotten even a syllable uttered by Aimée that afternoon in the woods, nor had he forgiven her. She fought a wave of fearful nausea, suddenly feeling extremely tiny in the great bed that was the property of this very man. "I, I realize that you have no reason to have sympathy for my plight, Your Majesty, but I beg you to listen before condemning me."

The king's anger had by no means subsided, but he was becoming more conscious of this maiden's extraordinary loveliness in spite of the fact that she had humiliated, insulted, and spurned him once before. There was an enchantment about the girl that was almost irresistible. Still, he glared at her before perching on the side of the bed. "I am listening, but my patience is thin. Make haste."

Briefly, Aimée explained that she was Honorine's sister, gave her name, and then went on to describe the events leading up to this moment of confrontation. "I know that I have behaved unforgivably, Your Majesty, and that my only hope is that you will treat me with your legendary understanding and mercy. I would not be so foolish as to request another moment of your hospitality, but if you will allow me to leave quietly—"

"Leave?" François laughed softly. "Leave? My dear Aimée, it is I who would be foolish to let you go. Any female resourceful enough to do what you have done all alone is a jewel. I prize intelligence in the ladies of my court, and yours is undoubtedly without peer. You have won my lasting respect and admiration. Tell me that you'll stay."

She blinked sparkling green eyes. How could this be happening? "I—I don't understand, sire."

His smile was playful as he reached for one of her tiny hands. "But I think that you do. I am not an ogre, *chérie*; in fact, some have said that my spirit is unusually magnanimous and forgiving. It would be easy for me to puff up with excessive pride and deal with you harshly, but that would benefit neither of us. I like to think that I am a wise enough man to seek out the humor in a situation rather than resorting to anger and revenge, which would be perfectly justified, I ought to point out." The king's eyes twinkled as he thought of St. Briac's advice about humor versus rage. His friend would be proud of this performance.

Aimée realized that an appropriate response was expected of her. "I do not deserve your forgiveness, Your Majesty. Never have I encountered such benevolence."

"Were I less impressed with your quick wit and courage in carrying off your little masquerade, my response might be different. However, as it is, I believe I am glad that Honorine is in Nieuil, and her irrepressible, outrageous"—He paused to shift closer to her—"and very beautiful sister is here with me instead. Having you as part of my court promises to be an entertaining experience, Aimée."

With a sickening jolt, it dawned on her just what sort of entertainment he intended her to provide. She wore only a shift of peach-hued silk, and the king was gazing appreciatively at the swell of her breasts and the creamy lines of her bare arms and throat. Wildly, she considered a confession that she was not nearly so resourceful as he believed, that she could never have deceived him so neatly without the aid of St. Briac. But the words never came near to being spoken, for Aimée could not betray Thomas, even if her silence meant letting the king into her bed. Besides, it was obvious that François had made up his mind. He was pleased with the morning's surprises, and now he was ready for other pleasures.

She watched with horror as one strong hand caressed her arm. There was nothing she could do; the king was going to honor her with his lovemaking, and she must receive his gift with joyous gratitude. His forgiveness of all Aimée had done in the past only intensified her entrapment.

"How lovely you are, my little wood sprite." He smiled to let her know that he was going to make a private joke out of that afternoon in the woods when Aimée's rudeness had verged on a criminal offense. "Already you are stealing into my heart. I find you captivating."

Somehow he had moved near enough to gather her into arms covered with jewel-encrusted plum satin. Tears rose in Aimée's throat and stung her eyes. Obviously the king meant her no harm. His touch and voice were gentle, and he doubtless believed that her gaze was averted out of maidenly shyness and gratitude. A new knot twisted inside her as she wondered whether he would be able to tell that she was not a virgin, and if so, what his reaction would be.

"Do not be nervous, *ma chérie*. You have nothing to fear."

When François bent to kiss her tenderly, Aimée felt as if she were falling down an endless black tunnel with no hope of rescue. His left arm was around her back while the other slid to her side; warm fingers explored the contours of her breast. She nearly sobbed aloud but managed to keep silent as her instinct for survival won out. Trying not to think of what was to come, Aimée concentrated instead on the mouth that was pressed to her own. He was kissing her with infinite gentleness and skill, yet she was revolted. How could this experience be so drastically different from what she had shared with St. Briac. Where was the fire that had danced over her nerves that night in the garden?

"Sweet...sweet," the king was murmuring thickly as his lips traveled downward over her neck, shoulder, and the first blossoming of her breasts. Aimée held her breath, certain that her heart would burst. He had begun to lower the bodice of her shift, when a knock at the door caused them both to start.

"Who is it?" François demanded impatiently. "What do you want?"

"Sire, is that you?" a familiar voice demanded. "What a surprise."

"For God's sake, St. Briac, what is it? Have you nothing better to do than wander the halls and knock on doors at random?"

"Oh, I did not choose this chamber at random, sire," he answered cheerfully. "I've come to visit Aimée. Is she there?"

"Incroyable," the king muttered. Climbing off the bed, he straightened his doublet and strode over to open the door. "Have you taken leave of your senses? What business have you with Mademoiselle de Fleurance, and how do you know her?"

St. Briac grinned and strode past François with an impudence that made Aimée want to laugh and weep at the same time. He had *come.*

"I have a confession to make, sire. Perhaps you should sit down." St. Briac perched audaciously on the edge of the bed and reached for Aimée's hand. *"Bonjour, miette.* You are well today?"

She blinked in confusion at his fond words and tone. What was the man up to? "Yes, I am well," she replied hesitantly.

St. Briac turned her hand over and kissed the palm, looking up at her with eyes that were reckless and unmistakably angry. "I have missed you," he whispered.

In spite of her spinning thoughts, Aimée felt the inevitable current of warmth from his hard, hot mouth. Never had he looked more appealingly masculine to her, clad in the fitted unembellished doublet, the whiteness of the fraise contrasting with the cocoa-brown velvet and the neat line of his bearded jaw. There was a dangerous undercurrent in St. Briac's demeanor that filled Aimée with excitement and apprehension.

"For God's sake, Thomas, I demand that you explain yourself! Quit fawning over Mademoiselle de Fleurance and make your confession." The king shifted uneasily in his chair.

"It is not easy." He sighed as if distressed and then stared toward the windows. "How can I find words to tell my king, my cherished friend, that I have helped to deceive him? I knew from the first night, in Gençay, that it was Aimée and not Honorine de Fleurance who had joined the court train, yet I did not come to you with the truth."

Horrified, Aimée burst out, "But it was not his fault, Your Majesty! I am to blame. I begged him and even resorted to tears, and still he refused ever to tell a lie to you for my sake."

"*Voyons*, there is no more reason for either of you to be concerned about Aimée's little masquerade," François insisted. "She and I have talked it over and agreed that it was an amusing adventure. I find I am quite charmed by her resourcefulness and have begged her to remain with us here at court." He stood and continued firmly, "And now, my friend, if you are done confessing, I must ask you to leave us."

St. Briac looked at Aimée for a long minute, searching her face and eyes. Then he sighed harshly. "I fear that I cannot do that, sire. There is more that I must confess. You see . . ." He paused to rake long fingers through his chestnut hair. "You see, I find that I am in love with Mademoiselle de Fleurance. I believe that she returns my feelings, and in truth, she has already given me her maidenhood. I came here this morning to ask her"—a muscle tightened in his jaw "—to be my wife."

PART II

Ah! my heart, ah! what aileth thee
To set so light by liberty,
Making me bond when I was free?
Ah! my heart, ah! what aileth thee?

SIR THOMAS WYATT
(1503–1542)

CHAPTER 11

 *May 5, 1526*

"*Did you mean* it?" Aimée managed to ask softly after François had left them alone. He had promised to give them an answer that night.

St. Briac, who had been pacing like a caged panther ever since the door closed, whirled around now. "*Mean it?*" he echoed in a low voice deadly with sarcasm.

Instantly on guard, Aimée cringed against the pillows as he advanced on her. This caustic, dangerous-looking St. Briac was so unfamiliar to her as to seem frightening. Why was he acting this way, and what had she done to deserve it?

"I would laugh were this entire situation not so pathetic. *Mean it?* Could you doubt my eternal love for you, Mademoiselle de Fleurance? Have I not told you often enough?" When he arched a brow above narrowed eyes, Aimée thought that surely Satan was there before her. "*Naturellement* you've been aware that I have dreamed only of making you my wife since the first moment we met. I cannot bear to live one minute deprived of your sweet company."

"Stop it!" Aimée choked on burning tears. "Why are you saying these things? Why did you do this—tell the king that you want to marry me—if in truth you hate me so? Once you swore that you would never tell him less than the truth on my account. Now you suddenly burst in after not speaking to me for days, lie outrageously and in a way that ensnarls your own life, then attack me as if I had coerced you into behaving this way."

"Shall we call François back and claim that I was momentarily deranged? Too much sun? Doubtless he'd be happy to believe it; he could resume his seduction. Is that what you want? Perhaps I was too hasty; tell me that you were eager for his lovemaking, and I'll gladly take back every word I spoke about wanting to marry you."

His voice was like a whip, and she cringed with each lash. "No, you're right. I did *not* want the king to make love to me. He was kind and gentle, and I knew I had no choice after he had been magnanimous enough to forgive me, but I thought I would be ill. I thought I would die! And"—She let out a little sobbing hiccough—"and all he did was kiss me before you came. You were like an angel, appearing from heaven to save me—"

"Oh, no. Spare me this, I beg you!" Feeling himself weaken slightly in the face of her appeal, St. Briac turned away and groaned in frustration.

"I still do not understand," Aimée whispered tentatively.

"Why I begged your hand in marriage? Because, my naive troublemaking vixen, nothing short of honorable intentions on my part could have dissuaded the king of France from claiming you as his own. What should I have said, 'Excuse me, sire, for interrupting you in the act of seduction, but I happen to know that this young lady would prefer not to engage in lovemaking with you'? Or I could have told him that you were already deflowered—by me!—but that it was a mistake and I had no further interest in you yet would prefer that he keep his hands to himself. *Or*—"

Aimée put up a hand, conscious all the while of a nagging pain in her breast. "I understand. It was the same dilemma I was faced with. One doesn't deny the king."

"Unless we were friends, I couldn't have interfered even with a marriage proposal. Only because he is fond of me will François consider it."

None of this answered the question uppermost in Aimée's mind, the one she was terrified to pose. "But you did not have to do this for me, monseigneur. You care not for me but for the duchess de Roanne. I do not understand, and I would appreciate hearing the reason."

"*I* don't *know!*" Every muscle in St. Briac's body was

clenched as he towered above her. "It must be this damnable excess of conscience that has plagued me all my life. Just this once I would that it had deserted me!"

He exited, slamming the paneled door, and the floodgates broke inside of Aimée. Collapsing, she turned her face into the pillows and wept until she was spent.

"Are you joking? Perhaps you fell asleep or forgot the time and that is why you did not join me for our rendezvous in the woods!" Ghislaine turned away from her fireplace, haloed by the dancing flames, and stared hopefully at St. Briac. "*Vraiment, mon cher*, I would not dream of interfering if I could believe that you were serious about this abrupt betrothal, but I confess that I am stunned."

"No more than I, Ghislaine," he muttered. His attempts to explain Aimée's situation and his own involvement had sounded bizarre even to his own ears. No wonder Ghislaine thought he had spun the tale for her amusement. "The marriage proposal was not something I planned. I was not contemplating it as we spoke on the steps this morning. If Gaspard, that devil's agent, had not told me that François was in Aimée's chamber, none of this would have happened."

"But Thomas, I still do not understand why you feel such responsibility for the fate of this girl who has been unknown to me and as yet unseen."

He stared at Ghislaine as she crossed the room, arms outstretched with typical warmth and generosity. She already had dressed for tonight's banquet and looked especially lovely in a gown of rose silk, its long fitted sleeves and bodice sewn with crystals and pearls. Her toffee-hued waves of hair were tamed by a golden caul studded with more pearls, making a focal point of the large, luminous blue eyes that were the duchess's most striking feature. They were invariably clear and honest; St. Briac needed to ask few questions when he could search her eyes.

"I wish that I could explain," he whispered, gathering her into his embrace. If the story of the passionate encounter between himself and Aimée at Chenonceau would have clarified the situation, Thomas would have offered it, but he knew that that was not the reason for this entanglement. It had begun the first moment he saw her in the Nieuil woods. "If only she had not begun this foolish masquerade, we would never have come to this. I told her—the instant I discovered what she was up to—that it was insane, that she was asking for trouble she couldn't imagine, that it would end with the king in her bed or worse!"

Ghislaine drew back to gaze up into the face she loved so well. How tense he was, how unaware of her own presence. "Your Aimée is very headstrong, I take it. I wonder why she arouses such protective instincts in you."

"*Protective?* The principal emotions I feel in her company are frustration and rage. The vixen has caused me nothing but trouble. I wish our paths had never crossed. I swear, if I could wake up tomorrow and find her returned to Nieuil, I would feel only profound relief."

"I hope then, for your sake, Thomas, that you will not be forced to live with Mademoiselle de Fleurance for the rest of your days."

He gave a derisive snort and reached up to rub the back of his neck. "I don't intend that it will come to that, *ma chérie.*"

"Well, as you know, I cannot protest if it should, since I am a married woman myself. In any case, we can go on as in the past, can't we?"

St. Briac was touched by the stricken expression that passed over Ghislaine's usually serene countenance. "*Mais, oui! Sans doute, ma petite.*" He kissed her long and deeply yet without desire.

"It is late, Thomas," she whispered when at length they drew apart. "You must dress. I will see you when we sup."

His eyes were distracted as he lifted both of Ghislaine's pale hands and kissed her fingers, each of which gleamed with a unique and beautiful ring. "I am grateful as always for your gift of listening without judging, criticizing, or arguing with me. You are my peace."

Ghislaine sighed to herself as he departed and wondered why trouble rather than peace seemed to have captured her lover's attention and passion.

Gaspard LeFait was waiting with a large linen towel when his master stepped dripping from the *cuvé*.

"You will be late if you don't hurry," the little man muttered.

Fed up with his own bad temper, St. Briac managed not

to reply. Instead, he dried off briskly in front of the fire and looked around for his clothes.

"I suppose you will be dining with your beloved fiancée," Gaspard ventured while producing the garments.

"Guard your tongue," came the low response.

"At times it has a will of its own, monseigneur."

"So I've noticed." St. Briac drew on hose and then pulled a snowy shirt over his head.

"In truth, I cannot stop it now from saying that this day's events astonish even me."

"Indeed?" Sighing, St. Briac tucked the shirt into snug haut-de-chausses of black velvet.

The sigh struck deep inside Gaspard. What had become of his merry, devil-may-care master who always faced trouble with a jest? "Will you listen to no one? How could you have allowed yourself to become ensnarled in such a coil? I sensed from the first that the black-haired chit would complicate our lives, but I never would have dreamed that she'd *change* them—or *you*, monseigneur."

St. Briac raised dark turquoise eyes to stare hard at his manservant. "My life is my own, Gaspard, as are its complications. I'll deal with both one way or another."

The little man tightened his lips but kept silent as he helped St. Briac don a black velvet doublet trimmed in silver. After it was laced, he straightened his master's pleated fraise and pulled bits of white shirt-sleeve through the slashings in the doublet.

"Monseigneur," Gaspard said at length, watching the tall man distractedly brush his hair. "Pardon me for saying so, but it is my feeling that this misadventure will not be resolved with your usual roguish ease. *Vraiment*, my feeling is that Mademoiselle de Fleurance is the greatest problem we— that is, *you*—have ever encountered. Even in battle I was not so concerned about whether you would emerge un-scathed."

St. Briac paused in the doorway and gave his manservant a wry smile. "Don't quote me, windbag, but for once you are absolutely correct."

Downstairs in the hall of honor, Aimée stood near the elaborate fireplace where tiny sculpted angels held up gilded carvings of a salamander and an ermine on the mantelpiece. She looked around, decidedly ill at ease, and sipped her wine. People whose names she could not remember milled about, garbed in rich fabrics crusted with jewels. The colors were unlike the simpler ones she was used to: copper, violet, cendre, gentian, topaz yellow. The king wore cloth-of-silver set with sapphires and diamonds; his jerkin was royal blue velvet with more diamonds and ermine trim. Even standing off to one side with Anne d'Heilly and a small group of rapt admirers, François was the focal point of the hall. This was the first banquet given on a grand scale since the court's arrival at Blois. Celebration was in the air, and spirits were high.

Aimée regarded the king for a long minute. After his entrance that evening, to the loud fanfare of several trumpets, he had surprised the uneasy Aimée by working his way gradually to her side. With good humor François introduced her to everyone in sight and told the story of her masquerade as though it amused him endlessly. The members of the court, pink-cheeked in the rosemary-scented firelight, nodded politely before drifting away in the eventual wake of their monarch. Now she stood alone and felt their eyes on her from a distance, sensed their curious whispers and condescending appraisals of her person. François had said nothing of St. Briac or his astonishing marriage proposal. What had he decided? What did she *want* him to decide?

Her eyes strayed back to the mantelpiece and rested on the ermine. Queen Claude had been raised here at Blois, the daughter of Louis XII and Anne de Bretagne. François had undertaken the creation of the newest wing so that his wife might continue to live in a fitting manner at her childhood home. This was the first time François had been here since her death during the Italian campaign; Aimée wondered whether he mourned the poor young queen who had died at twenty-five after giving her husband seven children in eight years of marriage. Had he loved her? Everyone knew that there had always been royal mistresses, most principally Françoise de Foix, the comtesse de Châteaubriant, who eventually had fallen out of favor after several years and now was in exile at her husband's estates in Britanny. Aimée found this style of life bewildering and wondered whether Queen Claude had, too. By all accounts she had been sweet, loving, and charitable, though not a beauty. Had her plainness been her undoing with François? Aimée sighed. Perhaps the poor little queen had died of a broken heart. "*Potius*

Mori Quam Foedari" was the motto inscribed beneath the graceful ermine: "Better death than disgrace."

"*Bon soir*, Mademoiselle de Fleurance. Pardon me for saying so, but I could not help noticing that you appear a bit forlorn. Would you mind company?"

Instantly on guard, Aimée looked around to discover the kind, lovely face of Marguerite d'Angoulême. They had met in the flurry of introductions performed by the king but had exchanged only a word or two of polite greeting. Aimée remembered now what St. Briac had said about François's beloved sister: "The lady is not only graceful but compassionate and intelligent as well."

"It is very thoughtful of you to offer..."

"Marguerite. You must call me Marguerite; everyone does."

Aimée beamed, put at ease by the older woman's warmth and friendliness. "I would be honored—and I am Aimée."

"I saw you looking at the ermine, Aimée. Lovely, is it not? Just as was the woman whom it symbolizes."

"How sad that the queen died at such a young age."

"Do you think so?" Marguerite smiled serenely. "I prefer to think that our Lord let her remain with us until her work was done and that now she is with Him. Perhaps you have heard that Claude's body has been waiting here at Blois until my brother could return for the funerals for her and their little daughter, Louise. There is evidence that the queen has performed miracles here since her death."

"Really?"

"At any rate, you must not grieve for her, Aimée; she had a very rich life. As the king's daughter, she could not inherit the throne, but was it not fortunate that she was still able to become queen when my brother assumed the crown? Perhaps it was part of God's plan that King Louis would have no surviving son. His daughter was able to bring the monarch's own blood to a match with François, who everyone agrees was destined to rule our land. It must have been a joy for Claude to give life to their children, and she would have been proud to see her own sons conducting themselves with such bravery now in Spain. The queen graciously did not only God's work but that of France as well. Singular achievements for so brief a stay in *this* world, *n'est-ce pas*? And now she is enjoying her reward."

Aimée blinked, mesmerized by Marguerite's gentle, calm voice and point of view. "I hadn't thought of it that way."

"You are still very young. I am doubtless twice your age, Aimée, and have learned that wisdom and trust in God grow with time." Her eyes shifted to the gown Aimée wore, signaling a change in the tone of the conversation. "How are you enjoying all this excitement? It must be quite different from what you are accustomed to in Nieuil. I wonder that we did not meet at the hunting lodge last month."

"That is another complicated story," Aimée murmured ruefully. "I am only glad that I no longer have to fear discovery by the king. How kind and understanding he has been."

"I don't wonder, child. You are as fresh, unaffected, and lovely as a spring rain. That gown is a treasure."

Aimée glanced down at the relatively simple creation of rich emerald velvet edged with golden embroidery. Just above her hips rode the same golden girdle she had worn to the king's hunting lodge at Nieuil, but her necklace was a single diamond on a delicate gold chain, and the crispenette that tamed her ebony curls was sprinkled with diamonds among the more numerous pearls. Still, Aimée felt that her finery paled in comparison with the sumptuous clothes worn by everyone else at court.

"It's really nothing, Marguerite," she apologized, blushing a bit. "In truth, I feel like a sparrow in a crowd of peacocks."

Although Marguerite's gown was as lavish as any, she scoffed lightly at Aimée's words. "Nonsense, my dear. It is your very simplicity that makes you shine, like a perfect gem that requires no excessive embellishment. I can see why my brother is so taken with you."

Aimée flushed and tried to smile, but Marguerite exclaimed softly, "Ah, speaking of masterful simplicity, there is a brilliant example." She paused to emit a decidedly girlish sigh. "Do you see that man who has just entered at the far end of the hall? He is taller than anyone else, with broad shoulders, and is clad all in black velvet except for the white at his slashings. Black! Who else but St. Briac would dare it and bring it off so effortlessly?" All at once, Marguerite seemed to remember Aimée and collected her wits. "No doubt you have yet to meet the seigneur de St. Briac, but perhaps you glimpsed him as we traveled north. He is quite a man!"

Rosy-cheeked and speechless, Aimée stared across the hall and instantly met the gleaming blue-green eyes of St. Briac. He glanced quickly away, a muscle moving in his jaw, and appeared to be intent on conversation with Bonnivet and Florange. A sigh rose in Aimée's throat. "*Bien sûr*, Marguerite," she murmured wistfully, "quite a man, indeed."

CHAPTER 12

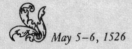 *May 5–6, 1526*

Boards of polished walnut had been laid over trestles before the crowd was seated for the lavish repast. Aimée stayed close to Marguerite as they approached the table, but to her chagrin the king announced that she would be sitting on the other side, next to the seigneur de St. Briac.

Moments later, eyes averted, she felt him settle down beside her on the long bench. The fresh scent of his soap intoxicated her, and she found her downcast gaze fixed on St. Briac's hard thigh, sheathed in black velvet, which rested just inches away from her body. *Silly fool*, Aimée scolded herself. *Do you want him to think you are a tongue-tied child undone by his mere proximity?* Straightening her back, she looked up to find that he was engaged in conversation with a blushing lady on his left. Aimée turned her attention to a goblet of strong Hungarian wine.

"So, *miette*," he said at length in a tone both soft and cold, "we meet again. Fate can be so confounding."

Aimée turned her head, and their eyes locked. St. Briac's expression was unreadable, as though he were making an effort to erect a high barrier between them. She wondered fleetingly if the lighthearted wit that once had seemed an intrinsic part of the man still lurked anywhere within him.

Rising to the challenge, Aimée let her almost feline eyes flicker over his black costume.

"*Bon soir*, monseigneur," she greeted him, deliberately casual. "Are you in mourning?"

St. Briac's lips twitched of their own accord, and he cursed her inwardly for making him smile. It seemed that no matter how he tried, he couldn't hate the minx. "In mourning?" he echoed, remembering what she had said to him on the barge. "For my lost innocence? Perish the thought, especially at this late date."

Aimée pursed her lips, struggling against laughter without success. It spilled out charmingly. White teeth gleamed, dimples winked, and leaf-green eyes tilted upward to melt St. Briac's shield of ice. He shook his head with a wry smile of surrender.

"Why is it so difficult to remain angry with you, *miette*? I was looking forward to making you suffer through this entire evening. I was going to be cold as marble, ruthlessly cruel."

"I am sorry to disappoint your plans, monseigneur," Aimée interrupted primly. Bubbles of happy delight rose inside her. "Truly, I am repentant."

One side of his mouth quirked upward. "Yes, that's obvious."

Distraction appeared in the form of silver-clad pages carrying giant dishes that held pyramids of meats in all forms, roasted or boiled, mixed with fish or vegetables. Sauces arrived in separate bowls. St. Briac was surprised to look up and find the king gazing speculatively at both him and Aimée. He raised a brow in question, but François merely gave him an infuriating smile before turning to respond to some remark of Louise de Savoy's.

During the meal there was little opportunity for St. Briac and Aimée to share any private conversation, which was a relief to both. Aimée picked her way through dishes of soup; rillons, a kind of potted pork from Tours; beef paté; shad with butter sauce; artichokes; cauliflower; fillets of veal with cream sauce; cheese from Vincennes, freshly curdled and drained in little baskets woven from wicker; and finally a colorful assortment of every imaginable variety of fruit. There was still much that she had not tasted, more courses than she could count. The silver plates were changed with each new dish, the goblets were replaced and filled with different wines, and there was a new type of eating utensil that Aimée had never seen before. St. Briac explained that it was called a fork, and was used to spear rebellious bits of food so that they would not be spilled on one's clothes. He tried to remain matter-of-fact, but the sight of Aimée staring suspiciously at the ivory-handled implement made him want to laugh. Instead, he smiled and hoped no one had seen.

Lofty conversation swirled about them. The guests were discussing astronomy, the law, medicine, Charles V and the possible outcome of the treaty which had yet to be signed, the fate of humanity, explorations of new worlds. Aimée and St. Briac listened with half an ear; neither could admit it, but their attention was focused on each other, and both were wondering what decision the king had reached concerning their betrothal.

Across the table, one voice rose above the others. The chevalier de Chauvergé had leaned forward to speak to the king.

"Your Majesty, I must inquire whether you have given further thought to Georges Teverant and his involvement in the Semblançay affair. Your very wise mother and I were just discussing this, and we agree that it is a problem that merits your immediate attention."

"Does it?" François asked mildly, lifting his serviette to wipe a droplet of cream sauce from his lips. "I am not quite as convinced as you seem to be, my dear Chauvergé, and your constant pestering is beginning to irritate me. I'll admit that there is much that Semblançay has done that concerns me, yet Teverant appears to be an honest enough young man. It doesn't seem to me that it would serve justice to punish him for the sins of an old yet powerful man."

"But sire, Teverant was Semblançay's assistant, his agent in dishonoring you."

The king's almond-shaped eyes flickered only briefly in Chauvergé's direction. "I am well aware of the facts and will interpret them as I see fit. When you are king, Chauvergé, I trust that you will be able to do the same." He reached for a fig in a gesture of dismissal.

"Your Majesty, don't you realize that Teverant would not have departed from the court before we reached Blois if he were not guilty?" The weasel-faced chevalier was too upset even to heed the look of warning from Louise de Savoy.

"Perhaps he left because he was afraid certain people

might pressure me into having him arrested." The sharp note of annoyance in François's voice made everyone at the table fall silent. "I find this conversation tedious. Let us enjoy the music." He spoke over his shoulder to a hovering page. "Bring some sweetmeats and more wine, and send in the tumblers."

Intimidated by the monarch's obvious anger, Aimée tried to make herself smaller in case he might decide to vent some in her direction. For some minutes there was no sound except the lilting melodies produced by a trio of flutes, a spinnet, and a viol. Servants scurried across the tiled floor to do the king's bidding. Furtively, Aimée stole a glance at St. Briac and was surprised to find his expression even stormier than François's. Dark turquoise eyes gleamed dangerously as they regarded Chauvergé from under concealing lashes, and a familiar muscle twitched in his jaw.

The tumblers, clad in bright colors, cavorted for the guests and made a fine diversion from the tense scene of a few moments before. Aimée stared with a child's delight and appreciation. She pressed her hands together, eyes alight, unaware of the watchful gazes of St. Briac, the king, and the duchesse de Roanne, who sat across from them but far enough down the table so that Aimée had not noticed her presence. When one of the tumblers cartwheeled to Aimée's side and impishly tweaked her rosy cheek, she responded with an enchanting peal of laughter.

St. Briac couldn't repress a smile; he stared at her profile—the fringe of sooty lashes above sparkly green eyes, the delicate retroussé nose, and the rose and white of her lovely uninhibited smile. The minx wasn't conscious of the picture she made; she had no inkling that every man in sight was spellbound by her innocent joy. A now familiar sigh rose in St. Briac's chest, and he wondered again why life had to be so complicated, why pleasure and trouble had been presented to him in one confusing package.

It was long past midnight when the last of the dishes were removed. Guests lingered, sipping sweet red wine as they contentedly awaited the king's departure from the table. None would dare to leave before him. At length, François did push back his chair and stand; then he raised his goblet.

"I want to tell all of you first how truly blissful it is to be here at Blois with those I care for. The welcome I have received everywhere in France has raised my spirits to new heights, but this first celebration here is especially meaningful for me." He paused, eyes twinkling, before continuing. "To add further to my high spirits, I have an announcement to make. Our friend Thomas Mardouet, seigneur de St. Briac, is pledged to wed the newest member of our court, Aimée de Fleurance. I ask you all to raise your glasses in toasting their love and future marriage."

St. Briac felt as if the king had struck him in the chest with a lance. Cheerful voices called out congratulations amid the buzz of shocked whispers. Bonnivet, who sat at his left, pounded him on the back.

"Well done, *mon ami*," he exclaimed. "I was about to try my luck with that refreshing nymph myself, but I see that you were ahead of all of us. How did you do it?"

Thomas opened his mouth, but no words came. Florange appeared behind them, kissing Aimée's hand and delivering courtly wishes of congratulations before bending to whisper in his friend's ear.

"I never thought I'd see the day, you rogue. It's not surprising, though. The maiden is exquisite, and you were long overdue for love."

Finally, as the chaos diminished, St. Briac looked over at Aimée. She was pale and appeared stricken; his heart went out to her.

"Are you all right?"

"No, I don't think so." Her voice sounded remote, and there was no joy in her eyes. "I believe I wish to return to my chamber."

The king had wandered away from the table, surrounded by the usual cluster of admiring hangers-on, and so St. Briac said, "I'll escort you. Allow me a moment to say our farewells to François."

When they came into the deserted, starlit courtyard, the silence was heavy. St. Briac was perplexed to find that he felt a bit offended by her gloom. Was this turn of events worse than her former betrothal to Armand Rovicette, for God's sake? The chit behaved as if François had just sentenced her to a slow and painful execution.

"Is the thought of marrying me really so devastating?" he muttered at last.

Aimée came to a complete stop. Her spine stiffened, and she made a little strangled noise. "I might ask you the same, monseigneur!"

"What the hell does that mean?"

She glared up at him, but the sight of his chiseled face, silvered by the moonlight, was irresistible. She stared down at the thick cobbles under her slippers and stalked away. *"Men!* You are all too dense for words!"

In three strides, St. Briac had her slim arm in his grasp. "I don't consider that childish insult an answer."

"Are you planning to break my arm if I don't provide an appropriate response?"

"You little witch, I don't know why I ever endured your company in the first place let alone was so insane as to rescue you from every predicament you could manage to ensnare yourself in!"

"Stop throwing your less than gallant behavior in my face every time I raise my voice to you! If you think I'll smile at you in silent adoration for the rest of my life just because you *grudgingly* came to my aid once or twice—"

"Arrgh!" St. Briac threw back his head and gave a smothered yell of frustration. He was about to answer in a more articulate fashion, when light from the hall of honor spilled onto the courtyard and two more couples appeared. To his consternation he saw that one couple was the duc and duchesse de Roanne. "Endeavor to close your mouth, mademoiselle," he ground out, "until we reach the privacy of your chamber. I am not anxious to make this quarrel public."

"How dare you? You cannot order me around, especially in that tone of voice! I shall speak if I—" Aimée's rage flared to new heights as he pulled her along with one hand while the other was clapped roughly over her mouth, muffling her protests.

Finally St. Briac led his new fiancée into her chamber and closed the heavy door behind them. Freed of his suffocating grip, Aimée whirled around. *"Parbleu!* I pity the poor, unsuspecting maiden who finally does become your wife, monseigneur, and I thank our Lord that I have the wits to escape such a fate."

"What are you raving about now?"

"It is obvious that you despise me, that you have only suffered my company out of some misguided sense of responsibility. You said it yourself this morning: *Conscience* obliged you to save me from the king by offering to marry me!" Unable to bear his unwavering gaze, she turned and walked over to a carved walnut dresser before continuing.

"I have my pride, monseigneur, and I am not so desperate that I would wed a man who doesn't care for me."

"And for whom you feel nothing?" he pressed in a low voice.

"I would not say that, but I certainly don't *love* you," Aimée retorted with all the emphasis she could muster.

"And just how do you suggest we extricate ourselves from this coil?" For some reason, St. Briac was struck by a wave of anger at her words. He was not a vain man, but neither was he obtuse, and over the years scores of maidens had angled to become his wife. Who did this vixen think she was to spurn the first proposal he ever had made, especially after the king's public announcement? "I am an adult and am perfectly willing to take responsibility for my words and actions. I was sober when I told François that I would marry you. No one has held a sword to my back and forced me into this situation—not in the Nieuil woods or during the journey here, not in the gardens at Chenonceau, and not this morning when I knew that the king meant to bed you."

Aimée stood frozen, trying to discern the nuances of emotion in his husky voice. Now she wished that she had not turned away from St. Briac's eyes, for they might have provided the answers she craved. "I understand what you are saying, monseigneur, but the fact remains that you have acted not out of love but for other reasons. Truly I do appreciate all that you have done to help me. You are a man of character."

"But?" He could not comprehend the fury he felt.

"But what is between us is no basis for a marriage. I want and need and deserve more. So do you. It would be unfair to both of us."

Who was this perfect man going to be who would supply all the qualities Aimée wanted, needed, and deserved in a husband? St. Briac wondered angrily. "Far be it from me to condemn you to a lifetime of suffering my company, mademoiselle, yet I must ask you again how you plan to avoid that fate."

Aimée was chilled by his frigid tone. Still, when he crossed the floor to stand behind her, she imagined that she could feel the heat from his powerful body. Swallowing, she discovered that her mouth had remained dry.

"Have the courtesy to face me, *s'il vous plaît*," St. Briac said harshly.

She turned slowly, looking small and pale in the faint candlelight. "I will find a way. I shall discover some means of leaving Blois without causing any harm to your reputation and honor. It may take me a few days to think of a plan, and in the meantime, I suppose we shall have to continue this charade..." Aimée's voice trailed off as she became increasingly conscious of the energy in the air between them. He was so tall. Never had St. Briac seemed quite so strong and powerful as he towered over her, and there was something about his hard visage that sent a shiver down her spine.

"Ah, I see. Mademoiselle de Fleurance will prove once again her legendary resourcefulness. I shall wait with interest to discover what scheme you devise that will save us both from a fate worse than death, but in the meantime I think it would be wise to practice our acting skills so that we will be able to carry off this charade. That was the word you used, wasn't it?" Deliberately, he reached out a dark hand to remove the crispenette that already had come loose during their journey out of the courtyard. Aimée's curls spilled down, silky and gleaming.

She knew that she ought to react indignantly, but she was unable to fight the hot flush of excitement that swept over her body. St. Briac's gaze was insolently caustic as he bent down to caress her lips with his. He felt the gasp that she tried to smother yet did not touch her anywhere else for a long, tantalizing minute. The fragrance of violets stirred his senses almost as keenly as the taste of Aimée's sweet, pliant mouth. Yearning to kiss her in earnest, St. Briac still held back until she finally parted her lips with a soft whimper. Steely arms pulled her upward into an embrace that seemed to fuse them together with its fire. Aimée felt as if she were being consumed by his mouth, and she reveled in the swirling blaze of sensations. She couldn't think, only feel: the texture of the hair curling at the back of St. Briac's strong neck, the muscles under his velvet doublet that seemed to crush her breasts, the urgent pressure of his mouth as their breath mingled in a kiss more devastating than anything Aimée had ever imagined.

Her arousal intensified when she felt the undeniable evidence of his own against her loins. St. Briac's hardness seemed to burn through their clothing; she waited instinctively for him to carry her to the bed. They would make love until dawn, and the charade would be over. It would be the beginning of a true betrothal, its flame kindled by joyous love.

When he released her, Aimée was so unprepared that she nearly fell against the dresser.

"Brava, mademoiselle. That was most impressive." St. Briac taunted her with an eyebrow arched above icy blue-green eyes. "*Vraiment*, even I was nearly convinced by your performance, so I've no doubt that you will be able to fool the rest of the court until you settle on a plan to escape." He walked to the doorway but turned to add, "This charade promises to be more amusing than I had anticipated. *Bon soir*, Aimée." Firelight flickered over the planes of his bronzed face as he opened the door and gave her a last grim smile. "Sleep well."

CHAPTER 13

 *May 6, 1526*

After a night so restless that Aimée was certain she hadn't slept at all, her body surrendered at dawn; she found a dreamless peace from the tormenting thoughts of St. Briac and his outrageous behavior. During hours spent alone in the darkness she had rehearsed dozens of speeches that she intended to deliver as soon as they were face to face again and out of earshot of others. For now, however, Aimée lay sprawled on her back in the middle of the big bed, oblivious to the morning sunshine.

Suzette winced as she put out a hand and jiggled her mistress's shoulder. "Mam'selle, *réveillez-vous*! It is past nine o'clock, and there are some impatient ladies here to see you!"

Aimée returned slowly to reality. She felt dismal in spite of the warm, buttery light that poured across her bed. "Tell them..." She paused to lick her lips. Last night's wine must have been more potent than it had seemed. "Tell them to go away, whoever they are. It is most rude to arrive at this hour without an appointment."

"But I cannot, mam'selle! Your—your"—Suzette finally coughed out the incredible word—"fiancé has sent them with strict instructions to fit you for as many new gowns as you desire—now! I tried to put them off, but they insisted that they would wait until you awakened." Suzette was dying to ask a dozen questions about the betrothal announcement, but the irritated expression on Aimée's face gave her pause. The court servants could talk of nothing else this morning, and all of them were counting on Suzette to provide details. "I, I want to offer my congratulations, mam'selle. How exciting and romantic that you and the seigneur de St. Briac have fallen in love, and even I was not aware!"

Aimée crawled out of bed and put on her robe. "I am not in the mood for girlish conversation, Suzette. I didn't sleep well last night."

"I'm not surprised. I saw the seigneur leaving this chamber when Paul brought me back after midnight, and I daresay that I wouldn't be able to sleep either after being held in that man's arms."

Turning toward the basin of warm water that waited for her on a carved chest, Aimée rolled her eyes but refrained from verbalizing her feelings. Like it or not, she would have to keep up appearances, as St. Briac had put it, even with Suzette. "You may tell those women that I will receive them in ten minutes."

The session with the dressmakers was an ordeal. To Aimée's chagrin, St. Briac had given specific instructions about the gowns he wanted made for his bride to be. Every suggestion of her own was politely brushed aside until she thought she would scream with frustration. Aimée couldn't recall feeling quite so ill tempered and restless even at the worst times at home. When at last the final measurements were taken and notations made, the women began to assemble their fabric samples, chattering animatedly among themselves about the wardrobe they would create. Tense and agitated, Aimée wandered over to the window. She felt like a bird locked in a cage.

Staring down at the assortment of servants and nobility that milled about the sun-splashed courtyard, her eyes widened at the sight of St. Briac and the duchesse de Roanne. They were strolling toward the arched opening to the gardens, her hand through his arm as they talked. Outrage blazed in Aimée as she watched Ghislaine pluck a grape from the cluster he held and then put it in his smiling mouth, her fingers lingering suggestively. How dare they! In broad daylight! Was this his idea of keeping up appearances? Flaunting his married mistress right under her window! It was too much to be borne.

Aimée flung open one of the paneled doors on the front of her dresser and yanked out the first gown she saw. It was simply fashioned of faded yellow linen; it had been one of her favorites for long walks in the Nieuil woods. She had been wearing only a chemise and did not even bother to add a petticoat now before pulling the dress over her head.

"Suzette!" The little maid scurried in from her adjoining cabinet, and Aimée snapped, "Fasten this, *s'il vous plaît.* I am going out."

Suzette fumbled with the back of the gown while her mistress angrily combed her touseled black curls. "Out? Alone?"

"Yes, alone. It is not the first time I have gone out alone, and it won't be the last!"

"*D'accord*, mam'selle," Suzette whispered, wondering what could be putting her mistress in such a temper. She had never seen her leaf-green eyes flash quite so stormily. "What if the seigneur de St. Briac comes in search of you? What shall I tell him?"

Aimée donned a pair of kid slippers and passed the dressmakers on her way to the door, ignoring their open-mouthed stares. "I'll tell him myself, I can assure you!"

She was conscious of neither surroundings nor faces as she crossed the courtyard. Even the panorama of the gardens, laid out in tiers that staggered away from the shimmering Loire, could not soften her with their spring beauty. The kitchen garden was closest to the chateau. A half dozen men labored there, planting vegetables and pruning fruit trees in the sunshine. Below it spread bright, extravagant flower beds of narcissus, tulips, hyacinths, primroses, dwarf irises, and lilies, trimmed by boxwood that had been sculpted painstakingly into the shapes of hearts, fans, love letters, masks, and broken hearts. At the farthest edge of the gardens were the cages that housed the royal menagerie of exotic animals from all around the world.

Although there were other couples wandering over the grassy paths, Aimée had no trouble picking out St. Briac's tall form. He and the duchesse had paused and appeared to be engaging in an earnest conversation that she was eager to interrupt. A breeze from the river sent her touseled ebony curls swirling behind her as she scrambled down the hillside, but Aimée was unaware of her disheveled appearance, not even realizing that the bodice of her two-year-old gown fit just a bit too tightly and revealed more of her ripe breasts than was seemly.

"Thomas!" She put deliberate emphasis on his Christian name. "Here you are." Ignoring the surprised faces that turned as she approached, Aimée gave the duchesse de Roanne a venomous smile. "I do hope you'll forgive me for stealing my fiancé away for a while. We have so much to talk about."

St. Briac stared in astonishment, his brow gathering as he tried to discern what the vixen was about. "Aimée! I—"

"Don't say it, *mon cher*, or I'll be blushing in front of the poor duchesse," she interjected in a voice that dripped honey. "Considering what we shared last night, it would be embarrassing for anyone to overhear our private conversation." Enjoying his discomfort, Aimée put a hand up to his face and sighed rapturously. "What a day to be in love."

Ghislaine lifted an eyebrow at her lover but said only, "I would not dream of intruding on such a tender scene. Allow me to offer you my heartfelt congratulations on your impending marriage, mademoiselle, and bid you a good morning."

St. Briac looked pained, but Aimée continued to smile until Ghislaine was out of sight. Then she whipped her hand away from his face and took a step backward.

"You are the most disgusting, vile man it has ever been my misfortune to know," she hissed.

"You actually *are* mad," St. Briac exclaimed. "What is going on? Would it be possible for me to get a rational explanation?" Meanwhile, his eyes roamed over her. "While you are at it, you might also explain why you look more like a peasant than a lady of the court."

"I don't owe you anything, monseigneur, least of all an explanation for my behavior! *Your* behavior in my room last night was worse than a dog's! I will never forgive you for treating me in such a humiliating fashion, and furthermore—"

"Are you in the habit of kissing dogs with such enthusiasm?" His eyes twinkled irrepressibly.

"Oh, no you don't," Aimée cried. "Don't you dare make fun of me. I am furious, and I intend to have my say!"

"By all means." He nodded with mock humility. "I would appear to be a captive audience. Do you mind if I sit down?" She merely glared as he sauntered over to a nearby stone bench and settled comfortably upon it. "Do go on, mademoiselle, but I must beg you to strive for brevity. I have a crowded schedule today."

Aimée realized that he thought her a child in the midst of a tantrum, but nothing could soften her rage.

"First of all, I want to emphasize that I will not allow you to continue last night's insulting treatment of me. You physically attacked me." She tried to ignore the sight of his eyebrows flying up in disbelief. "And then you verbally mocked me in a way that only reinforced what I already suspected. You hold me, and probably all women, in contempt!"

"I do?"

"You are mocking me again right now, monseigneur. I do not appreciate having my opinions and feelings made sport of."

St. Briac bit his lip to suppress at least a dozen suggestions for ways she might avoid that in the future. Instead, he murmured contritely, "I beg your pardon, mademoiselle. *Continuez.*"

"Well, as if last night were not bad enough, you proved your arrogance beyond a shadow of a doubt when you sent those dressmakers to me."

"I am repentant." He fought a grin. "Shall I cancel the order?"

"No, that is, I..." Aimée paused to take a deep breath and gather her thoughts. "A gentleman would have allowed me to dictate the style and color of gowns I wished rather than force his taste on me."

St. Briac shrugged. "That is one way of looking at it. Another way is that I am paying for your new clothes, and although I may not be an expert, I have been at court long enough to know more about its current fashions for ladies than you." Cool turquoise eyes slid downward to the bodice that threatened to burst if Aimée breathed any more agitatedly. "Speaking of gowns, mademoiselle, I don't mean to be *arrogant* or *insulting* or *vile*, but I find this one decidedly worrisome. Isn't there some way of putting more of your bosom inside that dress? I realize that only a *dog* would say this, but you are making a spectacle of yourself."

Instinctively, Aimée glanced down and saw that her nipples were on the verge of exposure. Hot blood rushed to her face. "You are the rudest man I ever met!" She longed to slap him but sensed that she'd regret it later.

St. Briac held up a hand. *"Ça y est!* One more unflattering description of my character and I'll lose count." A rustling noise made him turn just in time to see Bonnivet approaching with the comely daughter of a rich count. In the next instant Aimée found herself being lifted by strong hands and then planted on St. Briac's lap. "Time to be sweet, *miette*," he warned in an undertone, inclining his head toward the couple who were drawing nearer by the moment. It didn't appear that Bonnivet had recognized them yet. "Don't look so desperate. You only need to pretend that you find me irresistible. For appearances' sake, you know."

It was becoming harder to suppress the urge to giggle at one of St. Briac's witty remarks. Aimée was determined, though, that he would not win this skirmish, nor would she be left blushing in humiliation after he managed to turn the tables on her. "Speaking of appearances and spectacles, you certainly made both this morning in the courtyard." She was smiling shyly against his neck, but her whispered words were razor sharp. "The sight of you slobbering all over the duchess's décolletage in front of nearly the entire court was quite revolting."

St. Briac burst out laughing just as Bonnivet and his young lady paused in front of them. Such was his abandon that Aimée momentarily feared she would topple from his lap onto their visitors' feet.

"Mon ami," Bonnivet exclaimed. "I cannot tell you how wonderful it is to see you so happy. Love has transformed you."

"Has it?" Thomas had finally managed to stifle his hilarity; he was wiping tears from his eyes as he spoke. "It's kind of you to say so. Isn't that kind, Aimée?"

An elbow nudged her ribs. Wondering how much more of this she could stand, Aimée nodded brightly. *"More* than kind, *mon ange!"*

Introductions were made all around, but it was difficult for Aimée to concentrate on Michelle Whatever from Tours—or was it Angiers?—with St. Briac's arms fast around her waist, his mouth dipping intermittently to tease an unsuspecting area of her face, his wonderfully male scent tantalizing her nose. In the interest of performing for Bonnivet and the girl, Aimée let herself laugh aloud at his antics. Sometimes she would poke or pinch him out of sight, but that only made him more outrageous. At length Bonnivet bade them *bonjour* and led his young maiden back toward the chateau, pausing only once to glance back curiously at the betrothed couple.

"Wasn't that amusing?" Thomas inquired blithely before adding, "As always, your acting was superb. During the midday meal Bonnivet and his friend from Tours will spread the story about the charming scene of love they stumbled upon." Even though he found himself unnervingly aware of the warm, soft linen and trim waist that curved against his arm and fingers, St. Briac did not release Aimée. Her glossy, violet-scented hair, the satiny brow that grazed his bearded jaw, her profile, so delicate yet lively, just inches away...even the sensation of her feminine derriere shifting uneasily on his lap made it difficult for him to end this latest act in their charade.

"You were very convincing yourself, monseigneur." Aimée coolly tilted her nose upward. "Perhaps overly so."

"Really?" He chuckled lightly, his eyes dancing. "Well, I suppose it was inevitable. With such a bundle of charm cuddling in my arms, I scarcely needed to act at all."

"You are *too* kind," Aimée retorted sarcastically, certain that he was teasing her. However, when she tried to rise, arms that felt like bands of steel held her fast. Narrowing her thick-lashed green eyes, she looked upward and tried to resist the magnetic attraction of St. Briac's face. "In case you hadn't noticed, your friends have left, so if you don't mind—"

"Oh, but I do. Don't I deserve some sort of recompense for all my hard work on your behalf?" Mischievously, he kissed her ear and thought that it was as soft and sweet as a baby's.

"You are only trying to aggravate me, monseigneur, or worse, to make me laugh and forget that I have been angry with you." Aimée was struggling mightily against the quickening of her heart. Why must he torment her so? "*Quand même*, what would your precious duchesse de Roanne say if she could hear you now?"

"If I were not aware of your abysmally low opinion of me, I might think that you were jealous, *miette*." St. Briac still couldn't resist teasing her. "In any event, you needn't be. Your décolletage is much lower than Ghislaine's, I assure you."

She longed to let laughter spill out and then kiss him with

impetuous passion, but last night had provided a cruel lesson. Aimée glared upward into his merry eyes. "Loose me, monseigneur. *Maintenant*."

"Don't say that you doubt my word! Shall I demonstrate? If you don't mind getting wet..."

It was too much. If this situation continued, everything she was determined to accomplish would be undone. Putting both hands up to his shoulders, Aimée pushed with all her might and instantly found herself sprawled on the path.

"You didn't need to use force, mademoiselle. You had but to stand and you would have discovered yourself freed."

She was so stunned that it took a minute to regain her wits. St. Briac stared at her with a nonchalance that held no further trace of laughter; in fact, it was the coldness of his expression that sent tears to her eyes and hot blood to her cheeks. Scrambling up, Aimée brushed bits of grass from her faded skirt and cried, "I hate you! I mean it!" before rushing blindly back toward the chateau.

The town of Blois with its bent, jostling streets and crowds of animated people provided just the sort of escape Aimée needed from the web that was drawing itself about her at the chateau. At first she had run through the deep arch and down the cobbled ramp without any thought but flight. Now the sights and smells of this bustling town at work and play nearly made her forget that she had no business wandering these steep, twisting lanes by herself, particularly in such a state of dishabille. The Blésois seemed not to notice Aimée, however; they were absorbed in their own pursuits.

Growing up in the countryside, she had had little opportunity to enjoy the bright chaos of towns as large as Blois, which boasted nearly ten thousand citizens and attracted visitors from far and wide. Its charm was haphazard. Walled houses leaned so near one another over the brick streets that their dormers could have whispered secrets. Aimée saw more than one windowed gallery built to bridge the distance. She clambered up the precarious hillsides, staring about curiously, passing into alleyways that sometimes became flights of steps. An occasional gargoyle jutted out to startle her from a shadowed corner, but then there would be a basket of flowers hanging from a diamond-paned window or a carved angel beaming down. The homes of the wealthy and powerful mingled with shops whose signboards clattered in the breeze as Aimée walked east on the rue du Puits-Châtel.

Mouth-watering aromas wafted out from a boulangerie, a roast shop, and an auberge. Fruits and vegetables were sold in bins along the streets. It seemed to Aimée that there were more varieties and that they looked even more succulent in the sunlight than those at last night's court banquet. A grumbling sound from her stomach reminded her that she had yet to eat this day; obviously St. Briac had killed her appetite temporarily, but now it was reviving.

"Do you care for *une pomme*, mam'selle? Or *une pêche, ou la poire, très délicieux!*" A withered old woman tempted her with perfect examples of an apple, a peach, and a pear; Aimée could almost taste them.

"*Je suis désolée*, madame. Truly, I wish that I could buy your beautiful fruit, but I have no money." Her smile blended regret with appreciation. *Je vous dis au revoir.*"

"*Attendez*," the old crone ordered in a dry croak. "Don't rush away in such a hurry. That's the problem with young people these days. You think that you already know everything, and you are in *such* a great hurry that you can't wait an extra moment to hear whether you're right or wrong."

Aimée stopped and turned halfway toward the woman, her spring-green eyes wide with consternation. "I shall strive to retain my patience and composure until I hear what it is you want to say to me, madame."

"I won't keep you, mam'selle," the shriveled hag answered with a smile that revealed few teeth. "You look hungry, though. Take these along with you and eat every bite. My fruit're worth your time and appreciation!"

"*Mille mercis*, madame," Aimée cried gratefully. Already she was wondering whether to bite into the peach first or perhaps... "When I can, I'll return and pay you properly."

"*Peut-être.*" The old crone shrugged. "The fruit is my gift to you, but if some day you want to give *me* something—like a coin or two—I would try to accept graciously."

The blue eyes that twinkled at Aimée bespoke a younger woman, and for an instant it seemed that the wrinkled hag was just that: a girl who had retained her compassion and sense of humor in spite of time's inevitable passage and what must have been a great deal of disillusionment. This encounter alone had made the flight from the chateau worthwhile. After another round of farewells, Aimée set off up the hill, some of the fruit cradled in her left arm while she took the pear in her other hand and bit into it with relish. Juice drizzled down from the corners of her smiling mouth.

The sight of what had to be two *filles de joie* lounging sinuously in front of a tavern made Aimée forget her pear for a moment. Bosoms spilling from cheaply made gowns, they gave inviting smiles to every passing man until one, who was not only middle-aged but appeared well bred, linked arms with both of them. The trio went into the tavern amid a chorus of laughter.

Aimée suddenly felt dizzy. When she tried to steady herself, it seemed that her legs would give way. Somehow she found her way to the half-timbered front of the tavern and leaned against it, praying that the world would right itself. The barely eaten pear fell at her feet, while the apple and peach rolled away down the hill, to be confiscated by a thin little urchin who acted as if she had discovered diamonds in the street.

Sweat broke out on Aimée's brow, and she feared that she might faint. At that moment two handsome, well-dressed men approached her.

"*Bonjour*, mademoiselle," the first man, who was fairer and more slight than his companion, said in greeting. He gave Aimée a charming smile. "We noticed that you seem to be in distress. Can we offer assistance?"

The other man, of medium height and powerful build, spoke up. "We would be less than gentlemen to leave you to the mercy of cutpurses and common thieves if you are ill, mademoiselle. Let us help you to our chamber above the tavern, where you can lie down until you feel better."

Aimée tried to focus on their earnest faces. "Your chamber?" she repeated in confusion.

The blond man took her arm. "It's the best place for you," he said soothingly. "Hubert and I have a large soft bed where you can rest until your dizziness passes."

"Well." She allowed herself to be led to the doorway, thinking that it would be lovely to lie down. Oddly, it seemed that she could fall asleep right there on the street. She glanced over at Hubert for reassurance but discovered that he was eying her nearly bared breasts in a way that sounded a warning in her clouded mind. "I don't think...that is—"

The larger fellow caught himself and gave her a sincere

smile. "Don't fret, mademoiselle. My friend and I will take good care of you."

Aimée's tongue felt thick, but she managed to whisper, "No, I'd better not. I must be getting back. They'll worry."

"Nonsense. You're in no condition to go anywhere right now." Annoyance crept into the blond man's voice as he tightened his grip on her arm. "Come along like a good girl."

"No!" She tried to pull free, but her muscles wouldn't obey. "Let me go!"

Hubert caught her other arm with fingers like steel. "Behave yourself now or you'll regret it."

The two of them were pulling her into the dark, musty tavern when the sound of a familiar voice made Aimée's heart soar.

"Kindly do the lady's bidding and unhand her."

All three of them turned to discover the towering figure of St. Briac, his face clenched with rage.

CHAPTER 14

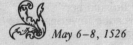 *May 6–8, 1526*

"*This does not* concern you, m'sieur," Hubert declared angrily. "My friend and I are only looking after this lady, who is feeling ill. Go on about your business."

"The lady *is* my business. Loose her." St. Briac's narrowed eyes were jewel-hard.

"And if we do not?" the blond man taunted.

"Well, then I should be forced to kill you," he answered lightly, his fingers closing around the hilt of his sword.

"*Both* of us?" scoffed the muscular Hubert. "I would be entertained by watching you try, m'sieur." He released Aimée's arm, leaving her in the custody of his blond friend, and drew his sword from its scabbard.

Aimée watched dazedly as the two men made perfunctory salutes with their weapons. It was frustrating not to be able to coordinate either her mind or her body. Not only couldn't she fashion a scheme to help St. Briac, she didn't even have the strength to carry one out. It did not seem possible for him to fend off two men, for certainly the one who held her now would step in with his rapier if his companion required assistance. Thomas was considerably taller and more powerful than either foe, but after all, he did have only one body and one weapon.

Blades gleamed and clashed in the sunlight; almost instantly it became obvious that Hubert was outclassed. St. Briac met each lunge with a lightning-quick parry and soft, mocking laughter. His own thrusts were clean and sure. He seemed to be playing with the man, trapping the other sword under his blade repeatedly but not forcing Hubert to drop the weapon. Finally St. Briac maneuvered his terror-stricken opponent against the tavern wall. Hubert struggled to hold him at bay, their blades crossed in a test of strength that the smaller man was losing rapidly. He cast wide, pleading eyes in the direction of his blond friend.

"Oh, unfair!" St. Briac laughed. To Aimée's dismay, he appeared unconcerned at the prospect of an extra man joining the battle against him.

The blond man paled, for he was not eager to challenge the formidable stranger, yet Hubert left him no choice. "Do not move," he snarled at Aimée. Releasing her, he put a hand on his sword hilt and stepped forward, only to feel the tip of a dagger prick his back through his doublet and jerkin.

"No, no, cowardly dog, it is *you* who must not move!" A new male voice delivered the warning in a tone of cheerful menace.

Aimée was so faint that she crumpled against the tavern's door frame when her arm was released, but the sound of Gaspard LeFait's voice nearly revived her. When had he come up behind them?

Hubert had lost his sword and found himself pinned to the wall, with the point of St. Briac's blade nudging his throat. Out of the corner of one eye he glimpsed a wiry little man who held a dagger to his friend's back.

"Isn't this fair enough for you yet?" Hubert rasped at St. Briac. "Finish me off and put an end to this public humiliation."

St. Briac knitted his brows and appeared thoughtful. "Hmm. I find I am in no hurry to spatter my handsome doublet with your blood." He glanced over to his manservant, greeting him for the first time. "Well met, Gaspard. My thanks, this once, for your meddling. It was timely."

"My pleasure as always, monseigneur." The little man grinned.

Just then four of the king's best archers rounded the corner, a high-spirited group out for a day's amusement. St. Briac recognized them all and was well aware that they had held him in a state of esteem bordering on worship ever since his heroic exploits during the battle of Pavia.

"Bonjour, mes amis," he called gaily over one shoulder, still holding the sword point to Hubert's throat.

"Monseigneur!" the archers chorused, and drew their weapons simultaneously. "How may we assist you? Has there been trouble here?"

St. Briac addressed the young man who had spoken last by name. "As a matter of fact, Bonnard, I believe that you and your able comrades may be able to resolve this situation. By all rights, I should claim my victory over this man by inflicting a mortal wound, but you know how unpleasant those can be. I hesitate to offend the sensibilities of this young lady"—he gestured toward Aimée with his free hand, and the archers bowed to her in unison—"and to ruin this doublet, of which I am uncommonly fond. Would you be so kind as to take these two villainous types off our hands and see to it that they are dealt with accordingly?"

"Certainement, monseigneur. We would be honored," exclaimed Bonnard. "May I be so bold as to inquire what crime they have committed?"

"They tried to waylay this lady, who is my betrothed, against her will. Fortunately, I came along just in time, but then they refused to release her into my care."

The archers gasped at the idea of such folly.

"We hadn't a clue that you knew the wench," protested the blond man. "And you didn't tell us you were a nobleman, either."

St. Briac cocked a sardonic brow at the quartet of eager helpers and shrugged. Moments later, after rounds of farewells and thanks had been exchanged, Hubert and his blond companion were led off, each in the firm grip of one of the archers. At last, St. Briac could turn his attention to his fiancée. Long-deferred annoyance bubbled to the surface.

"I should have let them take you away to be locked up as well! Is that what it will take to check your rebellious behavior? I certainly do not intend to play nursemaid and watch your every movement, so it would seem that you must endeavor to act thoughtfully, in the way of ladies and *adults,* until we can contrive to unsnarl this—" He broke off at the sight of Aimée closing her eyes and dropping her head back against the building. It was bad enough that she continued to sit on the street throughout his tirade, evincing

no signs of intimidation or remorse, but this was too impertinent. "I will not discuss this if you're going to act like a
child. Get up. I'll save the remainder of your lecture for the
privacy of your apartment at the chateau."

Aimée tried to look up and focus on St. Briac's face, but
it was so far above her. Through a fog, she heard Gaspard
murmuring, "Monseigneur, I am not sure that the lady is
being rude. I suspect that she is unwell."

Strong, warmly familiar hands encircled her waist and
lifted her up. She wobbled, trying to smile.

"Aimée, have you been drinking?"

"Drinking what?" she queried woozily.

St. Briac met Gaspard's confused gaze over her head and
lifted both brows sharply. Each of them slid an arm through
one of Aimée's and then around her back so that her feet
scarcely brushed the cobbles as they started down the hill.

Out of a shadowed doorway darted one of scores of the
peddlers, quacks, pardoners, and dealers in relics that haunted
every town in France. This man was part of the last group;
the sight of what appeared to be a hopelessly ill girl drew
him like a magnet. No sooner had he crept up beside the
trio, keeping pace with them and holding out a bone frag-
ment, than St. Briac waved him off.

"Doubtless part of some saint," he observed cynically as
the dealer in relics slunk back into his doorway. "One touch
and our poor, tragic Aimée would be restored to good health."
Thomas's tone was mocking, but privately he was beginning
to feel concerned about her condition. What could be causing
it? Had those villains hit her on the head, and if so, could
they have inflicted any lasting damage? She had shown no
reaction at all, not even a hint of a smile, at his jest. Tightening his arm around Aimée's back, he quickened their pace.

Conscious of the uncomfortable silence, Gaspard picked
up on his master's remark. "*Mais oui!* Do but put your money
down, and those merry rogues will sell you a cartload of
laths from the Ark of *père* Noah, the snout of St. Antho-
ny's pig, and the crest of the cock that crowed *chez* Pilate."

At this, Aimée's mouth twitched ever so slightly, and she
made a tiny sound. Heartened, St. Briac stopped and stared
down at her face.

"Aimée? Can you hear me?"

"Mmm." She blinked at him, her face screwing up as she

made a supreme effort to focus, think, and speak. "I feel so odd."

"Why? What happened to you? Did those men hit you or give you something to drink?"

Licking her lips, she whispered, "No. I ... don't know why ..." One hand fluttered toward his face. "Thomas, how did you ..."

"Pure chance, I assure you, *miette*," St. Briac muttered wryly. "I assumed after our little, ah, altercation in the gardens that you had returned to your room to lick your wounds. Eventually, in a burst of generosity, I went up to smooth things over, but you weren't there, and Suzette hadn't seen you since you departed the first time. So I left the chateau, questioning people all along the way, and finally tracked you down. Are you grateful?"

Aimée nodded clumsily but added with a lopsided smile, "Still, you should have known by now, monseigneur, not to assume anything where I am concerned."

St. Briac had to grin, however reluctantly, and allow her a soft, *"Touché, chérie."*

For an instant Aimée's eyes twinkled in response; then they closed as she went completely limp against his wide chest.

Her nose twitching, Aimée made a moue and wondered vaguely why she smelled brandy. Was it worth the effort to open her eyes and investigate?

"Oh, mam'selle, are you awake? I don't believe it! Tell me that you can hear me."

Aimée managed a weak smile and a nod but didn't feel up to more. A wave of disappointment washed over her at the sound of Suzette's high-pitched voice. Why had she expected St. Briac to be there with her on the bed? There had been dreams, warm, wonderful, enchanted dreams in which he had cradled her near, whispering her name, reassuring her, rubbing her back while pressing feather-light kisses to her damp brow. The dreams had almost made the awful, strange feelings in her body worthwhile; in truth, she was reluctant to leave St. Briac behind and return to Suzette and the real world.

"I beg you to open your eyes, mam'selle, and tell me that you are well again. We've been so worried."

Thick ebony lashes fluttered as she attempted to focus on Suzette. "We?"

"Everyone has been so afraid. *Eh bien*, will you not try to drink some of this brandy? It was sent by the king himself, and you can believe me when I tell you that he has been here countless times to see if you had improved."

Aimée managed to swallow some of the fiery-smooth liquid from the cup Suzette held to her lips. "Tell me, how long?" she whispered, sinking back into the pillows.

"It's been nearly two days since the seigneur de St. Briac carried you up here and put you to bed. I was out searching for you myself then, but even though Paul and I didn't get back until evening, monseigneur thought of everything. He took perfect care of you. He'd never admit it himself, but I'd wager that he was as scared as the rest of us that you might never wake up. Don't you know what caused this? You can tell me if you drank something."

Conscious of a strange, penetrating weakness, Aimée slowly shook her head. "No. I don't know." She realized that she was naked beneath the covers, which was normal for a person in bed, yet she couldn't help wondering whether St. Briac had undressed her.

"There are people waiting to see you, but I'd better tell monseigneur before anyone else. Don't go back to sleep." With that, the rosy-cheeked maid scrambled up and rushed out the door.

The prospect of seeing St. Briac kept Aimée awake. When he came in a few minutes later and smiled down at her, she wondered whether he could hear the thudding of her heart.

"So, you are going to live after all," he announced, teasing her gently.

"Are you sorry? My demise would have solved a number of problems for you."

Dimples cut into his bearded cheeks as he laughed and sat down on the edge of the bed. Aimée looked incredibly lovely and deceptively helpless, her black hair curling over the pillow and framing a pale face dominated by luminous spring-green eyes. "That's true, but I would hope that we could find less dramatic solutions for our problems." He paused, reaching out to caress her cheek before inquiring seriously, "How do you feel? Are you clearheaded?"

Aimée longed to turn her mouth and catch one of his fingers between her teeth. Just the sensation of his strong hand on her cheek, however impersonal, made her shiver beneath the covers. And the scent of him that drifted up to her nose was eerily reminiscent of those poignant dreams. "Since I am unsure of what my illness has been, it is difficult for me to answer your question. I feel very weak and tired, but I suppose that the mere fact of my consciousness is a good sign."

"Can't you give us a clue as to the cause of this strange malady? I could swear you were poisoned."

"I don't see how." Aimée closed her eyes, searching her memory. Then she gave a tiny, confused shrug. "I drank nothing after leaving this chamber. Those men offered me nothing, but I was already light-headed and weak when I encountered them. I found it difficult even to think, let alone speak."

"I don't understand it." He sprang up and paced across the room, his tall, broad-shouldered physique silhouetted against the sunlit window. "What could have caused this mysterious illness?"

"I don't know," Aimée replied softly. "Have you been so very worried?"

He turned and stared at her through narrowed eyes. The long hours during which she had lain unconscious in his arms filled his thoughts. It had seemed that she might never awake, never shake her finger in his face again or throw one of her insolent rejoinders at him. To say that he had been worried would have been an understatement, yet he was not prepared to admit even that much to Aimée. "It would be cruel of me to say that I felt no concern for your well-being," he told her lightly. "I'll allow that I've become rather used to you, in a perverse sort of way."

She grinned. "Spoken like a true romantic lover."

Smothering a chuckle, St. Briac retorted, "A man would have to be a fool to shower you with ardent declarations of love. You'd only make a joke of them—and him."

Suddenly grave, Aimée stared across the room at him and whispered, "Not if the man were sincere, monseigneur."

"Well." He swallowed and then cleared his throat. "Now that you are awake at last, you can turn your attention to your scheme to get away from me and this charade we are tangled in. No doubt you will find the man of your dreams then."

"Yes." The word sounded oddly choked. Turning her face

against the pillow, Aimée suddenly wished she were asleep again, immersed in a dream filled with St. Briac's embrace, whisper, caress, scent, hard warmth.

A tapping at the door roused them both from revery. Suzette poked her head in. *"Excusez-moi.* There is an old woman here to see you, mam'selle. She's been waiting since yesterday morning. Could you give her a minute?" The girl lowered her voice and hissed. *"Vraiment,* it will be a relief to see her business accomplished so that I can have some peace. I'm sick of the sight of her."

"I don't remember seeing an old woman loitering about," St. Briac interjected testily.

Suzette blinked in surprise at his tone. What had gotten under his skin? "I don't suppose you would have, monseigneur. After all, you've been playing nursemaid these past two days while I've stood waiting in the hall."

Aimée held her breath, noting the way his face darkened before he turned back to the window. Could that have been a blush? Before she could ponder that or Suzette's curious statement, the door opened, and the shriveled hag who had given her the fruit tottered in.

"Bonjour, oh, *bonjour,* mam'selle. Now that I see you are awake, I can die happy. Perhaps God will have mercy on me after all." The old crone sank shakily to her knees beside the bed and pressed dry kisses to Aimée's hand. "It is your forgiveness that means most to me, *pourtant,* and I could not be so bold as to ask for it. I don't deserve it."

Aimée gave St. Briac a tiny bewildered shrug and then said to the woman, "I do not understand. What have you done to seek my forgiveness?"

St. Briac, still grouchy, crossed the room and demanded, "Yes, old hag, stop speaking in riddles and tell us what you mean."

She glanced up fearfully, cringing as if she expected him to strike her. Then she burst into tears and covered her face with gnarled fingers. "I did not know that *you* would be here, monseigneur. I beg you to spare my life."

Recognition dawned on him. "Now I remember. You were the one who told me where I might find Mademoiselle de Fleurance. Why would I seek to punish you for coming to my aid?" St. Briac shifted his attention to a confused Aimée. "How do you know this old woman so well? I thought that she had merely witnessed your abduction by those two swine."

"There isn't much I can tell you. Before I went up the hill and encountered the two men, and began to feel faint, this kind lady took pity on me and gave me some of her fruit to appease my hunger. We exchanged pleasantries, nothing more. I was charmed by her generosity since I had no money to pay her."

The hag was seized by another wave of sobs. St. Briac stared down at her, thinking, and gradually his visage hardened. "Aimée," he asked with slow deliberation, "did you eat the fruit?"

"Why, only a bite of the pear. When I began to feel dizzy, I dropped the rest, and they rolled away."

In one swift movement he reached down, grasped two shriveled arms, lifted the old crone into the air, and shook her. So terrified was she that it seemed her eyes would pop out of their sockets. "I don't intend to wring the truth out of you word by word," St. Briac ground out. "Enlighten us *tout de suite!*"

The tale spilled out in hoarse gasps. She was so poor that she had feared she might freeze to death the past winter. It was then that she had met Hubert and his blond friend. They had offered her more money than she earned in a month selling fruit just to give certain pears to young ladies whom they would point out ahead of time. As the weeks passed and she grew more reluctant, they paid more, assuring her that they put only a mild sleeping potion into the fruit. It was only a bit of fun, they said. The girls were always pure, innocent types, easily persuaded to trust the pair that invariably rescued them when dizziness struck.

"I wanted to stop, truly I did. I shudder to think what those two did to those sleeping maidens. But lately I began to worry what they might do to me if I crossed 'em. Mean eyes they had. I had decided that last time would be the end, though; I'd take my fruit to another part of town rather than be part of such wickedness. I've had dreams where the Holy Mother has come right into my chamber and told me—"

"Never mind that. Just finish about Aimée." St. Briac had set her down but continued to hold one bony arm in a punishing grip.

"Well, that last girl was mam'selle here, and it broke my heart to have to hand her that poisoned pear. That's why I gave you the apple and peach, too, mam'selle. I said a prayer that you'd eat them first and throw that accursed pear away." She turned beseeching eyes on Aimée, who couldn't help feeling a pang of sympathy for the pathetic old soul. "You were so kind to me, as if you truly cared, and I was sure God was going to strike me dead for what I was doing. When I saw you start up the hill and bite into the poison side of that pear—" Between fresh sobs, she exclaimed, *"Mère de Dieu! Pardonnez-moi, je vous prie!"*

"So that's why you were so eager to tell me which way Aimée had gone?"

"I tell you the truth, monseigneur. If you had not come along when you did, I was going to go after them myself. I probably would have been murdered, but I would have had to try. Never have I despised myself so much."

"Good," he replied coldly.

"Thomas," Aimée interjected softly, "you have to give the poor woman credit for coming here to confess, not to mention leading you to me in the first place. If not for her, you might never have found me!"

"Sang de Dieu!" he swore. "If not for *her*, you would not have spent the last two days so deeply asleep that I feared the condition might be permanent." Hearing the raw pain in his own voice, St. Briac abruptly fell silent and stalked back to the window.

"Has it never occurred to you that if she had not carried out that dreadful task for those two monsters, they would have found someone more willing and with far fewer misgivings than this woman? If that had been the case, I probably *would* have died."

"And if *I* were a dog, I probably would have fleas," he shot back sarcastically. "Any other farfetched conjectures that you would like to elaborate on? What do you expect me to do, grovel at the feet of that witch and shower her with gratitude? She's a criminal, Aimée, and she will pay for what she did to you and Lord knows how many other innocent maidens."

The old hag began to whimper anew and mutter prayers under her breath. "No more than I deserve," she babbled in Aimée's direction. "Penance!"

With calm determination, Aimée propped up her pillows and sat against them. "Madame, what is your name?" she inquired of the woman.

"Marie, mam'selle. Marie Lissieu." She bowed an unkempt gray head before the young girl's bed. Aimée grimaced at the lice that were visible where the lank strands were parted.

"Marie, I want you to go into the corridor and wait with my maid, Suzette. You won't leave, will you?"

"Oh, no, mam'selle. Not until you bid me to do so."

When the door had closed behind the old crone, Aimée turned her attention to St. Briac. "Would you be so kind as to come over here where I may converse with you, monseigneur?"

For a moment he was tempted to dismiss her requests and do as he pleased. If he stormed from the room and saw to it that the witch was stoned to death, there wouldn't be a thing Aimée could do. She was weak as a kitten and hadn't the strength to chase him past the edge of her bed. Still, some impulse he couldn't identify caused him to go and sit beside her, waiting like a sullen boy for her to deliver her lecture on the spiritual joy achieved through compassionate forgiveness.

"You needn't sulk," Aimée complained instead.

"I'm not sulking, I'm waiting. Say whatever it is that I must hear. I haven't all day."

She tried not to smile. "I really am quite sincere about this, Thomas. It is very important to me that we be merciful in our treatment of that pitiful old woman. For you, who have never wanted for anything in all your life, it's easy to sit in judgment on people who act out of desperation because they are hungry or cold or lonely. It's important that we not forget about those people while we perch up here in the king's chateau, garbed in velvets and jewels and eating more than our bodies can comfortably hold." She paused for breath and blinked back the tears that glittered in her leaf-green eyes and made spikes of her abundant lashes. "To me it is not incredible that Madame Lissieu sank so low as to hand out poisoned fruit to unsuspecting maidens. What is remarkable is that she was still able to care for someone like me, who has all that she lacks. She risked her life to come here and beg my forgiveness."

St. Briac rubbed long fingers along his jaw. This was the most extraordinary female he had ever encountered or even imagined.

"I suppose you want me to let the old crone go free," he muttered, arching a dubious brow.

"Yes. Now that those men are in prison, as *they* certainly should be, Madame Lissieu will do no more harm." Aimée put out a small white hand and touched his bronzed one. "And Thomas?"

"I don't like your tone. You want me to do something even more outrageously foolish."

Aimée laughed, well aware of the charming picture she made. Just to make certain, though, she pretended not to notice that the edge of the sheet had slipped down to uncover the rosy nipple of her right breast. St. Briac had definitely noticed; his eyes seemed to burn away the teasing covers before he averted his gaze. A telltale muscle moved in his jaw.

"I would appreciate one more generous gesture on your part, monseigneur. I would feel so much better about the fate of Madame Lissieu if I knew what she was doing."

Wincing, he shook his head but murmured bravely, "And?"

"And I thought it would be wonderful if she could have a place on the household staff. I'm sure there must be any number of things she could do, and that way we would be certain not only that she was behaving herself but also that she was no longer hungry, cold, or lonely."

The words had poured out in a persuasive rush that left St. Briac momentarily stunned. "Are you mad?" he choked out at last. "What a question. I've known the answer since the moment I met you, when you halted the king of France in the midst of a hunt. You dare too much, Aimée. You push too far."

"I don't mean to," she replied. "It seemed a fine, honest solution to me. Sensible, in fact."

"Sensible? *Sensible!*" he repeated loudly, as if unable to believe his ears. "You've never had a sensible thought in your life. I've yet to see you behave sensibly for even an instant. And you have the audacity to tell *me* what's sensible? This is too much!"

"You needn't announce it to all of France," Aimée muttered, and then added stubbornly, "And I still say it's a sensible idea."

St. Briac was holding his head in his hands and shaking it from side to side in disbelief. "I suppose you'd also like a slice of the moon for supper."

"Thomas?" She put a hand on his crisp, dark hair. "If you do this for me, I will promise you something that will make you very happy."

"Don't keep me in suspense," he retorted sarcastically, his turquoise eyes peeking suspiciously over his fingertips.

"If you will see to it that Marie Lissieu is given a position on the household staff here at Blois, I will find a way to leave here in less than a week without damaging your reputation."

He experienced an unsettling twinge in his chest at her words but dismissed it as relief. Straightening, he gave Aimée a pleased smile and held out a hand to take one of hers. "Music to my ears, Mademoiselle de Fleurance. I would say that's a fair exchange of favors."

When she returned his smile, it felt as if her face might crack. As they shook hands, Aimée said lightly, "Not only fair, monseigneur, but eminently sensible."

CHAPTER 15

 *May 12, 1526*

Lilies of the valley, apple blossoms, purple and white lilacs, and gilly flowers mingled their fragrances in the warm breeze that wafted over the courtyard. Aimée inhaled appreciatively as she made her way across the giant cobbles to the Saint-Calais chapel, which stood behind the section of the Louis XII wing that paralleled the river. The king did not attend mass until ten, and so there was still time for Aimée to say a few prayers alone. She was feeling in need of divine inspiration after days of struggling to formulate a suitable plan for her departure from Blois. There were so many aspects to consider, involving so many people, that there seemed to be no ideal solution. She had just three days to discover one. St. Briac had kept his part of the bargain; Marie Lissieu was now a laundress at Blois. It was Aimée's turn to live up to her promise.

The silk skirts of her hyacinth-blue gown whispered as she made her way down the nave of the chapel. Stillness and peace always seemed so much richer and more meaningful to Aimée inside a church. As a child, she'd imagined that the quiet meant that God was listening, waiting to hear all her needs and feelings. Smiling, she approached the chancel. Morning sunlight streamed through brightly tinted stained-glass windows, intensifying the golden spell. A movement off to one side caught Aimée's eye then, and she realized with surprise that a man was kneeling there, his head bent in prayer. For a moment she thought it might be St. Briac, for the dark hair, broad shoulders, and partially visible beard struck a familiar chord. Yet the golden jerkin, trimmed with sable and set with emeralds, was a bit lavish for St. Briac's tastes.

All at once the head came up, swiveling to seek her out, and Aimée flushed with embarrassment as she realized how curiously she had been staring. She gasped. "Oh, sire! I—*pardonnez-moi!* I did not mean to disturb you! I am surprised that you would be here alone, that is, I did not expect—"All of this was sputtered out in an agitated whisper.

François rose lightly, smiling, and walked to the nave to clasp one of Aimée's hands. "I slipped in for a moment of privacy before mass. I wanted to speak to Claude, my cherished queen, before I depart for Cognac tomorrow. They don't like me to wander about on my own, but I exercise my royal temperament from time to time in order to get my own way."

Aimée found this warm little speech quite intriguing. He had come alone to speak to Claude, the queen she imagined he had used up like so much wine or rich clothing. So disarmed was she by his manner that she heard herself asking, "Has your wife's death truly caused you such pain? Did you cherish her so fervently?"

Misunderstanding her, François smiled indulgently and reassuringly. "Don't worry, mademoiselle. If I know Thomas, he will cherish you just as fervently once you become *his* wife. As for Claude..." For an instant tears sparkled in the faraway hazel eyes that stared over Aimée's head to the altar. "No one but she knew just how devoted I was. If I could bring her back with my life, I would gladly do so."

Stupefied by this totally unexpected display of emotion, Aimée felt an urge to weep. "Your Majesty, I am so sorry. I should not have pressed you on this subject. Please forgive me."

He shook his head quickly and focused once again on the raven-haired beauty. "Nonsense. It is I who should beg your pardon. I'm afraid I simply haven't been myself since those months of captivity. A bit of *crise de foi*, you know." The king gave her a charming smile. "And that's enough about me. I must go and meet the others before mass, and I'll leave you to the privacy you came here for. *Au revoir*, Mademoiselle de Fleurance."

Aimée watched him stride jauntily toward the doorway and put on a bejeweled and feathered velvet hat, as he emerged into the May sunshine. *Crise de foi*, the king had said matter-of-factly: crisis of the spirit; melancholy. Resolving to pursue the subject later with St. Briac, Aimée returned her attention to this patient God who was still waiting to listen to every problem. She quickly selected a kneeling bench near the altar, for there was little time. Genuflecting, Aimée made the sign of the cross and let her prayers pour out. Before long, an inspired plan took shape in her mind.

High in the canopied beech tree that grew near the chapel door, a blackcap and a chiffchaff warbled loudly in a way that made Aimée wonder whether the two males were in competition. It wouldn't have surprised her a bit if they were more intent on outdoing each other than on impressing their lady loves. Even as she paused in the doorway, smiling, a tiny rust-breasted stonechat flew upward to hover momentarily on a perch in the beech tree. He delivered a scratchy and jangling song and then fluttered off toward the garden.

Aimée's hyacinth silk skirts swirled in the morning breeze as she followed the stonechat's lead. Her destination was the François I wing, but her progress was interrupted by the appearance of an unfamiliar coach in the courtyard. Two sumptuously garbed women were being assisted into the sunlight. As Aimée drew nearer, she wondered idly whether they were mother and daughter. Certainly all the evidence pointed to that conclusion, for one was white-haired and the other young, and they shared an unnerving resemblance to an Egyptian greyhound a visitor once had brought to Nieuil. Their faces were long, but not in the usual way. Instead, the distance from ears to tips of noses seemed startlingly protracted, while the span from beady eyes to chins was measured in a blink. Perhaps, mused Aimée with a mischievous smile, that was because the poor women had no chins to speak of. Passing them as she started up the curving stone stairway, she noticed that their rib cages were outlined against their rich satin gowns. Could there be a race of people related to the greyhound?

The peculiar-looking women soon were forgotten as Aimée stepped from the balcony into the corridor that led to St. Briac's apartments. She wondered how she would discover the right door but was spared the embarrassment of knocking on them one by one by the sound of familiar, muted voices. She traced them to the second door, which was slightly ajar, and then paused to listen to St. Briac and Gaspard LeFait exchanging lighthearted insults amid what sounded like a great deal of rustling and knocking about. Thomas's tone of exasperated amusement sent a shiver down her spine. What delight she had felt when it had been directed at her, even when edged with annoyance. It seemed an eternity since they had shared such badinage. The few times they had seen each other since their conversation in her sickbed, St. Briac had been the essence of friendly charm, a solicitous, courteous acquaintance and no more. His eyes had been as carefully averted as his manner had been guarded.

With a sigh, Aimée focused her attention on the task at hand. It did no good to brood over what was better forgotten. Soon enough she wouldn't be seeing him at all. "Monseigneur?" Peeking hesitantly around the door, she turned crimson at the sight of him pulling on hose. His muscular thighs were naked; from the side she glimpsed a lean hip and buttock. A snowy linen shirt was unlaced to reveal the dark breadth of his chest. Stepping back behind the door, Aimée gulped and quavered. "My apologies, monseigneur. I did not realize . . ."

The sound of St. Briac's chuckle was audible as a chest lid thumped shut and Gaspard scurried over to the doorway. "Mademoiselle de Fleurance," he implored, a pair of fawn haut-de-chausses draped over one arm, "if you could just wait one minute, my master will be dressed and fit for company."

"*Mais, oui! Certainement!*" Aimée agreed hastily, wishing she could cool the fire in her cheeks.

"There's no reason for you to wait, *miette*!" St. Briac was calling merrily. "I've nothing to be ashamed of, and besides, you've seen it all, anyway."

Aimée gasped, and Gaspard rolled his eyes and shook his head hopelessly. Hurrying back to his master, he vented a series of whispered admonitions, which were met with laughter. A few moments later, St. Briac bade her enter, and Aimée straightened her shoulders, pushed the door open, and walked into the spacious chamber.

"You'll pardon me for my earlier state of dishabille, I

trust," St. Briac was saying casually as he laced the front of his doublet. It was a handsome garment, fawn, with two long panels of sage green down the front. "I must have forgotten our appointment."

Aimée's cheeks grew warm again. "We had no appointment, as you are well aware, monseigneur. I merely came to discuss a matter of importance to both of us."

"Ah." He nodded with mock sobriety, knitting his brows in a way that made Aimée want to smile, and turned to Gaspard, who had gone to fetch his shoes. "Mademoiselle de Fleurance and I are about to engage in an important discussion, so I suppose you should leave us, Gaspard. I would appreciate it if you would inform the duchesse de Roanne that I will be unable to escort her to mass."

The little manservant nodded, bowed, and cast a smile at Aimée before backing out the door.

"Well, won't you sit down?" St. Briac gestured toward a magnificent upholstered chair decorated in gold and silver passementerie. "Can I offer you a glass of wine or some food?"

Aimée took the chair and watched as he perched on the edge of his rumpled bed, pushing aside a richly embroidered silk curtain. For some reason the sight of him on the unmade bed caused her heart to race. "No, I don't care for anything, thank you. I—" She fussed with a fold in the skirt of her gown and then raised her wide green eyes. "I am sorry to have upset your plans with the duchess, but as you probably realize, the time is nearly at hand for me to meet my part of our bargain. That is what I wanted to discuss with you."

"*Miette*, you mustn't worry about Ghislaine or the time limit on our bargain." His gaze had softened as he regarded her thick-lashed leaf-green eyes, dusky cheeks, and charming hyacinth gown against the background of the ornate chair. Ebony curls spilled over her shoulders, loose and abundant. "I don't intend to send you into the streets at week's end."

"I'm sure you wouldn't, but I did give my word, and I know how anxious you are to be rid of me." She lifted her chin proudly. "No doubt the duchess will be overjoyed to have you all to herself."

St. Briac arched an eyebrow. "Am I to assume that you are leaving? I do hope you will confide your plan since it will certainly involve me."

"Of course I will tell you; that is why I am here." Brightening, Aimée rushed over to the bed and perched beside him, but St. Briac moved slightly away and regarded her suspiciously. "Don't look at me that way, monseigneur! My plan is perfect. I don't know why we didn't think of it sooner."

"Probably because *we* are so dull-witted," he muttered sarcastically.

"You needn't act so apprehensive. You won't have to do anything except uphold my story here at court ... and make me a small loan, which I will absolutely repay."

"I can't wait to hear how you will do that, but first I would appreciate a few more details of this brilliant plan."

Aimée grinned, pausing for effect, and then leaned over to his ear and whispered, "We shall say that I have had a vision, while I was ill, perhaps. I've realized that my first duty is to God, and so I am going to enter a convent."

St. Briac blinked at the triumphant expression on her face. "That's it?"

"The main part."

"I am still waiting to hear the *brilliant* part. Please tell me also why you need to borrow *my* money if you're going to a nunnery."

"I'm not *really* going to one, Thomas," she exclaimed. "We're just going to tell them that's where I've gone. It will be a perfect reason for us not to marry, and no one will think the worse of you. You will just have to act excessively noble about losing me to God, and then the entire matter will be forgotten before you know it."

"I hate to bring this up," he said with a wince, "but where *are* you going in truth? I don't think a convent would be such a bad idea, personally."

She waved a tiny hand as if to dismiss this subject as incidental. "I'm not exactly certain about that yet, but I can assure you that my destination will not be a convent. I was thinking of Paris. I could use the money you lend me to establish a little shop of some sort."

"Aimée, this plot you've hatched sounds as insane as the one that landed you here at Blois. I can't let you go off alone to Paris. Look what happened to you in less than an hour the other day."

"Oh, I wouldn't go alone. Suzette would come with me, and I thought that Paul, her young man, might accompany us, for safety's sake, of course."

"Of course," St. Briac echoed ironically. "Never let it be said that you would overlook something like safety!"

"Monseigneur, I don't see why you are being so mean about this. I thought you would be overjoyed to hear that I am going at last and that you won't have to be bothered with me any longer. There's no need for you to worry about my fate once I leave here; I'll manage somehow. I always have before."

"It isn't *your* fate that concerns me so much as that of my money," he returned grouchily, springing up to pace across the room in a way now very familiar to Aimée. "I would like to hold out some hope that it might be returned to me eventually."

"Oh, you needn't worry about that," Aimée said airily. "I'm like a cat; I always manage to land on my feet."

St. Briac held his bowed head in his hands and groaned. "When did you plan to embark on this journey into the cold, hard world, my clumsy little kitten?"

"Just as soon as we can set the stage. The king has already seen me in the chapel alone this morning, so that's a start. I shall just have to spend a great deal of time there and act very pious until tomorrow. Then I will go to the king with my story before he departs for Cognac."

He looked over at her, lounging confidently on his bed, and bit back a smile. Pious! Hell itself would freeze before she could convince *him*, but François might be more gullible. "I suppose you will wear that ridiculous gable-hooded head-dress for effect."

Aimée giggled, her green eyes twinkling. "That's a good idea. I shall have to unearth the thing from the depths of my chest at once."

Running a hand through his ruffled hair, St. Briac walked back to the bed and sighed in capitulation. Aimée held her breath, watching his dark hand reach out to trace the edge of her neckline from throat to the first swell of one breast. If only he wouldn't touch her, everything would be so much easier. Somehow she lifted her eyes and found his turquoise gaze almost brooding as he towered over her.

"I suppose I shall have to agree to this madness," he murmured at length. "At least you are beautiful, *miette*. If all else fails in Paris, you can always become a courtesan, and then I'll be certain of repayment of this loan."

Hot blood rushed to Aimée's cheeks, but she couldn't

move. Instinct told her that he was about to join her on the bed, and she hadn't the willpower to resist the prospect of one of his intoxicating kisses or the bliss of his embrace. This might be the last time.

"Monseigneur!" There was a sharp knock at the door, and then Gaspard burst in, breathless. "You must come with me at once. The king requests your presence in his study."

"What's wrong? You behave as if we are under attack."

"Something like that," Gaspard muttered. "I haven't time to explain, and the rumors I've heard may be wrong. You'd better come quickly and find out for yourself." He turned to Aimée, who had risen from the bed and was looking on in confusion. "Mademoiselle de Fleurance, I think it would be wise for you to remain here. You may be needed as well."

St. Briac took a narrow spiral staircase down to the second floor and then followed the corridor to his friend's study. Outside the massive door, he glanced back at his worried-looking manservant. "Will you say nothing to prepare me?"

"Guard your temper, monseigneur, and keep your wits about you."

Baffled, St. Briac shook his head and lifted the latch. Inside the paneled study he found François sitting uneasily in his favorite carved chair. As the king rose to greet him, Thomas glanced around the room. Florange was there, sitting in the arched window, and Louise de Savoy and Chauvergé shared a bench against the far wall. Two odd-looking women occupied chairs in the center of the study.

"Is something amiss, sire?" he inquired softly.

"I don't know," François replied with a tight smile before indicating that St. Briac should take the chair next to his own. "Before you sit down, *mon ami*, let me introduce Madame Blanche Dagonneau and her, ah, lovely daughter, Cécile-Anne."

Somehow Thomas managed to keep his face a blank as he kissed each long, bony hand in turn. "It is a great pleasure to meet you, madame"—he nodded toward the white-haired woman—"and mademoiselle." Looking from one to the other, he was reminded of something but couldn't put his finger on it. In any case, they certainly were the most peculiar-looking women he had ever seen.

"Oh, but monseigneur, we have met before," Blanche Dagonneau proclaimed in a high-pitched voice; then she tittered coyly. "Perhaps you were too young to remember, but before my dear husband's demise, our estates connected with yours. Your parents were such dear friends of ours, and after M'sieur Dagonneau passed on, your wonderful father bought our land, which enabled me to take Cécile-Anne to live with my brother's family in Burgundy."

"Well, that's very interesting." St. Briac smiled and then aimed an intensely quizzical look at the king.

François gave him a sickly smile in return. "It seems, *mon ami*, that before Madame Dagonneau left the village of St. Briac, she and your parents arranged for you and Cécile-Anne to be married when you reached the proper age."

First St. Briac's brows flew up, and then his eyes widened until white showed all around blue-green irises. Finally, his mouth dropped open. *"Sang de Dieu!"*

CHAPTER 16

 *May 12, 1526*

Gaspard's advice came back to St. Briac in a rush. Of course, the little man was right; it would do no good for him to toss his wits away with both hands. He certainly would need them to beat the Dagonneaux at their own game.

"You will pardon me for that little outburst, I hope," he said politely, looking first to the king and then to the two women, "but this news comes as a bit of a shock to me. You see, I find it puzzling that neither of my parents ever mentioned this arranged betrothal to me. I was nineteen years old when my mother died and twenty-four when I lost my father." St. Briac paused for a moment, making an effort to remain calm. "I'm certain, though, that once I see my parents' signatures on the documents you have brought, the matter will become clear to me."

Madame Dagonneau's eyes darted away from his level gaze. "I had the documents you speak of, and I would have them here today, but they were lost in a fire at my brother's chateau."

"Oh, I see." He nodded, his brows flicking upward almost imperceptibly. "A pity."

Madame Dagonneau bristled. "Do you question my word, monseigneur?" she retorted shrilly.

That was the rub. It was impossible for St. Briac as a

person of position at the court and in France itself to accuse a respectable woman of lying. He didn't care about his own reputation, but such behavior would reflect unpleasantly on François. There seemed to be only one logical solution to this ludicrous predicament. Attempting to fill his voice with polite charm, he said, "*Au contraire*, madame, I only ask that you accept my apologies for not being able to fulfill the promise my parents made. I am, after all, thirty-three years old. Had I but known about this, er, arrangement, the situation now would doubtless be different, but as it is, I am already on the brink of marriage to another woman, and we are deeply in love."

The king caught the sidelong glance delivered by his friend and spoke up instantly. "Sad but true, madame and mademoiselle. The seigneur's fiancée is right here at Blois with us. She's a charming girl, and we are all quite fond of her."

"How unfortunate." Madame Dagonneau sneered. "Not for you, of course, monseigneur, but for my dear Cécile-Anne, who has dreamed of nothing else except becoming your wife." She gave her daughter a nudge, and the girl attempted a mournful expression. She had yet to speak one word.

"Too bad you had to come all this way." St. Briac lifted both eyebrows and shook his head resignedly. "However, as I said, if I had only known about dear Cécile-Anne earlier, I, uh, well..." He coughed, wondering how to finish the sentence, but was saved by Blanche Dagonneau's voice.

"*Oui, oui*, it is too unfortunate. I trust that you will be so kind as to introduce us to your betrothed?" She drew out the last word, curling her upper lip.

Before the king could dispatch a page to the Louis XII wing, St. Briac exclaimed, "Of course. In fact, my manservant is in the hall. I will send him to fetch her." Stepping to the doorway, he spoke a few terse words to Gaspard before rejoining the others.

The group in the study engaged in uneasy small talk, all except the silent Cécile-Anne, as they waited for Aimée to appear. Chauvergé smirked at St. Briac, enjoying his discomfort to an unseemly degree. At last there was a knock at the door, and Aimée peeked in.

"*Bonjour*, sire. I hope that you will pardon my appearance, but Gaspard, that is, M'sieur LeFait, said that it was imperative that I come immediately, so I didn't take the time—"

"You look lovely as always, Mademoiselle de Fleurance," the king interjected, smiling. "Please join us."

St. Briac was torn between despair and delight at the sight of her. Aimée's gleaming black curls swirled around the square-cut bodice of her gown; her appearance was fresh, lovely, and quite unconventional. Unlike the Dagonneau women, she did not wear a high frilled collar that would have signified a chemise under her gown, nor was there evidence of a shakefold to hold out her skirts or a jeweled girdle or any jewels at all. Both Blanche and Cécile had carefully coiffed hair. The mother wore a caul, the daughter a transparent white veil over what appeared to be brown hair. Next to them, Aimée looked like a serving girl brought in from the country to play the part of St. Briac's fiancée. Worse, as far as St. Briac was concerned, her facial expression warned him that she was completely unaware of what was afoot in the king's study. As she came to stand beside him, she cocked her head in bafflement. He had to smother laughter before declaring, "Aimée, my dearest love. My apologies for interrupting your toilette. I know that nothing less than a summons from me or our king would bring you out before you had fixed your hair and everything else." He cleared his throat, but the sight of her eyes widening in outrage forced him to continue. "Come closer, *chérie*, so that I may introduce you to our guests. They have come all the way from Burgundy."

Aimée was dumbfounded by St. Briac's strange behavior. Why was he acting like such a dolt, especially in front of these two women? Close up, they looked even more like greyhounds. Just as she was about to speak, St. Briac grasped one of her arms, and she felt a pinch. What was going on? Aimée glanced up sharply, about to speak, but he was smiling at her worshipfully, and yet there was something in his eyes that gave her pause. For now she decided it would be best to act as eccentrically as he, just in case.

"I'm so embarrassed that I was unable to have my hair dressed," she exclaimed girlishly. "I only hope that you and our guests will be able to forgive my appearance."

St. Briac could scarcely keep a straight face. "How could we not, my darling? You would look beautiful in tattered rags."

Even François was looking dubious by this time, and Florange put a hand over his mouth to hide a grin. Fearing that someone might lose control, St. Briac led Aimée forward with a flourish.

"Allow me to present my beloved fiancée, Mademoiselle Aimée de Fleurance. My darling, this is Madame Blanche Dagonneau and her dear daughter, Cécile-Anne."

Greetings were exchanged all around, though Cécile-Anne did no more than smile woodenly and nod, and then St. Briac drew Aimée back into the circle of his embrace.

"Well, it has been a great pleasure to meet all of you, although matters unfortunately did not turn out as my dear Cécile-Anne and I had hoped," Madame Dagonneau announced mournfully. "I only hope that you, sire, will allow us to remain here at Blois for a few days in order to rest and make new plans."

"*Naturellement,*" the king assured her. "In fact, I hope that you will join us all now for our midday meal in the hall of honor downstairs."

Everyone moved toward the doorway and milled into the corridor until only François, Thomas, and Aimée remained in the study.

"A few days," St. Briac repeated Madame Dagonneau's words with a loud sigh. "Couldn't they leave this afternoon? I shall go mad."

"Will someone tell me what is going on? Why are the two of you behaving this way?" In her impatience, Aimée forgot that she was speaking to the king, but even upon realizing what she had said and how, she left it alone. He was only a man, after all.

François gave her a brief explanation of the events leading up to her summons to the study. It seemed that her presence at Blois was not such a problem after all; she had saved Thomas from marriage to a human greyhound. Fully aware of the king's presence, she gazed soulfully up at St. Briac.

"My darling, what an ordeal for you." Aimée patted his bearded cheek. "Thank the saints that I was here to settle that matter speedily. Of course, in a few days—"

"Aimée, *ma chère miette,*" St. Briac interrupted adoringly, "why don't you go down and join the others now. I have one or two matters to discuss with the king, and then we will be along as well."

"I shall count the minutes, *mon grand ours,*" she cooed

in response, sliding two fingers from his cheek to caress the contours of his mouth. Delighted by St. Briac's sudden blush, Aimée turned then, bade both men *adieu*, and strolled from the chamber.

"She calls you her great bear?" queried the king, overcome with curiosity.

Hoping that his beard would hide his deepening flush, St. Briac could only shrug helplessly. "You know how women are," he offered lamely.

"Hmm. I must say that I have been somewhat confused about that particular woman and about her relationship with you, Thomas. I'm glad to see that I was right in supporting your betrothal. I know how long you have searched for the right mate and how important a happy marriage is to you."

"Yes, sire." He pasted on a smile. "At the moment, however, I am rather concerned about Madame Dagonneau and her dear daughter."

François grinned, his hazel eyes slanting upward, at his friend's sarcastic use of Blanche Dagonneau's favorite adjective. "I confess, *mon ami*, that I have to repress an urge to scratch those two behind the ears. I suspect that if we did away with their silks, satins, and pearls, we could add them to my hunting dogs, and no one would notice the difference!"

They laughed together until the king had tears in his eyes. Then St. Briac crossed to a wide dresser and poured goblets of wine. "You are wicked, sire."

"I do hope so," François retorted merrily. Raising his glass to Thomas's, he said in a more sober voice, "Tell me, though, do you recall the woman or her family? Do you believe what she says?"

"I have vague recollections of the Dagonneau name and their singular looks, but I can't be certain of the true connection until I speak to my Tante Fanchette. As for the other, no, I do not believe it. It's madness! How ridiculous for that woman to turn up with her ugly, dull-witted daughter and announce to me—at my age—that I'm to marry the girl. What did she expect?"

The king straightened the puffs of silk shirt that showed through the slashes in his doublet. "I'm as puzzled as you are, *mon ami*, but I do have a few clues. Upon prompting, Madame Dagonneau told me that you were ten at the time of this supposed betrothal, and her dear Cécile-Anne was three. That makes the girl twenty-six years old now. Why do you suppose it took her so long to pursue this arranged marriage?" François arched a brow at his friend. "I've an answer of sorts to why she decided to pursue the entire idea, whether real or recently invented."

"I beg you not to keep me in suspense, sire." St. Briac's tone implied that he would prefer to discuss any subject other than this.

"You doubtless could have guessed. Madame Dagonneau's brother died, and not long after, her funds from the sale of her property to your family ran out. What to do?" Mischief and pretended innocence informed the king's expression.

"Why me?" St. Briac groaned. "I feel like a giant stag sitting placidly in the middle of a clearing during a hunt."

"It probably has something to do with your matchless physical attributes. No doubt Madame Dagonneau is trying to improve their breed." François steadfastly refused to laugh until his friend had surrendered; then the two of them shared a long minute of merriment. "Ah, Thomas," he sighed at last, "I shall miss you during the coming week. I fear there will be few occasions for laughter once I leave Blois. Only the thought of you trying to fend off the sly advances of Blanche and Cécile-Anne will bring a smile to my face."

"Won't you be kind and send them away before you leave?"

"You know perfectly well I cannot be so rude, but I must confess that if I could find a reason, I would do so. My instincts tell me that the Dagonneaux will still be here when I return in a month or more."

"Not if I have anything to do with it," St. Briac muttered darkly. Seeing that his friend had wandered to a window and was gazing distractedly over the courtyard, he changed the subject. "My apologies, sire. I should not be troubling you with my trivial problems when you have such important worries."

"*Pas du tout*. I have enjoyed the diversion. Thinking about that cursed treaty just upsets me and solves nothing."

"The viceroy of Naples will be waiting for you in Cognac?"

"I'm afraid so. Under any other circumstances I would be overjoyed to see him."

"Do you know what you will say?"

"Well, a definite no about Burgundy. There can be no discussion on that point. There's nothing to be gained by calling an Estates General and taking votes; I've made up my mind. I'll have to be firm with the viceroy, saying that my subjects will not allow me to hand over Burgundy."

"Sire, might it not sound a trifle farfetched for you, who have always declared your absolute authority, to now champion the principle of popular consultation?"

Glancing over one broad shoulder, François gave his friend an ironic smile. "Let them think they weakened me with their tower prisons. I don't care. Those promises I made during my captivity can have no binding force. I will tell the viceroy, however, that I wish to remain friendly with Charles V and that I will honor most of the other clauses of the treaty. We shall have to adjust the rest according to reason and honesty."

"And what of your sons?" St. Briac whispered.

A shadow crossed the king's bold visage. "I cannot ransom them with Burgundy. The payment will have to be monetary." After a long pause, he managed to turn and smile. "So, Thomas, it seems that we will both have plenty to keep us occupied during the coming weeks. I would press you to join me, but it would be criminal to deprive all these ladies of your company."

"You are too kind, sire. No doubt I'll be the envy of every man at court," he replied in a tone of self-deprecating sarcasm.

François had started toward the doorway, but he paused to answer candidly. "I'm certain that every one of them will envy you the night you share Mademoiselle de Fleurance's marriage bed. She is a rare female, *mon ami*. I think we were right in calling her a wood sprite that day in Nieuil. So often I find myself thinking that she seems almost magical ...enchanted. Do you know what I am trying to say?"

"*Oui*. I know." Each word was weighted with meaning.

"I have the impression that if one tried to embrace her, she would disappear, but obviously that's not true."

St. Briac rubbed his brow in bemusement. "No, you may be right, sire. Aimée could still do just that."

Downstairs in the sunlit hall of honor, St. Briac ate a hurried midday meal. Aimée was not present, and inquiries to Florange, Marguerite, and Bonnivet revealed no clues to her whereabouts. Equally disconcerting were the unwavering stares leveled at him by Blanche and Cécile-Anne Dagonneau. Although they were seated across the board and at least a half dozen places to the south, they paid more attention to St. Briac than to their food. Not once did he look at them or acknowledge their presence in any way, yet he could feel their beady gray eyes boring into him until he was unable to swallow another bite. The king was deep in conversation with his mother and sister when St. Briac leaned over to make his excuses; François waved him off with a smile.

First Thomas checked his apartments. Gaspard had not seen Aimée. Neither had Suzette, who had just returned to the Louis XII wing, flushed with passion after a picnic with Paul. St. Briac doubled back to wander the gardens, but there was no sign of her. Finally he sighed and walked in the direction of the chapel. There she was, visible instantly, kneeling alone at the altar. The silly gable-hooded headdress was unmistakable, and the cloak Aimée wore hid every line of her sweet body.

"Mon Dieu," St. Briac beseeched silently. "What have I done to deserve persecution from these women?"

He stalked down the aisle and joined Aimée, who looked up in surprise.

"I ought to have more sense than to ask, but I cannot help myself. What do you think you are doing?" St. Briac demanded in a heated whisper. One dark hand went to the nunlike hood that nearly concealed her luxuriant hair, but he suppressed the urge to pull it off.

Aimée scowled at him and pushed his hand from her head. "Your memory is short, monseigneur," she hissed. "Can you have forgotten so quickly our conversation of this morning?"

"That is no longer relevant."

"It's not? I was not aware. I knew only that we had a bargain and that I must fulfill my part by week's end."

"And leave me at the mercy of those two women? The circumstances have changed."

"Can this be the great strong *seigneur-chevalier* who rides into the thick of battle without blinking an eye in fear? Does the stalwart knight require rescuing from a pair of silly women who look like greyhounds? And is it possible that *I*, usually the object of scorn and the recipient of insults, have been chosen to do the rescuing?"

"Aimée, I am in no mood for your sarcasm," St. Briac warned.

"What a pity." She moved to resume her prayers.

"What do you want from me? Must I beg you to help me drive those two away? That mother's sly mind gives me the chills. I would be able to turn them away much more easily if they *were* men; as it is, I must tread more carefully, and the problem is far thornier."

"D'accord," whispered Aimée. She bowed her head, and thick lashes cast crescent-shaped shadows on her cheeks. "I will postpone my departure until you have safely eluded Madame Dagonneau's snares. I will not approach the king about my overwhelming desire to enter a convent before he leaves for Cognac on the morrow. I shall, however, continue to lay the groundwork for my plan and will carry it out at the first available opportunity." Hearing St. Briac emit a small groan that mixed exasperation with relief, Aimée concluded, "I'm certain that such a strong, intelligent *man* as you are will have no trouble at all solving this minor though vexing problem. I will keep silent for a few more days, and by then I trust that Madame and Mademoiselle Dagonneau will have left Blois and I will be free to do likewise."

What St. Briac did not reply, Aimée cast a sidelong glance at his splendidly masculine profile, which was set off by the pleated fraise of his shirt and the mellow light that poured through the stained-glass windows. After a moment, dark brows arched high above pained eyes, and he sighed in surrender.

CHAPTER 17

May 13, 1526

On the morning of the king's departure for Cognac, the courtyard was aswarm with activity. Most of the nearly six hundred members of the royal household would be attending the progression southward, and St. Briac had to maneuver among them as he slowly headed toward the council chamber. Wagons and coaches were being loaded with everything from furniture and tapestries to gold and silver plate.

The council chamber, which was located at the juncture of the François I and Louis XII wings, was a magnificent hall with a high vaulted ceiling. St. Briac identified various members of the king's entourage by the official colors they wore as they milled about, concealing François from view. There were archers in red and blue, *gentilhommes de la chambre* wearing white, the guard of honor with fiery salamanders on their surcoats, officers of the crown clad in the velvet, silk, and fur of officialdom, and the first chamberlain in his clothing of red and gold. Near the chamberlain, St. Briac glimpsed the bold profile of his royal friend, whose costume, of course, was the richest of all.

"Thomas," the king called out over several heads, and in the next instant the crowd parted so that he could pass.

"Beau sire," St. Briac greeted him with a short bow. As

usual when on the brink of an adventure, François was in high good spirits. The feathers in his velvet hat bobbed jauntily above his merry hazel eyes, and a smile gleamed white in his dark beard. One of the pet monkeys from the royal menagerie lounged in the crook of his arm, wearing a jeweled collar and nibbling on a preserved plum.

"You are looking forward to your journey?"

"Oddly enough, yes," the king replied. "I welcome the diversion, which confuses even me, since I was so anxious just a dozen days ago to reach the peace and solitude of Blois. I would seem to be restless; 'tis an affliction I cannot control."

"No affliction, sire," St. Briac said with a smile, "but a facet of your dynamic character. You are not one to loll about."

The two men had wandered toward the wide doorway that opened onto the courtyard, and François looked pleased as he digested the compliment. "I shall miss you while we are away, Thomas, but it eases my mind to know that you will be here to look after things." His gaze wandered over St. Briac's fitted dark-blue doublet and breeches, which were minimally embellished by black velvet at the wrists, collar, and waist. Instead of jewels, he wore black boots that suggested plans for outdoor recreation later in the day.

"*Eh bien, cher ami*, I realize that you will be kept occupied by Mademoiselle de Fleurance and the Dagonneaux, but I might suggest that your time would also be put to good use by having some new clothing made. Were it not for the great physical beauty of your face and form, you would not be admitted to my court clad thusly." He gestured with a flourish toward the courtyard. "*Regardez.* Why, even my pages and grooms and squires are garbed more lavishly than you."

One side of St. Briac's mouth bent upward in a smile. "I find lavish clothing to be a hindrance when I am not engaged in lavish pastimes, sire, but I shall endeavor not to disgrace you with my shabby appearance in the future."

The king laughed, glancing down at the monkey who was wriggling to be set free. There was no need for him to protest that Thomas never looked shabby. His clothing, however plain, was unfailingly well tailored and immaculate, made of the finest materials. Just a few more gems, a bit more fur . . .

"It looks as if they are nearly ready for you," St. Briac

remarked. "Before I bid you farewell, I would ask one question."

Alert to the solemn tone of his friend's voice, François put the monkey down and straightened to meet keen blue-green eyes. "I am listening."

"I realize that I have no right to press you on this matter, but knowing that you are going away, I cannot help feeling concerned about Georges Teverant. I don't trust Chauvergé, and since I won't be with you to balance his influence, I must beg you not to be swayed into making any decision against Teverant without discussing it first with me." St. Briac almost winced as the sentences poured out in a rush. No one had the right to speak this way to the king of France, implying that he might be misled like some witless fool. "I realize that you already are aware of Chauvergé's capacity for causing trouble, but I just had to speak to you about this for my own peace of mind."

"Chauvergé will not be going with me, so you needn't worry that I will be led astray without your steadying influence," the king said in an acid tone. "How have I ever managed to rule France without your help, St. Briac? What disasters will overtake this land after you and your new wife return to your chateau to live?"

"I apologize if I was impertinent, sire, and I pray that you will allow me one more impertinent question."

The king's only response was to tighten his mouth and wait.

"I really cannot explain why I am so concerned, except that I had the strangest dream last night about Teverant. Please reassure me that no action can be taken against him without your assent, sire."

"I don't know why I allow you to waste my time with this trivial nonsense when I can think of nothing except the fate of my beloved sons and the treaty which I cannot agree to. If I refuse to sign it, they may die! And you continue to rant at me about Georges Teverant."

"Sire, I assure you that I am very sensitive to the important worries that plague you now, but I beg you to understand that that is exactly the reason why I am concerned that Chauvergé might be able to take advantage of you. Catching you in a moment of distraction—"

"I've already told you that he is staying here," François nearly shouted.

St. Briac inhaled harshly. It was impossible for him to tell the king that his suspicions about Chauvergé applied equally to Louise de Savoy, who would not remain at Blois. Besides, why was Chauvergé electing to stay here? Obviously Louise and Chauvergé had decided to split up and use their ingenuity in different areas for the time being, but now that the king had been alerted, there seemed less chance of his making a decision about Teverant in a moment of distraction or frustration. As for St. Briac, he would pretend to amuse himself with his current feminine diversions while keeping a suspicious eye on Chauvergé at all times.

"I am sorry for upsetting you, sire. I beg you to accept my apology and bid me *adieu* with a smile of friendship. You know that I do not intend to offend you." St. Briac paused, the corners of his eyes and mouth crinkling impishly. "Had I more time, I would have been able to draw those few rude sentences into hours of conversation that would have seemed completely innocuous."

The king had to laugh. "*Ça va, ça va*. I realize that you did not mean to insult me, but you were quite successful all the same."

The crowd had begun to move toward the courtyard. Squires held prancing horses, and pages were opening carriage doors.

"I suppose I must say my good-byes," St. Briac said quietly. "I wish you great success with the resolution of the treaty and will hope to see you back here soon."

"Within a month, I hope. You have my permission to marry before that if you absolutely cannot wait, but I do yearn to be present for that ceremony, Thomas."

"Well, I am eager to be home at St. Briac again, but if you can return before mid-June, we will wait for you to, ah, join in our happiness." What am I saying? St. Briac wondered wildly to himself. Before he was forced to invent any more fantasies about marriage to Aimée, he reached out to clasp his friend's hand, and then they embraced. The two men walked together into the sunny courtyard just as Anne d'Heilly and Marguerite stepped off the circular staircase. Thomas bade them all farewell and left the king with his ladies.

The duc de Roanne nodded to St. Briac when they passed in the third-floor corridor. It was a shame that Marcel was going off to Cognac with the court train and Thomas would not be able to take advantage of his mistress's freedom, yet a part of him was relieved. He had been too busy to mull over the evaporation of his feelings for Ghislaine, but they obviously had changed.

"Ah, Thomas," the duchess exclaimed when he appeared in her open doorway. Still in bed, she lay swathed in silky covers that did little to disguise the ripe curves of her naked body. Her toffee-colored hair was drawn back neatly into a chignon. "Marcel has gone with the rest of the court to Cognac. Won't you join me?"

St. Briac perceived the tense undercurrent in her light-hearted invitation and felt a pang of regret. "I wish I could, *chérie*, but—"

"I was only teasing, silly," she broke in hastily. "But do come sit with me and tell me all that has been happening. How is that charming girl everyone thinks you are going to marry? Have you found a resolution to that problem? And Thomas, you must tell me about those two women who have come from Burgundy. I've been hearing the most incredible rumors."

Relieved, St. Briac let a smile spread over his face and sat on the edge of the bed. After kissing Ghislaine lightly on her brow, he said, "You anticipate me as always. Aimée and those two women are the reasons for my visit."

Ghislaine listened as he told her all that had occurred since the arrival of the Dagonneaux at Blois. At the end of the story, St. Briac paused, and she waited, aching inside.

"So, you can see my dilemma. I had hoped to have Aimée gone by now, and if these two women had not appeared, she probably would have left today." He laughed without humor and brought a forefinger up to rub a crease from the bridge of his nose. "As much as I long to see the last of Aimée, I need her now to ward off the advances of Blanche Dagonneau and her dear Cécile-Anne."

Ghislaine gazed out the window pensively. "The girl has a ready wit," she mused. "Her sense of whimsy will stand her in good stead."

He gave the duchess a quizzical glance before replying. "It's not always at the forefront of her qualities. When last we spoke, I was more struck by Aimée's stubbornness and insolence."

"Your wife would need both to survive a lifelong relationship with you, Thomas."

"You are spouting madness," he thundered, and then continued with more restraint. "I have said again and again that Aimée and I will never marry. It is all part of the plan, first to get her away from the court without gracing the king's bed and now to keep me safe from the schemes of the Dagonneaux, *mère et fille*. She is as unhappy about this new development as I."

"And you aren't in love with Mademoiselle de Fleurance?"

"In love? With Aimée?" St. Briac laughed loudly. "That question is so ludicrous, I won't even bother to reply."

Ghislaine lifted her perfectly curved eyebrows but didn't argue the point. "I suppose, then, that all this means you will have to stay close to Aimée and far away from me until Madame Dagonneau and her daughter become discouraged and return to Burgundy. I *am* disappointed. I've been anticipating our time alone."

Hearing her voice grow husky on the last word, St. Briac knew that he would have to kiss Ghislaine or she would be certain that he was in love with Aimée. The last thing he needed now was her pestering him about actually wedding that green-eyed vixen.

"You cannot be half as disappointed as I, *ma belle*. Nothing could have pleased me more than to spend every minute until the duke's return here in these apartments with you." St. Briac's tone was sincere, for he dearly wished that he had been speaking the truth. How much simpler life had been when the warm, lighthearted passion he and Ghislaine shared had been his primary romantic outlet. She was turning now in the bed, tugging at the side of his doublet, and St. Briac saw the gleam of sadness in her blue eyes before he lifted her into his strong embrace. They kissed for a long, bittersweet minute, so poignantly that sparks of desire nearly caught fire. He thought he tasted tears in Ghislaine's mouth, but then a noise in the hallway distracted them. She pulled the silky coverlet back over her breasts, while St. Briac sprang up to look out into the corridor. He'd forgotten that the door was ajar.

"Was there someone there?" Ghislaine asked anxiously.

"I saw a man's back disappear onto the inner staircase, so at least we know it wasn't Blanche and Cécile-Anne Dagonneau. With Aimée in the midst of her prenun act, the last thing I need is to be seen kissing a married woman. I'd never get rid of those two."

"The court has left? It couldn't have been Marcel?"

"I heard them riding off as we spoke. Besides, it wouldn't have come as a terrible shock to him, would it? He's always known and as far as I can tell hasn't much cared! With me to keep his wife warm in bed, the duke has been free to concentrate on his position at court." St. Briac crossed to the bed as he spoke, but he didn't resume his position.

"You shouldn't speak so harshly of those who strive for what has always come easily to you, Thomas," she replied defensively. "You could have anything you want here at court, so the lack of challenge bores you. Perhaps once Marcel attains a few of his goals, he will remember that he has a wife." Ghislaine glared at the sight of St. Briac arching a derisive brow. "Truth to tell, I think that Marcel does care more than either of us ever guessed. Perhaps he feels more secure at court, because he has been paying quite a bit of attention to me lately. You may not believe it, but my husband asked me to come with him to Cognac."

"Well, then, obviously you should have gone," retorted St. Briac, more annoyed with his own temper than with anything Ghislaine had said. "*Nom de Dieu*, you should know better than to plan your life around me."

"Don't flatter yourself, monseigneur. You have never been my reason for living, and you never will be. I have far too much sense to fall in love with a man like you."

Her eyes, blue and calm as the Loire, deflated his anger. "Yes, I know that, Ghislaine." Kneeling, St. Briac lifted her white hand and pressed his mouth to it tenderly. "I never meant to quarrel with you. I wouldn't hurt you for the world."

"Of course not, and you haven't. My eyes have been wide open right from the first, Thomas. I've never been your victim." Gazing at his irresistibly masculine face, Ghislaine hoped that he couldn't see how potent her longing was. "I shall be very inconspicuous until you and your Aimée manage to dissuade the Dagonneaux with the evidence of your true love. I can't help wondering, though. What will you do if they are not willing to be convinced? What if they don't leave Blois?"

St. Briac released her hand and straightened with a ragged sigh. "We'll convince them, no matter what it takes. You can depend on that, Ghislaine."

* * *

The chateau was quiet now that the king and most of his court and staff had departed for Cognac. St. Briac dreamed idly of a hard, exhausting ride into the woods that spread westward from Blois as he descended the great staircase on his way to the stables. However, no sooner had he attained the courtyard than voices called out in greeting.

"*Voyons.* It is the seigneur de St. Briac," exclaimed a woman.

"Well, Thomas, this *is* a surprise. On your way to rendezvous with your lovely fiancée, I'll wager." This speaker was male and all too familiar.

He froze for a moment in dread and then turned slowly to discover Chauvergé with Blanche and Cécile-Anne Dagonneau. The trio stood close together between the shadowed buttresses that supported the massive staircase. St. Briac was reminded of reptiles lying in wait for their prey under rocks.

Greetings were exchanged all around, but he kept his distance. Chauvergé wore a sly, gloating smile that put St. Briac on his guard. Was it possible that the weasel had nothing better to do with his time than plot against him? Unlikely, yet . . .

"Shall we see you at the midday meal, monseigneur?" Blanche inquired sweetly.

"I believe I shall be dining with Mademoiselle de Fleurance. I'm not certain." He tried to smile, but only one side of his mouth curved upward. Cécile-Anne sighed dreamily, thinking how boyish he looked.

"We shall look for you all the same, won't we, Cécile-Anne?"

"*Mais oui, maman!*" Nodding obediently on cue, the girl reminded St. Briac more than ever of one of the king's trained dogs.

"Before you rush off, monseigneur," Chauvergé spoke up, "I've been meaning to ask you. What news is there of your good friend Georges Teverant? Very odd, his disappearing from the court train that way. Where did he go, do you know?"

"No. I regret to say that M'sieur Teverant did not consult me before taking his leave."

Chauvergé wanted to pursue the matter, but Aimée de Fleurance interrupted the conversation. She emerged from the entrance to her wing, wrapped in a dark cloak and wearing the gable-hooded headdress St. Briac disliked so intensely.

"Good morning, my love," he called, and went to greet her. Through a clenched smile he cautioned, "Guard your tongue."

Aimée barely managed to conceal her elation at this encounter with St. Briac; she had no room for thoughts of the others. Pleasantries were spoken back and forth, but for some inexplicable reason, Aimée barely heard. Her concentration was centered on St. Briac: the tilt of his head in the sunny breeze, the set of his wide shoulders, the sensation of his fingers around her arm. It was as though the longing had built up to a point where it no longer would be denied, or perhaps it had something to do with the fact that nearly all the court had departed for Cognac, and they were alone. The Dagonneaux and Chauvergé seemed insignificant, merely sources of amusement for the occasional dull moments.

"Aren't you dressed awfully warm for a day like this?" Blanche was inquiring. How could such a dowdy maiden inspire the devotion of a man like St. Briac? Could there be some truth in the things the chevalier de Chauvergé had just told them?

"I am on my way to chapel, Madame Dagonneau," Aimée said primly. "I'm already late, so I do hope you will excuse me. *Au revoir.*"

St. Briac experienced a sharp, brief yearning as he thought of the stallion that waited in the stables to take him flying through the woods. That pleasure would have to wait, for at this moment his only choices were the clinging Dagonneaux and the newly pious Aimée de Fleurance.

"Excuse us both, *s'il vous plaît*," he said. By the time his smiled reached Chauvergé, there was a definite hint of mischief in his eyes. "I have some prayers of my own to say."

St. Briac had to run lightly to catch up with Aimée, but then their steps were perfectly synchronized. The others watched their departing backs, the shared moments of laughter, and finally the sight of St. Briac pulling off the gable-hooded headdress to let glossy ebony curls spill down to Aimée's hips.

CHAPTER 18

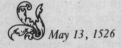 *May 13, 1526*

Excitement bubbled up inside Aimée as she walked by St. Briac's side, his hand riding on the small of her back. She didn't fight the pleasure but let herself flow with its effervescent current.

As they passed around the Louis XII gallery, out of sight of the courtyard, St. Briac inquired, "You aren't really going back to chapel, are you? After already attending mass with François at dawn?"

"I have to convince everyone that I have become unusually devout, and you know it. The entire court attended that mass, so there wasn't anything extraordinary about my presence, was there? This additional excursion to the chapel makes a point that few people can miss."

"Look, Aimée, I wish that you would put this plot of yours aside for a few days."

"No." She shook her head stubbornly. "I am compromising quite enough for your sake as it is."

The line of his jaw hardened. "How noble you are. I, on the other hand, am less virtuous of character. I'll leave you to your prayers and go to the stables this way to exercise Sèbastien."

Aimée suddenly caught his sleeve and raised her head, alert to approaching voices. St. Briac glanced back just in time to glimpse Blanche's skirt fluttering around the corner of the gallery. Before Aimée had a chance to think, much less protest, she was swooped up into sturdy arms. The impact of St. Briac's chest against her soft bosom sent an involuntary jolt of delight coursing through her nerves. He had lifted her off the ground, and so Aimée had to hold on for security; the feel of her slim arms rounding his neck made St. Briac smile before he kissed her.

She gave a smothered gasp that was lost in a tidal wave of keen sensations. *Parbleu*, how wonderful his mouth felt slanting over hers. Aimée drank in the taste of him, the scent of his bearded cheek that almost tickled her nose, the feel of his crisp, clean hair curling in her fingers that clung to the warmth of his neck. She opened her mouth, and their tongues teased, caressed, embraced with mounting passion. The pounding of her heart drowned out Cécile-Anne's squawk of surprise and Blanche's horrified whispers. Chauvergé hastened to steer the women toward the courtyard even as St. Briac pressed Aimée against the brick wall so that their hips met. He felt her arch instinctively nearer, and her hungry moan mingled with his breath. When at length he lifted his head and smiled down at her, Aimée's cheeks were dusky with passion, her eyes luminous with arousal. St. Briac ached to make fierce love to her; it took every ounce of control he possessed to murmur, "I fear we've cracked your reputation for piety, *chérie*. We could destroy it completely here and now, or—"

Reality hit Aimée with a painful thud. She squirmed against the big, steely body that pinned her to the wall and blushed when she felt his hardness taunt her in response.

"You animal," she ground out. "Let me go. They saw us, didn't they? They must think I'm a wanton!"

"As long as you reserve your wantonness for your future husband." St. Briac laughed as he put his hands around her waist and set her gently on the ground.

"Don't call yourself that. I wouldn't marry you if you were the last man on earth!"

He pressed a finger to her lips, and they both felt a flash of sensual lightning at that simple tactile connection. "Shh! That's supposed to be our secret. As far as the rest of the world is concerned, we are madly"—a chestnut brow arched suggestively—"*passionately* in love. You cannot wait to become my wife so that we can share all the joys of the marriage bed."

"You are disgusting!" Aimée took a gulp of air, her leaf-green eyes enormous in her delicate face. She was furious that he had managed to undo all her efforts to convince Chauvergé and the Dagonneaux of her pure devotion to God. St. Briac had wanted them to think she was crazed with desire for him, and he'd probably succeeded effortlessly. "You had no right to force yourself on me that way. Now go ride your silly horse and leave me to my penance."

Turquoise eyes gleaming merrily, St. Briac sketched a bow. "As you wish, *ma chère religieuse*."

"I'm not going to be a nun any more than I'm going to be your wife, so stop teasing me, you jackass!" Spinning around, Aimée stalked off toward the doorway to the chapel.

Behind her St. Briac cleared his throat. "Mademoiselle?"

She whirled around, two bright spots of color on her cheeks. "What is it now?"

He held out her gable-hooded headdress, which had fallen unnoticed to the ground, and dusted it off with mock solemnity. "Yours, I believe."

Inside the cool, silent chapel, Aimée knelt off to one side in the nave and bowed her head. She was expecting to calm down, but instead her mind whirled with images of St. Briac and what he'd said. The more she thought, the more she seethed. Worse, she could not resolve her feelings or arrive at answers for the questions that jumbled together inside her. It was easy enough to pretend that she hated the man and never wanted to see him again, but there were voices deep within her heart that told a different story.

"Mademoiselle de Fleurance?" a silky voice murmured beside her. Aimée jumped a bit in surprise, only to find Chauvergé settling to his knees nearby. "I hesitated to disturb you, but I wasn't certain if I would be able to speak to you privately after you left the chapel."

Too taken aback to protest, Aimée only stared, waiting.

"I'll be brief. I only want to assure you, on behalf of Madame and Mademoiselle Dagonneau, and myself of course, that we do not condemn you for the scene we inadvertently witnessed between you and the seigneur de St. Briac."

"Well, I appreciate that," Aimée answered numbly. Why was he saying these things?

"I told those ladies that they must not think the worst of you, only of St. Briac. Oh, yes! You don't have to say a word, mademoiselle. I've known that devil's spawn nearly all my life. He's free with his charm, but does he care who is hurt in the process? The answer, needless to say, is no. He uses people with no more conscience than an animal. He is using the king—has always used him—and he's using you now, I'm sorry to say."

Aimée was speechless. She watched as Chauvergé narrowed his eyes and waited to see what he would say next.

"You are young, naive, trusting, and that is what troubles me, mademoiselle. It is one thing for St. Briac to trifle endlessly with the affections of a woman like Ghislaine Pepin, for she is worldly and aware of the risks involved. I must tell you, though, that I feel quite ill when I think that I happened to see St. Briac in her bed this very morning, kissing her, just minutes before he forced himself on you outside this chapel."

For a moment Aimée couldn't breathe, and when she did, the air burned her throat. She was too stunned to notice the smug smile that curved Chauvergé's thin mouth upward.

"I won't take any more of your time, mademoiselle," he was saying smoothly. "I just wanted you to know that we realize you were not at fault."

Aimée barely noticed when he padded away down the aisle, silent as a cat. She told herself that there was no reason to be upset. Hadn't she known all along that the duchesse de Roanne was St. Briac's lover? She was not a child; she was well aware of the duties of a mistress. Still, a part of her hadn't wanted to face the idea that he was still sleeping with Ghislaine. It was painful to believe that Thomas could be so cavalier as to make love to a married woman and then, minutes later, share such intense intimacy with her. Was Chauvergé right? Was it all an act produced by St. Briac's magical charm?

Only one board was laid for supper that evening, just space enough to accommodate the two dozen members of court who remained at Blois. St. Briac and Florange came early to the hall of honor and stood before the cold, mammoth fireplace, drinking potent Alsatian wine.

"I'm happy to discover a friend among this group," St. Briac said ironically. "I feared that I would go mad with

Chauvergé and those Dagonneau women following me everywhere."

Robert de la Marck, seigneur de Florange, was an exceptionally handsome young man, but he felt quite overshadowed by St. Briac. His friend was looking especially splendid in a doublet and haut-de-chausses in a warm, sandy hue sewn lavishly with golden thread. A single emerald hung from a chain around his neck, nearly lost in the folds of a soft brown velvet jerkin set with pearls and a modest display of smaller emeralds. "I'm flattered that you're pleased to have me near, *mon ami*, but have you forgotten the two very agreeable ladies who stayed behind on your account? The duchesse de Roanne is temporarily free of the bonds of marriage, and your own future partner in that state of bliss is here as well. In fact, Mademoiselle de Fleurance appears even as I speak."

The hall of honor had been filling gradually. Ghislaine stood off to one side with another nobleman and his wife, while Aimée paused in the shadow of the courtyard. St. Briac gave his friend a smile and went to greet the lady who, God willing, would save him from Cécile-Anne Dagonneau.

Aimée stepped forward into the torchlight and candlelight, pleased when she heard St. Briac draw in his breath in surprise. Never had she looked more beautiful, not even the night they met, when she'd appeared at the hunting lodge in crimson velvet, gold, and pearls. This gown was one of the ones he had ordered. Midnight-blue velvet was fashioned into a square-cut frame for Aimée's creamy breasts, then hugged her tiny waist and parted to reveal an elaborate silver petticoat. Silver gleamed through the slashes in her puffed sleeves, and more silver thread traced a pattern of flowers over the bodice. Each bloom was set with a ruby or diamond. A perfect sapphire nestled between her breasts, while the shining black locks that had blown against St. Briac's face that afternoon were swept back and caught in a silvery crispinette.

"How beautiful you are, *miette*," he told her gently. "I am pleased to see that you have forsaken that headdress and your chapel gowns."

Aimée steeled her heart against his magnetism. "I have not forsaken them, monseigneur, only put them aside temporarily. And—" He was lifting her hand, his own fingers warm and strong, and she watched, speechless, as his mouth found and burned first her palm and then the treacherous pulse that throbbed at her wrist.

"You were saying?" He looked up at her with ironic perception.

"I was saying that, well, that nothing has changed, so you needn't begin acting smug. I still fully intend to carry out my part of our bargain."

"Naturally." St. Briac gave her a smile that made her seethe.

"I would be most appreciative if you would wipe that smirk off your face," Aimée whispered sharply.

"Your servant, *ma belle étoile*," he answered soothingly.

The mockery that laced his tone only infuriated her more. Beautiful star, indeed! Even in her agitated state, Aimée realized that he was alluding to their interlude under the stars at Chenonceau, but she knew that if she accused St. Briac of this, he would feign horrified innocence.

"St. Briac, you must not be so greedy as to hoard this beautiful lady's company. Take pity on the rest of us." Florange had come up beside them, smiling with mischievous charm. "Mademoiselle de Fleurance, could I persuade you to join me at the table? The meal is about to be served."

St. Briac opened his mouth to protest but changed his mind. Aimée's eyes were tilted up at the corners in a feline way; she was waiting for him to beg her to sit with him instead. The little vixen then would choose Florange anyway and go off gloating. "By all means, *chérie*, do join my friend. A few hours of his company will only make you appreciate me more."

Florange had to laugh at this, but Aimée, oddly enough, did not. She tossed a glance to her fiancé that could only be described as icy, and replied, "I doubt that."

St. Briac smothered a sigh as he watched them turn toward the table. He had the uneasy feeling that this evening would do little to convince the Dagonneaux of an indestructible love between him and Aimée. Damn Florange! Why couldn't he mind his own business? And why did it seem that Aimée was incapable of behaving in a way that did not create trouble for him?

A hand rested on St. Briac's clenched forearm. He looked down into the warm blue eyes of Ghislaine Pepin.

"My darling," she murmured, "you look upset. Surely

you are not jealous that Florange has stolen your . . . betrothed for a few hours?"

"What? Don't be ridiculous!" Bending down to the duchess's ear, he whispered, "Truth to tell, I am elated. Now I have an excuse to be with you."

Across the hall of honor, Aimée seated herself on the bench beside Florange. She pretended to ignore the intimate little scene between St. Briac and his mistress, but from the corners of her eyes she saw every smile, imagined every whispered secret they exchanged, and felt a hot ache in her breast each time they touched. How foolish she had been to think even for a moment that Chauvergé had not spoken the truth to her in the chapel. Remembering the painstaking effort she had put into dressing tonight, dreaming all the while of dazzling St. Briac so that he would be blind to the duchess's charms, Aimée felt her cheeks grow hot with humiliation.

"Will you have wine, mademoiselle?" Florange proffered a silver cup that just had been filled by a servant who wielded a pewter vessel with a long spout.

She took the cup and drank deeply of the crimson liquid. Florange was smiling at her as he tasted his wine, but there was an intent concentration in his blue eyes that put her on guard.

"Don't be nervous, mademoiselle. I don't mean to stare, but I confess to a lively curiosity about the woman Thomas has chosen to be his wife. You see . . ." He paused, searching for the right words, and brushed back his blond hair. "I love him as a brother. Although we grew up together and are nearly the same age, I have always looked up to him. From the time we were boys, wrestling, fighting with wooden swords, and riding ponies together, he has been at peace with himself. Always sure, brave, secure in his strength and wits, ready with a jest during the darkest moment of a battle."

Aimée's discomfort intensified. Florange was looking down across the board to the place where St. Briac and his lover sat, whispering side by side.

"I hope you'll forgive me for separating you from him tonight," Florange was saying sincerely as he signaled for the nearest servant to replenish her wine. "I fear I've been selfish, but I wanted to get to know you, especially after watching your charming performance in the king's study when Thomas was presented to those Dagonneau women. You were delightful."

"I was?"

Florange laughed. "No false modesty, mademoiselle. You are far too clever to need compliments from me; besides, St. Briac must have showered you with dozens when all of us were gone."

"Oh, no, he thinks I'm too bold as it is. He won't encourage me." The words spilled out of their own accord, and the sound of Florange's laughter made her blush.

"Good for you. I'm sure that your spirit will stand you in good stead during a lifetime as St. Briac's wife. Don't let him intimidate you, mademoiselle. You are enchanting."

His flattery made her head spin. How wonderful it was to be admired. Surreptitiously, she glanced down the table and caught St. Briac watching her with narrowed eyes. Aimée returned her attention to Florange. They chatted on not only about his beloved friend but about all manner of subjects in which they shared an interest. More wine and good food combined to heighten Aimée's already soaring spirits. From time to time she caught sight of Blanche Dagonneau leaning forward to peer down the table at her. Lifting her chin, Aimée told herself that it was important for St. Briac's sake that she give a good performance so that those greyhound women would realize that she was a person to be reckoned with.

Plates of duck cooked with turnips had been placed before them when Florange said, "I suppose Thomas has told you the story of the occasion when we were knighted."

"Why, no, I don't believe so." She had been tempted to lie, for certainly he would have shared such an important story with his beloved.

"You are familiar with the great French victory at Melegnano?"

"*Quinze quinze*," Aimée affirmed, quoting the year that had been one of the most spectacular of François's reign.

"You must insist that St. Briac share with you the entire story of that battle and the events leading up to it. Afterward, though, our young king met with Bayard, *le chevalier sans peur et sans reproche*, on the bloody battlefield. François revered him."

Aimée waited as Florange took a drink of wine, looking out toward the courtyard. She could see grief in his blue eyes for the famous Bayard who had lost his life during the more recent ill-fated battle of Pavia.

"The two of them were alone," Florange continued, "but I have heard that the king told him that he wished on that day to be knighted by the most worthy knight—Bayard, of course. The chevalier argued that François was king of a realm and had been anointed by oil from heaven, so he was already a knight above all others."

Listening with wide green eyes, Aimée tried to imagine the scene on the twilit battlefield. "And?"

"François insisted, cajoled, and finally ordered him to do the thing. He knelt before Bayard, who lifted his sword and struck him once, twice, thrice on the shoulder and then murmured, 'The first king I ever knighted.' After a moment the chevalier was seized by exaltation himself. He lifted his sword to the heavens and spoke to it: 'You are blessed this day to have given knighthood to so fine a prince. Henceforth, you will be treasured as a relic and never drawn except against Turk, Saracen, or Moor.'"

"What a splendid tale," Aimée exclaimed, letting out her breath in a long sigh.

"It doesn't end there. You see, St. Briac and I had been out chasing the Swiss since the battle ended. We had worn full suits of armor and had been on horseback since dawn, when we rode up during the scene between Bayard and the king. François had heard that both of us were dead. So great was his relief when he saw us alive that he insisted that we should accept knighthood at his hand."

"*Parbleu*," Aimée whispered.

"Thomas and I dismounted, removed our helms, and dropped to our knees before our monarch. I remember little except the touch of the sword on my shoulder. My exhaustion was such that I could scarcely rise when the ceremony ended, but a wave of pride and joy swept over me that I had not experienced before or since. I recall turning my head and seeing St. Briac, his face smudged with grime and sweat, grinning at me." Florange smiled at the memory. "I'll admit to you, mademoiselle, that he assisted me when I tried to stand, and there was still strength enough in his arm for us both."

"It must have been a glorious moment for all four of you. I wish I could have seen it."

Florange smiled as he brought himself back to the present.

"That happened more than a decade ago, when you were but a child, mademoiselle. Now eat your duck before they take the plate away."

Aimée laughed as she saw that her duck and turnips were almost untouched. Picking up the peculiar ivory-handled implement that St. Briac had called a fork, she attacked the food. Florange stared as she ate, wondering whether it was the wine or the enchanting spell she cast so guilelessly that was to blame for his euphoria.

Farther down the table, St. Briac watched Aimée while Chauvergé, the duchesse de Roanne, and the Dagonneaux women watched him. He could hardly contain himself until the eighth course had been cleared away. The sight of a servant pouring more wine for Aimée was more than he could stand.

"Ghislaine, I find that I am fatigued. Will you excuse me?"

The duchess was wise enough to know when to retreat and wait. "*Naturellement, mon ange.* Your company during this long meal has been pleasure enough for one evening." She gave him an incandescent smile.

After bidding everyone within hearing distance a charming "*bon soir,*" St. Briac rounded the table and came up behind Florange and Aimée. She appeared oblivious to his presence until he reached over her shoulder and plucked the cup of wine from her slim fingers.

"Oh! How dare y—"

"Don't say I frightened you, my darling," St. Briac cut in. Just enough steel crept into his voice and eyes to give Aimée pause. "It's been a long day for both of us, and I feel that it's time I see you to your chamber."

Florange rose, extended a hand to his friend, and thanked him for granting him some time with Mademoiselle de Fleurance. Aimée had gone to stand beside St. Briac, but she couldn't resist a parting shot spoken to Florange but directed at her fiancé.

"I've so enjoyed our little interlude, monseigneur de Florange." Dimples winked as she added, "You must not thank Thomas, however. He does not own me, nor shall he ever, wedding or not."

CHAPTER 19

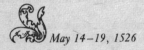 *May 14–19, 1526*

"Sometimes you make me so angry, I could just . . ."

St. Briac paused in the act of dragging Aimée across the courtyard and exclaimed, "Don't say that you are going to leave me in suspense and not finish your thought."

"I could hit you, that's what!"

He gasped in mock horror. "A frightening threat, mademoiselle, but one that I believe I am man enough to withstand. I insist that you fulfill your desire."

His last words had been spoken suggestively, but Aimée would not rise to the bait. Instead she gave him a wicked smile, drew back one delicate hand, and swung it at St. Briac's bearded cheek. The impact generated a less than impressive "whap."

"Do you feel better?" he inquired mildly. Silvery-blue starlight streamed over his massive physique and sculpted face. Her hand felt as though it had hit a giant tree.

"No, I don't feel better," she mimicked. "I will, though, as I inform you that I found your behavior in the hall just now insufferably pompous. How dare you treat me like your chattel? I am not some trained falcon that lights on your arm on command."

"Mon Dieu!" St. Briac's exclamation dripped sarcasm. "I had almost forgotten the magical pleasure of your company."

"Why did you force me to accompany you? I was having a perfectly lovely time with a man who thinks I am beautiful, charming, and enchanting."

He wanted to snap, So I noticed! but managed to bite his tongue. Instead, he gripped Aimée's slender shoulders as he spoke. "Now, *look*, I didn't tear you away from Florange because I couldn't bear to be separated from you a moment longer. There is something that I must discuss with you seriously tonight. I suggest that you cease these childish tantrums and come along with me to your chamber."

Aimée refused to run in an effort to keep up with his long strides, and so she trailed along behind, very sedately, she thought. She found St. Briac waiting for her in the doorway to her chamber. Sweeping past him, she waited until he had closed the door before murmuring sweetly, "I would offer you something to drink, for certainly that must be customary when a lady invites a man to her boudoir, but then, I didn't invite you, did I?"

"I'll pour my own," St. Briac assured her, caustically polite. "After all, I did pay for it." He went to the dresser and filled a pewter cup with red wine. "Will you join me?"

"I would be *rude* to refuse so charming an invitation." Aimée seated herself in a carved chair, feeling quite proud of her cool wits until she took the cup he proffered and saw that there was barely a swallow at the bottom.

"You've had more than enough," he informed her tersely. "I want you to remember our discussion when you awake tomorrow morning."

Aimée's spring-green eyes widened in outrage, but she held her tongue. Forcing a smile, she asked sweetly through clenched teeth, "Might I beg you, monseigneur, to indulge one tiny whim of mine?"

"Perhaps." He dropped into a chair opposite hers and stretched out his legs.

"It would make me very happy if you could begin our important conversation immediately and end it as soon as possible." Still smiling, Aimée leaned forward and whispered, "I yearn to be rid of you, monseigneur."

St. Briac's dark brows lifted as he appraised her, the corners of his mouth twitching slightly with amused admiration. "How much we have in common, *miette*. It was my own longing to bid you a permanent farewell that forced me to seek this private interview with you."

"*Vraiment?* Pray explain, monseigneur." Restless, rebellious, and hurting for some reason, Aimée rose and took her cup to the dresser, where she filled it and sipped defiantly as St. Briac spoke.

"I shall be brief, as you requested. I want to go home. I am fed up with this nonsense, particularly since the debut of Blanche and Cécile-Anne Dagonneau, and I want it ended. I've sent word to my aunt and brother that I shall be with them before the end of June." He turned to regard Aimée's lovely yet stubborn profile. "No more games. I want to be rid of those two women, but it seems that will not be accomplished with any ease unless you help. It's time for me to make the rules and for you to follow them to the letter."

Chin high, Aimée slowly turned her head and looked into his wintry midnight eyes. Pride demanded that she make an impertinent reply, but the words eluded her. St. Briac filled the silence.

"You know, don't you, that you owe me this much and more, *miette*. Ordinarily, I wouldn't demand payment on a debt such as ours, but this time I have no choice, and neither do you."

Aimée sighed, set down her cup of wine, and then twisted her fingers together. "But we already made a bargain. I've been perfectly honorable, trying to uphold my part, and it isn't fair of you to ask me to change all my plans."

"Was it fair for those women to burst into my life with that ridiculous story about an arranged marriage? Was it fair for me to be trapped into a betrothal to save you from the king's bed? For that matter, was it fair of you to ask me to help you in the first place?" St. Briac's voice was as cold and sharp as his sword. "If it weren't for you, I'd have been home by now! I'm tired of living my life to accommodate the needs of others." He stood, gripped Aimée's arm, and swung her around so that they faced each other, their bodies touching lightly. "I'm not asking you, mademoiselle, I'm telling you! Those cursed women will never leave Blois if you go on creeping into the chapel and snuggling up to Florange. From now on I expect you to devote all your energies to convincing the Dagonneaux that you are ardently and permanently in love with me. You live only to become the wife of the seigneur de St. Briac, *comprends-tu*?"

His fingers were hurting her arms; even the force of his

gaze was painful . . . yet exciting somehow. In spite of dozens of conflicting emotions, not the least of which were anger and hostility, Aimée had to admit that he was right. She owed him this much and more, and she would have to swallow her pride and do as he asked. "I'll try, monseigneur." She couldn't help adding petulantly, "You do realize, I hope, that no matter how adoring I may pretend to be, it can be difficult to fool people when such sentiments are contrived rather than genuine."

"I suggest, then, that you fall in love with me before tomorrow morning." Amusement flickered briefly over St. Briac's chiseled face, but his tone remained harsh.

Aimée blinked back sudden, bitter tears. If only he didn't behave as if he despised her. "I'll deliver a flawless performance, monseigneur, I promise. If you're certain that this is the way to end this fiasco, I shall participate wholeheartedly."

"I knew you would see it my way," he murmured. "And now, since each of us is so eager to escape the other's company, I suggest that we say good night so that we can enjoy the next few hours of peaceful solitude before our romantic drama begins."

Aimée followed his tall, broad-shouldered figure to the door, trying all the while to ignore the constricting pain in her breast. Why did St. Briac affect her so?

"Sleep well, *miette*." Opening the door, he stepped into the hallway and turned back to add, "I expect you to be alert and in prime feminine form tomorrow." One side of his mouth quirked slightly. "Dream of me."

A movement at the far end of the corridor caught Aimée's eye, and she glanced over just in time to see a familiar, long Dagonneau nose retreat around the corner. It seemed that she had no other course of action, and besides, it was already tomorrow. Suddenly she stood on tiptoe and wrapped her arms around St. Briac's shoulders, ignoring the startled expression that crossed his face. "They're here," she whispered, and then pulled his mouth down to her own.

St. Briac's shock lasted only an instant before his arms caught Aimée up and their bodies met full length. Their kiss caught fire immediately. He groaned silently deep inside, lost in the sweet, maddening enchantment that was Aimée: her woman's curves, soft and firm all at once, that taunted him beneath the close-fitting velvet gown; the heady fragrance of violets that clung to her neck and rose from her gleaming black curls; and most of all the feel of her fingers in his hair as she responded to his kiss, her mouth opening to yield its delicious secrets, her heart beating against his doublet.

At length Aimée drew back, her cheeks flushed. "We mustn't get carried away before our wedding day, my love," she cautioned in a voice just loud enough to drift down the corridor.

St. Briac had to smile at her audacity in spite of the aching hardness outlined against his breeches. "You torture me, *chérie*. How can I wait?"

"'Tis torture that will end soon enough." Aimée gave him a coquettish smile and disentangled herself, stepping back into the shadowed doorway. "Dream of *me*, Thomas."

As a bemused St. Briac turned away from the portal that had closed in his face, he heard a scurrying sound around the corner of the hallway; Blanche and Cécile-Anne Dagonneau were making a hasty retreat.

The next few days passed smoothly. Aimée was all that one could wish for in a devoted, adoring fiancée. She and St. Briac sat together at meals, strolled side by side in the gardens, and pretended to whisper words of love that in reality were closer to insults in each other's ears. All the while, Blanche and Cécile-Anne remained at Blois.

St. Briac avoided being alone with Aimée, keeping strictly to their bargain. The only emotion he showed her aside from the artificial ones he displayed in public was frustration at the smiling perseverance of the Dagonneaux women. She, on the other hand, found it difficult to sleep at night. Dreams of St. Briac were not at all what she craved, but there he was, each time she drifted off, kissing her, gazing down at her with eyes that smiled with both passion and love, opening her gown with long, gentle fingers.

Just such a dream drove her from bed one night. Aimée slid from her bed, telling herself that the warm air was to blame for her insomnia, and drew a satin shift over her head. A soft, flower-scented breeze caressed her on the balcony. She closed her eyes, luxuriating in the sensation of her hair ruffling over her bare shoulders and arms. Where was St. Briac? She imagined him asleep in his own bed, but the image of Ghislaine Pepin intruded. Aimée opened her eyes, studying the few still dimly lit windows in the François I wing. Then she saw St. Briac, fully dressed, stepping from the grand staircase into the courtyard. Blinking incredulously as her eyes became accustomed to the dark, she grew convinced. He wore only a loose white shirt, breeches, and boots, but there was no mistaking those shoulders, that stride, and, even at a distance, his moonlit silhouette.

What was he doing? Aimée's curiosity intensified as she saw him cast a surreptitious look in both directions before starting toward the arched entrance to the gardens. Her first thought was that the duchesse de Roanne must be waiting for him, but the realization that they could be alone in either of their apartments made her dismiss such a notion. She was still staring, puzzled, when another figure appeared at the top of the open staircase. Instantly, Aimée recognized Louis Arçet, chevalier de Chauvergé.

Her heart pounded. Something was wrong. She didn't know what it was, but she had to warn St. Briac. Without pondering the matter further, Aimée turned back to her chamber, pulling the shift over her head and almost instantly replacing it with one of the worn cotton dresses she had brought from Nieuil. Her bare feet fairly flew down the stairs, but she paused at the Louis XII wing's entryway until she saw Chauvergé exit through the arch that led to the forecourt. He hadn't seen St. Briac.

Aimée was not conscious of the pebbles that bit into her feet as she raced across the cobbled courtyard. Emerging into the gardens, she scanned them quickly until she spied St. Briac at the far end, near the kennels. In moments she was at his side.

"*Sang de Dieu*," he swore, recognizing her at last when she reached him. "What are you doing? Have you lost your senses?"

"I came to warn you. Chauvergé followed you, but he went into the courtyard since he didn't see which way you went. I don't know what is going on, but—" Aimée was panting. But what? "I just had a feeling that something was wrong when I saw him come down the staircase after you."

St. Briac was torn between relief and astonishment. Aimée's breasts were heaving in the half-undone bodice of her gown, her ebony mane of curls was tangled about her face, and her feet were bare. What in God's name was she doing awake and watching the courtyard halfway between midnight and dawn?

"I appreciate your concern, *miette*." His white teeth flashed briefly in the darkness. "Such efforts on your part were surely unnecessary, though. I doubt that Blanche and Cécile-Anne are spying on us at this hour."

"But Chauvergé—"

"Why do you assume that I am doing anything that would interest him? Can I not take a walk?"

"In the middle of the night?"

St. Briac arched a brow as if to say, "And what is your excuse?" Aimée's cheeks warmed with embarrassment.

"I'm sorry," she whispered. "I was only trying to help. Good night." Turning away, her head high as she attempted to retain some semblance of pride, she felt his large hand close around her elbow.

"Wait."

A night bird was calling softly from the trees below the garden. Aimée opened her mouth to reply to St. Briac, only to be silenced by a curt "Shh!" To her amazement, he then mimicked perfectly the voice of the bird. "You can help me after all, *ma petite étoile*." His voice was barely audible.

"But—"

"Shh. Don't speak. Just look at the stars. It would be a tragedy to waste them."

Aimée's astonishment was such that she couldn't have spoken if she tried. St. Briac was leading her to a secluded stone bench, drawing her down to sit across his lap, one arm circling her waist while the other hand found the slim column of her neck. He was kissing her then, and her mind whirled with confusion. What was happening? Was he sincere? Somehow, through the cloud of her bewilderment, Aimée sensed his distraction. Never before had St. Briac kissed her quite so methodically. Opening her eyes, she saw to her surprise that his also were open, narrowed past her face as he scanned the gardens that swept toward the chateau.

Aimée pulled her mouth free, but St. Briac held fast to the back of her head when she tried to turn it.

"It's Chauvergé," he breathed into her ear. "Be still until he leaves."

Unsure of what to make of this, Aimée remained passive in St. Briac's embrace, her nose and mouth pressed to his neck. Helplessly she inhaled his arousing scent and felt the blood pound in her veins. I must be dreaming this, she re-assured herself. They remained thus for several minutes while Aimée pondered the hard muscles of the chest that was crushing her bosom, the texture of St. Briac's clean hair, and her own acute yearning to have him pull her with him into a whirlpool of sweet abandon. Unfortunately—or for-tunately, as she thought later when sanity returned—St. Briac's thoughts and needs were focused elsewhere. His big body was as tense as a panther's about to spring, and he seemed totally oblivious to the soft feminine curves that yielded against him.

"At *last*. I swear that man's a voyeur. How long did he need to peer at us?" Setting her on her feet, St. Briac chuck-led softly. "Perhaps he was hoping to see more of you, *miette*. A pity we couldn't oblige."

"I don't understand. Won't you tell me what is going on?" Aimée's eyes shone up at him in the starlight.

He bit his lip, thinking, tasting the glib lie that was ready to satisfy her curiosity. For some reason, he traded it for a portion of the truth. "You must not repeat this to anyone, Aimée. Do you swear?"

"Yes, of course."

"I cannot tell you everything, but I will say that the reason I am here is to collect an important letter."

"From that night bird?" she queried shrewdly.

St. Briac grinned. "You are too bright for your own good. Yes, that is the messenger. This could be very important, and it is especially crucial that Chauvergé not suspect."

"Why don't I go back now. I will make certain that he is not lurking in the courtyard so that you can receive your letter in complete safety." A sudden smile lit her face. "I know! I will make the same bird call or at least a reasonable imitation to let you know Chauvergé is gone."

He had to laugh gently at her excitement. "A brilliant plan, *ma chère miette*." Aimée was already turning, eager to play this more active roll in the night's adventure, but St. Briac reached out and captured her waist with both hands. "I appreciate your enthusiasm, but first let me say good night and thank you. You've helped more than you know. *Mille mercis*, Mademoiselle de Fleurance."

CHAPTER 20

 *May 24, 1526*

Aimée was perched on the slope of a lush meadow that curved outward from Blois to melt into woodlands. Heedless of her gown of soft white batiste, she tucked her bare feet more securely beneath her derrière and selected another lapful of wild flowers. The garland was almost finished. Woven of violets, oxe-eye daisies, and tiny buttercups, it would contrast charmingly with her tumbled black curls. Aimée pushed her sleeves higher in defense against the May sunshine and sighed, wondering how long she had been here. Would the afternoon be nearly over when she returned to the chateau?

The joy which she had pressed to her heart day and night like a tender, secret poem was fading away, as were the early buttercups that drooped nearby. Last week they had all been fresh, their faces turned toward the sun.

Where was St. Briac? It was silly, she knew, to make so much of their little scene in the garden. He had trusted her enough to confide at least a portion of something important. He had smiled at her as an equal, had been grateful for her help, had even said "*Mille mercis*" in a tone that still warmed her. That next morning she had fairly danced out of bed, dressing with care before setting off across the courtyard in search of him. Aimée couldn't recall feeling happier in all her life. It wouldn't be hard to convince the Dagonneaux that she positively adored St. Briac. She could scarcely wait to see him, put her hand in his tanned fingers that would reach out to her, hear his laughter, smile up into his blue-green eyes that crinkled so irresistibly at the corners. She hungered for him, and Blanche and Cécile-Anne would certainly be dazzled when they watched the seigneur de St. Briac with his lady love.

But he was gone. Adding to her despair was Ghislaine Pepin, who had met her in the courtyard to deliver the news. The duchess was perfectly kind as she explained that Thomas had gone hunting for a few days with Florange and some other courtiers, to Fontainebleu, she thought. Yes, it was a spur of the moment decision, Florange's idea, it seemed.

Aimée suffered through nearly a week alone, her magical elation drying up like those early buttercups at her feet. She tried to make excuses to herself for the dull ache in her breast that worsened each day, for the poignantly real dreams of St. Briac that haunted her fitful slumber. The problem, she decided, was a lack of friends. No one except the faithful Suzette showed her any kindness. Once or twice the duchesse de Roanne had begun tentative conversations, but the mere proximity of the woman made Aimée freeze with suspicion. Chauvergé hovered about like an evil reptile, sending shivers of revulsion down her spine, and Blanche and Cécile-Anne Dagonneau had begun to sneer knowingly in Aimée's direction whenever the three were in the same room together. They could sense her weakness, she knew, and their increasingly superior airs made her despise them. How could St. Briac have left her alone this way?

If only there were one friendly face to greet her when she returned to the chateau: Marguerite d'Angoulême, Florange, Bonnivet, or even the king. Fastening the ends of the flower chain together, Aimée settled the finished garland among her curls and sighed. Suddenly a memory appeared in her mind: Marie Lissieu, the fruit peddler turned court laundress. Caught up in her own problems, she had nearly forgotten that poor old woman, who must be even more in need of friendship than she. Standing, Aimée shook the grass and flowers from her skirts and laughed when she realized that one foot had fallen asleep. It wasn't such a bad day after all.

Aimée arrived at the servants' wing out of breath and

clutching a nosegay of violets. The head laundress directed her to a large room where several women were bent over wooden washtubs.

"Marie? It's Aimée de Fleurance."

The old woman raised her head in surprise. "Mam'selle?" She had undergone a change, but it was not as wondrous as Aimée might have wished. Gray hair was knotted tightly at her neck, and she wore a dress that was clean though yellowed and worn from dozens of scrubbings. The lice were gone, but the poor woman still looked pale and starved.

"I brought you these." Aimée held out the violets. "Come and sit down. We'll have a nice chat."

"*Merci*, mam'selle. But my work—"

"It's all right. Aren't I a friend of the king? My needs come before those of a few soiled shirts." Her tone was light and teasing, but she added, "Truly, you must not worry."

They went into the corridor, its walls of white stone pierced by tiny windows through which streamed buttery sunlight, and sat together on a carved bench. Marie Lissieu stared at the cluster of violets that only served to emphasize her bony, emaciated hands.

"I must apologize for not coming to see you earlier," Aimée was saying. "I know how you must feel, living in a new place, among strangers. Is everything going well? Are you getting enough to eat?"

"You're so kind, mam'selle, to visit me this way after what happened. I couldn't believe it when I found out that you arranged for me to work here in the king's own household." Tears spilled over cheeks that were dry as parchment.

"You mustn't cry. It was nothing. Anyone would have done as much." Aimée embraced the withered, sharp-boned woman.

"Not anyone *I* ever knew," Marie sobbed. "Our Lord must have sent you to be my salvation. He forgives even a sinner like me."

Before Aimée could summon a reply, Marie went limp in her arms. The old woman collapsed across the bench, her mouth slack, her spindly arms hanging toward the stone floor like those of a corpse.

"*Nom de Dieu!*" Aimée breathed fearfully. She sprang up and had started in search of help, when the formidable head laundress appeared.

"Qu'est-ce que c'est?" the woman demanded, pushing past Aimée. "This lazy hag. She's good for nothing!"

"No, something is wrong. Madame Lissieu has fainted. She may be dying for all we know. We must get help!"

"Madame Lissieu?" mimicked the head laundress. "Madame Worthless, as far as I can see."

Angry now, Aimée was about to reply, when another voice spoke from the end of the corridor. "What is happening?"

It was Chauvergé, puffed up with authority. He strode over to Aimée and the burly head laundress, who was explaining that Marie never had done her job properly since the day she arrived. There was no place at court for such sloth.

"Non!" cried Aimée. "That's not fair. The woman isn't well; you can see that plainly. She needs a physician, some rest, and good food. Please, we must help her!"

"You must be mad," Chauvergé muttered coldly. "A physician for the most common of servants, one who didn't even earn her place here?" He gave Aimée a look that sent chills down her spine. "The old crone is obviously useless. She belongs back in the streets whence she came."

"I couldn't agree more," the head laundress barked triumphantly.

"Parbleu. How can you be so cruel?" Aimée was too distraught to ask how Chauvergé knew where Marie had come from. "What gives you the right?"

"Louise de Savoy has given me authority to speak for her in her absence," Chauvergé condescended to inform her.

Before Aimée could argue, another voice broke in. "Fortunately, my dear Chauvergé, the king has given *me* the authority to speak for him in his absence."

They all whirled around to discover Thomas Mardouet, seigneur de St. Briac, filling the arch at the end of the hall. For an instant Aimée couldn't speak or move. She devoured the sight of him: the boots and fawn breeches that skimmed his long, taut legs; the soft fawn doublet under which he wore a white shirt, its pleated fraise snowy against his golden-brown neck and bearded chin; and his masculine face, steely with anger. Even from a distance Aimée saw the splendid turquoise of his eyes and the way his crisp hair had been tousled by the wind. Then she was running into his arms.

St. Briac caught her up against himself. It was heaven to

feel the petite softness of her body and glimpse the joy that he could swear was genuine in her leaf-green eyes and blinding smile. While away St. Briac had suspected that he might miss the minx, and now he had to admit that his fears had been well founded.

"Miette," he said softly, smiling against her hair.

"Oh, Thomas, I am so glad to see you." Standing on tiptoe, Aimée could only reach his jaw, and so she pressed excited kisses over it. "They mean to cast Marie into the street. She is ill; she needs help!" Even as she spoke, she remembered St. Briac's contempt for the old woman whose poisoned pear nearly had killed her. It seemed impossible that he could step forward to help Marie.

Still holding Aimée close with one arm about her waist, St. Briac walked toward the others. "What is going on here? Does Mademoiselle de Fleurance speak the truth?"

Chauvergé managed a snide smile. "The head laundress has told me that this hag has been worthless since the day she began working here. Any fool could see what must be done."

"Perhaps." St. Briac stepped away from Aimée and bent over Marie Lissieu's prostrate body. He winced instinctively and then turned to stare hard at Chauvergé. "Obviously you must mean that the woman needs help." He cast a brief, insincere smile toward the head laundress. "Don't worry, I'll see to it that Madame Lissieu gets the proper attention. Lots of rest and good food should do her a world of good."

Aimée stared in wonderment as St. Briac lifted the old woman easily in his arms and carried her off toward the door. He was almost out of sight when she gave the remaining pair a happily victorious grin and then lifted her skirts and ran to catch up.

"Oh, monseigneur, how can I ever thank you?" Aimée couldn't bring herself to let go of his arm as they closed the door on a sleeping Marie Lissieu. "You were wonderful."

"I owed you that much after the other night." He paused to look down at her. "Again, *mille mercis.* You were a tremendous help."

The dejection Aimée had felt in the meadow seemed part of another lifetime. Glowing from his praise, she thought again of the old woman who now lay tucked into bed in a remote chamber of the Louis XII wing. St. Briac had even found a serving girl to keep an eye on Marie and bring her plates of nourishing food until she grew strong.

St. Briac led the way through the arch that opened onto the courtyard, slipping a hand over the small one that held fast to his forearm. "I'm sorry I had to leave without telling you good-bye. The decision to go hunting was made impulsively. Has anything else been amiss in my absence?"

She longed to give vent to the tears that made her heart ache, to tell him all she had felt during the past week, but pride erected a familiar barrier. "No, I've been fine. A trifle lonely perhaps."

"I expected you to keep busy hatching new plots for your liberation." His sarcasm was a reflex. This warm intimacy between himself and Aimée was flourishing too quickly.

"I thought you had ordered me to put away my schemes until Blanche and Cécile-Anne Dagonneau had been forced to retreat," she replied coolly.

St. Briac tilted his head back and wrinkled his nose at the wide blue sky. "Ah, this conversation takes me back to the battlefield at Pavia. Nothing like a good battle to make one's blood start flowing."

Her tone matched his for irony. "Let us hope that *this* battle finds you on the winning side, monseigneur."

"And which side will you be on?"

"Your tongue is sharp."

"No sharper than yours. Will I need my armor?"

For an instant Aimée thought of him kneeling on the battlefield at Melegano in full armor, removing his helm to be knighted by the king. He must have looked magnificent. "No doubt you would make an impressive figure, monseigneur, and perhaps could frighten the Dagonneaux away clad thusly, but in my opinion it is much too hot for armor."

"You're probably right." St. Briac rubbed his jaw, pretending to give the matter serious thought. "Besides, with my luck, Cécile-Anne would find my lance irresistibly attractive."

Aimée glanced up, wondering if he had intended his words to have a double meaning. Turquoise eyes sparkled merrily back at her, and she giggled. "Wicked man. You'll corrupt me."

"An intriguing prospect, mademoiselle." St. Briac stared at her for a long minute, thinking that she looked utterly delicious with that garland of flowers woven through her curls. Aimée's skin was peach-gold against the white of her gown, and now he noticed a faint dusting of freckles across the delicate bridge of her nose. "You've been out in the sun."

She flushed self-consciously, pushing her sleeves down to cover her wrists. "I plead guilty, monseigneur. *Parbleu*. If Maman could see me."

"You look charming. Like a fairy who frolics among the wild flowers."

"You sound suspiciously poetic, which makes me think you are insincere."

St. Briac put a dark, tapering finger under her chin, tipping it up until she was forced to meet his eyes. "*Au contraire, miette*. In truth, I fear that I am often too candid for my own good when you are near."

Afraid to reply in kind, Aimée tried to avert her gaze, only to see Blanche and Cécile-Anne standing on the second balcony of the grand staircase. "Don't look now," she whispered, relieved to have the diversion, "but we are being watched."

His white grin seemed to flash in the sunlight. "By two females who suspiciously resemble greyhounds? I know."

There was a sudden stinging where Aimée knew her heart must be. Had St. Briac been acting all this time for their benefit?

"It's time, I think, for you to welcome your future husband home properly," he was saying. "Brace yourself, mademoiselle."

At first she responded with what she hoped was reserve to St. Briac's kiss, but then sensation broke over her in waves that were impossible to deny. Aimée forgot the Dagonneaux, forgot everything except the hard body pressed to the length of her own, the arms that lifted her off the ground, the mouth that captured hers as if by right. She had longed to welcome him in just this fashion. Her hands clung to his broad shoulders, and as their kiss deepened, Aimée was filled with overwhelming joy.

"Monseigneur, do you think this is the proper place for such displays of passion?"

They broke apart to discover Blanche Dagonneau, her daughter in tow, standing inches away.

"Probably not." St. Briac, hot and aching with desire, could not keep the annoyance from his voice. "Aimée, *ma chérie*, why don't you wait for me in my apartments. I'll join you as soon as I've finished chatting with Madame Dagonneau and her dear daughter."

How dare he? To imply that she was already his bed partner before their marriage like some common strumpet who loitered outside the taverns in Blois! "I, well..." Her cheeks were stained by embarrassment; she could feel the heat suffusing her face. Of course, there was nothing she could do. As much as Aimée yearned to yank a branch from the nearest tree and bash St. Briac over the head with it, the presence of the Dagonneaux forced her to squelch her rage and try to smile.

"Off with you now. That's a good girl," St. Briac was saying in a cheerful voice. Only she could recognize the undertone of mockery.

Sparing barely a nod for Blanche and Cécile-Anne, Aimée stormed off toward the François I wing, muttering under her breath. Wait in his apartments, indeed. She'd wait all right, brandishing a deadly weapon!

CHAPTER 21

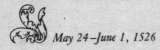 *May 24—June 1, 1526*

Aimée was still simmering with indignation when she entered St. Briac's apartments. Her fury was such that for a moment she didn't notice Chauvergé standing guiltily in front of a towering dresser, its doors wide open.

"Mademoiselle de Fleurance," he gasped. "I thought—I mean—weren't you and the seigneur de St. Briac out in the courtyard?"

"We were interrupted," she informed him sweetly. "Thomas will be along any moment. Was he expecting you?"

The chevalier stuffed something white back into the open cupboard and then closed the doors. "Actually, no. I just stopped by to, ah, apologize in case he felt any of the unpleasantness about that old woman might be my fault. The manservant—LeFait?—was unpacking, so I waited, and just now I noticed that the fellow left this dresser cupboard open, and I was closing it as you walked in."

"Indeed?" Aimée arched a finely drawn brow in flawless imitation of her betrothed. "I appreciate your elaborate explanation, monsieur. I'll be certain to pass it along to Thomas when he arrives."

"In that case, I'll just be on my way. *À demain*, mademoiselle."

"If not sooner," she replied, enjoying the sick smile that he pasted on while backing out the door.

Moments later St. Briac appeared. "Did I just see Chauvergé come out of here? He hurried off in the other direction at the sight of me."

"He was looking at what appeared to be a piece of parchment in the cupboard of your dresser," Aimée said coldly. "When I came in, he put it back amid effusive excuses about what he was up to."

"Hmm. 'Twould seem I haven't been giving our friend enough credit. He's even more treacherous than I'd guessed." St. Briac's brows knit thoughtfully as he opened the dresser and withdrew folded sheets of parchment. "The letter I received the other evening," he told her absently.

"I don't think he'd opened it yet."

"I pray not." St. Briac lifted the heavy lid of a chest against the far wall and drew out a carved wooden box. Unlocking it, he placed the letter inside and then turned the key and took it from the lock. Aimée watched as he returned the box to its hiding place, thought for a moment, and then withdrew a small doeskin pouch that appeared to be attached inside the waist of his breeches. The key then was concealed in the pouch. It occurred to Aimée that she should be pleased to be included in what was obviously a secret of some importance to St. Briac, but she wasn't ready to let go of the anger she had been nursing since he'd dismissed her in the courtyard.

"So." He looked up at Aimée as if mentally shaking himself back to the moment at hand. "Now that we've taken care of that, let's return to my welcome home greeting. Where were we before that rude interruption?"

She seized on this instantly. "The Dagonneaux's rudeness was pale compared to *yours*, monseigneur. How dare you treat me that way in front of them?"

St. Briac laughed and came toward her. "You don't mind, then, if I'm rude when we're alone?" he teased.

"You know perfectly well what I'm talking about—and don't think you can charm your way out of this. For you to send me off to your apartments, implying that I was to wait for you in bed—"

"Did I say that? I might have if I'd thought there was a chance you would obey."

"When pigs fly, monseigneur," she yelled.

St. Briac laughed again, highly amused. She looked absolutely ravishing with her flushed cheeks and starry-lashed, flashing green eyes. The charming garland of wild flowers was now slightly askew. "Now, Aimée, you know you don't really mean that. Be honest."

When he reached for her, Aimée warned, "Don't touch me, you animal!"

"I hope you intend to demonstrate a bit of creativity and make me something other than a dog this time." St. Briac drew her lightly into his arms and laughed as she pummeled his wide chest with ineffectual blows.

"I demand that you let me go!" The fires of Aimée's outrage were fueled by his obvious merriment.

This time, when they were interrupted by Blanche Dagonneau, St. Briac did not release Aimée. "I do hope that nothing is amiss," the woman exclaimed. She was poking her long nose around the door that St. Briac had forgotten to close. "We couldn't help hearing poor Mademoiselle de Fleurance's cries of distress."

"There's no cause for concern, madame," he assured her cheerfully. "Aimée just does that to tease me." Looking down at the seething female who suffered his embrace rigidly, St. Briac prompted, "Isn't that right, darling?"

She could barely bring herself to glance in the direction of Blanche Dagonneau and offer a muted, "Mmm."

St. Briac winked at the woman over Aimée's head. "She's a bit embarrassed, you understand. Women like to keep these little love games private. Would it be rude of me to ask you to leave us alone?"

It appeared for a moment that Madame Dagonneau's eyes might pop out on the tiled floor. "No, no, and I beg your pardon for interrupting," she choked at last.

"Would you mind closing the door? *Merci*, madame."

"I loathe that woman and her insipid daughter almost as much as I *detest* you," Aimée stormed. "If it had been anyone else, I can assure you that I would not have hesitated to beg for rescue. I will not give her the satisfaction, though. She's been driving me mad, hovering about while you were away with that infuriating self-satisfied expression on her canine face. Never have I longed to be rid of anyone quite so vehemently, unless it's you, and—"

"That's right, tease me some more. You know how it excites me." St. Briac was having a wonderful time.

"You're insufferable."

"I'm hoping that Blanche will be so alarmed by my depravity that she'll decide to spare Cécile-Anne the horrors of our marriage bed."

"I only thank God that *I* shall be spared them."

"Oh, cruel. Are you trying to hurt my feelings?" A wicked gleam came into his eyes that made Aimée's heart jump. "Tell me you didn't mean it, *miette*."

She knew that she was asking for trouble but could not bring herself to speak the words, even mockingly. St. Briac's arm tightened around her waist while the other hand traced her spine and felt the texture of her hair. Aimée told herself to protest and struggle, but already her bones were melting under his skillful touch. When St. Briac bent to taste one peach-gold shoulder, she was lost.

Somehow they were lying across the huge bed, and Aimée's skin was prickling all over as his mouth grazed her ear, the fragile line of her jaw, the curve of her throat, and finally the first swell of breasts that ached to be freed from constraint. Hearing her smothered moan, St. Briac obliged. Aimée thought she would faint with pleasure when she felt his long fingers caressing her bare flesh, carefully avoiding the rosy crests that puckered with longing. Helplessly, she buried her hands in his hair and drew him against her. For one endless minute St. Briac was quiet, breathing in the sweet, innocent fragrance that was Aimée, knowing that his warm breath was enough to heighten her arousal. Then his mouth touched her nipple, and she gasped. Slowly he kissed it, tasting with his tongue, until she arched her hips instinctively. St. Briac pulled her body gently against the length of his own, one hand cupping her buttocks through the thin stuff of her gown. She had buried her face in the hair that ruffled back from his brow.

"Thomas." Aimée was on fire, and he was the flame. His lips were burning her breasts, now her shoulder, the inside of one wrist, and finally her eager mouth. As they kissed and she felt the last of her reason spin away, St. Briac slid a hand up her leg, taking his time. In defense against the heat, Aimée had scorned her chemise, and now she was glad. Finally he brushed a tantalizing fingertip over the core of her longing. Her hands were caressing the lean strength of his shoulders and chest, and she had just reached the hardness that strained against his breeches, when he lifted his head. A soft, ironic voice came to her through a haze.

"When pigs fly, *miette*?"

The sunlight was hazy and golden, typical of early mornings in the Loire valley. Aimée, however, was oblivious to its warmth as she stood next to an outer wall of the chateau and stared down at the stables. More than a quarter hour had passed since she had watched Sébastien gallop across the meadow, returning with his master from what seemed to her an endless ride. When St. Briac had dropped lightly to the ground and led his horse into the stables, she had expected him to reappear in moments. Now she realized that he was not a man to leave the care of his steed to a groom, and so she waited. She smoothed the sky-blue silk of her skirts and wondered whether all traces of the tears she had shed during the night were gone from her eyes. Had the wind loosened her curls?

Unbidden, the memory of his face returned to haunt her for the thousandth time. St. Briac's caustic question, spoken at a moment when she was particularly vulnerable, had shattered the spell between them, had shattered her pride as well. Aimée recalled little of what had followed. It would seem that she had drawn away from his body, risen from the bed, somehow restored modesty to her bared breasts, and walked to the door. One image remained, scorched in her memory. Lifting the latch, she had looked back. St. Briac had said nothing. She could still see him, lounging back on the rumpled bed, staring at her calmly. His thick, curving brows had lifted almost imperceptibly, and there had been an unreadable gleam in his blue-green eyes.

Aimée shivered again in the sunlight. During the long hours since she'd left his apartments, pain had squeezed her heart mercilessly. Some of her tears had been shed to soothe her battered pride, but by dawn Aimée had been forced to confront the fact that the roots of her agony went much deeper.

"*Bon Dieu,*" she prayed now in a choked whisper, "*save me from falling in love with Thomas. I beseech thee!*" What terrified her most of all was the realization that it was probably too late and that after their adventure together was ended she would carry this pain with her for the rest of her life.

A shadow fell across the stable yard, and Aimée caught her breath at the sight of the familiar figure who emerged and paused to slip a coin to a groom. She straightened, putting aside pain and more bittersweet emotions. It was time to demonstrate to St. Briac that she would not be humiliated or beaten by anything he did. Lifting her chin, Aimée went to meet him.

He had accepted a clean square of linen proffered by the groom and was rubbing it over his neck, face, and damp hair. With a smile, St. Briac handed it back to the boy, who then disappeared back into the coolness of the stables. Distractedly, he unlaced his dove-gray doublet and the white shirt beneath and then glanced up to see Aimée haloed in sunshine as she descended the grassy slope.

"Miette." Surprise was accompanied by a catch in his throat. She looked perfectly lovely. Her silk gown seemed tinted to match the cloudless sky and was set off by a silver girdle sprinkled lightly with diamonds that grazed the curves of her hips. Even from a distance, St. Briac noticed that her gleaming black curls were arranged artfully and decorated with sprays of baby's breath and tiny pink rosebuds. Something was amiss.

"Bonjour, monseigneur. How was your ride? Did Sébastien behave himself?"

He cocked his head slightly in disbelief. Was this really happening? "Aimée, I'm surprised to see you," he murmured in bemusement as she drew near. The minx's eyes were positively sparkling with high spirits.

"I have a new plan that I couldn't wait to tell you about," she exclaimed.

"Really!" St. Briac stared, trying to make sense of what was happening. After his callous treatment of her the day before and her absence from the hall of honor that same evening, he'd expected to be forced to beg her on bended knee even to speak to him. "I, ah, was about to visit you myself." Feeling like a shy boy, he produced the nosegay of violets that he'd been holding in his left hand. "These are a peace offering."

The soft curves of Aimée's cheekbones took on a dusky stain as she accepted the flowers with her eyes downcast. Why did he have to remind her? This was not part of her scenario. "You were kind to think of me," she managed to whisper with what she hoped was finality.

"I have to apologize to you for yesterday," he was saying gently, bending down in the hope of seeing her eyes. "I am truly contrite. My behavior was worse than a dog's!"

Laughter bubbled up inside Aimée, and she blessed him for teasing her at exactly the moment when she needed it most. Blinking back tears, she met his hopeful gaze and said, "Nothing new, monseigneur."

"Thank you so much for reminding me."

St. Briac's smile was so captivating that she had to avert her eyes, but she couldn't help staring at the portion of his chest that was exposed by the unlaced doublet and shirt. How she ached to touch that bronzed, taut skin and feel the texture of the crisp hair covering it, curling against the base of his throat.

St. Briac's brows gathered anew as he looked curiously at the top of Aimée's head. Was she ill? One minute all confident enthusiasm, the next stammering shyly and staring at her toes.

He tried again. "Now that we've settled that, I would be grateful if you'd walk with me back to the chateau and fill me in on this latest brilliant plan en route. I find that I have a potent craving for a mug of cold ale."

Aimée swallowed hard and gave him a bright smile. "I suppose that Sébastien is already having his ale."

"He doesn't indulge in spirits." Eyes crinkling at the corners, he lightly took Aimée's elbow and started up the hill. "Now don't make me wait any longer to hear this new scheme. Will it prove our salvation?"

She repeated the memorized speech with zeal. "Oh, yes, I think so. I wonder it hasn't occurred to us before. You see, I believe that we have been playing into Blanche and Cécile-Anne's hands by allowing them to corner us and then pretending to be madly in love. They have put us on the defensive."

St. Briac glanced down at her animated face and wondered once again how Aimée's mind worked. Just when he felt he could predict what she might say or do, something like this would happen. "That's an interesting observation. What do you suggest?"

"The time has come for *us* to take charge, monseigneur. I have gotten so angry over them lurking about, lying in wait for us, hoping to catch us off guard. Why don't we wage this battle using their rules? We'll lie in wait for *them*."

A slow smile spread over St. Briac's face as they came into the courtyard. "I must admit, Aimée, that I have never met a female quite as cunning as you. Your schemes may not always work, but at least your heart is in the right place."

They laughed together, and happiness blossomed in her breast. "Don't you agree, though, that this plan is virtually foolproof? It should put an end to our ordeal faster than anything."

"Except marriage," St. Briac supplied softly.

"No more jokes now, monseigneur. We must join forces and resolve this problem once and for all."

Shaking his head fondly, St. Briac followed after Aimée as she marched purposefully across the courtyard. "Can I have my ale first?"

Minutes later, he found himself seated on a stone bench in the Louis XII gallery, just around the corner from the chapel. His right hand held the mug of ale he'd longed for, and his left curved around Aimée's waist. She was perched on St. Briac's lap like a bird about to take flight, leaning forward in an effort to see the chapel and forget the proximity of the man she yearned to touch.

"How long do you suppose it will be before mass is finished?" he inquired between sips of ale. Aimée's awkward silence was making him nervous.

"Why? Am I too heavy?"

He laughed. "Don't be silly, of course not. I just wish you would relax."

"One of us has to take this seriously." Relenting, she reached for his ale and took a long drink, pausing only to lick dry lips. "It must be nearly ten o'clock."

St. Briac leaned back, arching his hips as he drew a gold watch from a pocket in his haut-de-chausses. Aimée steadied herself on his lap but could not help glancing down at the evidence of his manhood that was outlined clearly by his movement. Suddenly her mouth was dry once more, and she drank again from the mug of ale.

"Ten o'clock exactly." St. Briac replaced the watch with its single hand and reached for the pewter mug. "Are you going to drink it all?"

Aimée was about to reply, when the sound of voices reached her ears. "They're coming," she hissed, and threw her arms around St. Briac's neck.

St. Briac had to smile under the impact of Aimée's open

mouth. He released his hold on the ale mug, hoping it wouldn't topple off the bench, and gathered her close, enjoying the enthusiasm of her performance. If this was her idea of taking the offensive, he was grateful never to have faced her in battle. Soon, though, his amusement waned, replaced by arousal. Aimée's hands were twisted in his hair, and her mouth was hot and fervent against his. Their tongues fenced while she pressed straining breasts to the hard expanse of his doublet. St. Briac wanted to moan as he felt the exquisite ache in his loins. Was she going to do this to him day after day? He went on kissing her, their bodies fused together with an intimacy that neither realized.

After what seemed an eternity, St. Briac had to come up for air. The courtyard was deserted. There was no excuse to continue what they'd been doing, and after yesterday, he was not about to test his luck. After a moment, Aimée leaned forward languidly, her cheeks flushed in a way that had become familiar to him.

"*Miette*," St. Briac murmured barely an inch from her pliant mouth, "they're all gone."

"Oh!" She blinked, blushed, and straightened her back. "I didn't realize."

Longing to pull the flowers from those carefully pinned curls, St. Briac could only smile at Aimée and let his hands drop away. "Did the Dagonneaux see us?"

For an instant she couldn't think who he meant. Yearning so potent that it seemed beyond her control suffused her body, and Aimée swayed slightly toward his face, his mouth. "The Dagonneaux?" she repeated absently.

St. Briac clenched his fists to keep them from reaching out to her. "The two women for whose benefit we were kissing."

"*Mais oui!*" Aimée shook her head almost indiscernibly. "I was only teasing, monseigneur. Of course, since we were, well, you know ... I could not see them any better than you, but certainly they were part of that group leaving mass. I must say that you gave a wonderful performance. Almost as convincing as my own!"

Blanche Dagonneau came to an abrupt halt at the bottom of the staircase that spiraled down through the center of the chateau, nearly causing Cécile-Anne and Ghislaine Pepin to collide behind her. Ghislaine glanced up in surprise, only to see Thomas and Aimée de Fleurance clinging together, whispering and smiling between feather-light kisses. Although her mind told her this was all an act, her heart sank.

The betrothed couple turned and drifted off arm in arm toward the hall of honor, and Madame Dagonneau whirled around to face her companions. "They're disgraceful. This has been going on without pause for days now. If those two are truly so passionately in love, why do they not set a date for their marriage so they can carry on this way in private?"

Cécile-Anne shrugged, red-faced, her eyes focused on the broad back of the seigneur de St. Briac, while Ghislaine wondered how to respond.

"Tell me the truth, madame," Blanche demanded. "Do you really believe that he intends to marry that wench? There is something about the way they carry on whenever we appear that makes me very suspicious."

The duchesse de Roanne knew what Thomas would want her to say, but she loved him too much to act against what she felt were his best interests. "I must confess, Madame Dagonneau, that I agree with you."

PART III

His heart sighs and fain would show
That which all the world did know;
His heart sighed the sighs of fear
And durst not tell her love was there.
Pain of all pain, lover's fear,
Makes his heart to silence swear.

FULKE GREVILLE, LORD BROOKE
(1554–1628)

CHAPTER 22

 *June 14, 1526*

All day long it had rained incessantly and forcefully, but as Aimée's coach rumbled toward the far edge of the forest of Boulogne, the downpour tapered off. Aimée had been dozing, lulled by the rhythm of the raindrops; when they ceased, she awoke.

"We're almost there, mam'selle," Suzette exclaimed. "The park's just ahead. Isn't this exciting? For years I've heard tales of the chateau called Chambord that the king's been building. Do you suppose it could be as magnificent as they say?"

"Knowing our illustrious monarch, I wouldn't doubt it," Aimée replied. She couldn't resist sitting up and drawing back the window curtain for a look.

The sun had just begun to set, and the effect was quite stunning as the rainstorm blew away, allowing the clouds to break open and let in streams of tangerine and violet light. The coach emerged from the oak and pine trees onto a long road surrounded by parkland. Aimée was anticipating her first view of Chambord almost as much as Suzette was, but her mind was also on the seigneur de St. Briac. More than a week had passed since she last had seen him, riding off on some obscure errand that she was convinced he had invented to escape the Dagonneaux.

No matter how enthusiastically Aimée and St. Briac had attempted to convince the Dagonneaux of their love, the two women persisted in remaining at Blois, never losing patience. St. Briac, on the other hand, grew more irritable with each passing day until finally he shouted at Aimée one night. They had just put on one of their displays of passion in the garden. The Dagonneau women had passed by without a word and returned to the chateau, at which point St. Briac whirled on Aimée and stormed, "That does it, I'm finished. I'm leaving. I have important matters to attend to, not a moment too soon, I might add. I feel like an idiot! How long can you expect me to go on this way? A letter came today from the king asking us to meet him at Chambord on the fourteenth day of this month. Perhaps I'll see you there."

With that he had stalked out of the garden, leaving Aimée to swallow scalding tears. The next morning she went to the stables at dawn to see him off, and St. Briac offered a stiff apology for losing his temper. What remained now in her memory, however, was the taut coolness of the lips that grazed hers in parting.

"Mam'selle, there it is!" Suzette was leaning out the window and screaming like a madwoman.

Aimée looked around the curtain and was rendered breathless by the splendor she beheld. The sheer white mass of the chateau stood out in stark relief against the intense green of the forest, bathed in the golden-rose glow of twilight like some incredible vision. Chambord was enormous, the solid expanse of its lower part crowned by a lacy jumble of staggered pinnacles, lantern lights, gables, bell turrets, and sculpted chimneys that seemed to rise like enchanted soap bubbles into the cloud-strewn sky.

"Can you believe it?" Suzette cried as the coach rolled closer to the entrance.

For a long minute Aimée was speechless. Finally she whispered, "No, I'm not certain that I do."

The Chateau de Chambord was designed in the basic feudal tradition, boasting a central donjon with four drum towers linked to outer towers by two-storied galleries supported by arcades. King François had his study in one of those outer towers. Tonight the spacious room was made cozy by the spicy aroma of mulled wine and a roaring fire that helped dispel the unseasonable chill.

The king and the seigneur de St. Briac sat side by side in chairs of carved walnut before the great stone fireplace. Thomas had arrived barely a half hour before, soaking wet and in a foul mood. Even the usually outspoken Gaspard had held his tongue as he followed his master through the mud from the stables. Meeting the king in the guardroom, St. Briac had accepted his offer of mulled wine, a fire, and conversation, but he remained distant. Now François related the news of his stay in Cognac while watching his friend from the corners of his keen hazel eyes. Thomas still wasn't dry. His chestnut hair and doublet remained damp, and beads of water gleamed on his riding boots.

"There really isn't much more to tell," the king concluded. "I've spent most of my time saying no to Charles V and working on improving relations with England."

"This antiimperial league you've joined with Venice, the papacy, and England—won't it endanger your sons?"

François attempted a shrug. "Charles V was invited to join as well."

"*If* he freed your sons for a ransom, paid his debts to Henry VIII in three months, restored Sforza to the duchy of Milan, and limited the size of the retinue he intended to take to Italy." St. Briac laughed in disbelief. "Why didn't you include a few more wild conditions while you were at it?"

Lifting his goblet of mulled wine, the king drank silently for a moment. "I have to think of France first. This Holy League of Cognac will be good for the country, for all of us who oppose the imperialism of Charles V. As for my sons..." He shrugged again in a way that fooled St. Briac not at all. "I don't really worry about them. They are being well cared for. The princes are only children, after all, and probably view this experience as a great adventure. By the time they return home, they'll be speaking Spanish, and I've no doubt that they will have established many friendships that will help them in the future. Even if they have to remain three or four years in Spain, it would not be a tragedy."

St. Briac nodded. "If you say so."

"Why are you in such a black mood?" demanded the king. "I was looking forward to seeing you, to being cheered by your ready wit. I might as well have Chauvergé beside me for all the pleasure your company has imparted."

"Well, then, why don't you send for him or one of your

other sniveling, obsequious cavaliers?" The instant the words were out, St. Briac was ashamed. It wasn't fair to take out his trivial problems with Aimée and the Dagonneaux on this man who worried about matters that affected not only France but the rest of Europe. He felt even more contrite when he remembered the king's broken arm.

"I don't care for sniveling any more than I do for your rudeness," François shot back.

"I apologize. I mean that sincerely." St. Briac rubbed long fingers against his aching brow. "Tell me, does your arm give you pain?"

"Not really. I feel more pain for the plight of my steed. It broke my heart to have to slit his throat. If only he hadn't chanced on that hole, his hoof landing at that deadly angle..." The king sighed and watched as St. Briac rose to refill their goblets. "As for my arm, I was fortunate to have my skilled *premier médecin* in attendance. He set it with an excellent willow splint. Over that are wrapped bandages strengthened with starch that must be changed periodically. My worst suffering was inflicted by the *premier médecin*'s two helpers, who yanked mightily, using a light winch, to make certain the bones would fit together correctly."

"A light wench?" St. Briac teased. "That must have been diverting."

François choked on his wine. "Not *wench*, winch!" He laughed.

Smiling with mock innocence, Thomas nodded agreeably. "Oh. *Certainement!*"

"Speaking of wenches, how is that captivating one you are betrothed to?"

"The last time I saw her she was fine, but that was several days ago. Frankly, I'm not certain if Aimée will even make an appearance here. We didn't part on the best of terms, and to add to my difficulties, I noticed that Blanche and dear Cécile-Anne *have* arrived. They were lurking in a corner of the guardroom when I came in."

The king arched a brow thoughtfully. "I begin to understand the cause of your ill temper."

"You don't know the half of it." St. Briac sprang up to pace across the study. "While you've been in Cognac, those two *chiennes* have nearly driven me over the brink of madness."

Just then, a familiar wizened face peeked around the door. "I hope I'm not intruding."

"How could you do otherwise, Gaspard?" retorted St. Briac.

The little manservant drew himself up stiffly. "*Pardonnez-moi*, monseigneur," he said in an injured tone. "I thought you might wish to know that Mademoiselle de Fleurance is here. She's gone to her chamber."

Relief and elation swept over St. Briac and were reflected for an instant on his face. "I'm so happy she didn't feel it necessary to *rush*," he observed.

"Would you kindly ask Mademoiselle de Fleurance to join us, Gaspard?" François inquired politely.

"*Toute de suite*, sire."

The king watched his friend pace like a caged tiger. At length he murmured, "I wonder if your frustrations are caused not by the Dagonneaux but by that enchanting wood sprite."

Suddenly alert, St. Briac halted beside his chair. "I don't know what you mean."

"Simply that celibacy does not agree with you, *mon ami*. Hasn't it occurred to you that perhaps you're just eager for your wedding night?"

"You are perceptive, sire, more so than I, I fear." Thomas gave him an ironic smile. "I'm sure there's truth in your observation, though at this point I care not about a wedding night. *Any* night—or hour!—would do."

The king chuckled contentedly. "You and I may be dispirited at this point in our lives, Thomas, but I find it truly heartening that we can still share moments of humor. Laughter breeds optimism, hmm?"

"That does seem to be the case." St. Briac sank back into his chair and reached for the goblet of mulled wine. Casting about for a more cheerful topic, he queried, "How fares Anne d'Heilly? Did she enjoy Cognac?"

"You would have to ask her that," the king replied coldly. "I will say only that Anne has done nothing to ease the burdens that weigh so heavily on my shoulders."

"Oh! Well, I'm sorry to hear that. Perhaps the situation will improve now that you are here at Chambord." St. Briac's words sounded lame in his own ears, and it was with great relief that he heard Aimée's hesitant voice follow a knock on the door.

"Sire? Monseigneur?"

The king bade her enter, and Aimée felt her heart leap unexpectedly at the sight of St. Briac. He had risen, along with his friend, to welcome her, but he was not smiling. Still, his mere physical presence made her giddy. It was as if a void that she had been trying not to recognize had filled suddenly with a warm, bittersweet rush of emotion.

"Have some mulled wine," François was saying, conscious of the tension in the air. "It's a pleasure to see you again, mademoiselle. I'd almost forgotten how lovely you are. I do hope your journey was not too unbearable on account of the rain." He bent to press smiling lips to Aimée's hand and then passed the goblet that St. Briac had filled for her. "Tell me, my dear, how do you like my place in the country?"

"I am spellbound, sire. I never even imagined that such a chateau could exist!"

While the king explained his future plans for Chambord, St. Briac's turquoise eyes studied Aimée from under hooded lids. Again she had taken uncharacteristic care with her appearance; all the haphazard edges were smooth. A gown of deep rose velvet and ivory satin encrusted with pearls displayed the graceful curves of her throat and breasts. He was surprised to see that she wore a modest shakefold under her gown that served to emphasize the dainty proportions of her waist. Once again, ebony curls were demurely tame under a crispinette, and a small mirror hung from the obligatory cordelière attached to her sapphire-studded girdle. St. Briac couldn't help wondering, a trifle suspiciously, why Aimée had suddenly become such an immaculate paragon of fashion.

"Will you not greet your betrothed?" François prompted him.

St. Briac lifted his eyes to Aimée's and found them poignantly wide and dewy. *"Pardonnez-moi.* I was only admiring Mademoiselle de Fleurance's extraordinary beauty. Her appearance is a match for any lady of your court. Who would believe that only a few weeks ago we mistook her for a peasant in the woods of Nieuil?"

There was an undercurrent in his tone that gave both the king and Aimée pause. François mustered his wits and spoke up first. "Who indeed? Mademoiselle de Fleurance is proof that even a king can be mistaken. You are truly fortunate to anticipate the joy of taking such a lady as your wife."

"Exactly so." St. Briac arched a wry brow and moved to kiss Aimée's hand. "How good it is to see you at last, *miette*. You are well?"

"Yes." Her mouth was dry. "I am very happy to be here. It is difficult to believe that Chambord is not even completed." Unable to endure a lull in the conversation, she hurried on. "Do you know, I could have sworn I glimpsed a bishop when I came across the courtyard. I've only ever known one, but I do recall that little arched cap and the long embroidered coat trimmed with fur."

"You are most observant, mademoiselle," François replied, charmed by her guilelessness. "The bishop d'Angoulême accompanied me from Cognac for a brief stay here."

"Well, then, he's the one I know. It's been a long time, but I thought I recognized him. The bishop d'Angoulême used to be our *curé* in Nieuil. He christened Honorine and me." She sipped her wine, welcoming the current of warmth that flowed down through the tightness in her breast. "It must be wonderful for you to have him here, and for Marguerite and your mother."

"Marguerite will be equally pleased to see you. Often, while we were in Cognac, she spoke of you with great affection."

"She is a wonderful woman, sire. I don't think I ever met a lady quite so lovely and warm. I envy her her peace with life."

François considered this. "I know that she strives for that state of grace, but I can assure you, mademoiselle, that even Marguerite continues to yearn like other mortals. I long to see her achieve complete contentment." He noticed then that his friend had wandered over to the fireplace, staring into it as he drank from the silver goblet. "Speaking of my sister, I have just remembered an appointment with her. I'll leave you two alone." Thomas had turned his head, and the king gave him a measured glance. "Until we sup, then."

Formal good-byes were exchanged before the heavy door swung shut and Aimée found herself confined in the otherwise empty study with St. Briac. Emboldened by the mulled wine and her irrepressible pleasure in his company, she crossed to the fireplace and put a hand on his forearm.

"You're wet. You came on horseback?"

"Yes." The memory of the long day's miserable journey was reflected in the look he bent on her. Still, his face seemed magnificent to Aimée, every curve and plane accentuated by the firelight. "I don't suppose you have any news that might cheer me? I saw Blanche and Cécile-Anne Dagonneau when I came in. I'd hoped that you might have accomplished alone what we were unable to do together."

"Well, I didn't. I can see that you are gravely disappointed, though. After all, if the Dagonneaux were out of your life, I would be too."

"Don't pretend that I've tried to force you out against your will, Aimée. From the night I discovered you at Gençay, you have cried incessantly to be free, not only free of your family but free of the court and of me."

"And then you could carry on your affair with the duchesse de Roanne?" she heard herself shout.

St. Briac rolled his eyes and then pressed a finger to Aimée's pouting lips. "I've a feeling that this discussion is out of control. Ghislaine has nothing to do with our predicament."

She stalked away to a window that overlooked the park, now cloaked in violet, and the forest that stretched to the horizon. Ghislaine Pepin had a great deal to do with *her* predicament, but that was not what he had referred to. Once more she asked herself whether it might not be best to find some way of abruptly ending her involvement with St. Briac in the hope of lessening the pain that would follow. Yet, discipline over the joy of the moment had never been in her nature.

"Thomas, look at this. There's something written on the windowpane!"

He crossed to her side and stared past Aimée's pointing finger. The last silvery-pink gleam of dusk illumined the words that had been scratched into the glass:

> Souvent femme varie;
> Bien fol est qui s'y fie.

"Women are fickle; foolish is he who puts his trust in them," St. Briac whispered aloud. His first thought was of the king, sitting at this very spot, turned with his diamond ring against the window when he'd entered the study tonight. Then he remembered the general melancholy of his friend, which had been a welcome mate for his own, and François's enigmatic remarks about Anne d'Heilly.

" 'Twould seem that even the heart of a king is vulnerable," he murmured, almost forgetting that Aimée stood at his side.

For some reason Aimée felt attacked, indirectly at least. Thomas's assumption that the harsh words had been engraved on the window by the king seemed to transform them into some kind of decree. Never trust a Frenchwoman, she thought crazily. Would St. Briac take such advice to heart?

"I would have expected such sentiments to be expressed by a woman," she observed at length.

"And why is that?"

"Isn't your sex more famous for its inconstancy?"

St. Briac stared at her for a long minute and then turned away. "It's debatable. I suppose in the end it comes down to the character of the individual."

"I couldn't agree more."

"The fire is making this room too warm for me. Why don't we go up on the roof? There is something I wish to discuss with you."

Full of misgivings, Aimée nodded and followed him out of the study. St. Briac led her down a long corridor and a flight of stone steps that opened into the guardroom.

"I suppose you must have seen this stairway when you arrived today, but it's impossible to appreciate it until you've climbed it to the top."

St. Briac was gesturing toward the enormous double spiral staircase that constituted the centerpiece of the chateau. Its two flights twined around a single core that featured openwork arcades.

"You see," St. Briac explained as they started up one set of white stone steps, "the flights cross each other's paths without ever meeting, and because of the pierced center, two people going up or down need never lose sight of each other."

"Yet cannot touch..." Aimée's voice was almost inaudible.

"Pardon?"

"Nothing. I was just talking to myself." Impulsively she threw him a dazzling smile. "It's a habit one falls into when alone too long."

They climbed upward, passing other people, who were almost but not quite within touching distance. The staircase rose uninterrupted like a pair of long-stemmed intertwining flowers toward the roof. There, to Aimée's astonishment, it emerged in a single spiral that revolved above the terrace inside a magnificent lantern that was at least a hundred feet high. All around her lay a kind of aerial village with little streets and squares that crossed each other around the huge lantern and the other fanciful ornaments that crowded the roof. There were as many chimneys as there were days in the year, and each seemed unique in size and shape.

"An interesting idea, don't you think?" St. Briac drew Aimée out from the staircase. "François conceived of this as a kind of fairyland where the court could escape from the tedium of staying here at Chambord, in the middle of nowhere. When we go out to hunt, the ladies frolic here on the terrace, waiting for us to return."

Aimée allowed him to lead her past a cluster of airy turrets and pinnacles, wondering how many times Ghislaine had stood on this roof and watched for Thomas, astride Sébastien, in the purplish-rose twilight. He spoke in the present tense, as though nothing had changed or ever would.

"What was it you wanted to say to me?" she asked, looking up at St. Briac as he stared out over the parkland. Night was on its way.

"I'll be brief. I long for a bath and some dry clothes, not to mention the food that awaits us at supper." He reached absently for Aimée's hand and regarded her for a moment. She noticed the way he bit the inside of his lower lip and knew that no trivial subject was on his mind. "Look, I'm tired, cold, wet, and fed up. I realized when I saw Blanche and Cécile-Anne in the guardroom here that I simply cannot take another day of this. There's no reason why I should have to."

She wished she could read his mind. "I agree, monseigneur. Have you a solution?" Certainly he couldn't blame her.

"Yes. The only one left, as far as I can see, at least the only one we can depend on. If both of us are able to carry this off, *miette*, the Dagonneaux should go bounding back to their kennels in Burgundy before the sun sets again."

The terrace was bristling with hiding places where members of the court might amuse themselves with secret assignations. As St. Briac explained his outrageous plan, the duchesse de Roanne stood nearby between a spire and a tall dormer window, listening. Bathed in the last vestiges of the plum-tinted sunset, she smiled to herself.

CHAPTER 23

 *June 14, 1526*

Aimée was filled with trepidation when she met St. Briac in his apartments that night after supper. Now scrubbed, fed, and looking especially handsome in burgundy velvet, he seemed even more determined that they should follow through with his plan.

"Ah, *miette*, we cannot fail," he declared merrily. "Within the hour all our problems will be solved."

She tried to smile but succeeded only in looking sick. "If you say so. Where is Gaspard?"

"I sent him away. That meddling windbag would make a tremendous scene if he knew what we mean to do."

Aimée could only nod helplessly. That was exactly what she'd been hoping for.

"You can get undressed in his cabinet if that's any consolation to your modesty. I'll build up the fire, and then we'll be ready." St. Briac strode to the mammoth stone fireplace and lithely dropped down to sit back on his heels, brimming with energy. "You'll find a shirt of mine to wear until we're in bed."

Aimée nodded again; still, she couldn't move her legs.

"Did you hear me?" He glanced back over one broad shoulder. "We haven't a lot of time." The fire blazed high with the addition of two birch logs, and St. Briac gave his full attention to Aimée. "You needn't look as if I plan to rape you. This will all be pretend, except for the very real effect our little drama will have on Blanche and Cécile-Anne. Here, have some wine." He poured a large goblet and took it to the spot just inside the doorway where she had remained fixed. "Drink it up like a good girl."

Numbly, Aimée obeyed and allowed him to lead her toward Gaspard's cabinet. A single candle flickered beside the manservant's narrow bed. "Do I have to take off *everything*?"

St. Briac replied patiently, "*Chérie*, if you wear your chemise, I doubt they'll be convinced. Now, hurry."

After extinguishing all light in the chamber except that provided by the fire, St. Briac peeled off his clothes, put them in the nearest chest, and crossed naked to the massive four-poster bed. The linens were fresh and soft against his skin. Sighing with pleasure, he reclined against the pillows and folded his arms behind his head. It was going to be an entertaining evening.

After several minutes St. Briac called, "Aren't you ready yet?"

The cabinet door opened, and a reluctant Aimée emerged, swimming in one of his shirts. Only shapely calves showed beneath the expanse of white; even her hands had disappeared inside the long sleeves. St. Briac had to smile when Aimée edged toward the firelight and he saw that she'd laced the shirtfront carefully.

"You'll have to take it off, no matter how many knots you've tied, *miette*," he murmured.

Aimée gazed heavenward, her eyes appearing even larger and more vividly leaf-green in the shadows. Golden firelight played over the delicate planes of her face, danced along the ebony curve of her hair that was still confined under the crispenette, and softly illumined the tantalizing outline of her breasts and hips, so sweet and ripe that St. Briac felt abruptly hungry. It was not, however, food that he craved....

Aimée sighed loudly. "I don't feel right about this."

"*Quel dommage*. Too late. Now get out of that thing and join me under these covers before our guests arrive."

She fumbled with the shirt laces until St. Briac sat up suddenly and brushed her fingers aside. While he opened the neckline deftly, Aimée found her gaze drawn inexorably to the taut strength of his shoulders. *Parbleu*, she thought.

How beautifully he is made! Muscles rippled over his dark torso, accentuated by the flickering glow of the fire, which also struck sparks of light against the soft, sable-hued hair that covered his chest and made a thin line like an arrow down the ridges of his belly to the part of him hidden beneath the covers. A sigh of longing mingled with panic inside Aimée. How could this be happening? She said a silent prayer that the Dagonneaux would be waylaid somehow for the rest of the night.

"*Vite*, mademoiselle," St. Briac whispered sharply. "If you continue to worry and ponder this, I'll have another fiasco on my hands, and I don't intend to suffer through one of those again. Take off that shirt and get into bed right now or I shall see to it that you do!"

When his hands reached for the hem of her last barrier against complete exposure, Aimée struck out. "Stop that, you brute! I'll do as you say, but kindly have the grace to close your eyes and avert your face."

The corners of his mouth lifted under the trim mustache, but he did as she bade, reclining against the pillows and turning closed eyes toward the doorway. After a moment, the other side of the mattress sagged slightly. St. Briac looked over to find Aimée staring at the expanse of blue above them and clutching the covers to her bosom with pale little hands. The thought of her body, naked and warm and soft, just inches away in his own bed, caused a tightening in St. Briac's loins. He swallowed in an effort to dislodge what may have been his heart from his throat.

"I wish you would relax, *miette*," he whispered with studied nonchalance. "Think of this as another of your lighthearted adventures. I'm certain that years from now we'll encounter each other by chance—in Paris, perhaps—and laugh about this night over a cup or two of wine."

She nodded, wondering why tears had to pick this moment to sting her eyes. "I, I'm sure you're right. But how will we ever explain our mirth to my husband and your wife?"

St. Briac's dark brows flew up in the darkness, but he played along with her fantasy. "I suppose we shouldn't mention our more, ah, intimate escapades when first we meet, but later each of us would have to think of an excuse to go out alone."

"A secret rendezvous?" Aimée whispered.

"Two old friends sharing memories that only we could

appreciate. Your husband and my wife would never understand. Why risk upsetting them?"

Aimée could envision it all in her mind, so clearly that it seemed a glimpse into the future. She would be in Paris with her kind but provincial husband, probably grasping two or three children's hands; as she turned a corner, there would be the seigneur de St. Briac and his poised, elegantly beautiful lady. St. Briac wouldn't recognize Aimée at first, for she would be worn down by the ravages of hard work and childbirth. She'd put her hand on his forearm, and he'd look into her eyes, and the past would come flooding back.

"Aimée, are you all right?"

Startled, she turned in the direction of his voice and found St. Briac raised on an elbow, gazing down at her. "Of course. I'm fine." Aimée prayed that he hadn't seen the tears that crowded her eyes. "Isn't it almost time for Blanche and Cécile-Anne to appear? I don't suppose we should be lying here chatting when they do."

"No." St. Briac was suddenly ashamed of himself for putting Aimée in this position and forcing her to go along with this desperate plan and ashamed of his own consuming desire to make love to her. Every inch of him ached to touch every inch of her. He felt like a cad.

"I suppose I should be in your arms when the Dagonneaux arrive," Aimée suggested softly, her eyes wide with apprehension.

Sighing, St. Briac tried to smile in an effort to put her at ease. "As long as we've gone this far, I daresay that would be wise."

Absolute silence followed, for neither of them could breathe as Aimée edged in his direction and St. Briac placed a tentative arm around her waist. Bare flesh! She was soft as satin, and when his fingers fanned out, he felt the first smooth curve of her derrière. St. Briac's entire body tensed under a wave of hot yearning.

Swallowing hard, Aimée put a small hand up to his steely shoulder. Panic and desire mingled to create a potent excitement that danced over her nerves. "I wish—" Suddenly she had to sneeze. She turned her face away, only to feel the warm strength of his other shoulder against her cheek. "*Excusez-moi*. I was going to say that I wish you would tell me more precisely what you think we should be doing when Blanche and Cécile-Anne come in."

"Doing?" St. Briac repeated, obviously amused. "Have you any suggestions? I'm amazingly flexible."

A rosy flush stained Aimée's face. She opened her mouth but then closed it, determined not to be tricked into humiliating herself.

"We could rehearse if that would reassure you," he suggested with a smile. "How would you like to begin? With a simple kiss?"

Time seemed suspended as St. Briac leaned slowly toward her. She could hear the pounding of blood in her temples before he touched his mouth tentatively to hers. A shudder of endlessly suppressed desire passed between their bodies, and then St. Briac's long, lean forearms and hands were gathering her near. She flinched instinctively as her naked flesh met his, creamy breasts against a muscled, masculine chest covered with crisp hair; the softness of her belly pressed to his narrow hips; her trim, satiny calves twining within his long male legs; and, of course, the shock of contact with St. Briac's hot, hard desire. Aimée heard herself moan before their mouths came together in an ardent burst of starfire. How wonderful he tasted. She'd almost forgotten yet never stopped craving the flavor of his mouth or the feel of it slanting over her lips, matching her hunger.

It was as if they were caught in some cataclysmic act of nature, a tremendous flood that swept into the room and captured them. There was no escape, only a kind of joyous surrender to this tide of sensation and emotion that was stronger than either of them. They kissed on and on, touching each other, wonderingly at first and then ardently. Aimée thought she would die from pleasure when St. Briac cupped one of her breasts within the firmness of his hand. His fingers strayed over all her body; he was like a starving man presented with a banquet. She understood; she felt the same. They both barely could control their desire to put an end to this torment and discover the bliss that awaited them, yet there was an exquisite pleasure to be taken from heightening the anticipation.

St. Briac was forcing himself to hold back and experience each long-imagined taste. His mouth burned the delicate outline of Aimée's ear, memorizing it as she shivered, and then traced her cheekbone, brow, nose, chin, and finally the silky curve of her throat. When she searched boldly for another delicious kiss, he reached around to pull off her confining crispenette and inhaled the violet fragrance of the curls that spilled across his cheek. Finally, his fingers caressing the fragile length of her spine, St. Briac tasted Aimée's shoulder and then one aroused breast. She began to moan in earnest, but he held her off, avoiding the pouting crest even as he drew her eager fingers away from his throbbing hardness.

"Wait for dessert, *miette*," he admonished in a fond whisper. "We'll both enjoy it more."

She blushed at the same instant her nipple was covered by St. Briac's warm mouth. The sensation was astonishing. Slowly he explored the sweet bud that seemed to swell with each touch of his tongue, waiting until Aimée was on the brink of sobbing before he finally began to tug and suck on her nipple.

"Parbleu," she gasped, unprepared for the storm of sparks that flickered downward to intensify the ache between her thighs. St. Briac was smiling, but the torture went on. He is cruel, she thought wildly, yet she prayed he'd never stop even while longing for him to press her back into the pillows and thrust so deeply inside her that her very heart would be jolted. He was teasing the tender curves of her other breast, but each time she tried to touch him, he brushed her hands away. Now he held them at her hips, his long fingers almost cupping her buttocks, and she sensed that he too was nearing the bounds of control.

"Oh, please, please," Aimée heard herself whimper.

Suddenly St. Briac was over her. Her hands freed, she wrapped them tightly around his neck and pulled him down for an endless, ravenous kiss. For an instant she focused on his firelit shoulders, neck, and hair. Her slim fingers traced the chiseled lines of his face, and Aimée smiled under his insistent mouth. This is joy, she thought as he finally allowed himself to settle between her warm thighs. She could feel the steely muscles in his buttocks against her soft legs and the heat of his manhood pressing her own heat. Finally! She wanted so much to touch him, to intensify the pleasure for them both. Her hand had just made contact with the aroused, rigid proof of his need, when a loud voice broke through the spell that enveloped them.

"I cannot believe my eyes. I'm sure I shall faint!"

St. Briac's eyes flew open. He turned his head and then buried it in Aimée's gleaming curls. *"Sang de Dieu, non,"* he groaned.

Of course, it was Blanche and Cécile-Anne Dagonneau, swooning in the doorway as if they were witnessing something unheard of in the history of civilized beings.

Aimée almost hurt when she felt St. Briac's warm body roll away from her own. A voice in her mind reminded her that this was what they had hoped to accomplish, but he had said that it would all be pretend and painless. The covers were still warm from him yet colder than he had been against her. She shivered. Pretend! They hadn't been pretending; they'd forgotten they were supposed to—at least Aimée had. A part of her realized that St. Briac was sitting up in bed, saying something to Blanche Dagonneau. Now, through half-closed eyes, Aimée saw that someone else was coming into the room. A man was catching Madame Dagonneau as she swayed dramatically once again.

"Is anything wrong?" inquired King François I. He then turned his royal attention from Blanche Dagonneau and her daughter to the chamber at large. His eyes had just fallen on St. Briac and Aimée, when his companion for this evening's stroll stepped in from the corridor.

"I don't mean to intrude, sire, but is there anything I can do to help? Do these two ladies require the *premier médecin*?" The bishop of Angoulême spoke solicitously and then gasped upon glimpsing not only the seigneur de St. Briac but also a young lady he had known since her birth, Aimée de Fleurance. The two of them were side by side, apparently unclothed, in the seigneur's bed.

"I demand an explanation!" the bishop thundered. "What is the meaning of this?"

CHAPTER 24

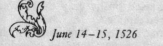 *June 14–15, 1526*

"*Aimée de Fleurance,* your parents are worried to distraction about you, not to mention Armand Rovicette, who thought to become your husband," exclaimed the bishop d'Angoulême. "I am shocked to discover you in this *situation.* If you are wife to the seigneur de St. Briac, I offer my humble apologies for this outburst, but somehow I sense that is not the case, and I beg you to explain."

As he spoke, looking hot in his brocade coat, there was a flurry of activity around him. The Dagonneaux regained their composure and watched the proceedings with shrewd, beady eyes. The king looked pained, glancing from his friend to the bishop and then to Aimée as though uncertain of his role in this drama.

"I thank you for your concern," Aimée spoke up. "But you must not blame the seigneur de St. Briac. I am here with him of my own free will, though we are not married. I beg you to spare me this public confession and allow me to explain to you privately tomorrow."

"Mademoiselle de Fleurance and I are betrothed," St. Briac declared firmly.

A hand reached in from the corridor to shake the sleeve of the king. "Go on," hissed Ghislaine. François had almost forgotten the conversation he had shared earlier with the duchesse de Roanne, but she obviously intended that he should not forget. Odd, he thought, in light of Ghislaine's own entanglement with St. Briac. It would have seemed to him that she'd be the last person to involve herself this way in his affairs.

"*D'accord!*" the king whispered in reply, with impatience creeping into his voice. Stepping forward, he touched the bishop's shoulder. "Pardon me for interrupting, but I must intercede on behalf of my friends. Obviously, you cannot excuse their impatience, but perhaps it will soften your heart to learn that they plan to be married very soon. The seigneur de St. Briac has been away from his betrothed for several days now, and I feel confident in assuring you that only the impetuosity of true love is to blame for this."

The bishop d'Angoulême raised bushy gray eyebrows. "Is this so, my child?" he asked Aimée.

"Of course it's true," St. Briac affirmed. If he hadn't been naked, he'd have shoved the lot of them into the corridor long ago. How could this be happening? Why was the king allowing this incredible scene to continue?

"I happen to know that these two lovebirds desire nothing more than to be united in marriage," François was saying. "If it will set your mind at ease, I suggest that you perform the ceremony as soon as possible."

The bishop stared hard at the uneasy couple in the enormous bed. "Tomorrow morning, during mass?"

"A marvelous suggestion!" the king exclaimed. Nearby, Blanche and Cécile-Anne Dagonneau made low, choking noises and collapsed against the paneled wall. "Thomas, your wedding will be the high point of our stay at Chambord." He turned to the bishop. "Shall we go downstairs and drink a toast to the happy couple?"

"Only if they promise to join us as soon as possible." He thrust out his chin toward the bed once again, obviously little mollified.

"They would be delighted, I'm sure. We'll see you two in the guardroom in a few minutes." François ushered the others out of the chamber and then gave St. Briac a wink before closing the heavy door.

Alone again, Aimée and Thomas lay back on their separate pillows and stared up at the blue tester. Her heart was pounding harder than she'd ever felt it; for a moment it seemed she would die.

"Well?" he said after a minute, his voice cold and flat.

"What are we going to do?" Aimée whispered. At least he couldn't blame her. This entire evening had been his idea, and it was his friend who had shoved them toward a marriage ceremony.

St. Briac sighed. He didn't move or touch her. "An excellent question, mademoiselle." He sighed again, his jaw clenching in the firelight. "I don't see anything for it. I suppose we'll have to go through with it."

With an effort, she managed to speak. "The wedding?"

"What else?"

"But isn't there anything we could do?" Was it actually possible that he would wed her?

"I don't see what, now that your dear bishop d'Angoulême has flown to your defense."

He did blame her! "I don't believe it. I wouldn't even be here except for your *inspired* plan that was going to untangle all our problems. Even then, we might have escaped matrimony were it not for the interference of *your* dear friend, the king."

St. Briac had to smile at her ferocity. Instinctively, he searched for the bright side to their predicament. "You needn't behave as if we've been sentenced to death, *miette*." Rising up on an elbow, he put out a finger to trace the tense, exquisite line of her face from temple to jaw. "Cheer up. Things could be worse. After all, it's not as if you find me repulsive. We'll find solace in our bedchamber, and I did have to get married *someday*. It's my obligation to provide an heir to the St. Briac line."

Boiling with outrage, Aimée shoved at his broad chest with all her strength. Caught off balance, St. Briac toppled off the bed and onto the cold tiled floor.

"You little vixen," he burst out, lifting himself up to glare at her over the side of the bed. "If you want to get physical, I'll be glad to—"

"I only meant to nudge you, monseigneur, in the direction of your clothes," Aimée interrupted sweetly. "Your helpful comrade the king, and the bishop d'Angoulême will be knocking at the door momentarily if we do not dress and join them in the guardroom. Are you not anxious to toast our impending nuptials? After all, you've found a captive breeder for the next seigneur de St. Briac."

* * *

"I am simply in a state of shock," cried Gaspard LeFait as he collapsed into a chair near the fireplace. "I cannot function!"

Awash in morning sunlight, St. Briac glanced into the looking glass and straightened his fraise so that the white pleats stood up evenly against his golden-brown neck. "Why is your tongue not impaired?" he wondered mildly.

"Only death could still it."

"A pity." All seemed in order. He wore a doublet and haut-de-chausses of violet-gray embroidered with silver. A jerkin of steel-gray velvet set with sapphires and a sprinkling of diamonds set off the breadth of his shoulders. Freshly barbered, St. Briac's handsome face was accentuated by his trim beard and mustache and by ruffled dark chestnut hair that curled against his neck. "Have you ever beheld a more magnificent bridegroom?" he teased his manservant.

Gaspard groaned dramatically and pressed thin hands to his eyes. "Don't say it until it's a fact."

"What did you expect, windbag? I couldn't remain childless."

"Not childless, perhaps, but at least wifeless."

St. Briac laughed. "Never fear, ticklebrain. I won't let Aimée turn you into the street."

The wizened little valet sighed in surrender. "It could be worse, I suppose."

"Indeed! I could be marrying Cécile-Anne Dagonneau." St. Briac chuckled and then inspected his watch. "I must be going. Am I presentable?"

"If you're truly going through with this madness, I suppose you should be reminded to wear this." Gaspard tottered over to the carved chest and drew out a splendid sapphire surrounded with tiny diamonds that hung from a thin-linked chain. "I don't need to remind you that it was your father's. He wanted you to wear it on your"—the manservant choked out the words—"wedding day."

St. Briac eyed the piece of jewelry a bit dubiously. It was more the king's style than his own, but the thought of his late father softened his heart. This wasn't the sort of wedding day his parents would have envisioned, yet for some inexplicable reason the prospect of marrying Aimée filled him with mischief rather than despair. At least she would not bore him.

"*Merci,* Gaspard. It was good of you to think of this, and

of my father, today." He put the chain over his head, and the sapphire and diamonds were almost obscured under his jerkin. "Are you coming to the chapel?"

"*Oui,* monseigneur, I suppose I must," the valet replied mournfully, trailing after his master.

With one hand on the door latch, St. Briac paused to glance back at Gaspard, his turquoise eyes dancing with merriment. "During the ceremony, please endeavor not to grieve aloud. The sound of your weeping might cause me to laugh at an inopportune moment."

St. Briac's lighthearted mood persisted long after he and Aimée were pronounced husband and wife. Hastily arranged wedding festivities continued all day, and it wasn't until a huge meal was served at midafternoon that the couple were able to converse with any semblance of privacy. Yet even seated beside St. Briac, his thigh pressing hers through her crimson gown and petticoat, Aimée was unnerved by the dozens of curious eyes turned their way. Chauvergé and Louise de Savoy had not stopped staring and whispering since the last moment of the nuptial mass. Why, she wondered, were the two of them so interested? The bishop d'Angoulême continued to direct looks of frank disappointment in her direction. Your poor parents, said his eyes. You've broken their hearts over and over again!

Oddly enough, in spite of the combined failure of her mother and father and sister to provide her with loving support, Aimée felt a mixture of sadness and guilt when she thought of them today. What sort of wedding was this and what sort of celebration that did not include members of either her family or Thomas's? As for St. Briac, it seemed to Aimée that his air of merriment confirmed her suspicion that he felt no serious emotion regarding their marriage. Her heart was leaden with melancholy.

"I've wanted to tell you all morning how beautiful you look, *miette.*" St. Briac spoke gently, close to her ear. "No man could wish for a more enchanting bride."

Aimée had decided to wear the same gown of crimson velvet with its pearl and gold embroidered hem that had marked her first evening with St. Briac back at Nieuil. Suzette had included all the same accessories in the small trunk they'd brought to Chambord: the golden girdle set with emeralds with its thin gold cordelière and dangling mirror, the sapphire necklace that now nestled between her breasts, and the crispenette of golden net sprinkled with pearls and rubies. While dressing, Aimée had tried not to think, but as her bride's costume became complete, she couldn't help remembering that first night at the king's hunting lodge. How embarrassed she had been, bumping into St. Briac and then discovering not only that he was the man she had encountered in the woods—and kissed!—but that he also was the seigneur de St. Briac and one of the king's closest friends. In spite of the friendly moments they eventually shared that evening, not to mention St. Briac's warm, teasing manner and farewell speech, there hadn't been any hint that they were destined to be lifelong mates, had there? Now, sitting beside her husband, the question returned to Aimée's mind. The answer must be no, and yet...

"*Chérie*, did you hear me?" St. Briac murmured, apparently amused by her dreaminess.

She tried unsuccessfully to steel her senses against the assault of his charm. "Of course I heard you, monseigneur," she whispered demurely. "I thank you for the compliment."

"We are married now, Aimée, and you shall have to call me Thomas," he reminded her, only half in jest.

Lifting starry-lashed green eyes that were crowded with questions, Aimée tried to smile. She wanted to be happy, but all her defensive instincts argued against that happiness; a warning voice invaded her mind and her heart.

Hours later, after a feast of boars head, venison, duckling, succulent oysters, cheeses, artichokes, oranges, strawberries, spices and confections and sweetmeats of every sort, and even a swan in its plumage plus more goblets of wine than prudence deemed wise, all accompanied by the entertainment of various acrobats, minstrels, and jugglers, the tables were cleared away, and the court turned its attention to dancing and merrymaking. Aimée tried to enter into the spirit of what should have been her most cherished day but found it almost impossible to relax. At one point St. Briac left her alone to watch the dancing after the king beckoned him. Aimée stood off to one side, stiff and ill at ease amid the fresh summer flowers and herbs strewn over the tiles. She felt like an impostor. Something told her to turn her head, and she discovered Ghislaine Pepin gazing at her speculatively. Instantly, Aimée's cheeks grew hot.

"Ah, *ma chère amie!*" It was Marguerite d'Angoulême,

looking beautiful in vermilion silk and sapphires. She embraced Aimée with apparent sincerity. "How fortunate you are to become the wife of the seigneur de St. Briac. No doubt you remember the night I spoke of him at Blois. Perhaps you were already in love then but too shy to tell me. Truly, I feel as if we are almost sisters, since Thomas could not be closer to me if he were related by blood. Does that make sense?" Gay laughter spilled from her pretty mouth.

"Of course," Aimée assured Marguerite dazedly. "You're very kind."

"You look tired, my dear. No doubt you're exhausted from all the excitement."

"A bit."

The king and St. Briac were approaching, chatting merrily as they sipped wine from jeweled goblets. After the amenities were exchanged, François told Aimée, "I must apologize for this unimpressive celebration. If your marriage hadn't come up so suddenly or if we had been at Blois or Amboise, where a proper celebration can be arranged on short notice, this display would be of a character more deserving of you and Thomas."

Aimée tried not to let the king see her discomfort, but she threw St. Briac a look that said, We are hypocrites.

Across the room, the duchesse de Roanne watched the newlyweds. Her heart went out to Aimée, for she felt more than a little responsible for the girl's plight. Last night's drama had been planned in part by St. Briac, but Ghislaine had engineered the surprise twist at the end. All her instincts told her that this marriage was right for both parties. Ghislaine had realized weeks ago that Thomas and Aimée shared one common trait: stubbornness. They'd decided that love would not be an ingredient in their wildly improbable relationship, and neither would be the first to admit the truth. She wondered whether they had faced it privately yet. The poignant expression Aimée wore suggested that at least one of them had seen the light. Ghislaine sighed and said a silent prayer that Thomas would find a lifetime of happiness with the woman who obviously enchanted and maddened him so. He deserved a bounty of love, contentment, and laughter.

"What makes you so certain that this marriage is a good thing?"

Ghislaine heard the muted question and glanced around to discover Louise de Savoy and Chauvergé huddled together just a few paces in front of her. What mischief was brewing between those two now? the duchess wondered while waiting to hear Chauvergé's reply to Louise.

"I don't see how anything *but* good can come from it." He sneered. "That headstrong little vixen will keep our friend occupied inside and outside of the bedchamber. Pardon me for so crass a statement, madame, but in St. Briac's case, how can one speak otherwise? The man's a stallion, and I'm convinced that his new bride is frisky enough to divert him for weeks at least from the possibility of serious thought."

"No doubt that is true, but if you are wise, you won't underestimate St. Briac. There's more to his manhood than the evidence between his legs."

Chauvergé blinked at the king's mother, who merely arched an eyebrow and averted her face to scan the crowd.

Torn between alarm and an urge to laugh at Louise's astonishing, astute observation, Ghislaine was caught off guard by the fingers that curved around her waist.

"Thomas," she gasped, knowing the identity of the hand's owner before turning to face him.

"I saw you looking so thoughtful that I decided to come over and console you, *ma belle*. Are you terribly heartbroken now that I'm married?"

The sight of his wry, teasing smile gave Ghislaine a bittersweet pang. "Your conceit is appalling," she managed to scold.

"Don't you mean appealing?"

The duchess couldn't help laughing at his audacity, but her thoughts quickly returned to the conversation she had just overheard. "You must curb your impulse to be outrageous now that you are a husband, Thomas," she told him lightly, and then continued, "and I trust that you will keep your wits about you."

St. Briac's brows lifted in bemusement when he saw Ghislaine incline her head toward Chauvergé and Louise de Savoy. "I appreciate your sage advice, *chérie!*"

She longed to take him aside or make an appointment for a private conversation, but the circumstances made that impossible. Instead, she could only whisper, "I am confident that even the duties of a bridegroom will not dull your interest in the events and people around you."

Chauvergé had started toward them, and so St. Briac could only smile and rejoin, "I see your meaning, madame, and I assure you that not even my bride could make me forget the people who have concerned me in the past." Eyes agleam with amusement, he raised her hand and kissed it. "Not even you."

"*Excusez-moi*, St. Briac." Chauvergé leaned between them like a snake. "I don't wish to interrupt, but I did want to offer my congratulations. Your new wife is very beautiful."

Thomas looked down at the man as though he found him malodorous. "I agree. Thank you for your good wishes."

"What a shame it is that your friend Georges Teverant could not be present for this festive occasion."

"Yes."

Chauvergé's cheek twitched. "Perhaps he'll be able to join the court later and meet your bride then."

Seeing St. Briac's face darken, the duchesse de Roanne interjected, "Monseigneur, I really think you should leave us now. Madame de St. Briac is looking rather bereft."

"A wise suggestion," he agreed, and then glanced coldly in the direction of the chevalier. "You'll pardon me?"

"*Naturellement!*" Chauvergé gave him a vulpine smile.

Barely suppressing a shiver of revulsion, St. Briac bade his longtime mistress *adieu* and then distractedly crossed the room to rejoin Aimée, François, Marguerite, and Anne d'Heilly.

Aimée blinked back tears as she watched him approach. Obviously her new husband was brooding about the love he and Ghislaine Pepin had shared. It seemed incredible that he could have flaunted their relationship before the court on this of all days. It wasn't that Aimée imagined a simple wedding ceremony would end that affair, but she'd hoped St. Briac would be able to restrain himself from enjoying the company of his mistress out of consideration for her feelings.

Marguerite looked at Aimée and was filled with pity. Such a sweet, bright, guileless maiden. It was sad if her heart should already be breaking on her wedding day. What could Thomas be thinking of?

"Your lovely bride has been missing you, monseigneur," she told him, ignoring Aimée's tiny, embarrassed gasp and St. Briac's rather distant expression.

He tried to put Chauvergé from his mind. "If I know Aimée, she was glad of the respite."

The new bride smiled bravely. She was searching for a properly light reply when Marguerite spoke up again.

"*Pas de tout*, Thomas. Shame on you. Every woman longs for the undivided attention of the man she loves on her wedding day."

"I'm sure that's true," Anne d'Heilly sighed sadly. The king glanced away as if something of importance had captured his eye.

"Oh, well, I . . ." Aimée wanted to press her hands to her hot cheeks. Why was Marguerite saying these things? "I certainly realize that Thomas will not remain at my side like a trained dog."

"No, like an ardent, loving husband," the king's sister exclaimed. "Thomas, look at your bride. She is exhausted. Why don't you take her away for some peace and quiet?"

This idea obviously appealed to him. "What an inspired suggestion. I find that I am rather tired myself." Already St. Briac could feel the soft sheets and the warm, satiny curves of Aimée's body. No more interruptions, no more denials, just sweet Aimée, giving herself without stint. He looked down at her, eyes warm with desire, and the reality of their marriage struck him. Never had she looked more winsome, vulnerable, or adorable. A golden band fixed Aimée's veil of filmy white silk to her ebony tresses, and her eyes seemed a more vivid green than the emeralds that grazed the curves of her hips. "It has been a long day," he heard himself murmur.

"I'm really not tired," Aimée protested. "Wouldn't it be rude of us to desert our guests?"

"Don't be silly," exclaimed the king. "We *expect* you to desert us!"

Marguerite gave her a little push that brought her abruptly in contact with St. Briac's tall, hard body. Aimée flinched as though burned. "But I don't think—"

"This isn't a day to think, just to enjoy," Marguerite assured her.

Deciding that the conversation had gone on long enough, St. Briac put an arm around his wife's tiny waist. He made the proper apologies, endured the appearance of Florange and Bonnivet to demand kisses from the bride, smiled through the seemingly interminable good wishes of other members of the court, and finally drew Aimée into the long corridor that would bring them to the staircase leading to his chambers.

"Consider, *miette*," St. Briac bent to whisper roguishly against her hair, "we are about to sample, unhindered, the sweetest benefit of married life."

CHAPTER 25

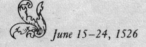 *June 15–24, 1526*

Aimée drew the shift of coral satin over her head with a sigh; it flowed like water down her hips. Once again she was shut in Gaspard's cabinet, having undressed by candlelight with deliberate slowness. There was nothing left to do now but stall some more. Sitting down on a hard chair with a high, carved back, Aimée thought of her parents. Their absence on her wedding day made the events of these past hours seem counterfeit. By tradition, Gilles and Éloise de Fleurance should have given their approval for this union, provided a dowry, however nominal, and shared in the execution of a marriage contract. They would have participated in a betrothal ceremony weeks ago and gotten to know Thomas as a son, and this morning Honorine and her mother would have helped Aimée dress. Before she and her new husband shared their marriage bed, Éloise would have searched it to make certain that no ill wisher had secreted anything there that might have impeded conjugal relations.

Instead, Aimée was alone, except for an impatient bridegroom who waited for her with a heart filled with lust rather than love. One disappointed tear coursed down her cheek as she gathered her courage and stood.

Somehow she'd expected to find St. Briac in bed, eager for her to join him. Instead, he was standing before the fireplace, one hand braced on the chimneypiece as he stared somberly into the flickering flames. Jerkin and doublet and shoes had been removed, but he still wore his white shirt unlaced over the gray-violet haut-de-chausses. For a long minute Aimée watched him and wondered about the reason for his reflective expression. The burnished firelight played over the curves and hollows of his splendid face and neck in a way that caused an unsettling flurry of sparks to catch in her breast. When he glanced up suddenly, his eyes eloquently searching her own, she felt faint.

"I'm sorry. I didn't hear the door." His smile was a flash of white in the shadows as one hand stretched out to gesture toward the bed. "Shall we?"

Together they walked to opposite sides of the carefully made bed. Drawing back the covers, Aimée found a nosegay of fresh violets on her pillow. Such a sweet gesture, yet she could not believe that tenderness had inspired it. Looking up, she saw St. Briac pull up his shirt to reveal the strong, handsome chest she knew well, yet she felt wary of this evening. Aimée took advantage of his preoccupation to divest herself of the satin shift and slide between the covers.

"Feeling shy, *miette?*" His tone was light but was underlaid with a challenge she could not fail to recognize.

"Am I not a bride?" she countered.

"Innocent? Unschooled in the ways of love?" St. Briac smiled at the sight of her averted eyes when he drew off the rest of his clothing. "We both know better. You know and want more than even you realize, Aimée."

"I suppose you think that I want *you.*"

Barely lifting his thick, arched eyebrows, he told her mildly, "Last night dispelled any doubts I might have entertained on that score."

"Your conceit is astounding, monseigneur," Aimée cried, her heart pounding frantically as he climbed into bed beside her. "Unlike you, I am a civilized human being. There is no love between us, and I won't be used to satisfy your carnal appetites just because of that farce we endured this morning in the chapel."

"Indeed? If I may be so bold, I would like to remind you that what took place in the chapel was no farce. You are my wife, *miette*. Aside from your own obvious desires, it is your duty to satisfy my carnal appetites."

She stared at him with incredulous spring-green eyes.

"My duty! *My desires?* Where you are concerned, I desire only to see the last of you, you jackass."

St. Briac's amused gaze took in the fiery beauty of her face and the swirl of ebony tresses that veiled ripe breasts. "You should have thought of that hours ago, my dear bride. Unfortunately, I won't be going anywhere for years and years...unless you put poison in my wine."

"I appreciate the suggestion!"

He tried to keep his irritation at bay. "I am not thirsty at the moment, though. In the meantime, won't you indulge a condemned man's most ardent wish?"

Aimée wasn't at all certain she felt comfortable with the web of conversation he was spinning. "And what is that?"

"I want to cease this foolishness. You are deluding yourself if you think you can put me off, Aimée."

There was no longer any humor in St. Briac's tone; it was cutting. Panic flared over her nerves. "Well, you are deluding yourself, monseigneur, if you believe that I am going to change because of a few words spoken by the bishop d'Angoulême. We may be married, but I cannot allow myself to submit docilely to your rutting attentions. You don't love me. This is a joke! You probably intend to use my body for your pleasure and keep mistresses as well. Will you be warming the duchesse de Roanne's bed on the morrow? Or tonight perhaps?"

St. Briac caught her face between his strong, dark hands. "Aimée, stop this."

An irresistible wave of pleasure showered her body solely because of the pressure of his fingers framing her cheeks. She wanted to sob in frustration, but every ounce of her resistance was swept away as St. Briac's mouth covered her own. Aimée gasped even as they kissed when he ran one hand, trailing fire over her back, down to draw her into his embrace. Without thinking, she pressed against him, twining her slim arms around his neck, inhaling his masculine scent, tasting his mouth. The force of St. Briac's passion seemed completely serious; it was as though he spoke to her with his body, expressing emotions that could not be articulated yet in any other way. He made love to Aimée with skillful lips and sensitive fingers, lingering over her throat, brushing back gleaming black locks to find the baby curls along her hairline, kissing shoulder blades and hips and the tender insides of her thighs.

"Nom de Dieu!" Aimée breathed, clinging to him just before their mouths fused once more and the hard length of his manhood found her sweet desire. She was like a bud that he had caused to blossom, still dewy and fresh.

"How beautiful you are," St. Briac murmured against her ear, smiling as he felt her shiver from the sensation of his warm breath. "My own Aimée."

This was the closest thing to a declaration of love she ever had heard from him, and it injected a current of joy into Aimée's painfully swelling heart. St. Briac's buttocks flexed under her hands as his hot flesh penetrated her body. She arched upward, eager to receive him, and for an instant the ceiling seemed dusted with stars.

In the middle of the night Aimée awoke to the sound of raindrops spattering the leaded windowpanes. The fire had gone out, and the room was chilly, but St. Briac kept her warm. They lay on their sides, and she was enfolded in his arms, the hair on his chest and legs soft against her. The sensation of him breathing, almost as if they were joined, was comforting yet disquieting. A sigh swelled inside her as she thought of the beautiful nature of their lovemaking and the fact that it had all been some sort of magical illusion, for St. Briac did not love her. If only the fragile spell were reality and he felt the same intense, passionate, consuming emotions that infused her every breath and thought. Then Aimée would be filled with joy. Perhaps it would be more than a human being could contain.

Her gaze wandered down to the steely arms that bent around her body, to the strong, elegant hands that continued to curve against her even in sleep. The contrast between them was stirring: bronzed skin against ivory, hard against soft. Aimée had to repress a yearning to lift St. Briac's fingers to her mouth and taste every inch of them. This seemed like an outrageous dream, the two of them sleeping together not only tonight but always! The concept of Thomas belonging to her was too huge to deal with.

His manhood shifted slightly, hardening against her derrière. Aimée tingled with arousal until it occurred to her that he probably was dreaming of Ghislaine. Still, the heat in her loins intensified until she ached with longing that made her despise herself. St. Briac's hands didn't move, nor did his breathing change, and so she knew he was still asleep. In frustration, Aimée carefully shifted onto her back, keeping one shoulder braced against her husband's body so that his slumber would not be disturbed. He continued to embrace her.

Something prompted Aimée to bring up her left hand and study her wedding ring in the darkness. It was a wide, heavy band of gold that had appeared mysteriously during the nuptial mass. Four words were inscribed on its outer surface: *Vous et Nul Autre*: You and No Other. If only St. Briac had chosen the ring and had it made for her, but obviously it was one that either François or the bishop had produced.

Tears burned Aimée's eyes. She tried to blink them back, but one ran down her temple like a stream of acid, and she was certain the droplet must have continued to St. Briac's chest. Apprehensive lest she might have awakened him, Aimée looked upward and let her breath out sharply. He was watching her with intent blue-green eyes.

A dozen confused explanations rushed toward Aimée's lips, but St. Briac spared her the trouble. "This is not a night for tears or doubts, *miette*. Accept the situation, and you'll feel better." With painstaking care, he gathered her near and kissed her deeply. Aimée's response was instant, erotic, and involuntary. Turning to press nearer to St. Briac's maleness, she wrapped her arms about him and lost herself in bliss.

In the morning, the newly married couple shared a *petit déjeuner* of fruit, cheese, and cold fresh milk in bed. Aimée felt dazed, but her husband was thinking that she had never looked more ravishing with black curls tumbling over her slim pale shoulders, lips deep-rose from kissing through the night, cheeks flushed to match the dawn, and green eyes curiously wide and dewy. After a while he felt hungry for something more substantial than fruit or cheese. Setting the dishes on a nearby chest, he returned to kiss his wife, who had just popped the last two raspberries into her mouth. They shared them, breaking the juicy berries between their tongues.

"Aimée, I'm feeling better and"—He caressed the bare, satiny curves of her hips, smiling—"better about this marriage. I find that being a husband is actually quite pleasant."

She couldn't stifle a giggle, but then her sensitive nipples were being crushed against his taut chest, and their mouths came together. Aimée decided that St. Briac tasted better than all the raspberries in France.

On the surface, even to them, the first days of their marriage were happy. They spent a great deal of time in bed, and sometimes in the aftermath of lovemaking Aimée was certain that they had communicated physically what had yet to be put into words. Still, the fact that St. Briac had not spoken of love ate at her. At first the dark thoughts sprang to her mind only when they were abroad in the chateau, sharing meals with the rest of the court—not touching. With the passage of time, however, doubts began to invade even their most intimate moments. She would wait, aching for the sound of any tender declaration from Thomas's lips, but it never came. Waking during the night, Aimée stared for what seemed like hours at the face of the man she adored so ardently and wondered whether it would be like this always. Would he never feel more than a mischievous affection mixed with physical lust? Would he never open his heart to her and share all of himself?

Moments of soaring hope mingled with despair for Aimée. On the second day of their marriage, St. Briac seemed to remember that there was a world apart from the bed he shared with his bride. Almost guiltily, he accepted an invitation from François to hunt boar in the forests surrounding Chambord.

"Poor Sébastien," he said wryly to Aimée after informing her of his plans. "He must think I've deserted him. Why don't you come along with me and greet the beast, if only to soothe his injured feelings."

Pleased to be included in the warm relationship between master and steed, Aimée agreed readily. The rainy days were over, replaced by billowy white clouds against a sky of azure. Walking beside her husband to the stables, Aimée inhaled the clean air and felt ebullient. Just the sight of St. Briac filled her with pleasure.

Sébastien whinnied at the sound of his owner's footsteps and instantly appeared at the front of his stall. His black coat gleamed, and he seemed almost to grin after snatching the chunk of carrot St. Briac proffered. They both reached up to stroke the stallion's mane, but Aimée's attention soon shifted to the horse in the next stall.

"Pretty, isn't she?" Thomas remarked casually.

The mare had come over to prance hopefully before him and then had put her beautiful sable-brown head into the adjoining stall and attempted to nudge Sébastien. He only eyed her with disdain and continued to munch his carrot.

"She's wonderful! Who is her owner?" Aimée exclaimed, experiencing a pang of envy for that lucky person.

"You are, *miette*." St. Briac smiled and produced another piece of carrot for her to offer the mare.

"You're teasing me," she protested, but took the carrot all the same and held it out to the splendid horse, which bent her head to nibble gracefully at Aimée's palm. Tears of spontaneous affection stung Aimée's eyes.

"I assure you that I would not jest about anything as important as your horse, my dear," St. Briac said gently. "Her name is Mignonne, and she's the reason I left Blois prematurely. I went to Vendôme to collect her from a friend of mine who's been raising her until now."

"But for me?" Aimée breathed in disbelief. "Surely you didn't intend..."

"Not when I originally arranged to purchase Mignonne, because I didn't know you then. But when I went to Vendôme, it was your horse I had to acquire. The two of you were made for each other."

It was a gesture of such astonishing generosity that Aimée felt momentarily paralyzed. She turned to stare into Mignonne's huge golden-brown eyes and then allowed herself to vent her feelings to St. Briac. Throwing herself upward, knowing his arms would catch her, Aimée wept against his bearded cheek and kissed him until she felt drained.

"*Mille mercis*, Thomas." She wanted to exclaim that she loved him but managed to restrain herself. "You are wonderful."

"I'm so pleased that you've noticed," he murmured with a rakish grin.

On what would prove to be the court's last day at Chambord, the delicate fabric of a loving marriage that St. Briac and Aimée had begun tentatively to weave unraveled abruptly.

The first tear occurred in the morning, when he missed their habitual exercising of Sébastien and Mignonne. On his way to meet Aimée at the stables, St. Briac passed the king's study and caught a glimpse of François leaning over something on his desk. Since last week's hasty wedding, Thomas

had seen little of his friend, and he felt more than a pang of
guilt thinking of all the indulgent hours he'd spent in bed
with Aimée while the king wrestled with problems of enormous significance.

"Bonjour, mon ami," St. Briac greeted him merrily, putting his head around the side of the door. "Not disturbing
you, I hope."

François had to beam at the sight of a familiar, engaging
grin and the sound of its owner's voice. "Of course not.
Welcome!" He came around the desk to hug St. Briac. "I
expect you've been too worn out to stumble down here for
a visit until now. Why has your charming bride let you loose?"

"Actually, she'll be looking for me soon in the stables. A
bit of exercise to offset too much time spent lying down."
Turquoise eyes twinkled wickedly. "You understand?"

"Not lately, unfortunately." The king smiled. "Before you
go, do come and see my new model of Chambord. It's quite
impressive." Sunlight gleamed off the ivory satin that showed
through the slashes of his blue doublet.

The wooden miniature of the chateau was charming and
fascinating, constructed with painstaking attention to every
detail. The two men looked over it for a while, commenting
on the areas still to be completed, while St. Briac searched
his mind for a graceful exit line.

"You know," the king said suddenly, as though he sensed
that his friend was about to desert him, "Charles V has
rejected the terms of membership offered by the league."

"What a surprise," Thomas murmured sarcastically.

"Let me read to you his exact words." He drew a piece
of parchment from under a book. "In response to our request
that he release my sons for a generous ransom, he writes,
'I will not deliver them for money. I refused money for the
father; I will much less take money for the sons. I am content
to render them upon reasonable treaty, but not for money,
nor will I trust any more the king's promise, for he has
deceived me, and that like no noble prince. And where he
excuses that he cannot fulfill some things without grudge of
his subjects, let him fulfill that that is in his power, which
he promised by the honor of a prince to fulfill; that is to
say, that if he could not bring all his promise to pass, he
would return again hither into prison'!"

St. Briac wondered what to say. The king's face was
flushed with outrage directed not only toward the emperor

but also, Thomas realized, at himself for the truth he saw in Charles's words. "Sire," he said gently, crossing to put a hand on his shoulder, "I am sorry."

"So am I."

Thomas realized that he could not possibly leave at such a moment. Instead, he poured large goblets of wine for himself and the king, and the two of them sat down before the cold fireplace.

Aimée rode alone that day, and though she tried to be understanding when she heard St. Briac's explanation, her insecurities rose to the surface. Rather than let him see them, she withdrew. Logic told her to forget the entire incident, yet it seemed they were caught in a game with rules neither of them had chosen.

Since Thomas had demonstrated that marriage would not affect his other relationships, Aimée felt bound to demonstrate that she felt the same way. After a quiet supper that evening, she engaged Marguerite d'Angoulême in spirited conversation. The king's sister had missed Aimée's company, and she suggested that they stroll together in the courtyard now that the weather was fine. St. Briac smiled politely in farewell to both of them, but he felt bored surrounded by men, the same friends with whom he had passed countless evenings in seeming contentment. At length, he wandered up the stone staircase that led to his and Aimée's chamber, only to encounter Ghislaine Pepin on the top step.

"Thomas," she exclaimed, her happiness tempered by the instant reminder that their relationship had changed forever. "Marcel is still down with the other men, but how is it that your wife is not with you? I'd begun to think the two of you were joined at the hip."

"You know me better than that, *chérie*. In truth, I suspect Aimée is paying me back for missing our riding appointment this morning. I was waylaid by the king, and now she is very sincerely occupied in conversation with the king's sister."

The duchess laughed softly. "In that case, come with me to my apartments. We'll indulge in some long overdue conversation of our own."

As Ghislaine squeezed St. Briac's arm and led him down the darkened corridor, Aimée faltered on the steps below. She hadn't been too far behind, however, to miss the last of their tête-à-tête. Fighting an urge to be physically ill,

Aimée leaned against the cool stone wall and took deep breaths until she was certain they were gone.

Barely a half hour had elapsed when St. Briac left the chambers of the duchesse de Roanne, bound for his own. Ghislaine had made him smile with her lecture about his responsibilities as a husband, but at least that was better than every man's nightmare: a jealous, vindictive ex-mistress. It would seem that the situation between Ghislaine and Marcel had improved dramatically, and now she was determined that everyone else she cared for should also know romance in marriage.

It seemed doubtful that Aimée would have come upstairs yet. Women together had a tendency to stretch conversations to unheard-of lengths. Opening the door to their chamber, St. Briac was surprised to find that the candles had been doused and that Gaspard had retired to his new, separate room. A moonbeam slanted across the bed to lend added glow to a pale shoulder and the spill of Aimée's ebony tresses.

St. Briac slowly crossed the tiled floor and stared down at his sleeping wife. Her lush, thick eyelashes made dark crescents against the delicate bones of her cheeks. She seemed to pout slightly in her sleep, her lower lip outthrust in a way he found highly appealing, while one tiny hand was clenched into a fist beneath her chin.

Rounding the bed, St. Briac stripped quickly and slid between the covers. Enough of this foolishness, he thought. Time to make up before we let a simple misunderstanding escalate into a real quarrel. Already he could smell her faint violet essence; his fingertips ached to touch her.

"*Miette*," St. Briac said tenderly while reaching out to curve one hand over her hip.

"Keep your distance!" Whirling in his direction, Aimée felt a twinge of satisfaction at the sight of his stunned expression. "You are worse than the lowest animal. How dare you insult me by going to your mistress after we have only been married a few days? Of course, I realize that it's all a farce, that you are only acting a part when you pretend to be my husband. Well, that's how it shall be from now on, but there is no need for us to pretend when we're alone, is there? I'll be damned, monseigneur, if I'll let you touch me when your body is still warm with *her* scent!"

In the moonlight, St. Briac lifted a bronzed hand and pressed taut fingers to his brow for a long minute. It was almost impossible for him to believe what had just happened, the words that had assailed him from the mouth he'd been yearning to kiss. He wasn't certain which of the several instinctive reactions he was feeling would be appropriate. The strongest was an urge to slap Aimée across the face.

"I see," he managed to reply politely. "In that case, madame, I will bid you good night."

Aimée found herself presented with a dark, long back, one that she loved to snuggle against but now was forbidden to touch. At first she felt deflated. St. Briac's words and reaction had not been even close to her expectations. He'd acted as if she were the one at fault. Not only that, he'd stopped the fight between them without her permission.

Aimée sighed loudly and flipped back onto her side, away from her husband. Rage boiled inside her, followed by an uncontrollable urge to weep. Pressing her face into the down-filled pillow, Aimée swallowed sobs and waited for St. Briac to relent and take her in his arms. Longing for him, for his caring and tenderness and teasing, became a pain that consumed her. Still Thomas did not turn in her direction, and Aimée could not bring herself to reach out to him.

CHAPTER 26

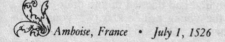 *Amboise, France • July 1, 1526*

July broke softly, caressing the Loire valley with breezes reminiscent of spring. It was a day to ride Mignonne and frolic in the woods, but Aimée found herself instead seated next to Marguerite d'Angoulême on a gallery overlooking one of the courtyards of the great chateau of Amboise. The king, bored with hunting and masquerades, had proposed an impromptu tournament, and within a day it was arranged. Tapestries hung from hooks along the galleries, lists had been drawn, and brightly colored tents were erected for the chevaliers' convenience.

Everyone looked splendid and seemed to be having a wonderful time, despite the fact that the afternoon was waning and they had watched more jousts than Aimée could count. François wore armor himself; a suit too magnificent to be risked in conflict, it was saved for parades and events like this. Casting a sidelong glance past her friend, Aimée had to admire the figure of the king. His armor was black steel elaborately inlaid with gold, with a medallion on the chest and a scallop shell collar that were the emblems of the knightly order of Saint Michael. A helmet shaped like the upturned head of a lion reposed near François's feet, and his face looked more dashing and dynamic than ever to Aimée as he watched the current match between two opposing sides of three knights each, his hazel eyes alight with enjoyment.

Aimée wished she could absorb some of that pleasure. It was hard for her even to work up enthusiasm over the prospect of seeing St. Briac joust for the first time. He and Bonnivet would be next in a solo match planned to demonstrate the skills of the two knights François valued most. Florange may have been as good, but he lacked the height and power of his friends.

Servants appeared with trays of cheeses from Brie and Montreuil as well as herring and an assortment of fruits. Aimée took a small wedge of Brie and a goblet of wine, which she sipped pensively. Her gallery and the ones above were crowded with members of the court. Aimée imagined that close to five hundred had flocked to join their monarch at Amboise. Even the young prince and two young princesses—all that remained of the king's family now that his older sons were in Spain and his wife and first two daughters had died—were here to join their father at last. Aimée was especially charmed by little Marguerite, who had just turned three. Her heart ached that such a sweet and loving child should be without a mother and have a father she scarcely knew.

Nearly oblivious to the chaos on the field before her, Aimée gazed around the chateau where François had grown to manhood. Spread over the rocky spur that divided the valleys of the Loire and the Amasse, the castle was a vast grouping of buildings that dominated the charming village below. It was supported by thick walls and flanked by two huge, squat towers, the Minimes and the Hurtault. The Minimes tower was a wonder conceived, of course, by François. The spiral ramp that wound upward through it was massive enough to accommodate not only horses but coaches as well. In the chateau itself there were elegant royal living quarters that boasted buttresses embellished with niches, fretwork balustrade, and dormer windows bristling with pinnacles. An enchanting gothic gem of a chapel called St. Hubert adjoined the queen's apartments and had been used daily by Claude, according to Marguerite. Gardens laid out by Parcello occupied a huge rectangle. The embroidered square flower beds were divided by paths that led northward to a fountain sheltered by framing. Parrots and magpies joined other exotic birds in the aviary, and three lions roamed almost at will by the moats. St. Briac had shown Aimée the armory that contained the battle-axes of Clovis, St. Louis, and DuGuesclin; the dagger of Charlemagne; the swords of Charles VI and Louis XI; and the armor of Jeanne d'Arc.

It should have been a wonderful place to be a new wife in love, but Aimée was eaten up with love while her husband continued to maintain a careful distance. How she regretted the impetuous words she had spoken in their bed at Chambord. Would he never forgive them? Worse, did he want to?

Suddenly Bonnivet strode toward them down the gallery, clad in full armor and holding his helm in the crook of his arm. There was a lull in the courtyard as St. Briac's match was prepared. Aimée stared at her husband's friendly opponent, confused and then alarmed.

"Is something wrong?"

Bonnivet pushed back disheveled fair hair and perched on the gallery's stone baluster. "Not quite."

By now François was leaning forward in his chair, waiting for an explanation. Bonnivet wrinkled his aquiline nose, trying to decide how to begin. His nature was so genuinely merry that he dreaded the prospect of an argument.

"I won't be jousting with St. Briac," he said carefully.

"Ah, I see." The king lifted chestnut brows. "I would appreciate more information, Bonnivet. I don't intend to wring every word from you. Explain!"

The massive knight suddenly looked uncomfortably warm. "You will no doubt recall, sire, that last evening Chauvergé demanded the right to oppose St. Briac."

"I do, and I also recall that I said his height and strength were no match for St. Briac's. Thomas agreed, and that was the end of it."

"Not quite," Bonnivet repeated uneasily. "He's been badgering us all through the tournament. We finally decided that if he is so determined to inflict pain on his own body, he should have that privilege."

François collapsed against the back of his high, carved chair with an explosive sigh. "How entertaining for the rest of us!"

"I couldn't help thinking, sire, that it might teach that weasel a lesson. Perhaps he'll learn not to tamper with Thomas in the future."

"Considering the fact that this has been going on for a score of years, I'd say that is highly unlikely."

Bonnivet could see nothing else to do but shrug, attempt a charming smile, and try unsuccessfully to make himself look small as he stole away to the nearest empty chair at the far end of the gallery. The king was still grumbling to himself when Chauvergé rode onto the field.

The heralds announced the contest with silvery trumpet blasts, but Aimée scarcely heard them. She did, however, see Chauvergé all too clearly as he paused before them, visor raised and lance lowered in pseudo-respect. She knew she should be relieved that St. Briac would face such a weakling, but there was something so malevolent in those glittering eyes that she felt a stab of fear. Chauvergé was so filled with hate, he would do anything to dispatch his rival.

Across the courtyard, St. Briac emerged from his tent as nonchalantly as if he'd been called to supper. The sight of him made Aimée forget all else. It was the first time she had seen him in armor; he looked utterly splendid. St. Briac's armor was a paler steel than the king's, inlaid with etched silver and marked with the same medallion of the order of St. Michael on the chest and the collar. Gentle winds from the Loire ruffled the dark hair back from his brow as he looked down to draw on his gauntlets. Aimée studied her husband's sculpted countenance, watching as he glanced upward, eyes crinkling, to regard the cloudless blue sky. His squire had brought Sébastien, and Thomas paused for the briefest moment to exchange a greeting with his strong black steed. Then, after donning his helm, he swung onto Sébastien as if the armor had no weight at all. He took up his shield, the device on which was an inlaid sun of beaten gold, and his lance and then rode calmly in the direction of the gallery where Aimée sat.

The king greeted St. Briac with grudging good humor. "Endeavor to allow the man to remain on his horse long enough to make this worthwhile."

"This will be my first joust with Chauvergé, sire. We may all be surprised by his skill."

"I do so hope that is the case."

St. Briac laughed softly in response and then turned his attention to Aimée. Sunlight blazed on the lifted visor of his helm, making it nearly impossible to read his eyes. As his lady, Aimée knew that she must demonstrate her favor, and so she stood, went to the rail, curtsied, and gracefully extended her fingertips. Sébastien stepped forward so that his master might reach up to her. The steel gauntlet made St. Briac's hand seem bigger and stronger than ever as it enveloped hers; somehow that reassured Aimée. In this situation, how could evil wim out over physical power?

"Do be careful, Thomas," she heard herself say in a tone that was transparently anxious.

St. Briac regarded her for a moment and then spoke lightly. "'Twill be child's play, *miette*, but it is reassuring to know that you care."

Aimée hoped he didn't see her blush as he released her hand, saluted the king, and rode off to his place at the north end of the lists. When both men were in position, another shrill trumpet blast rent the air; then they were charging full gallop toward one another. Lances struck shields, and the two horses were thrown back on their haunches, muscles bunching, by the jolting impact.

"Thomas is being kind," the king muttered to no one in particular.

St. Briac and Chauvergé rode back to their opposite positions, took fresh lances from their squires, and waited for the next clarion signal. When it came, the great steeds thundered toward each other, but just before the moment of impact, Chauvergé shifted his horse slightly to the left, toward the barrier, and at the same time raised his lance, aiming it at St. Briac's helm rather than his shield. Aimée heard her own silent scream in her mind, but she needn't have feared. Sébastien and his master possessed not only strength but wits. They instantly moved to counteract Chauvergé's maneuver, and St. Briac lifted his shield to take the force of the lance.

Watching him wheel around and return to his starting place for a third run, Aimée imagined she could see his angry features. Surely she recognized the hard, stubborn set of his shoulders within the suit of armor. Still, her fear was real now. Chauvergé knew that he was outmatched and intended to use his wiles not only to win but to injure or even kill his rival. Her heart pounding, Aimée leaned forward to look at the king, but he was leaning forward himself, staring intently as he waited for the third run to begin. She closed her eyes and said a prayer as the trumpets sounded again.

Sébastien charged like a bolt of lightning, much harder than before. St. Briac seemed a statue of steel and silver in the saddle, his lance never wavering. It was over in an instant. Suspicious that his opponent might employ a trick similar to his own, Chauvergé moved his shield slightly upward, but St. Briac aimed straight at his chest. The blow sent the smaller man flying into the air like a rag doll, his lance and horse scattering in wild disarray. Sébastien recovered with admirable dignity from his efforts to step daintily over the vanquished knight.

Dimly, Aimée heard the wild cheers of the crowd, saw François jump to his feet with elation, observed her husband as he dismounted and bent over Chauvergé's prostrate figure. She could scarcely breathe, so overcome was she with relief, shock, and a warm glow of pride that washed over her from head to toe.

The *premier médecin* rushed out onto the field, joining St. Briac. They conversed for a moment, crouched beside Chauvergé. Then Thomas stood and drew off his gauntlets and helm, still staring down at the other knight. Even from a distance Aimée could see the disgust and pity in his expression.

After returning Sébastien to his squire, St. Briac came bareheaded into the gallery. Her heart in her throat, Aimée watched his approach.

"Well done, *mon ami*," cried François, rising to hug his friend. "You taught Chauvergé a lesson that he will not soon forget! That is, if he isn't dead."

St. Briac smiled grimly and raked a hand through his damp hair. "No, I'm afraid he'll live." He paused, his face darkening in remembrance. "The ass."

"Cheer up, you're the hero of the tourney." The king turned to Aimée. "Come over here, madame. Your stalwart husband deserves a kiss."

A kiss! They hadn't kissed since Chambord, since before she'd seen him go off with the duchesse de Roanne that fateful night. Everyone was staring at her, and so Aimée tried to smile and make her way to her husband. He towered over her, smelling of horses and male sweat. His face, streaked with dust, had never looked more irresistible. She blushed under his penetrating turquoise gaze.

Looking down at his beautiful wife, St. Briac felt a pain in his chest altogether different from the kind inflicted by a lance. How he wanted her, missed her! Aimée's spring-green eyes, with their thick sooty lashes, were so luminous that he longed to drown in them.

"Don't be shy, you two," Bonnivet prompted jovially.

Aimée smiled, her face growing hotter by the moment, and then gathered her courage and stood on tiptoe to rest delicate hands on his steel-enclosed shoulders. The thought of their lips touching was so arousing that she almost felt faint.

"Congratulations, Thomas," Aimée whispered. "You were wonderful."

Her lips were soft and sweet as they came up to brush his. St. Briac almost groaned aloud. Desire rushed into his loins in a long-suppressed tide as he caught her up against his hard, armor-covered body. The fragrance of her hair and its silky texture in his fingers! His other arm easily encircled her slim back so that his fingertips were touching the first blossom of her breast. Aimée's arms were wrapped around his neck, and her mouth opened eagerly under his. They kissed long and hungrily, lost in a world of sensation.

"You can be shy again now," François suggested at length, wryly amused. He'd been a bit worried about these two lately, but obviously his concern had been unwarranted.

St. Briac was loath to release Aimée, but he did so. She slid from his arms down to the stone floor, her cheeks flaming.

"Let's go up to my apartments," said the king. "I find I am ravenous, and Thomas no doubt craves a cold mug of ale."

A select group from the court mingled in the royal apartments, all of them eager for a word with St. Briac. He tried to get away for a bath, but no one would let him leave, and so he remained in armor and found solace in frosty ale and a plate of bread, cheese, salmon, and pears.

Aimée kept her distance. St. Briac had to wonder whether she was more wary of him or of herself after that brief display of shared passion in the gallery. While conversing with Florange, he watched her with one eye as she swept hither and yon, her skirts of coral silk brushing the tiles. She had a word for everyone and gave to mere acquaintances the incandescent smile he rarely saw of late.

"Thomas?" a gentle, familiar voice spoke beside him.

"Ghislaine, it's good to see you. Where have you been keeping yourself?"

"Oh, I've been occupied with Marcel." Her smile was

contented. "He leaves tomorrow to go on ahead to our château, so I wanted to spend time with him while we had the chance."

"How romantic."

"Rather," she agreed softly. "At any rate, I know that you must be tired and hot in that armor, but before you go, I wanted to say that I was so proud of you today. You were magnificent."

"Strong words, *chérie*. One might think that you still care."

Ghislaine stared at him, wondering what was going on between St. Briac and his bride. They'd seemed rather aloof from each other these past days, but the kiss in the gallery would seem to tell a different story. "Of course I care, Thomas. I will always care." She put a hand on his cheek and leaned up to touch her lips to his. "I only want you to be happy."

Aimée watched them from across the room, tears stinging her eyes. Would this affair never end? She turned her face away and tried to listen to what Anne d'Heilly was saying about the contest that was about to begin in the courtyard between a boar and some dummies. It seemed that the king had longed to fight a duel with the wild boar himself, but Anne had managed to dissuade him.

Before St. Briac could speak or touch her, Aimée sensed his proximity. She whirled around and almost collided with his broad, steel-covered chest.

"I apologize for interrupting," he said easily, with a warm smile for Anne, "but I thought I should tell you that I am going to our apartments for a bath. Another minute in this armor will drive me mad."

"But what about supper?"

"I just had some food, and to be honest, I'm tired. Perhaps my bath will revive me, but I doubt it. Also, there's the matter of Chauvergé. He's sure to appear momentarily, and I don't think I could endure being in the same room with him tonight."

Aimée waited in vain for an invitation to accompany him.

"So," St. Briac said easily, "I will bid you ladies *bon soir*. Enjoy your suppers."

When he bent to graze her cheek with his mouth, Aimée felt as if she'd been burned. "*Bon soir*, Thomas."

Anne gave him a hug, too, and poured out another string

of compliments for his heroic joust. St. Briac suffered them patiently and then went to bid the king good night.

No sooner had he disappeared under the vaulted doorway than Chauvergé came in through another portal. Armor shed and freshly washed, he wore courtly garb and entered with chin outthrust as if challenging those present to make a derisive comment about the tournament. Accepting a goblet of wine, he walked over to Aimée and Anne d'Heilly.

"Good evening, ladies. Where is my worthy opponent? Was he exhausted by our match?"

"My husband has just gone to bathe. He couldn't get away until now." Aimée gave him a cold stare.

François had been on a balcony, watching the wild boar tear the dummies to shreds, but now he and his courtiers made their way to Chauvergé. After a few polite words of greeting, the king said, "I'm happy to see that you were not injured as severely as it seemed. I feared that you might have taken to your bed."

"'Twas but a scratch, sire," Chauvergé replied, trying to breathe normally to disguise the sharp pain in his chest. The *premier médecin* had decided that some ribs had been broken and had bound him up tightly. "St. Briac's supposed strength is an illusion."

Aimée's eyes opened wide at this, but the king spoke for her. "Was it an illusion when he unseated you with such ease?"

"He aimed for my chest rather than my shield, sire. Not a tactic of fair play."

Chauvergé's listeners glanced at one another with brows raised.

"I see," murmured Florange. "That was not the way it appeared to all of us."

"*Vraiment?* And how did it appear to you?"

"It looked as if you were trying to kill St. Briac on that second run, and only his quick wits and skill saved him. He gave you what you deserve, Chauvergé."

The chevalier snorted derisively. "Huh! The man was only making a show for his new wife." The sidelong glance he gave Aimée was so venomous, it made her blood chill.

Warming to the conversation, Florange retorted, "I do not think St. Briac needs to prove his manhood to his bride. Perhaps it's the other way around? Perhaps you were longing to end his life so that you might slither into madame's bed?"

Everyone gasped at this, but the "Young Adventurer" stared calmly at Chauvergé until the latter burst out. "Ridiculous! You act as superior as St. Briac. Let me tell you something, Florange. I wouldn't have this woman even if I *had* killed St. Briac. Everyone knows that she was his whore before he was forced to make her his wife."

Louder gasps greeted these words, but Aimée was too stunned to make a sound. She felt as if he had struck her too with his lance, unfairly and with malice. Anne quickly put an arm around her shoulders to steady her, while Aimée managed to retain her composure and meet Chauvergé's reptilian eyes.

The king spoke first, his voice cold and clear. "You have gone too far this time. If St. Briac were here, he would surely kill you for the insult you have delivered. As it is, I must remind you of what you know full well—that I have always sworn that any man who would be so crass as to reflect on the honor of one of the ladies of my court would be hanged." François paused, narrowing his hazel eyes at the smaller man. "If you wish to avoid that fate or a worse one when St. Briac hears of your words, I suggest that you remove yourself from my court immediately."

Chauvergé put his nose in the air and was about to reply, when a scream rang out and they all turned to see the wild boar charging straight into the royal apartments.

CHAPTER 27

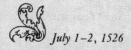 *July 1–2, 1526*

It appeared that the boar, which seemed to be mad, had demolished the barricades that had been erected around the courtyard and had stormed up the stairway. Members of the court rushed toward the nearest wall, chair, or table in mad confusion; only the king remained unperturbed. As the beast roared into his apartments, François calmly drew his sword. Pausing only briefly to study his adversary, the boar bared his tusks and charged. With seeming ease, the king sidestepped the long snout and razor-sharp tusks and drove the point of his sword home. The boar snorted in pain and surprise before falling, neatly spitted, at the feet of François. The massive, hairy form rolled heavily down the steps and landed in the courtyard below.

In the wild scene of acclamation that followed, Aimée slipped out of the room. She felt dazed, more by the behavior of Chauvergé than by that of the boar. Walking toward the apartments she shared with St. Briac, she wondered whether to tell him what had happened. There seemed no graceful way to do so, since the bulk of the confrontation had concerned her. Should she whine that she'd been insulted, forcing her husband to take up arms once again against a foe who didn't warrant his merest glance? No, and if Chauvergé was indeed absent from the court after tonight, the problem would be erased.

His words had bothered her almost more than the exchange that followed them. Did people think she was merely a wench St. Briac had been forced to make his wife? Did the entire court whisper behind her back?

Their bedchamber was empty, but Aimée heard voices in the *étuve*, the small chamber where they bathed and performed other duties relating to cleanliness. She sat down on the bed in a position that offered a view through the narrow doorway. St. Briac's broad shoulders and dark chestnut hair were visible above the high, sculptured *cuvé*. Aimée watched as Gaspard poured a large ewer of clear water over his master's soapy head before turning to notice her.

"*Sacré bleu!*" exclaimed the little man. "Your wife is here. I'd better go."

"Why?" St. Briac queried in seeming irritation. "She's not bothering you."

"It's not my place," insisted the valet. "Besides, we're finished. You didn't want me to dry you off?"

"Of course not! Go on, then. I'll see you tomorrow."

On his way out, Gaspard bowed and mumbled a greeting to Aimée before hastening toward the door. She couldn't help wondering which her husband dreaded more: his valet's departure or the thought of being naked and alone with her.

"I hope you didn't cut your evening short on my account," St. Briac said after a minute's silence.

"No. Actually, the boar that was providing entertainment in the courtyard stormed the king's apartments."

"Really!" St. Briac swiveled to peer at her over the *cuvé*, water dripping from his neat beard. "Why don't you come in here and tell me about it?"

Uneasily, she complied. Perched on a low stool, Aimée scarcely could concentrate on what she was saying, so overwhelmingly conscious was she of her husband's nearness. Her eyes drank in the sight of his glistening, naked chest and shoulders, the strength of his neck, the aristocratic shape of the fingers that curved around a wedge of soap.

St. Briac listened with interest as she related the tale of the boar, all the while soaping muscular calves covered with crisp dark hair. To Aimée, even his feet were beautiful.

"So," he commented when she had finished, "'twould

seem that I am not the only hero at Amboise today. Thank God."

Her smile answered his as she watched him reach across to a nearby chair and retrieve a large folded linen towel. Aimée panicked as she realized he was about to get out of the water. During the first days of their marriage, she had often bathed with St. Briac, but those times now seemed part of a silly romantic dream. There was not supposed to be such intimacy between them anymore.

"Well," Aimée said, choking, "I'll leave you now."

Only a hint of amusement lit his eyes as he stood up, dripping, and watched her hurry from the *étuve*. After drying off with the first large linen towel, he reached for a dry one and applied it vigorously to his hair. When it was barely damp, St. Briac ran long fingers through to brush it away from his face and then walked naked into the bedchamber. Aimée stood by the fireplace, eyes averted and cheeks flaming. She expected her husband to make a caustic remark about her embarrassment, but he remained silent. Out of the corner of her eye, she saw him drawing back the counterpane before he slid between the sheets with a sigh.

"You are going to bed?" Aimée asked in surprise.

"That does seem to be the case."

"But isn't it rather early?"

"I am tired, and there is nothing else to do, is there? Why don't you go back and have your supper."

"I don't want any. Actually, I had enough to eat during the tournament. Probably as much as you had afterward, and I certainly was not as famished as you must have been." She tried to smile politely, to pretend that they were having a normal husband-wife conversation. "You must have worked up an enormous appetite. Jousting looks like very hard work."

St. Briac's only response was to lift both eyebrows as if to mock her mindless chatter.

"Well, I suppose I'll go to bed, too," Aimée announced with false brightness.

"Not on my account, I hope."

Her step faltered, and then she turned to unlace the front of her gown, trying to blink back hot tears. St. Briac cursed himself but couldn't help turning his head to watch as she undressed. Off came the complicated layers of clothing: gown, shakefold, petticoat, corset, and finally chemise. In the dim candlelight Aimée's body was exquisite, delicately curved and with the hue of a soft pink rose. When Aimée crossed to place her discarded garments in bureau and chest, St. Briac caught a tantalizing glimpse of her high, sweet breasts. Under the covers, his ache became a maddening torment, and he turned his face away before the full view of her approaching the bed drove him past the brink of control. Just the sensation of the bed sagging slightly as she got in made him shut his eyes tightly against the pain of her nearness. The fresh scent of violets teased the air.

"Are you asleep?" she queried hesitantly.

"No," St. Briac said through gritted teeth.

"Oh." She sighed audibly, wishing she could find the courage to touch him, to weep against his broad chest and tell him how desperately she loved him. The fear that he might reject and despise her held Aimée back.

Seeking to distract himself, St. Briac said abruptly, "We're going home day after tomorrow."

"Home?"

"Yes, to St. Briac. Our home, remember?"

Aimée felt like a dull-witted child. "Of course I remember. I just thought, well, that is, thank you for letting me know in advance. Suzette will have to pack."

"You knew that I wanted to be home before the end of June. I've only lingered this long because I felt that the king might need me."

"You're a considerate friend," she answered, wanting to cry, What about me? What about my wishes? Is that really going to be my home or will I live there as a barely tolerated guest? Don't my needs deserve the same care you devote to the king's?

"I feel a certain obligation to be available to him if I can, especially during times like this, when he has problems that involve all our futures."

Something broke inside of Aimée. She turned her head to look at him, and it seemed the intensity of her gaze forced St. Briac to meet her eyes. "Thomas," she whispered finally, "are we going to go on together like this always?"

He blinked and then swallowed almost imperceptibly. "Madame, you spurned me for the last time while we were at Chambord. I won't make love to you again until you tell me that it is your own desire to be my wife in every way for the rest of our lives. I will not be turned aside again."

Before she could answer, St. Briac swung his legs over

the side of the bed. Muscles flexed in his back and firm buttocks as he rummaged through his bureau for shirt, breeches, and hose. Aimée watched him dress, struck dumb by what he had said and what he was doing. Pulling on his boots, St. Briac gave her a look that was unreadable.

"I suddenly find that I'm not tired anymore. *Bon soir*."

Outside, St. Briac took hard, deep breaths of the cool night air. In spite of the exertions of the tournament, new energy surged through his veins. He strode through the high vaulted archways that led to the gardens. Lanterns hung from the chestnut trees that lined the flower beds, bobbing and flashing in the starlit summer wind. At the fountain, Thomas splashed cold water on his face. He retraced his steps and climbed up to the ramparts, three stairs at a time.

Amboise was still. It was growing late, after all. St. Briac stared down at the huddled jumble of blue roofs, thinking that their inhabitants were probably a lot more content than those of the king's chateau. Bracing his arms on the stone barrier of a parapet, he narrowed his eyes pensively at the curving sweep of the Loire. It really was the most bewitching river. Just when one imagined that it was sensuous, kind, and lovable, it would fly into a fearful fit of temper and rage over its banks. Yes, it was surely a feminine river.

Now, however, the water was content, even alluring. A silvery full moon splashed its glistening light over the ripples, and on the far bank a curtain of poplar trees trembled in the breeze.

St. Briac closed his eyes and rubbed one dark hand over them. *Nom de Dieu*, he thought. What does it mean when even my river reminds me of Aimée?

In the morning Aimée awoke to an empty bed. She'd lain awake for the longest time that night, waiting, but must have fallen asleep before St. Briac's return, for his pillow was rumpled. Burying her face in it, Aimée inhaled his clean, intoxicating scent. She tried to sigh but emotion swelled and caught in her breast, refusing to be released.

Suzette helped her mistress bathe and dress, and then they talked over plans for the next day's departure. Finally, after nibbling at a roll and a few slices of orange, Aimée went in search of St. Briac. Outside in the courtyard, a tennis court had been laid out. Her husband was engaged in a spirited match that pitted Florange and him against Bonnivet and Henri de Navarre, Marguerite's suitor. Poor François observed from the gallery, sidelined because of his broken arm.

Aimée watched for a while, conversing with the king. Eventually, when it seemed St. Briac would never notice her presence, she returned to her apartments to supervise Suzette's packing. During the afternoon Gaspard appeared to organize his master's belongings, but there was no sign of St. Briac.

Although Aimée's mood was far from festive, she made up her mind to enjoy the ball that was planned for that evening. There was no telling how long it would be before she and Thomas would visit the court again.

St. Briac still had not made an appearance when Aimée began to dress. She chose a gown of soft, moss-green velvet, its puffed sleeves slashed to reveal creamy satin. The girdle that rode just beneath her waist was filigreed gold, sprinkled with emeralds and pearls, and more emeralds sparkled over her golden crispenette. A diamond necklace added a stunning touch. When Suzette held up a looking glass and exclaimed, "Madame, you'll be the most beautiful woman in the chateau tonight," Aimée had to smile. She did look pretty. Her eyes seemed more brilliantly green than the emeralds, her ebony hair was lustrous, and the curves of her breasts showing above the bodice of her gown looked soft and, she hoped, inviting. Perhaps this would be the night when St. Briac would lose his heart to her.

Finally it was time to go down for supper. Aimée was filled with disappointment. Where could Thomas be? With that woman? Suzette trailed despondently after her mistress, the corners of her mouth drooping in imitation of Aimée's expression. At the door, Aimée reached for the latch. It opened, and Suzette crashed into her mistress's back. She looked up in surprise to discover the seigneur de St. Briac filling the doorway. Aimée was caught between husband and maid.

"*Pardonnez-moi*, ladies." He gave them his usual merry smile, but it seemed distracted somehow.

"Monseigneur, we thought you'd never come," cried Suzette.

Aimée turned and gave her a threatening look. "You may leave us," she said sweetly.

"Oh. *Bien sûr.*" The little maid curtsied to them both. "I'll be going, then. Enjoy the ball." St. Briac stood aside to let her pass, and she couldn't resist a parting remark. "Doesn't madame look glorious? You must be so proud."

"Very," he assured her, amused.

When they were alone, Aimée muttered, "Sometimes I could box that girl's ears."

"I've longed to do the same to Gaspard many times."

She watched him cross the chamber, noting that his boots had mud on them and that his doublet was streaked with dust. "Where have you been all afternoon? I was beginning to worry."

St. Briac glanced at her over one shoulder. "How touching." He arched an eyebrow for emphasis. "I was out riding."

"You might have taken me with you."

"I thought you were packing. Besides, I needed the solitude."

Hot blood rushed to her cheeks. How could he be so relentlessly cruel? What could she ever do to mend things between them? "Well, I'll leave you to your bath, then. Will you be joining us for supper?"

"Yes, in a while." St. Briac watched her go, well aware of the pain in her eyes, and he almost spoke her name. The urge to hold Aimée was overwhelming, but he had to steel himself, just through tonight. For the next few hours St. Briac needed Aimée to stay as far away from him as possible.

The mood of the court was so festive that Aimée almost forgot her despondency. François was especially jovial, for the wild boar he had skewered so heroically the night before was the centerpiece of their supper. The beast had been grilled over the fire on a huge gridiron, larded with foie gras, flamed with fine fats, and doused with the fullest-flavored wines. It was being served in one piece, head and all. Wine flowed freely up and down the boards. Aimée found herself drinking liberally as more and more time passed with no sign of St. Briac.

When at last he did come in, everyone greeted him enthusiastically. His dark, freshly washed chestnut hair gleamed in the torchlight, and he looked especially splendid in a doublet and haut-de-chausses the color of dark Burgundy wine. However, as St. Briac worked his way around the table to his own place next to her, Aimée couldn't help thinking that he seemed preoccupied, that he was going through the motions with his friends, just as he had been doing with less success when the two of them were alone.

"I do hope you'll pardon me, sire," he said, settling down next to his wife.

"What have you been doing all afternoon?" the king asked.

To Aimée's total surprise, St. Briac reached for her hand under the table. When he began to reply to his friend's question, she understood why. "Believe it or not, I've been asleep in our chamber. I suspect I might be a bit ill; I haven't felt like myself since last night." Long, hard fingers squeezed Aimée's delicate ones in warning. "I did want to make an appearance, though, since this will be our final supper with all of you—"

"You and your charming bride must travel to Fontaine-bleu this autumn," François interrupted in a tone of royal command. "I can't hunt without you, Thomas, and that will be the best hunting of the year."

"Well, we'll see." The sight of the king's eyebrows flying up made St. Briac smile. "Probably."

"*Definitely.* I shall be expecting you."

"Barring any unforeseen circumstances, you may do so." A servant brought St. Briac a plate of food and some wine. He made properly impressed comments about the size and ferocious appearance of the boar and then inquired casually, "Where is Chauvergé? He's not so rude as to be late, I hope."

François made a face at his friend's sally and then exchanged barely perceptible glances with Bonnivet, Florange, and even Aimée. She could see that the men had reached the same conclusion she had: Only trouble would come of relating last night's incident to Thomas.

"Chauvergé's left, I think," Florange put in between bites of artichoke.

"Left! Why?"

"Perhaps he didn't feel wanted," the "Young Adventurer" suggested laconically. From across the table, Bonnivet contributed a sage nod.

St. Briac knitted his brows but kept his tone light. "Don't tell me he's finally seen the light."

Everyone laughed, more wine was poured, and the evening wore on. Aimée's mind was in a whirl. They were all telling each other lies, yet her instincts told her that St. Briac, in spite of his nonchalance and innocent manner, knew a great deal more than anyone else about what was going on. The question remained: What *was* going on?

"I do hope," Thomas said as the sweetmeats and strawberries were being served, "that you all will understand if I retire early. I feel a bit of malaise lingering on, and I want to be fit to travel tomorrow."

Aimée's heart sank. "But what about the ball?" she cried impulsively.

He turned to meet her eyes. "You must stay and enjoy it."

"Oh, no, I'll go with you." All she yearned for was his nearness.

Once again St. Briac caught her hand as if they were lovers, and once again the pressure of his fingers warned Aimée to keep silent. "I insist. This may be your last ball for a long time."

She tried valiantly to smile. "If you're certain you don't mind." It was a test of her love to play along with his game, whatever it was, and Aimée hoped he appreciated her efforts on his behalf.

She soon found an excuse to leave. If Thomas was ill, Aimée explained to the king, she should at least spare a moment from her own pleasures to check on him.

Her feet fairly flew down the stone corridors. A guard by the stairway leading to the royal apartments only blinked as she passed, but upon reaching her own door, Aimée found that it would not open.

"Monseigneur is ill. Go away," cried Gaspard when she knocked.

"Open the door, Gaspard. It is I, Madame de St. Briac."

He opened it a few inches and stuck his nose out. "I cannot. Go back to the ball."

"No! I insist that you allow me—" Aimée broke off at the sound of a familiar voice around the corner. Immediately she pushed hard against the door, knocking the little valet off balance, and entered the chamber. "Chauvergé!" she whispered to Gaspard.

She strained to hear what Chauvergé was saying; he sounded a bit breathless as he spoke to the guard. "Tell me something, won't you, m'sieur?"

"*Certainement*, if I can."

"Do you know where the seigneur de St. Briac has gone? I've been looking for him everywhere."

Gaspard groaned when he heard the guard's stuttering reply. "Why, uh, no. That is, he's ill, I think. Yes, that's it! Ill. In his apartments. You won't want to disturb him." Obviously the man was not a skilled liar.

"Is he? I did check there already, but his manservant wouldn't let me in."

"That's because he's ill." The guard was warming to his part.

"Of course. St. Briac has always been a rather frail specimen. You'll excuse my curiosity, but I could have sworn I saw him stealing down the stairs. I followed, hoping to speak to him, but it must have been a mirage, because there was no one there when I reached the bottom." Chauvergé's silky voice was chatty now.

"Well, there couldn't have been because he's in his apartments. Ill, you know."

"I remember. Look here, I seem to have a flask of brandy. Won't you join me?"

"*Merci*, m'sieur. Very kind of you to offer. My bones do begin to ache standing here all night."

There was a long pause, during which Aimée turned and scanned the bed she knew would be empty and then shot Gaspard an accusing glance. What in heaven's name was going on?

Chauvergé spoke up again in a conversational tone. "I've heard that there is a tunnel to Clos-Lucé hidden somewhere in the depths of this chateau that the king had built during the years when Leonardo da Vinci lived there. I know that the king visited him constantly when he was in residence here, and I suppose a tunnel would have made all that much easier. Here, have another drink." He paused, patiently biding his time, while Gaspard let out a smothered moan of worry. "Do you suppose there's any truth to that rumor?"

"Oh yes, m'sieur," the guard affirmed, proud of his knowledge. "We all know about the tunnel. Sometimes the king still uses it just to go over and look at things that great man left behind when he died. Books and sketches, you know. That sort of thing."

"Really! That's very interesting. I'd love to have a look at that tunnel, just out of curiosity. Where is it, exactly?"

The guard's tone changed abruptly. "Oh, I can't tell you that, m'sieur. It's a secret."

Next to Aimée, Gaspard let out his breath in a great whoosh of relief, while back in the corridor Chauvergé's voice turned brittle. "A secret! Ah, well, too bad. I'll bid you good night now. Back to the ball for me."

"Back to the ball?" Aimée whispered incredulously. "What's he talking about? He can't show his face there. Everyone thinks he's gone."

"Chauvergé's not going to any ball. He's bound for Clos-Lucé the usual way. No doubt he's decided that would be equally effective now that he's figured out where monseigneur's gone and how—and probably why!"

"Would you kindly enlighten *me*, then?" Aimée cried in exasperation.

"No time for that, madame. You'll have to go and warn monseigneur. I'd do it, but my old legs won't carry me very fast anymore, and we must beat Chauvergé. That weasel is doubtless running or even riding with all possible speed. The tunnel's much faster, though." Gaspard threw open the door and gave her a quick stare, eyes wide in his wizened face. "Come on."

This was obviously no time to argue. Lifting her velvet skirts, Aimée followed Gaspard past the guard and down three flights of stone steps. On the way, Gaspard paused momentarily to pluck a torch from the wall before hurrying onward. At the bottom he followed a maze of darkened, narrow corridors before pausing in front of a recessed wall made of great rectangular stones. Aimée watched awestruck as the little man reached out with a pale, wrinkled hand to push at a particular spot on a certain stone. A door swung open in front of them.

"Here's the tunnel," Gaspard announced, pointing into blackness. He handed her the torch. "You'll need this. Now you must *hurry*, madame, if you care at all for the fate of my master."

CHAPTER 28

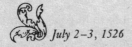 *July 2–3, 1526*

Aimée found herself alone at the top of a narrow series of steps that staggered downward into what appeared to be the bowels of the earth. Gaspard had pushed the wall shut behind her, and the torch provided only the frailest comfort. The air was chilly and damp; she was certain she heard rats scurrying at the sound of her approach. Still, there was nothing to do but obey the command of St. Briac's manservant. If her husband was in danger, Aimée would have braved an army of rats to assist him.

She managed to lift her gown and petticoat high with her free hand, throwing them over her arm and holding them fast with tense fingers. In the next instant she hurried down the stairs, under a brick archway, and into the tunnel. The floor was dirt, as were the walls; only the supporting stones above hinted of civilization. Holding the torch aloft, Aimée could see no farther than the next step she would take, yet she ran on as if her life depended on it. Her lungs began to burn and her legs to ache before she finally came panting to another flight of steps.

Spider webs tangled in Aimée's face as she started toward what she hoped would be a door. Gaspard had said nothing about another secret entrance. What if she couldn't get in?

At the top of the stairs there was a wooden portal but no

latch. Tears stung Aimée's eyes. "Thomas!" It was almost a shriek. "*Thomas*, let me in! It's Aimée!"

To her astonishment, the door swung open immediately, and St. Briac loomed above her, silhouetted against a cozy candlelit background.

"Aimée, what are you doing here?" His handsome face was incredulous as he took the torch in one hand and wrapped his other arm around her trembling form.

She wanted to burst into tears, but swallowed them all and managed to gasp, "It's Chauvergé. He's coming. He tried to find the way to the tunnel when he guessed where you'd gone, but then he left, and Gaspard is certain he's coming on the road."

An attractive, earnest-looking young man rose behind a table in the middle of what must have been Leonardo da Vinci's bedchamber. A massive bed hung with red velvet stood against the far wall, and beside it hung Leonardo's painting of St. John the Baptist.

"Aimée, this is Georges Teverant. Georges, allow me to present my wife." St. Briac held her close against him.

They recognized each other from the hunting lodge at Nieuil. Teverant thought back to his friend's reaction that night to the sparkling, winsome maiden. So this was the new bride everyone was talking about! Teverant smiled; he would have enjoyed hearing about what happened between Nieuil, when St. Briac had declared that the girl was to marry someone else, and their own wedding.

"*Bon soir*, m'sieur," Aimée was saying. "I have heard a great deal about you. But now you must hide before Chauvergé arrives!"

"It is a pleasure to meet you, too, madame. It makes me very happy to see my good and faithful friend wed to such a splendid woman."

"Enough charm, Georges." St. Briac laughed. "Let's put you in the tunnel until this business with Chauvergé is taken care of."

Teverant went obediently, accepting the torch that Aimée had brought. When the door swung closed behind him, she saw that it blended perfectly with the carved linenfold wainscoting.

"I thought Chauvergé had left," St. Briac hissed when they were alone.

"Apparently not. He's been lurking about, watching you, I think."

"Damn, then he may have seen Teverant this afternoon." Muscles clenched in his jaw. "I'm beginning to wish I had killed him during the tournament. It wouldn't have been terribly difficult."

"Thomas, what are you going to say when he finds me here? Shouldn't I join M'sieur Teverant in the tunnel? Why don't we all just go?"

"If Chauvergé is on his way here, he's seen the lights by now." St. Briac crossed the room and took some books from a chest beside the bed. "I've no intention of running from him like a scared rabbit. I'll merely say that I was feeling better and you persuaded me to show you Clos-Lucé before our departure from Amboise." He opened the books across the table. "Come over here and sit down, my brave *miette*, and try to look interested in these notes and sketches in Leonardo's own hand."

At any other time she would have devoured such treasures, but no sooner had she seated herself than the outer door burst open and Chauvergé fairly jumped across the threshold.

St. Briac was standing behind Aimée's chair, leaning forward as if pointing out something in one of the books. He straightened unhurriedly and arched an eyebrow at the intruder.

The scene was ended in less than a minute. St. Briac made his explanation without a telltale blink, and the other man had no choice but to accept it. Even Aimée offered some sharp parting words before Chauvergé stormed away.

"I heard that you had already left Amboise, m'sieur. Perhaps the king will be interested to learn that you are still about."

His face twitched as he glared at her. Then, spinning on a spade-shaped shoe, Chauvergé was gone. When the door had slammed shut behind him, Aimée stood impulsively and leaned against her husband's wide chest.

"How I detest that man."

St. Briac allowed himself to gather her into his embrace, and the same wave of emotion washed over them both. Just the feel of his body enfolding hers made Aimée's senses reel.

"I feel the same way, but keep in mind that he is no threat

to us, only a nuisance. I don't mean to sound vain, but I could outwit Chauvergé in my sleep."

Aimée was certain that was true, yet there was always the possibility of an unexpected move on Chauvergé's part and the element of his venomous hatred for St. Briac.

"Can we leave now?" she sighed at last. She hated to let go of him now that she finally was back in his arms.

"I'm sorry to say it, but I shall have to stay here and finish my conversation with Teverant. I can't explain right now, but I must do what I can to help him. He's not used to the tactics of people like Chauvergé and Louise de Savoy and needs me for a bit of advice. They've scared the poor fellow to death."

"Of course. I understand." Aimée gave him a valiant smile, thinking at the same time of the return walk down the cold, wet, dark tunnel alone.

The last person Aimée needed to encounter was Ghislaine Pepin, but she nearly bumped into her, rounding the corner to her bedchamber.

"I'm sorry," exclaimed Ghislaine with a friendly smile. "I must not have been watching where I was going."

"*Mais, non*, madame," Aimée returned coolly. "I was at fault."

"Well, there was no damage done. We'll compromise and excuse each other."

Aimée glared at the woman whose calm beauty, wit, and poise had won St. Briac's heart. She was certain he had gone to the duchess last night when he left their bed, but those thoughts were too painful to entertain for more than a moment. Ghislaine Pepin had a husband of her own; why couldn't she leave Aimée's in peace?

"I'm very tired. *Bon soir*, madame."

The duchesse de Roanne laid a gentle hand on Aimée's arm. "Wait, please. I wish that you would not hate me. I think that perhaps you misunderstand a great deal."

"Do I?" Leaf-green eyes flashed in the candlelit hallway.

"I bear you no animosity. I think it is wonderful that Thomas has found a wife."

"As long as that wife is young and stupid enough to tolerate his mistress?"

Ghislaine started to gasp but then closed her mouth and regarded Aimée for a long moment. She smiled slightly. "You are foolish as well, madame, if you know your husband so little. He is devoted to his marriage now. The reason Thomas was hesitant to wed was that he had grown cynical after observing the activities among husbands and wives and their lovers at court. His heart is as fair, strong, and true as the rest of him; when he married you, he made you a gift of it. Betrayal would not enter his mind."

Bewilderment, joy, and suspicion struggled inside Aimée. Could she believe what this woman said, or was this some sort of ploy? "You obviously do not understand what kind of marriage Thomas and I have. He didn't wed me by choice."

"Of course he did!" Ghislaine laughed. "How silly you are. He may have needed a little nudge in the right direction, but he wanted to be your husband as much as you yearned to be his wife. The man's in love with you, *chérie!*"

Aimée blinked. There was a huge lump in her throat. "Has he told you this?"

"He didn't need to, and I certainly shouldn't need to tell you. It's been obvious to everyone, even the king, since you first arrived at Blois. Believe me, I would not have let Thomas go so easily if I hadn't known you were the right woman for him."

"*Parbleu.* I'm so ashamed when I think of the mean thoughts I've had about you, madame."

The duchess smiled and touched Aimée's cheek. "I love Thomas, too. I always will. And because I love him, I want him to be happy. Let me tell you something else that should gladden your heart, *chérie*, and help explain how I knew you were the one even before he did. Thomas and I haven't slept together since the two of you arrived at Blois. He didn't realize it, but he was in love with you even then." She paused and put up a hand to smooth back a toffee-hued curl, her blue eyes wistful.

"You are very generous to tell me these things, madame."

"Everything that's happened has been for the best, for all of us. When I realized Thomas would never make love to me again, I took a page from his book and examined my own marriage. I've decided his way was the best. Marcel and I are discovering how much we really love each other, and that love is making me happier, in a deep sense, than I've ever been."

"How wonderful for you." Aimée smiled. She wanted to throw her arms around the duchess.

"You'd better have a bath, *chérie*, and wash those spider webs from your hair before Thomas returns. He wouldn't like them in his bed." Ghislaine kissed her lightly on the cheek, smiled, and then turned to leave. "Trust him, Aimée."

It was the middle of the night. Silvery blue moonbeams poured through the arched window and drenched the bed where Aimée lay on her back, sound asleep. Nearby stood St. Briac, staring down at her as he unlaced his doublet.

One of her slender arms was flung upward over her head, tangled in flowing ebony tresses. The silken sheet barely concealed her pert nipples as they swelled with each breath. Exhausted though he was, St. Briac ached anew at the sight of her. His garments shed and folded away, he slipped carefully into bed and rose on an elbow to study his wife's beauty. He had known dozens of lovely women in his life, but only Aimée had ever affected him this way, like a sorcerer's spell that he was powerless to resist, one minute the fount of impossible bliss, the next an agony of yearning.

Aimée stirred in her sleep and rolled in St. Briac's direction. Her fingertips brushed his chest, burning him. Walls of resistance collapsed in quick succession within St. Briac and he was flooded by waves of relief, irresistible desire, and love that would not be denied an instant longer. For the first time in his life, he greeted surrender. There was no world outside of Aimée. Relaxing his arm, he lowered his head to the pillow and waited, his heart pounding as if this were his first time near a woman. Aimée's nose nudged his bicep. He felt the sweep of her thick lashes near his shoulder.

His love for her was wedded with physical desire that approached pain. Unable to bear another moment of such agony, St. Briac gently slid his free hand around her tiny waist, and his fingers curved over the swell of Aimée's hip. Spring-green eyes opened, staring up at him with liquid love and yearning that mirrored his own.

At first Aimée thought she must be dreaming, but every sensation was too acute. Her breath came in little gasps as she contemplated St. Briac's fingers on her bare hip, the strength of the warm body turned toward her own, waiting, and most of all, the unmistakable light that gleamed in the depths of his eyes. Words, poised on her lips for what seemed an eternity, rushed out.

"Oh, Thomas, I am so sorry." Tears blurred her vision,

and she blinked them back, wanting to memorize the tenderness of his chiseled face. "I've been a fool."

St. Briac's strong hand moved upward to caress her back. "I wouldn't go that far, *miette*." He smiled. "Forget about it. Forget about everything except the two of us."

"But—"

"You don't need to speak. I know."

When his mouth came down to capture her own, Aimée thought she would die, so poignantly exquisite was her pleasure. They kissed and kissed, rediscovering the tastes and textures each loved best in the world. St. Briac did not hurry toward complete fulfillment, instead allowing them to experience each delicious sensation in the knowledge that the final ones would be all the sweeter. When his lips and tongue explored her delicate ear, Aimée whispered, her voice near a sob, "I've missed you so!"

"Mmm. No more than I've missed you, *miette*." Her skin was velvety against his hard body, her hair like silk; her fresh violet fragrance reminded him of lying in a meadow at the peak of springtime. As he kissed her nape and shoulders and throat and finally her breasts, her hands wandered over every inch of him she could reach. She gloried in the lean, muscular form so different from her own. St. Briac's body was the half that made her whole. She had been starving without him.

He was kissing her nipples slowly and sensuously, and Aimée felt the tension build between her thighs. So much desire had accumulated within her since Chambord that her arousal now almost hurt, yet pleasurably so. When at last St. Briac moved to trail his mouth over her hips, belly, and derrière and lingered over the backs of her knees, Aimée moaned aloud. They were kissing again, and she explored the breadth of his shoulders with her fingertips and then the hard curves of his chest, her slim fingers running through its soft mat of hair. She traced the ridges of his belly wonderingly and felt the long muscles in St. Briac's thighs before finally grazing his manhood.

"*Sang de Dieu!*" He choked. "You are asking for trouble."

"I suppose I am." She laughed softly. His hand had long ago parted her legs to touch and tease her. "Fair play, Thomas."

They continued their love play, enjoying each moment of pleasure and anticipation. When at last he pressed Aimée

back into the pillows, she could hardly wait to feel him inside
her. Their eyes met, and he framed her piquant face with
dark hands, kissing her deeply. She wrapped her arms around
the wide span of his back, nearly overcome with love that
she still couldn't bring herself to voice. Even the wise Ghislaine might be wrong, after all, and Aimée would not chance
spoiling the perfection of this night.

Easily, St. Briac found his way into her and paused, savoring the sensation of Aimée's moist, warm tautness surrounding him. She was less patient, however, and arched
her slim hips upward to meet his so that they were totally
united. St. Briac gasped and then slid his hands down to cup
her buttocks, feeling her legs twine about his own. As they
moved together, their rhythm was that of the perfect, ulti-
mate embrace. Each found a shuddering, exquisite release
that was all the more blissful because of the sharing.

Afterward, St. Briac felt more drained than he ever had
after a battle or tournament. Aimée was shivering against
him, and he held her close, his heart overflowing.

"Ah, *miette*, how desperately I love you," he whispered
into the cloud of her hair.

Aimée's heart thudded crazily. She couldn't believe her
ears, but she lay against his chest and heard his own heart-
beat tell her that it was true. This time she didn't swallow
her tears. She wept and pulled St. Briac's head down and
kissed him joyfully.

"Oh, Thomas, *I love you!*"

PART IV

Give place you ladies, and be gone,
Boast not yourselves at all,
For here at hand approacheth one,
Whose face will stain you all.

If all the world were sought so far,
Who could find such a wight?
Her beauty twinkleth like a star
Within the frosty night.

Her rosial colour comes and goes
With such a comely grace,
More readier too than doth the rose
Within her lively face.

Truly she doth as far exceed
Our women nowadays,
As doth the gillyflower a weed,
And more, a thousand
ways . . .

JOHN HEYWOOD
(c. 1497–c. 1580)

CHAPTER 29

 Château du Soleil
St. Briac-sur-Loire, France •
August 16, 1526

Fanchette Mardouet stood at one of the long windows of the tapestry-hung gallery, munching on a crust of the baguette she had removed from the oven just minutes before. When a few crumbs dropped to the floor, which was laid out in squares of magnificent black and white marble, she stooped to pick them up and then deposited them in a pocket of her apron.

A coach had drawn up to the gatehouse, far away from the chateau at the foot of a long sloping drive. Visitors? No one in the village of St. Briac owned so fine a carriage, nor did Fanchette recognize it as belonging to any of their aristocratic neighbors along the Loire. "Christophe?" She raised her voice. *"Venez-ici, maintenant!"*

The boy, all of fourteen and feeling like a man, did not need to be told twice. His aunt was the kindest, most fun-loving woman he knew (except perhaps Aimée), but since his birth her command had been law. Even Christophe's brother, who had ridden many times into battle beside the king of France, obeyed Fanchette's raised voice.

Christophe clattered down the curving stairway and hurried into the long gallery, all legs since his most recent spurt of growth. He was nearly six feet tall, but his shoulders and chest were those of a boy. He'd been feeling especially puny since Thomas's return to Chateau du Soleil.

"Here I am, Tante Fanchette. What may I do?"

"There's a coach at the gatehouse that I don't recognize. Do you know where Thomas and Aimée have gone?"

"They were out riding earlier, but I think I heard him say there was something to be done in the vineyards." Christophe's mouth turned down slightly. "I don't understand why Aimée must spend so much time outside. Aren't wives supposed to stay in the house?"

"Aren't growing boys supposed to be outside themselves?" Fanchette retorted a trifle sharply. "Books are all well and good, but you'll never look like your brother if you don't exercise your muscles."

As usual, his aunt had gone right to the root of the matter. Christophe blushed.

"Well, this is your chance. I want you to find those two and bring them home. Perhaps this visitor is a friend of theirs."

At that moment Thomas and Aimée were seated side by side on a bench in one of the chateau's wine caves that opened into the white chalk of the Loire hillside. The cave was enormous, filled with casks and barrels and pleasantly cool and damp on this sultry August afternoon.

"Well?" queried St. Briac. "What do you think?"

She peered at the wine in her cup. "I'm not certain. Let me try again." Her green eyes dancing at him over the rim, she tipped the cup and drained it. "Very good. Very, *very* good."

"I'm so relieved that you approve." He gazed at her with fond delight, and Aimée basked in the warmth of his eyes. It was a look St. Briac wore often these days, usually when she wasn't watching. The joy of life with Aimée was almost more than he could believe. She was a miracle of charming high spirits, brimming with love for him, and the most beautiful, enchanting woman God had ever created. Whenever he looked at her, it was impossible to keep his eyes from crinkling at the corners.

Putting her tiny feet beside his on the stool in front of

them, Aimée beamed. "Aren't you going to offer me some
more wine? I'd like something red."

St. Briac merely lifted a brow at her and then went to a
new barrel, where he poured her third cupful of wine plus
another for himself. The afternoon had wicked possibilities.

Taking the cup proffered by her husband, Aimée waited
until he sat down; then she snuggled near, put her arm through
his, and rested her hand on his thigh. St. Briac glanced over
at her in amusement. Clad in a gown of pale yellow muslin,
with a garland of daisies and buttercups somewhat askew
on her tumbled black curls, Aimée was the picture of a
meadow nymph.

"This was a very good idea you had, Thomas," she announced. "Tasting the wine, I mean. It's important that I
understand the subtleties of each one, don't you think?"
Taking a generous sip of the red wine that, like those from
Chinon, tasted faintly of violets, she added, "We should do
this more often."

"You are enjoying yourself?" St. Briac asked wryly.

"Immensely."

"Well, you know, this is supposed to be a very serious
matter."

"Oh. Yes, I suppose so." She widened her lovely black-
lashed eyes at him and attempted to look properly grave.
Slowly Aimée lifted her cup and sipped carefully, rolling the
wine around her tongue. At length she swallowed and then
nodded. "Ah, yes, this is excellent. A gentle wine. Reminiscent of the Loire itself, I think."

St. Briac put his head back and laughed in delight. "That's
enough."

Her hand drifted over his thigh, and she propped her chin
on the hard curve of his shoulder. "I love the way you look,
Thomas."

"I'm glad to hear it." He smiled, and his eyes filled with
affectionate amusement. "I've been a bit worried about that."

Aimée wrinkled her nose at him. "There's not another
man at court who wears a beard as well as you do. Not even
the king."

"None of us would have beards if it weren't for François.
You've heard the story of that beard, haven't you?"

"No, tell me."

"It was January 1521, and a group of us were in Romo-
rantin. The king declared that we should stage a mock battle,

using snowballs, against the Comte de Saint-Pol. We'd all drunk far too much that night, so it seemed a worthy project, and we set out for the comte's chateau. The battle ensued. The people in the chateau struck back with apples, pears, and eggs, but someone got carried away and dropped part of a log from the fireplace. It struck François on the side of the head and rendered him unconscious."

Aimée gasped. "How terrible. But obviously he recovered."

"Slowly. It took two months before he was completely restored. The physicians had to cut his hair to tend the wounds, and there was a long scar on the side of his face as well. The king grew a beard to cover it, so of course we all grew beards, too. Soon Britain and all of Europe followed suit."

"How incredible that one man could affect fashion so completely."

"Not just any man, *miette*, but our own François."

"We're fortunate to be his friends, aren't we?" Aimée took another sip of wine.

"I believe so."

"I must be the most fortunate woman in the entire world," she exclaimed suddenly. "Not only is the king of France my friend, but I am married to *you*. You're even more compelling than he is, Thomas. Handsomer, too."

"You've had too much wine," laughed St. Briac.

"I'm just in love," she sighed, and then put her cup aside and moved over to his lap. St. Briac's thighs were like steel beneath her. "I could drown in you and die happily."

"Don't be silly," he whispered before reaching up with both hands to bring her face close to his. They stared at each other for a long minute and then kissed sensuously, luxuriously.

Just the feeling of St. Briac's strong, elegant fingers laced through her hair sent shivers of desire down Aimée's spine. She wrapped her arms around him and caressed his crisp hair, loving especially the curls behind his ears and along the back of his neck. She pressed her ripe breasts against the flat breadth of St. Briac's chest and sighed into his mouth.

"Ah-*hem*!" Christophe tried to clear his throat with authority, but his voice cracked. It was the first time he had ever seen his brother kiss Aimée this way, and he could scarcely believe his eyes. Was Thomas forcing her?

Aimée scrambled quickly to her feet and smoothed her skirts. Behind her, St. Briac rose unhurriedly, one side of his mouth curving upward at the sight of the blush that stained his wife's cheeks.

"I hope this is important, Christophe," he said. "You know, it's not really necessary for you to announce yourself every time you happen upon Aimée and me. In this case, we wouldn't have minded if you had made a silent retreat."

"Oh, really?" the boy shouted. Then, realizing how ridiculous he sounded, he continued in a slightly less strident tone. "It just so happens that Tante Fanchette sent me to fetch you. A coach that she doesn't recognize arrived at the gatehouse, and whoever was inside has probably been in the chateau for hours by now. I've been looking for you everywhere."

"We were tasting wine," Aimée explained, her composure returning.

"Oh, really?" Christophe repeated sarcastically.

"*Mon frère*," said St. Briac in a carefully even tone, "I must remind you that I am the older of the two of us. Considerably older, in fact."

"I know that." His voice cracked again.

"I'm glad to hear it. Your behavior would suggest otherwise." St. Briac lifted an eyebrow, but there was no trace of amusement in his blue-green gaze. "Shall we go?"

Christophe rushed on ahead of them and ran all the way back to the chateau. Once out in the sunshine, alone again with her husband, Aimée's mischievous mood surfaced. She took hold of St. Briac's arm with both hands and smiled up at him.

"Don't let Christophe spoil our enjoyment of this afternoon. He's just a boy, and he's terribly envious of you for being a man, especially such a splendid one. No doubt he's afraid he'll never measure up."

St. Briac bent to kiss her, but his eyes remained narrowed as he watched the gangly retreating figure of his brother. "You're right about one thing, *miette*. Christophe envies me, but not because I'm a man—at least that's not the main reason. It's not my age or my body or my mind he dreams of possessing—it's *you*."

Aimée opened her mouth to protest and then closed it. No longer was there any pretense between her and Thomas, and she was not about to allow a boy of fourteen to create that barrier between them again. From the first moment she and Christophe had met in early July, his adoration had been apparent. Still, it seemed a harmless thing. Aimée was glad that Thomas's family cared so much for her, and there was something rather sweet about Christophe's protective attitude.

"You must not be so dramatic about this, Thomas," she told him gently. "He's but a youth, filled with longings he cannot understand or satisfy. After years alone with Tante Fanchette, what could you expect when a young woman came to live in his home?"

"You just passed your nineteenth birthday last week," St. Briac reminded her. "You're barely five years older than Christophe. Not only that, you are a great deal more than a young woman. You're captivating." The last was stated plainly, as a fact. Aimée chose to ignore it.

"There is a huge difference between Christophe's age and mine, and well you know it. At my age a girl is a woman, but a boy is not yet a man."

"I am fully aware of that, Aimée, but that does not mean that my dear brother realizes how wide a gulf he has yet to cross. No doubt Christophe feels he has more right to your favors than I, since I am well on my way to being elderly."

She cuffed at his chest as they walked up the lush, sloping hill. "Stop this. You are being ridiculous."

"I wish I were," St. Briac said pensively. "I remember what it was like to be fourteen so well that I can read Christophe's mind. His thoughts would not bother me so much if they were not about my wife."

"Were you really fourteen once?" Aimée inquired with an irrepressible grin. "Barefaced, callow, and without a hair on your chest? I don't believe it!"

St. Briac had to laugh. Taking her cue, he let the subject rest.

The chateau loomed ahead of them. It was the most romantic castle Aimée had ever seen. Built of white, evenly matched stones and topped with lacy pinnacles, soaring rooftops, and lofty chimneys, it seemed to exemplify the Renaissance. Terraced gardens led downward toward the Loire, laid out with flower beds and trees that bore oranges, *bon chrétian* pears, and peaches. Behind and off to the sides almost as far as the eye could see spread thousands of rows of grapevines curled about their trellises. All this beauty was set against a background of the dark and mysterious forest of Chinon.

St. Briac's arm encircled Aimée's waist as they climbed the steps from one of the garden tiers that would bring them into the open courtyard of the chateau. Once the dwelling had been closed off in the protective, medieval tradition, but Thomas had razed the north wing to provide a view of the Loire and the entry of sunlight into the chateau. The several machicolated towers were only for decoration now; no one attacked Chateau du Soleil anymore.

Aimée had felt at home instantly. Seeing St. Briac with his family, at work in the vineyards, and mingling with the people of the village that lay below and off to one side of the chateau, she knew what he had meant back at Nieuil when he said that all he needed was this. His friendship with the king was important to him, and court life was diverting, but this was the center of St. Briac's life. And now Aimée could share it with him.

They went in through the doorway to the east wing, passing under the sun that had been carved into the white stone. Behind the gallery was the great hall, where Fanchette came to meet them now.

"Thomas, Aimée, at last. We thought you would never arrive. Look who is here."

Seated in a carved chair near the fireplace, the blond and flawlessly beautiful Honorine de Fleurance smiled at them in greeting.

CHAPTER 30

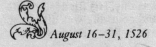 *August 16–31, 1526*

One of the best surprises Aimée had received upon arriving at Chateau du Soleil had been Marie Lissieu. After their marriage, St. Briac had quietly arranged for the old woman to be sent to his home to be near Aimée. Aimée saw this unselfish gesture as another expression of the love he had not yet been able to voice, just as his earlier gift of her horse, Mignonne, had been. He still harbored no fondness for Marie but allowed his wife her own point of view. He had given Aimée what she wanted before she even asked.

In early August, Suzette and her squire, Paul, had been married. Paul was now Aimée's squire, courtesy of another generous man, François I. The newlyweds had traveled back to Nieuil to visit relatives, and Marie Lissieu was playing maid until Suzette's return.

The night of Honorine's surprise appearance, the old woman scurried about their bedchamber, seeing to Aimée's bath and clothing. St. Briac occupied a massive carved chair near the window, a book open in his lap as he pretended to read while his irritation grew. Finally, as if sensing the hostility from a corner of the chamber, Marie declared that she was finished and bade them good night. In the doorway she collided with Gaspard LeFait.

"Didn't anyone ever teach you to knock?"

Gaspard drew himself up, eying the woman with disdain. In spite of her clean clothes and neat hair, Marie still retained vestiges of the person St. Briac had called a hag. "*Pardonnez-moi*, madame."

Marie sniffed and edged past him. Shutting the door, the manservant sought St. Briac and exclaimed, "How can you tolerate that woman's presence?"

"Aimée likes her." He shrugged. "There's no accounting for tastes. She likes me as well."

"I've a letter for you, monseigneur. It looks important." Gaspard raised his thick gray eyebrows meaningfully.

St. Briac accepted the folded piece of parchment and then lay a finger over his lips and lifted it to point toward the *étuve*, where Aimée was having a bath. Opening the letter, he scanned it, his brow gathering.

"Gaspard," he said softly, "you'll have to go to Paris on an errand for me. Teverant's been imprisoned. Learn what you can, and if there's any danger of his being executed, I must know immediately."

"*Oui*, monseigneur. I'll leave at dawn."

When his valet had gone, St. Briac leaned back in the chair and pressed his fingers to his eyes. Chauvergé's absence from court had seemed to bode well for the fate of Georges Teverant, but now it appeared that Louise de Savoy was a worse threat on her own. François knew enough to distrust Chauvergé, but how could he suspect his own mother? Complicating the matter were all the problems of real consequence that the king was dealing with these days. Louise could have put a paper before him, asking him to sign it, and a preoccupied François might have done so without so much as a glance.

"Thomas," Aimée called gaily from her bath, "come and talk to me."

St. Briac shook his head as if to send worry spinning away. There was no point brooding about Georges Teverant until Gaspard returned with the news. Something probably would have to be done, but not tonight. The sound of his wife's voice always made him smile, and even now he was powerless to resist her magic. Shedding his clothes, St. Briac went into the *étuve*.

"*Talk* to you, *miette?*" he greeted her. "I'll do better than that."

Aimée laughed with delight at the sight of his magnificent

naked body. The large *cuvé* had plenty of room for both of them. She drew up her knees as he settled into the hot water and lifted his brows at her.

"I fear I'll smell of violets after this."

"It won't be the first time, *mon ange*," she countered sweetly.

With a devilish grin he reached into the water for the soap, touching her intimately in the process. Aimée pretended to be shocked. "Bathing is a very serious matter, Thomas. Possibly even more serious than tasting wine. I must demand that you show the proper respect for cleansing your body."

Laughter rose from deep in his chest. "I'd rather not."

Aimée's long ebony curls were pinned up, and she leaned back now, her neck against the rim of the *cuvé*. One graceful leg came up to push at St. Briac's chest. "What do you think of Honorine?"

He caught her slim foot in his hand and began to nibble on her toes. "I'm not sure. She's not at all like you, is she?"

"Absolutely not. Stop that. It tickles." Reclaiming her foot, Aimée persisted. "Did you notice her watching us all evening? That, combined with her speeches about how much I have hurt our parents with my behavior, makes me very uneasy."

"I'm certain that it was I who fascinated Honorine, *miette*. No doubt she is consumed by lust."

"I wouldn't joke about that if I were you," Aimée scolded. "You may well be right. I saw the way she fawned over you that first night at Nieuil, and I cannot believe that Honorine has come here out of sisterly love. I know her too well."

St. Briac was soaping his body, one eye on his wife. "Perhaps you are overreacting, Aimée. All Honorine may want is an *entrée* into the court of François."

"I don't like her pleasant demeanor, though. She *must* resent me for taking her place when she had the chance to join the court in April. Now I've not only done all that she might have done, but I'm married to the seigneur de St. Briac."

"Yes, you are," he replied agreeably, his fingers caressing the slender curves of her legs under the water.

"Don't you see, Honorine must be filled with jealousy, probably even hatred."

"Should I try to reassure her?" St. Briac inquired innocently.

"You are too outrageous, Thomas. I don't know why I even try to carry on a conversation with you."

By now his hands were cupping her full, wet breasts, and he felt the nipples pucker against his palms. "Neither do I, *ma chérie.*" He smiled. They slid together, legs intertwined, and kissed. St. Briac's mouth dipped down to find the rosy peak of Aimée's breast, and under the water she felt him harden fully against her thigh.

Later, in the huge four-poster bed with its draped hangings of dark blue velvet that contrasted so strikingly with the white stone walls, Aimée cuddled against her husband's chest and released a sigh of contentment.

"Oh, well, it will all work out somehow. I'm going to share *petit déjeuner* with Honorine tomorrow morning, so perhaps we can clear the air then. Why don't you take Christophe on some manly errand so she and I can be alone."

"*Certainement, miette,*" he replied. "Should he and I clear the air as well?"

"Thomas, you must forget about that. As you said today, you were once fourteen. He can't help it if his emotions have outgrown his age at this moment."

St. Briac sighed. "Consider, Aimée. My brother is lying alone in his bed as we speak, probably dreaming about you. Tonight, each time I touched you, he glared at me as if I were committing an unpardonable sin. How can I forget about it? Will this go on for years?"

"Of course not! Soon Christophe will find a girl his own age to moon over, and then I will seem as elderly as you imagine yourself to be."

He gathered her close, inhaling her fresh, clean fragrance. "You are probably right. I'll give him some time. We must both be patient with our siblings, *n'est-ce pas?*"

Aimée nodded agreement against his neck. She murmured, "Aren't you going to tell me about the letter Gaspard brought you tonight?"

"Your ears are very large, *miette!*"

"I only overheard by accident, but I did expect that you would confide in me."

"I cannot. Not because I don't love and trust you but because you have the most unnerving habit of becoming embroiled in any situation that holds even a hint of danger.

I appreciate all the help you have given me in the past, but now I want you safe. Keeping you ignorant would appear to be the only way to protect you."

"Oh, unfair," Aimée cried, pushing herself away from him. "What about *my* concern for *your* safety?"

"At this point there's no reason for concern. I'm staying right here with you and allowing Gaspard to discover what, if anything, needs to be done. In any event, I can take care of myself, but I wouldn't want to have to worry about taking care of both of us."

"You underestimate me, Thomas. I have taken care of myself ever since leaving Nieuil, haven't I?"

"Oh yes, of course. How could I have forgotten?" St. Briac said sarcastically.

"All right, you may have helped a bit," Aimée allowed, and then stared at him for a while in the shadows. "This is about Georges Teverant again, isn't it?"

"Perhaps."

Realizing that he would never tell her if she pressed him, Aimée relented. "Keep your little secret, then. I don't mind."

St. Briac rose on an elbow and looked down at his wife. She was lying on her back on her side of the bed, arms folded over her breasts. He had to smile. "I'm not trying to deceive you, my darling. For now, please trust me."

"Well, I'll try."

"Aren't you going to kiss me good night?" He ran his hand over the silken sheet, caressing downward from Aimée's breast to her thigh.

"I shouldn't," she declared, and then turned into her husband's strong embrace.

In the morning Aimée walked down the wide curving staircase that led into the gallery. She loved that room with its row of windows that opened onto the courtyard and the coffered ceiling painted in blue, red, and gold. Fanchette met her at the doorway to the great hall.

"Your sister's waiting for you, Aimée," she told her.

"Merci, chère tante." Aimée turned to her sister. "Have you been up long?" she asked. "I'm sorry if I've kept you waiting."

Honorine gave her a ladylike smile. "I didn't mind. I've been looking around your new home."

"Have you!" Aimée took in her gown of pale blue silk set

off by slashings, embroidered sapphires, and lace trimming. Her own garb was vastly more elegant than it had been at Nieuil, but she still could not match her sister and was glad of it.

Servants brought goblets of cider from Normandy and a platter of cheeses, golden apricots, mirabelle plums, sliced peaches, and small prune tarts. Honorine selected a sliver of creamy goat cheese and an apricot.

"Where is your handsome husband this morning?" she inquired.

Instantly on guard like a lioness, Aimée still did not betray her tension. "He and Christophe have gone hunting, I believe." She tried to chew a bite of tart.

"I must say, we were all so surprised to hear of your marriage. Maman and Papa were aghast. It might not have been so shocking if the bridegroom had been anyone except the seigneur de St. Briac. However did you manage it?"

"I didn't manage it at all, Honorine. We fell in love. How did the family learn that I had wed?"

"Well, the bishop d'Angoulême came straight to us after he left Chambord. Then we had another visitor, who suggested that I should come to see you. He said he knew your husband and was certain that you had plenty of room."

"Indeed? What was this gentleman's name?"

Honorine blanched. "I, I am not certain. M'sieur—ah, Camaret, I think. He said he knew you both."

Arching delicate brows, Aimée responded, "I've never heard of the man, but of course we are glad that you've come. I was just about to write and extend an invitation to you and our parents."

"It's kind of you to think of them, but I suspect that they are far too upset to see you now."

"I'm not sure I understand. Even though I did not wed Armand Rovicette, I have made a marriage that is far more advantageous from our parents' point of view. I would think they'd be ecstatic. They need not worry about money for the rest of their lives."

"That's true, though I'm certain they have not gotten around to considering that aspect of your marriage. They are still too hurt over what you did to all of us by leaving the way you did." Honorine widened her blue eyes to demonstrate her own lingering pain.

Old feelings rushed over Aimée. She wanted to lean forward and slap her sister. Instead, she looked down at her dish and murmured, "I'm sorry to hear that, but perhaps when they learn of my great happiness, they will change their minds."

"That is possible, I suppose," Honorine replied. "Oh, I almost forgot, Maman and Papa sent you letters." She reached over to pluck two pieces of parchment from a nearby table, both folded and sealed with wax.

"Why didn't you give them to me before?"

"I forgot. There were other things on my mind."

Aimée was almost too irritated to reply, but she managed a few cool words of parting before taking the letters and retreating to her chamber. She opened the one from her mother first. It held no surprises. Éloise minced no words in telling Aimée just how great a disappointment she was as a daughter. Every wound she had inflicted on her parents and sister was listed. She ended with:

> I doubt whether you can ever make amends to us, and no doubt now that you have everything that we do not, you will forget that your family even exists. I can only pray that you will discover some spark of selflessness in your soul and try to help your poor sister. I don't expect you to worry about me or my feelings. You never did in the past!
> Your Mother

Anger and guilt swirled together within Aimée. The latter she fought, for she knew Éloise had hoped to fill her with remorse. She told herself that she would rise above her mother's petty efforts at manipulation. She would be gracious and invite her parents to St. Briac, take them to court, and make them proud of her. Smiling to herself, Aimée reached for her father's letter. It pleased her to realize that Thomas's love had strengthened her self-esteem to the point where even her mother could not threaten it more than momentarily. Turning her attention to Gilles's few, plain sentences, Aimée read:

> Ma chère fille,
> I write this without your mother's knowledge. I had to tell you that I love you as ever and am pleased that you took command of your own future. I was

*impressed by St. Briac and, in spite of rumors that
would suggest otherwise, feel that your life with him
will be a happy one.*

*Do not let your mother upset you, but I do urge
caution with Honorine. She is bitter, Aimée, and I
worry about her reasons for this visit. You would
be wise to find her a husband to turn her attention
to.*

I miss you, ma petite, *and keep you in my prayers.*

Papa

Tears stung Aimée's eyes and splashed onto the parchment.

August ended in a burst of sultry heat. Aimée found herself beset by a strange illness that would not end. Her appetite had virtually disappeared, replaced by an urge to vomit
at the sight of even the most tempting dishes. However, she
experienced intermittent cravings for foods that the cook
was unable to produce. The heat drove her mad, and she
wanted only to sleep. Most alarming from St. Briac's point
of view was her occasional lack of interest in lovemaking.
On the nights when Aimée would brush her lips over his,
say good night, and roll in the opposite direction, he worried
that she was falling out of love with him. Could this be the
same minx who had not been able to keep her hands off him
just a fortnight ago?

Honorine was another problem. She continued to remain
aloof from Aimée, brightening only in the presence of St.
Briac or even Christophe, who had begun to regard her with
the same light in his eyes that he previously had reserved
for his sister-in-law.

Aimée hadn't shown the letters from her parents to
Thomas. It seemed enough to her that Honorine was staying
indefinitely in their home; she didn't want to bother him with
the quirks of her family. At times she would ponder her
father's warning, but she felt too lethargic to worry for long.
So far Honorine had done nothing spiteful, and so it seemed
a waste of time and energy to brood about problems that
might never materialize. It would have helped if she could
have planned to introduce Honorine to the court in the near

future, but she couldn't think about such an undertaking now.

Toward the end of August Honorine received a mysterious note, the contents of which she would not disclose. It caused her to leave the chateau for the entire afternoon, and Aimée was still very curious about that. By now, she knew every person in the village; none of them would have any reason to contact Honorine.

On the last day of August, Aimée lay on her bed and tried to ignore the heat. The Loire was an enchanting river, but there were days when its golden haze could be deadly. All through the afternoon, Aimée had dozed on and off, even refusing St. Briac's invitation to accompany him on some errands in the village. She suspected what was wrong but wasn't ready to tell Thomas just yet. A few days ago she had missed her monthly flow for the second time. In July she had decided that the excitement and upheaval in her life had been the cause, but now she believed otherwise. Only Tante Fanchette, watchful as ever, seemed to know what was afoot.

Aimée had considered telling Thomas that she suspected she was with child, but some instinct made her hold back. There was always a chance her symptoms were caused merely by nerves, and so it would be better to wait until she was certain, she told herself. Another, less acknowledged reason had to do with St. Briac's secret. Gaspard had returned to the chateau only yesterday and then had disappeared again this morning. Until Aimée knew for certain what the two of them were up to, she was determined to keep a secret of her own. If Thomas thought his wife was *enceinte*, he would watch her every move like a hawk, pampering her outrageously. Aimée wanted to keep her options open in case he needed her help.

"Chérie?" called Tante Fanchette from the corridor. "May I come in?"

"Of course." Aimée adored St. Briac's aunt. The strong-willed old woman had run the chateau for fourteen years yet hadn't shown the least hint of resentment when her nephew brought home a new bride and mistress for his home. Aimée and Fanchette lived happily side by side, sharing responsibilities. If not for Fanchette, Aimée could never have spent so much time with St. Briac.

"I've brought you a bit of wine and cheese. Perhaps they'll

settle your stomach." She crossed the room and handed the plate and cup to Aimée, who sat up to accept them.

"I hope you are right. *Merci*."

"Thomas is home." Fanchette sat down on the side of the bed, watching until Aimée obediently took a bite of cheese. "He's eating downstairs with Christophe, but it was his idea that I bring this food up to you. He's quite concerned, you know."

"There's certainly no reason to be. I'm not really sick."

"I know," the older woman said with emphasis.

"What I mean is, I think this is just nerves. Anxiety, I suppose. So many changes in my life, and now with Honorine here—"

"If you say so, *chérie*," interrupted Fanchette. "It's your decision." She stood up. "Your sister is waiting in the corridor to see you. Shall I tell her she can come in?"

"Yes, certainly."

"I want you to eat that cheese, now! You need to keep your strength up. If this goes on much longer, your loving husband will be sending to Paris for the king's *premier médecin!*"

Aimée heard her words and took them to heart. Alone for a moment before Honorine came in, she decided she must gather her resources and show St. Briac she was not ill. It was cruel to make him worry, and what Fanchette had said about the king's personal physician might not have been an exaggeration.

"Bonjour, ma soeur," exclaimed Honorine. "Still unwell? What a pity. You've been missing all the laughter and lively conversations between Thomas and me."

Suddenly Aimée's wine looked more attractive. She took a large swallow and then shuddered. Her sister drew a chair up next to the bed and smiled in a way that made Aimée instantly suspicious.

"I'm glad to hear that my husband has been keeping you entertained. It's probably better that I haven't been present very much. The way I've been feeling, I might have put a damper on all your high spirits."

"Thomas really is the most charming man. There's no one in Nieuil or even all of Angoulême to compare with him."

"I'm aware of that, Honorine," Aimée replied in a carefully even tone.

Suddenly the younger girl smiled archly and inquired,

"Tell me something. Do you believe that fidelity in marriage is possible?"

"What a question! Of course it's possible."

"Even for a man like your Thomas?" pressed Honorine.

"*Especially* for a man like Thomas." Aimée didn't know what kind of game her sister was attempting to play, but she wanted no part of it. "Was there something you wanted, or did you just come up here to chat?"

"Well, I didn't want you to think we'd forgotten all about you, Aimée."

She took a deep breath. "Look, Honorine, wouldn't it be more pleasant if we could get along together? I realize that you have reasons to be angry with me, but that has gone both ways over the years. We're sisters."

"I'm happy you remember," Honorine replied stiffly.

"Would it help if I said that I'm sorry about taking your place with the court train? Not sorry about what happened to me, of course, but sorry if I hurt you in the process of saving my own life. I want to try to make amends. In the autumn, when I'm feeling better, we'll take you to Fontainebleau. The king will welcome you with open arms."

"You would do that for me?" Honorine's blue eyes widened and then were clouded first by confusion and then by wariness.

At that moment the door opened again and St. Briac entered. He wore boots, fawn breeches, and a white shirt and fawn doublet that were unlaced to reveal a glimpse of his dark chest. Aimée's eyes grew warm and soft at the sight of him.

"How are you feeling, *miette?*" he asked, apparently not noticing Honorine.

"Much better, especially now that you are here."

"That's just what I wanted to hear." St. Briac smiled. He crossed to the bed and sat down to remove his boots. "Oh, hello, Honorine. I didn't see you. Have you come to cheer up our invalid?"

"Of course, monseigneur. I wouldn't want her to waste away upstairs while the rest of us are having so much fun."

He gave her a quizzical glance and then stretched out on the bed beside his wife. "Well, if you don't mind, I'll take over now."

Honorine stood up. "I was about to take a walk to the village in any case. I'll see you two later."

"*Au revoir*," Aimée said distractedly. She was wondering why her sister had gone to such pains to use St. Briac's Christian name in their conversation when she obviously had not worked up the courage to call him Thomas to his face.

As the door closed, he reached for her hand. "Are you really better?"

"Much. The cheese helped, I think." Impulsively, Aimée lifted his hand to her mouth and kissed each tanned finger. "And how could I feel ill when you are near?"

"Ah, *miette*," St. Briac murmured, bending to kiss her mouth, "you are delicious."

Aimée put aside her wine and cheese and snuggled against the length of St. Briac's hard-muscled body. Their lips met again lingeringly, and she whispered, "That's because I taste of you, my love."

CHAPTER 31

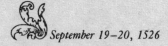 *September 19–20, 1526*

Autumn drifted into the Loire valley early that year, painting the leaves scarlet, yellow, and burnished orange and making the river look bluer than ever. The nights were chilly, and so Thomas and Aimée slept cuddled together under thick covers.

On this particular morning she dreamed on, burrowing facedown in her pillow, only gradually becoming aware that she was alone. A stretch toward her husband's pillow was no help; it was cold. Sitting up, Aimée pushed long, glossy curls back from her face and blinked sleepy eyes.

"*Bonjour, miette.* Were you looking for me?"

"Yes," she complained. St. Briac stood near the bed, drawing on doeskin gloves. He was garbed in riding attire. "What's happening? Why are you dressed like that?"

"I'd appreciate it if you would endeavor not to look so beautiful, Aimée. You'll lure me back into bed."

"Good! But first answer my question."

He sat down on the far edge of the bed. "I have to go to Paris for a few days."

"I knew it! I thought I heard Gaspard come in last night. What is all this about?"

"This is precisely the time I cannot tell you, as much as I'd like to. Even the detail of my destination is one you must

298

not divulge to anyone, understand? As for the rest, you will have to trust me again. No harm will come to me, and I should be back here with you for good within a few days."

"I don't like this, Thomas."

"I'm sorry to hear that, but there's no time to discuss it right now. I have to be off."

"Don't you care if I am angry? Can you leave me this way?"

St. Briac leaned over and caught her tiny fingers in his gloved hand. "My darling, if I thought there was even a remote possibility that your anger would last and do any damage to our marriage, I would not leave. However, I know you better than that. I'll return very soon, and then we'll be free to discuss all this in as much detail as you'd like. You'll have to be patient just a little longer."

"I don't like it," she muttered again.

"Well, I can only hope that you still like me well enough to kiss me good-bye."

She would have preferred to refuse for dramatic effect, but that was out of the question. This would be their last physical contact for several days, after all. Aimée scrambled naked from under the covers, and St. Briac met her halfway. He bent her across his lap and gave her a kiss of such burning ardor that it took her breath away.

"Now you've done it," St. Briac scolded. "Look at me."

She grinned triumphantly at the hard ridge that strained against his breeches. "Yes, I see. Quite a manly display. What are you going to do about it? Keep Gaspard waiting?"

"Oh, no. That meddler would doubtless burst in and pull me off at the critical moment." Smiling, St. Briac kissed his wife once more, briefly. "I'll just have to suffer this way for a few days. If I haven't changed when next I slide into bed beside you, *miette*, you'll know how true I've been."

Good sense told Aimée to withhold laughter, but where Thomas was concerned, that was impossible.

It was one thing to laugh with St. Briac when he was still nearby but quite another to remain in good humor once he and Gaspard had ridden away. Aimée was in a dismal mood all day. She trailed around the chateau looking forlorn and would not be cheered by anyone. Even Christophe, following after her like an eager puppy, caused Aimée to raise her voice in irritation. He told himself that there was nothing personal in her anger. It was just one more symptom of her mild but lingering illness.

Honorine's company at the noon meal did not improve Aimée's disposition. The younger girl complained that she was bored and then burst out, "Thomas has probably gone off to frolic at court while we sit here and rot. I don't believe you ever intend to take me to Fontainebleau. You're just trying to make me so miserable here that I'll go back to Nieuil and leave you alone."

Struggling to be patient, Aimée protested, "That is not so. I can't explain right now, but soon the situation for all of us should improve. If you can wait just a little longer—"

"Wait! I'll go mad. You don't care about me at all." She jumped up from the table and headed toward the door.

"Honorine." Aimée rose, waiting until her sister stopped and slowly looked back. "You're wrong. I do care."

The girl blinked, her blue eyes swimming with confusion, and then turned away and ran from the room.

Late in the afternoon Honorine received a mysterious message and then announced that she was going to freshen up and go out for another walk. When Aimée wondered aloud what business her sister might have in the village, she replied, "I've a right to friends, too, haven't I?"

Honorine lifted her chin and swept up the curving stairway. Aimée went into the gallery and stood staring out over the courtyard. There was an unseemly amount of subterfuge going on in her home, but it bothered her even more that she was not part of any of it. Was it possible that Honorine's secret errands might be linked in any way to St. Briac's?

Honorine descended the stairs, every blond curl once more in place. She wore a charming gown of iris-blue satin set off by a modest display of diamonds.

She spoke to Fanchette. "I'm going out for a bit. It's such a lovely day. Tell Aimée I will see her at supper." She passed by the gallery without noticing her sister.

Moments later, Aimée watched her emerge from the east wing doorway and turn the corner of the courtyard. She made up her mind in an instant to follow Honorine. Nothing might come of it, but Aimée was eager for any diversion that would take her mind off St. Briac's absence.

"I believe I shall take a stroll myself," she announced hastily to Fanchette and Christophe.

"I'll come with you," the boy exclaimed.

"No, no, don't do that! What I mean is, this is the first time I have been separated from your brother since our marriage. I feel a bit melancholy and would appreciate some time alone."

Narrow cobbled streets twisted through the sunlit village of St. Briac, which rambled down almost to the edge of the Loire. Aimée tried to remain inconspicuous as she followed Honorine at a distance, silently acknowledging the greetings of nearly every person who saw her. The villagers stared after her curiously, for the new bride of their seigneur was usually one to stop for a bit of cheerful conversation.

There was definitely something strange about her sister's behavior, Aimée decided. She was glancing right and left in a most furtive manner as if she expected someone to leap out and drag her away. Then it suddenly seemed that someone might have done just that, for Honorine disappeared into an alleyway. Aimée lifted her skirts and ran to catch up. Next to the alley was a boucherie where huge pieces of beef, whole ducks and chickens, and even pigs and wild boars hung in the window. Aimée hid between the shop and the alley, listening.

"Where were you yesterday?" Honorine was demanding. "I waited for hours."

Did her sister have a lover? If so, why were they meeting in alleyways? Aimée's curiosity was satisfied abruptly when another voice spoke up.

"I was unavoidably detained, my dear, but I do appreciate your patience. How are things going?"

Aimée sagged against the boucherie window and put a hand over her mouth to silence a gasp. *Chauvergé!*

"It's all been terrible, m'sieur," Honorine replied angrily. "Try as I might, I have not been able to make any trouble at all in my sister's marriage. Those two are more in love than any couple I have ever seen. Not only couldn't I manage to raise any doubts in Aimée's mind, I couldn't even persuade St. Briac to flirt with me. He was always perfectly charming, but the gleam that comes into his eyes when Aimée is present was never turned in my direction." She paused. "I've even begun to wonder if Aimée might not be so—"

"What?" Chauvergé demanded sharply, hearing the soft tone of her voice.

"Nothing. I'm just tired. Forgive me for babbling."

"Well, I must say I'm surprised that you haven't had more success, but at least you've been keeping them both occupied, and that's all I care about. Right now I want St. Briac safely clasped in the bosom of his family. After all this is over, I will come back for you, *ma belle*, and take you to the royal court, just as I've promised all along. You'll put Anne d'Heilly herself in the shade. Now, however, I must be off to Paris."

Aimée thought her heart would burst as she waited, praying that Honorine would not give St. Briac away. There was a long pause.

"I ought to tell you, m'sieur, that the seigneur de St. Briac is not exactly clasped in the bosom of his family as we speak. He, uh, rode off on a journey himself this very morning."

"Rode off on a journey? Where?"

"I couldn't say, m'sieur." Honorine's voice was barely audible.

"Damn! I don't know how he knows what's afoot, but he does. You *imbecile*! Why didn't you tell me at once? Why didn't you stop him? How could you allow this to happen?"

Out of the corner of her eye, Aimée saw the village *curé* approaching with the kind of smile that told her he would stop to chat at length. Since she had already heard enough from Chauvergé and Honorine to know what had to be done, Aimée rushed to head off the curé, apologized for her haste, and fairly ran all the way back to the chateau.

Gasping for breath, she shouted for Tante Fanchette and Christophe. When they appeared, Aimée declared, "I am going to have to ride after Thomas. I've learned that he is in danger, and I am the only one who can warn him. I must leave immediately."

"That is out of the question," cried Fanchette.

"I'll go instead," Christophe exclaimed, his voice cracking with excitement.

Aimée's eyes were like emeralds. "No, I will go. There isn't time to argue. You two can help me, though. I'll need a groom to accompany me, one who has ridden to Paris with Thomas before and knows his usual route and stopping places. I will also require boots, breeches, and a doublet that will fit me reasonably well. For safety's sake I must pass myself off as a boy. Do you have any old clothes, Christophe?"

"I have them all packed away," supplied Tante Fanchette.

"I'm sure we have what you need. About two years ago, believe it or not, Christophe was just about your size."

"Good. Bring them to my chamber. I'm going to gather other essentials." Aimée turned back to add, "I'll need Mignonne saddled, of course."

"I'll see to it," Christophe assured her.

Upstairs, Aimée hurriedly packed a few essentials, including soap, comb, undergarments, and an extra gown and slippers, in a leather bag belonging to St. Briac. Within minutes Fanchette brought in three separate sets of doublets and breeches.

"You can try them on and use those which fit best."

"Merci, chère tante," Aimée said, and gave her a kiss on the cheek.

"Don't try to placate me with your charm, my dear. I'm worried to death about this."

"You mustn't be!" She pulled the first pair of breeches on and then off. They were too large.

"Will you promise me to be careful? There's more at stake than your own life, you know. I would like to see Thomas's child born."

Their eyes met, with Aimée's acknowledging the truth for the first time. "You shall. I've been feeling wonderful all this month, and I'm certain that the baby is as strong as his, or her, parents."

"I hope you are right," Fanchette replied.

"You must believe that I would not go if I didn't believe my husband's life was in danger. We'll explain it all to you when we return, but I must be off now to warn him."

"D'accord. You and Thomas are too much alike. Neither of you listens to a word I say."

"Of course we do. We just don't always have the good sense to obey." Aimée held out her arms. "How do I look?"

She wore breeches and a doublet of sage-green velvet that made her eyes look even greener. The white fraise of the shirt disguised the delicate shape of her neck. Aimée pulled on one of the two pairs of boots Fanchette had brought and declared them a perfect fit.

"You look like a beautiful girl dressed up as a boy," said St. Briac's aunt. "Have you forgotten your breasts, *chérie?* They are more noticeable than ever these days."

"Parbleu!" Aimée gasped. "Thank you for reminding me."

"I'll leave you to bind them and pin up your hair. You

should find a hat or two among Thomas's things that will serve. He never wears them, so it's time they saw the light of day."

"*Mille mercis,* Tante Fanchette. What would I do without you?" Aimée put her arms around the older woman and was relieved to feel her reciprocate with feeling.

"Godspeed, my dear girl. I'll keep you and Thomas in my prayers until you return."

A few minutes later, Aimée was in the *étuve*, staring into a mirror as she drew on a velvet plumed hat she had never seen before. 'Twill serve, she thought. The strips of petticoat that flattened her breasts under the shirt and doublet were uncomfortable but not unbearably so. She was ready to gather up her things and leave, when Honorine burst into the bedchamber.

"Aimée? Aimée! I must talk to you. I have to confess!" She began to weep with such force that she barely noticed her sister's appearance when she emerged from the *étuve*.

"Don't waste your breath. I already know everything. You've betrayed not only me but my husband, and I'll never forgive you for that, Honorine."

"Oh, Aimée, please listen to me. You must! I didn't realize when I came here just how strong the bond was between us. I felt that *you* had betrayed *me* when you took my place with the court. When M'sieur Chauvergé came to Nieuil and urged me to journey north with him, there was a great deal of bitterness inside me. I had just heard that you were married to the seigneur de St. Briac, the most magnificent man I'd ever seen in all my life. I thought I hated you, I was so filled with envy. I thought that if I had come with the court instead of you, he would surely have married *me*. Chauvergé said that your wedding had taken place under strange circumstances and that he was convinced Thomas did not really love you. He said that he had reasons of his own for wanting to cause trouble for St. Briac and that if I would help him, he would see to it that I occupied a place of importance at court. I was so bored and unhappy with Maman and Papa at Nieuil. Worst of all, Armand Rovicette began hovering around *me* after you left. Wait, don't leave! Just let me say that I have come to regret everything I've done. Walking back from town today, I determined to tell you all in the hope that there might be some way to salvage the situation.

Aimée, I love you and need you. I want to be your sister, if you'll have me."

Aimée closed her eyes for a long moment and then turned to stare at Honorine. The torrent of words reminded her of all the speeches she had wanted to make to St. Briac after Chambord, begging for his forgiveness. She'd never worked up the courage, but Honorine had, and she admired her for that. More important, Aimée wanted a sister.

"All right, let us forget about everything that's happened since you arrived here. I'll give you the benefit of the doubt until you do just *one* thing that makes me suspicious." She paused, picking up her bag of belongings. "You know, you've been a fool, Honorine. You've endangered Thomas's life for nothing. Chauvergé couldn't get you a position on the kitchen staff at court. If he dares to show his own face to François again, he'll be hanged."

"But he was with the king and Louise de Savoy at Nieuil. He's one of the foremost *gentilhommes de la chambre!*"

"Not any more. But I haven't time to discuss it. I have to find my husband before Chauvergé does."

Honorine caught her arm. "So that's why you're dressed that way. I feared as much. Aimée, I beg you, let me come with you. You may need my help."

Aimée took a breath and made up her mind. Since she was with child, her sister's presence might be of help. If Aimée felt more than a twinge of pain, she'd feel like a murderess to keep on riding. The chances of that happening were small, but if it did, the repentant Honorine could go on in her place.

"All right." She gestured toward the bed. "There ought to be some clothes there that fit you. Get dressed, put on the other hat that I left in the *étuve*, and meet me in the stables." At the doorway, Aimée turned back to add, "Hurry! And don't forget to bind your breasts. You'll find strips of my petticoat on the bed."

For thirty-six long hours Aimée, Honorine, and their groom, Pierre, traveled with only the briefest pauses for food and sleep. Tante Fanchette had packed three bags with provisions that could be eaten during pauses to water, feed, and rest the horses. Aimée and Honorine had succumbed to fatigue around midnight the first day and slept on blankets under a grove of rustling, golden-leaved birch trees. Aimée couldn't sleep for long; she was too tense. Knowing St. Briac, she had to assume that he was setting a punishing pace for himself. If they ever were going to catch up, their own pace must be even more rapid.

Honorine frequently looked as if she wanted to complain, but she rarely followed through. One look at her sister's resolute expression squelched her bone-deep fatigue. If it took this torture to prove herself to Aimée, Honorine was determined to meet the challenge and win.

Pierre, a young, fair-haired man of around twenty, had ridden several times to Paris with St. Briac and knew every auberge the seigneur preferred. They tried them all. On the morning of the second day they found one in the tiny village of Montoire. The innkeeper confirmed that St. Briac and Gaspard had indeed slept there the night before, but they had left in a hurry before dawn.

They rode on down long, flat, narrow roads lined with plane trees or oaks, their leaves bright against the crisp blue sky, over rolling hills still carpeted in green, and through charming hamlets that tempted the trio to pause and sample hot food and enjoy friendly conversation. Aimée's resolve never wavered, however, and her companions could only match her pace in silence.

Finally, at about ten o'clock on the second night, they drew up before a half-timbered auberge in the village of Illiers.

"I'll wager that he's here, madame," declared Pierre. "We've rested here often in the past, and it's just the right distance from his last bed if he's been riding hard."

Aimée swung down from Mignonne's back and handed the horse over to a stable hand. "Have a care with her. She's very precious to me and has put in a long day." She slipped the boy a coin. Her heart pounding with nervous anticipation, Aimée went into the auberge. There were still men quaffing ale and wine before the fire, but St. Briac was not among them. Of course, he would not waste precious time so frivolously, yet she steeled herself for disappointment.

"M'sieur," she said to the innkeeper, trying to lower her voice convincingly, "I am in search of my brother. He is the seigneur de St. Briac. Do you know if he is staying here tonight?"

"*Mais oui!*" exclaimed the old man, peering at her curiously. "He went to bed long ago."

Aimée almost smiled at his expression. The poor fellow must have wondered how St. Briac could have such a frail, effeminate sibling. "Well, he's expecting me. I'll just go on up if you will point out his door to me. Also, could you provide rooms for my two companions?"

"*Certainement*. But wouldn't you like some supper first?"

"Yes," cried Honorine and Pierre in unison.

"For myself, I am not hungry," Aimée said gruffly. "I would like to see my brother."

"Of course, m'sieur. Follow me." The innkeeper glanced back to speak to the other two. "I'll be back in just a moment and will fetch your suppers *tout de suite*."

"Fine, fine," murmured Pierre as he collapsed in the nearest chair. Honorine followed suit, longing to unbind her breasts and take down her hair.

Aimée followed the old man up a dark, narrow flight of stairs lit only by his candle and another that sat on a table on the landing. After pointing out a corner room to her, he turned and descended to attend to his guests.

She'd hurried all this time as if the devil himself were chasing her, but now Aimée felt her courage ebbing away. What would he do when he saw her? There was only one way to find out, she told herself, and in any case, her longing to be close to St. Briac was even more potent than her fear of his temper.

Slowly, Aimée eased the latch up and pushed the door open. The chamber was spacious and moonlit; instantly her eyes went to her husband, asleep in a comfortable-looking bed. Her heart turned over as she was reminded of the last time she had tiptoed into his chamber while he slept. He looked much the same now, brown and hard and splendid against the white bedclothes. It surprised Aimée that her entrance had not wakened him, but then she remembered the long hours he had ridden for two days and realized the depth of his fatigue.

Nearing the bed, she saw that he had one arm outflung toward the other pillow, the one which usually was occupied by her. Tears pooled in her eyes.

"Thomas."

Instantly on guard, he sat up and reached toward the sword that always remained propped at his bedside. Then St. Briac narrowed his gaze in the moonlight. The figure leaning over him appeared to be that of a boy, but there was no mistaking the leaf-green eyes and creamy skin he knew so well.

"Aimée! *Non*. It *can't* be you," St. Briac moaned.

CHAPTER 32

 September 20, 1526

"This must be a dream," St. Briac said to himself. "That's it, a bizarre dream. If I just lie down and go back to sleep, this apparition of my wife will disappear." He dropped back onto his pillow and covered his face with his hands.

Aimée smothered nervous laughter. "Thomas."

"I'm asleep."

Wincing, she leaned down and pried his hands away. Turquoise eyes stared up at her in the starlight

"Tell me you're not real," he begged

"I'm very real, I'm afraid."

"I cannot believe it. It's impossible!" St. Briac bolted upright again and grasped her wrists. "In the name of God, Aimée, *why*? Why couldn't you behave yourself and stay put, just once? Must I chain you to our bed?"

"If you will only listen to me, you'll understand that I had no choice. I had to—"

"And what are you doing in those ridiculous clothes?" St. Briac interrupted. "At first glance I thought you were a boy. Where are your breasts?"

"Let me speak. I can explain everything."

He put his head in his hands and made a low sound of

frustration. "I must be losing my mind. All right, go on. I'm listening."

Hastily, Aimée related all that had happened at home in the hours after his departure, including the story of how Chauvergé had lured Honorine to Chateau du Soleil so that she might attempt to cause trouble between the newlyweds and keep St. Briac's mind off Georges Teverant.

"You forgave her?" he exclaimed, incredulous.

"I had to, Thomas. I think this experience has made a change in Honorine. She seems to have grown up overnight. All these long hours that we've been traveling to reach you, she's held up heroically." She paused. There was a look in her husband's eyes that told her he wasn't really listening. His thoughts were focused elsewhere. "What are you going to do about Chauvergé?"

"There's nothing I can do. We'll go on as planned. I'll just have to proceed with even greater caution now that I know he will be lying in wait for me. Under a rock, no doubt."

"Thomas, you must tell me now what is going on. You owe me that much."

He stared at her. *"D'accord.* I suppose you are right, but don't imagine that I've forgiven you for tearing across France on this insane chase. Next time send a servant or even Christophe with a message for me."

"I wouldn't have trusted anyone else to find you in time. No one else *cares* the way I do."

St. Briac's heart melted when he heard the raw emotion in Aimée's voice. He gathered her into his arms and smiled when she threw her arms around his neck and kissed him. There were tears on her lips.

"I've missed you so, Thomas. It seems that we've been apart a year instead of less than two days."

"I've missed you as well, *miette.* I've been aching for you."

Their mouths came together again, tasting, speaking in a language that had no words. Finally, Aimée fitted herself cozily into St. Briac's embrace and said eagerly, "Now, tell me all about Teverant."

"First we must dispose of that silly plumed hat and take down your hair." He longed to feel it against his face, and so he removed the offending chapeau and hairpins himself.

"As for Teverant, he's been imprisoned in the Conciergerie for over a month now. You remember why, I'm sure."

"Louise de Savoy has been trying to make him a scapegoat for the Baron de Semblançay."

"That's right. After I learned of his arrest, I sent Gaspard to Paris to find out what he could. He returned to say that a date had been set for Teverant's execution: the twenty-fifth of September. So, you see, it was Chauvergé's job to see to it that I was kept occupied at St. Briac until then. When I learned that François actually had approved an execution, I decided to write to him. He's been in Paris lately, staying at the Louvre. I thought he would listen to reason, but when Gaspard arrived with his extremely slow reply, I saw that Louise has truly exerted her will in this case."

"What did François say? He has always seemed to be the epitome of a just man."

St. Briac sighed harshly. "Basically that there had been too much talk about Semblançay and his helpers getting away with their crimes. He's decided that an example must be made so that the other money men will not think they can slip their hands into the till and go unpunished. Also, there's the related matter of Jean de Poitiers, seigneur de Saint-Vallier."

"Was he the man who was nearly executed?"

"Yes. After Charles of Bourbon fled to Italy and joined forces with Charles V to crush France, the scapegoat issue surfaced, much as it has in this case. François felt he had to stamp out any embers of a conspiracy, particularly while the country was in danger of invasion from Bourbon's allies. Saint-Vallier was the logical choice, since he'd been a party to the signing of Bourbon's treaty with Charles V, but he was very old and frail. Everything proceeded as ordered, though. The poor man was trembling with fright as they led him to the scaffold. This was in January 1524, as I recall. There was a huge crowd, of course, and Saint-Vallier, his hands tied, begged the headsman to be quick and merciful with his ax. He knelt, the ax was raised, and at that moment a messenger rode up waving the king's reprieve."

"Do you mean that François *intended* to wait until the last minute?"

"Exactly. It was his way of punishing Saint-Vallier but still showing mercy. However, now he says that he's been criticized for being too softhearted, not only in that case but also with the heretics who subscribe to the beliefs of Martin Luther. Louise has convinced the king that this time an example must be made and that there is no room for mercy."

Aimée's brows gathered as she pondered this. When she asked her next question, she already knew what St. Briac's answer would be. "What do you intend to do, then?"

"Why, I must see to Teverant's escape from the Conciergerie, of course. What else *can* I do?" Aimée's prolonged nearness had begun to distract him from more serious matters. Now that the story was told, he turned his attention to her clothing. "I must say, I find this very odd," he remarked as his fingers untied the laces of her white shirt.

"What do you mean?" Aimée could think only of her husband's statement about rescuing Teverant. Worry and fear spread inside her like a dark stain.

"I've never undressed anyone before who was wearing a doublet," St. Briac replied, laughing.

He had such a stimulating low, masculine laugh that Aimée was powerless to resist its magic. They were alone together, and the night spread out before them, filled with love and promise.

It wasn't until much later that Aimée returned to the subject of Teverant. They were lying together, legs entwined, her face nestled in the place where St. Briac's shoulder curved into his neck.

"So you are off to Paris tomorrow?" she ventured.

"Mmhmm." He stroked her hair back with lean, tender fingers and kissed her temple.

"And I?"

"Back to St. Briac, of course. Go gently this time."

"Thomas?" She lifted her face and pressed feather-soft kisses to a spot below his ear that she knew to be particularly sensitive.

"I don't like the tone of your voice, *miette*. Why don't we go to sleep?"

"I cannot go to sleep when all I can think about is how much I need to go with you to Paris. Wait! Don't say no yet. I have the most extraordinary plan, but you can't carry it out without Honorine and myself. If you will just listen with an open mind—"

"Non! Absolutely not! And that is my final word!"

* * *

Two days later St. Briac, Gaspard, their groom, Aimée, and Honorine rode through one of the gates in the walls and ramparts that enclosed Paris.

St. Briac had succumbed to his wife's pleas against his better judgment, partly because her plan to use Honorine to foil Chauvergé was a good one. During their journey from Illiers, his attitude had combined helpless affection with gruffness. It wouldn't do, he told himself, for Aimée to think she could talk him into anything.

He glanced casually in her direction, and his heart softened once again. The minx was incorrigible but undeniably enchanting. She sat up very straight astride Mignonne, looking silly and adorable in her doublet and plumed hat as she gazed around with excitement. There was little cause for excitement, but Aimée always seemed to find a spark of beauty in the most awful surroundings.

Paris stank. Thomas recognized the odor when they were still a league away. Once a visitor was trapped within the walls, the reason became apparent. There were no real streets to speak of, only a labyrinth of narrow passages pooled with filthy water and piled with rotting garbage. Houses, mainly of a sordid nature, crowded together and rose up three, four, or even six stories so that virtually no sun could invade the streets below. Paris had outgrown its walls long ago, and the people had been forced to build higher and higher. Even the bridges were piled with dwellings that overlooked a river into which citizens daily added their slop. The Seine provided drinking water for the city; St. Briac thought it was no wonder half the population seemed to be swilling wine so eagerly.

Aimée was seeing Paris from a different perspective. She was aware of the foul odors and other general unpleasantness, but she chose to concentrate on the congregation of gothic rooftops, the turrets hanging at angles to the city walls, the pointed gables, and the clustered towers of the Louvre that came into view as they made progress toward the Seine. Many of the houses were disgusting, but occasionally they came into a passage lined with carved and painted housefronts, their projected stories nearly meeting above the travelers. Aimée found it exciting to be among crowds of people again after the tranquility of Chateau du Soleil. Horses and coaches and even herds of swine with their inevitable abbot or prior thronged the streets. Beggars cried for food, children chased through mud puddles, and a chicken came flying toward Honorine's face.

"What a horrid place," she cried, flailing at the unfortunate bird.

"Well said," murmured St. Briac wryly. "Don't forget that you ladies wanted to come to Paris. Now you'll have to hold your breath and endure for a while, Honorine." He paused, wrinkling his nose as they passed a boucherie with a large pile of offal outside its door. "Is it any wonder the king spends so little time in his capital city?"

They were turning onto the rue de la Huchette, not far from the banks of the Seine and the Île de la Cité. Suddenly Aimée pointed above the rooftops, her green eyes sparkling.

"*Regardez!* Is that the cathedral of Notre Dame?"

An airy spire rose into the air above the maze that was Paris. "Yes, that's it," said St. Briac. "Look to your left and you'll see Sainte Chapelle. Just north of it is the Conciergerie."

This was a reminder of their purpose in Paris, and the little band fell silent until they reached le Chien Rouge, a small but relatively clean-looking auberge bracketed between the many eating houses that lined the rue de la Huchette.

"My sister has a nice house on the Right Bank," St. Briac remarked as they dismounted, "but with Chauvergé sniffing around, there was no question of us staying there. I thought it would be best to choose one of the last places he might suspect."

Once again St. Briac managed to obtain a corner room, while Honorine occupied the chamber next to them and Gaspard shared quarters with Pierre farther down the hall. Thomas had sent his groom back to Chateau du Soleil to inform Tante Fanchette that Aimée was safe and would return in due time in the company of her husband.

No sooner had all three doors shut than Honorine's flew open and she burst in on St. Briac and Aimée.

"There's a rat in my room," she screamed. "He ran under the bed when I came in."

"How shocking," St. Briac murmured. "Why don't you leave your door open for a bit, and perhaps he'll run out."

Honorine looked as if she might burst into tears, and her sister took pity on her. "I'm not terribly impressed with these conditions, either. Let's see if we can't persuade the inn-keeper to let us wash our bedding and borrow a broom."

The two girls set to work. Later, after the sheets and blankets had been strung outside the windows to dry, St. Briac and Aimée set off to procure some supper for them all. He'd decided it would be safest if they kept their number to a minimum when venturing out, in case Chauvergé happened to spot them, and he was particularly determined that Honorine not be seen with him, Aimée, or Gaspard until Teverant's escape had been effected.

They walked south to an outdoor market. On the way, St. Briac pointed out the University of Paris, also known as the Sorbonne, where he had been a student more than a dozen years before. This was a detail of her husband's life Aimée hadn't been aware of, and she wondered what other surprises there were in his past.

Finally, their arms laden with two crusty baguettes, a generous wedge of cheese, and some pears and apples, they headed back to the rue de la Huchette. There St. Briac purchased a capon *au gros sel* and a small cask of Burgundy wine at an eating house. The capon was fished out of the ever-ready pot, where it had been boiling with a mass of other capons.

"A far cry from the suppers at court," remarked St. Briac, "but when one is hungry, nothing smells better than one of these."

The innkeeper grudgingly lent them bowls and cups, and all five crowded into the corner room to eat. Afterward, sipping more of the dark wine, they discussed plans.

It would be mainly up to Gaspard and Pierre to venture forth, in disguise, of course, and learn whatever they could at the Conciergerie plus, crucially, the whereabouts of Chauvergé. St. Briac knew he would have to spend most of his time at the auberge, for his face and size were too easy to recognize. Aimée shared his frustration and begged to take part in the skullduggery, clad in her boy's garb.

"No!" St. Briac turned on her and uttered the word in a tone that would brook no argument. "And do not ask again."

"Oh, all right." Aimée pretended to pout and then gave him a mischievous smile. "I suppose my time would be better spent keeping you entertained in our room, *n'est-ce pas?*"

"An ingenious plan. What an inventive wife I have."

Over the next thirty-six hours Gaspard discovered that

Chauvergé had taken rooms not far from the Louvre on the Right Bank. The manservant spent a full day haunting the streets and talking to friends. Finally, by chance, he happened to glimpse Chauvergé inside a hired coach. Because the traffic was so snarled, he had no trouble following on foot. After the chevalier had disappeared into a prosperous auberge, Gaspard went in to confirm from the innkeeper that Chauvergé was lodging there.

Pierre meanwhile concentrated on the fate of Georges Teverant. He made friends with one of the guards at the prison and learned that the execution was set for noon on the twenty-fifth. He also managed to discover in which cell Teverant was being held. The guard, after a mug of ale, went so far as to take Pierre to view the prisoner. Later, the young groom reported that Teverant appeared thin but coherent. Best of all, Pierre was able to draw a map showing the quickest way to the condemned man's cell.

Because an execution usually brought out half of Paris in a macabre mood of celebration, St. Briac had decided that the morning of the twenty-fifth would be the best time to rescue Teverant. There would be such chaos in the streets that there would be little problem getting him away.

St. Briac spent hour after hour in their room at the auberge, poring over papers he had spread on a small table. An inkhorn and several swan quills enabled him to cover sheets of parchment with notes, times, and other details pertaining to Teverant's escape. Aimée was usually at his side, studying the map of the Conciergerie with him and discussing their plans over and over. Long conversations were held with Honorine about her role in the drama. St. Briac rehearsed with her patiently, for it was his one worry that she would panic and ruin everything.

Finally, Aimée lay by her husband's side in the lumpy bed on what would be their last night at the auberge. Both of them were too tense to make love. She studied his chiseled profile in the violet shadows, noting the intensity of his blue-green eyes as they stared at the ceiling. Within a few hours all their painstaking plans would become reality. Aimée closed her eyes and said a silent prayer that justice would be served.

CHAPTER 33

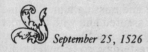 *September 25, 1526*

Honorine stood outside the carved door that separated her from the chevalier de Chauvergé. She carried a basket filled with warm, crusty rolls and oranges. Her heart pounding with trepidation, she raised a pretty white hand to the door but could not bring herself to knock. The innkeeper of this prosperous, well-kept auberge had assured Honorine that Chauvergé was still abed, and so there was no need for fear on that score. Pierre waited outside in case she needed to be rescued. At that moment St. Briac and Aimée had probably already left le Chien Rouge to carry out their part of the plan. The rest was up to her, and Honorine was terrified that she would botch it.

St. Briac had rehearsed with her over and over again; she knew every word by heart. But what if Chauvergé did not play his role as they'd anticipated? A vision of St. Briac as he had appeared at dawn came back to haunt her. "You'll be fine," he'd said firmly. "If all else fails, use your wits, *ma soeur*. They won't fail you." Being called sister by a man who had every reason to bear her a grudge had filled Honorine with love and gratitude. She was determined not to disappoint him.

Her hand moved and knocked. An instant later, a nervous-looking manservant threw open the door.

"*Bonjour, messieurs!*" Honorine cried cheerfully. "I hope I'm not too early." Beyond the manservant, she could see Chauvergé seated beside a table with a basin on it. He wore breeches but was bare-chested with a towel draped around his neck. From the look of the razor held aloft by the valet, it appeared he'd been shaving Chauvergé's neck. "Oh dear, I hope I'm not disturbing you."

"Not at all," cried the chevalier, standing. "We've finished. Jean, you may leave us."

When the servant had gone, Chauvergé threw off his towel and came forward to greet Honorine. "What a delightful surprise. What brings you to Paris? And how did you find me, my beauty?"

So far, so good. Honorine made her little speech about being bored at her sister's house and missing him. "I came to Paris to see *you*, m'sieur," she assured him with her most charming smile. "My own lodgings are nearby, and my maid happened to see you leave here yesterday, so I could hardly wait to come myself. I've brought *petit déjeuner*." Setting the basket on the chest, she plucked out a roll for his inspection. "Freshly baked. And don't the oranges look heavenly?"

"Not nearly so heavenly as you, mademoiselle." He caught her shoulders and bent his head. Honorine suffered the briefest of kisses before drawing lightly away and laughing.

"Not so fast, m'sieur. You take a girl's breath away."

Chauvergé puffed out his thin chest and smiled. "I've missed you, too, my sweet, and am delighted to see you, of course, but I cannot tarry long. Today, as you may already know, Georges Teverant will be executed. I must be away to the Conciergerie before long."

"Have you not time to share a roll and an orange with a maiden who has journeyed so far to be with you?"

"Well, perhaps. To be frank, I would like to share much more than that with you, mademoiselle." He gave her his version of a rakish smile.

Honorine reached quickly into the basket and began munching on a roll.

"Why don't you come over here and sit down beside me, my beauty?" He made no effort to finish dressing but lounged back on his huge four-poster bed. When Honorine complied, perching nervously on the edge, Chauvergé leaned forward and peered over her shoulder. Her gown was cut low to reveal a tempting display of creamy bosom. Saliva filled his mouth at the sight.

"Aren't you hungry, m'sieur?" Honorine inquired after a moment.

"*Mais, oui!*" He chuckled in a way that made her concentrate all her attention on the roll, which was growing smaller by the moment. "Tell me something, Honorine, what news is there of the seigneur de St. Briac? Is he in Paris, too?"

"Oh, no, at least I don't think so." Again she recited a prepared speech. "I came upon him at an auberge in—" Suddenly the name of the town St. Briac had given her was blocked from her memory. "—Illiers," she supplied helplessly. "He had taken a terrible fall from his horse and was confined to bed. Heaven knows when he'll be able to travel."

"That's odd. I stayed at that auberge myself during my journey here, but I must have arrived after St. Briac, since he had a day's head start. He was not there. In fact, the innkeeper told me he'd left that morning."

"Well, perhaps I'm confused about the village. I may have it wrong." Panic had crept into Honorine's voice, and Chauvergé heard it.

"In any case, there's nothing he can do to upset my plans now. I must be off to the Conciergerie to keep an eye on the condemned man, but first let us explore the reason for your visit." His thin lips curved upward. It had been so long since he had had a woman, particularly one as fair and pure as this one. "You know, my sweet, you can stay right here and wait for me. When this day's business is done, we will leave together to join the court at Fontainebleau and begin our wondrous future."

Honorine wanted to scream or strike out when she felt hands like claws dig into her shoulders, pulling her back onto the bed. There was nothing she could say or do to stop this horror. It was, after all, her duty to keep Chauvergé occupied as long as possible. St. Briac had said specifically that she was not to allow him to touch her, but what choice did she have?

Chauvergé was kissing her, thrusting his tongue into her mouth. He tasted awful. Her upper lip was being pressed so hard against her teeth that she gave a small, involuntary cry of pain.

"I'm sorry if I am too ardent," he said in a passion-muffled tone, moving to slide his wet mouth down her neck. "You are so beautiful, and I've waited so long."

"But m'sieur, this is not right. That is—we are not married!"

"A lady concerned about such minor points would not have arrived alone at my bedchamber at an hour when I was likely to be asleep." Chauvergé chuckled. He began to knead one of her breasts; it seemed that his loins might burst.

"But I only came to bring you the food."

"Hush! I have no appetite for anything but you." In his eagerness to open her bodice, he tore some of the lace but ignored it as Honorine's breasts spilled free of their confines. Chauvergé made a low, grunting sound of approval and then began kissing them and finally sucking voraciously on one pink nipple.

Honorine thought she must be dying. Dimly, she heard him slobbering and smacking, felt his teeth on her sensitive flesh. However, not until one of Chauvergé's hands pushed its way between her thighs and squeezed her most private place did Honorine come to life. Something swollen and disgusting was rubbing against her thigh, and when she realized what it must be, she forgot St. Briac, Aimée, and all their plans.

"Stop that! Loose me!" Like a wild animal, Honorine pushed with all her might and managed to send the man toppling sideways. Instantly, she was off the bed and running across the chamber toward the razor that the manservant had left behind.

"You didn't come here because you missed me, you slut," he shouted. "St. Briac sent you, didn't he? I guessed as much from your little story about his riding accident but decided that I should have my pleasure anyway. That damned St. Briac has never fallen from a horse in his life."

"Don't touch me," was all Honorine could say. Tears streamed down her face.

"Give me the razor. You won't use it, and you know it." Chauvergé rose from the bed and advanced toward her. "Give it to me and I won't hurt you."

When he clamped a hand around her wrist, Honorine released the razor, sobbing. In the next instant, Chauvergé struck her across the face with all his strength, and she fell against the corner of the chest, hitting her head. He stood there, staring at her crumpled form for a moment, wondering whether he could afford to relieve the ache in his loins. No, not this time. If St. Briac was attempting to rescue Georges Teverant this morning, there wasn't a moment to spare.

Not long after Honorine knocked on Chauvergé's door, St. Briac and Aimée drew alongside the Conciergerie in a rickety wagon filled with casks of wine and driven by a dubious-looking Gaspard LeFait. A casual acquaintance would not have recognized any of them. St. Briac wore a matted gray wig and powder in his beard. His clothing consisted of scuffed, spade-shaped black shoes, tan hose, brown breeches, a soiled shirt, and a dingy leather jerkin. He sat slumped over so that he appeared much shorter, and his eyes were those of a dull-witted fellow.

Aimée was clad in the costume of a strumpet. She wore a cheap gown of scarlet silk cut so low that only her nipples were concealed. Fake gems glittered on every finger, and several necklaces were looped around her neck. Her hair was piled into elaborate curls studded with glass jewels, and she reeked of cheap perfume. She had had the most fun of all painting her mouth red and rouging her cheeks until St. Briac had been forced to pull her from the mirror.

Gaspard's role was to be even more apelike than his master. His wig was long and black, as was the fake beard Aimée had glued carefully to his face amid cries of outrage. His clothing was gray and tattered. St. Briac had instructed him to play mute, for he feared that if Gaspard were to open his mouth, all would be ruined.

The Conciergerie once had been part of the old palace, traded by Charles V for the Louvre nearly two hundred years earlier. Since then it had served as the seat of the Parliament and then as the supreme court of the kingdom; now it was used as a prison. The magnificent façade of the Conciergerie bordered the north bank of the Île de la Cité. Their wagon passed first the rectangular Tour de l'Horloge, which John the Good had had constructed in 1334, complete with the first public clock in Paris. Farther on were three more towers, all circular with high pointed roofs. St. Briac drew the wagon to a halt in front of the pair that flanked the entrance to the Conciergerie. Immediately several guards clattered down the steps to meet them.

St. Briac was pleased. They still had a long way to go, but at this point all was on schedule. None of these guards appeared particularly intelligent, and there were crowds gathering already on the bridges and the streets in anticipation of the noontime execution.

"Bonjour, messieurs," he greeted the men, his body hunched forward and his speech decidedly that of an ignorant peasant.

"What do you want? What's all this?" one of the guards demanded, gesturing toward the casks of wine that crowded the wagon.

"The chevalier de Chauvergé bade us bring you this wine. He said that the king suggested it. Thought you all deserved to celebrate, too. Finally there will be an execution that won't be called off at the last minute."

"About time," agreed one of the guards.

"You say it's for us?" queried their spokesman doubtfully.

"That's right, m'sieur," Aimée spoke up, flashing her most alluring smile. "Enough wine to quench the thirst of every guard who toils within the Conciergerie. Our king and the chevalier de Chauvergé are very generous, *n'est-ce pas?"*

"Who's that?" the head guard asked St. Briac, his eyes widening at the sight of Aimée's bosom.

"My, uh, sister," he told him stupidly, wanting to deliver a punishing blow to the leering man's jaw. "The chevalier thought you might enjoy her along with the wine."

"What a day," cried another of the guards. "Why aren't there more executions?"

St. Briac was climbing down clumsily from his seat and taking the casks that the mute Gaspard handed him. "Have you cups? I can open one of these for you right here, and my sister and the lackey will take another inside to the rest of the guards."

One of the men dashed inside and returned with several battered vessels. The head guard succumbed. "Oh, all right. As long as the king's insisted, I suppose we might as well drink a bit."

In moments the cask had been pried open and cups dipped inside. The guards were so happily toasting the occasion that they barely noticed Aimée and Gaspard passing them with another cask of wine.

"Wench, hurry back to us," shouted one of the guards. She gave them all a wink and followed Gaspard through the high arched doorway.

Inside, the pair passed through a vaulted vestibule and

then found themselves in the breathtaking Salle des Gens
d'Armes, which once had served as a meal hall for soldiers
and knights. It was a huge room, divided by columns and
piers into four aisles with gothic cross vaults. Torches flickered against columns highlighted with gold and azure, lend-
ing an eerily magnificent air to the place. Almost immediately
they were greeted by more guards. Aimée explained their
mission, assuring the men that not only had the head guard
outside given permission for this celebration, so had the
chevalier de Chauvergé and King François himself.

"You must call the others. It would be unfair to deprive
even one man of this morning's pleasure." She gave them a
coquettish smile and hoped they wouldn't decide to partake
of her instead of the wine.

The other guards were summoned, and they thundered
down a spiral staircase from the great kitchens above. The
rest came from the prison itself. More cups were procured
from the kitchens, and soon Aimée was dipping them into
the red wine and passing them around. When the guards
insisted that she join in, she laughed and said she wanted to
be alert so that she might share the enjoyment of each of
them. Their eyes lit up lustily at this. Gaspard meanwhile
slouched against the wall as if he were too stupid to know
what wine was.

Almost in unison, the guards began to yawn and then sit
down. Finally, too dazed to realize what was happening,
they dropped over against the pillars and one another, sound
asleep. Aimée pressed a hand over her mouth to stifle a
giggle. Gaspard came forward to slip a ring of keys from one
man's hand, and then the two of them were running down
the west bay of the Salle des Gens d'Armes toward the
corridor that would lead them into the men's quarters of the
prison. The passages were lit dimly, and Aimée had to hold
up her skirts and dodge rats as she hurried along. Prisoners
called to her from the tiny screens in the doors to their cells,
but she hardened her heart and rushed onward toward
Georges Teverant. She and Gaspard climbed a great circular
stairway to the next floor, and by this time the stench was
nearly unbearable. Aimée knew the layout of the Conciergerie by heart, though this was her first time inside the place.
Teverant was being held in the third cell on the left, and
when they called for him through the mesh that covered the

square in his door, she saw him rise from his knees as if he'd been praying.

Pierre had even described the key to her and St. Briac, and so they had to try only a few before finding the one that brought Teverant to freedom.

"Madame de St. Briac," he breathed incredulously, staring at her improbable costume and wondering whether it actually was she. "I don't understand."

"Thomas and Gaspard and I have come to rescue you, Georges. We cannot talk now, though. Hurry!"

They ran back down the dark corridor and were starting to descend the stairway, when Aimée saw St. Briac coming toward them. Her heart leaped with joy to realize that he could take the responsibility of this escape from her shoulders, but then a shadow at the foot of the stairs caught her eye.

"Thomas," she cried. "Behind you!" Of course there would be at least one guard who had declined to celebrate.

St. Briac whirled around and drew his sword in one smooth movement, pricking the other man's chest before he could lift his weapon. "Well met," he said with a laugh. "You'd have been better off with the wine, my friend." Taking the keys from Gaspard, he held his sword to the guard's back and prodded him upward toward Teverant's empty cell.

Moments later Aimée sensed rather than heard her husband as he drew up alongside them in the vestibule. He and Teverant embraced briefly, exchanging broad smiles, and then St. Briac caught Aimée up against him with one arm and pressed his open mouth to hers.

"I love you, *miette*," he told her, his voice sincere and merry all at once.

"And I love you, monseigneur!"

"I've told you not to call me that!" St. Briac grinned before taking her hand and pulling her through the doorway that opened onto the sunlit Quay de l'Horloge. The quartet of guards was sprawled across the steps, sound asleep, half-full cups of wine tipping in their hands.

"There's no time to move them," St. Briac said tersely. "Climb in. We're away!"

Sébastien and Mignonne pulled the wagon. Earlier, they had played their parts to perfection, looking as lazily vacant as their driver, but now they took off at a gallop. Deftly, St.

Briac maneuvered the pair through the gathering crowds and the crush of vehicles.

He had planned to return to le Chien Rouge, but the sight of a heavy coach advancing toward them altered the situation drastically.

"It's Chauvergé," Gaspard shouted from his perch among the wine casks.

Teverant was hiding among them, and for an instant St. Briac thought it might be possible that Chauvergé would not recognize them. However, the sight of the weasellike chevalier leaning out and pointing while screaming wildly at his driver quickly dispelled those hopes.

"Damn!" St. Briac swore under his breath, and then turned the horses north, over the bridge to the Right Bank.

CHAPTER 34

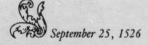 *September 25, 1526*

The Quay de l'Horloge was crowded with spectators eager to watch the condemned man being led to his death, and so Chauvergé's coach lost precious time turning around. As St. Briac urged his horses across the bridge, Gaspard cried, "Ha! There's a herd of swine blocking the other end of the bridge. We're safe!"

"I wouldn't count on that," St. Briac muttered. He guessed that Chauvergé would know where they were bound. Thus, rather than taking a roundabout route in the hope of losing him, he counted on their time advantage to see them through. "We must see to Honorine first. She may be hurt."

They lost all sight of their pursuer before reaching Chauvergé's auberge. St. Briac breathed a sigh of relief on spotting Honorine coming out of the doorway, leaning heavily against Pierre. His relief turned to alarm when he got a closer look. Her gown was torn and her hair bedraggled, and there was a dark, puffy bruise spreading over one side of her jaw.

"Honorine," shouted Aimée. "Here we are!" She began to get up, but her husband held her down. "Thomas, look at her. What's that monster done to my sister?"

"I fear we'll have to leave the questions for later, *miette*." St. Briac began to climb down, but Georges Teverant was already in the street, rushing forward to catch the swooning Honorine.

"There's room in back for her to lie down," he said quickly.

"I, I'm all right," protested Honorine. Although still dazed and aching, she could not help instinctively noticing the good looks of her gallant savior. "Are you Monsieur Teverant?"

"Don't try to speak, mademoiselle." With St. Briac's help, Georges carefully placed her in the back of the wagon and climbed up after her.

"You're safe," she whispered. "I'm so glad of that."

Time was short. St. Briac lost not a moment springing back up beside Aimée, who was craning her neck to check on her sister. Returning to le Chien Rouge was impossible, and so he steered the horses through the maze of Paris streets. Finally, they turned into a drive next to a tall, narrow house and found themselves outside some rather dilapidated stables.

"Gaspard," called St. Briac immediately. "Take this wagon and the horses and find another stable some distance away. We'll call for them before dawn. Chauvergé is certain to look for us here." He glanced toward Pierre. "Go with him and then return here separately. We'll see if we can't persuade my sister to provide some hot food and cool wine."

"*Mais oui, monsieur,*" Pierre cried eagerly, while Gaspard moved to obey just as quickly but with far less enthusiasm.

Nicole Joubert and her husband, Michel, lived with their daughter and baby son in a narrow wooden house four stories tall. Once the bottom floor had been a shop, with the merchant living above and the workmen occupying the higher floors. Now, although it was owned by just one family of greater wealth, the narrow front remained. It was a common problem in the walled city of Paris. Houses were extended in every possible direction: in upper stories and basements, in hanging rooms, in attics and recesses. Tiny staircases like ladders often linked these rooms.

Nicole's home conformed to this pattern, but she had made it charming, bright, and cozy. The first thing Aimée noticed when they came into the kitchen through the court-yard door was that flowers seemed to be everywhere. A tall, slim young woman with glossy sable curls swept up on her head was kneading dough at a *miex.* She wore a snowy-white apron over a plain rose-colored gown, and at the sound of their approach she turned to display an elegantly beautiful face smudged with flour.

"*Oh, mon Dieu*! Thomas, *mon cher!*" Her large blue eyes shifted to Teverant, and Nicole gasped. "Georges, I cannot believe this."

St. Briac stepped forward to embrace her and apologize for the intrusion. Then he led Aimée over to meet her sister-in-law. Greetings had to be kept brief, for he feared that Chauvergé might burst in at any moment. "We'll talk later, *chérie*, but for now you must hide us. Have you an appropriate nook or two that might accommodate us until after the chevalier has made his search?"

Nicole glanced from St. Briac and Aimée to Honorine and Teverant. Her eyes softened at the sight of her ardent suitor from years past, and she was heartened to see that he did not return her gaze. He'd stared for a moment, but now all his attention seemed to be concentrated on Aimée's pretty, trembling sister.

Michel had gone out to purchase a duck for their afternoon meal, and so they could avoid the awkwardness of that situation for the time being. Her husband and Georges had met just once before, on the night when Nicole had been forced to tell the smitten Teverant that she did not love him. She'd never regretted her choice, but there had been moments when marriage wore thin and she longingly remembered the reverent adoration Georges had displayed.

Nicole's four-year-old daughter, Thérèse, appeared and tugged at her mother's skirts. St. Briac came forward immediately to scoop up his niece, carrying her along as they climbed the stiflingly narrow spiral staircase that wound upward through the house. Nicole and Thomas talked on the way. He told her as much as he could in those few minutes, while behind them Teverant solicitously helped Honorine reach their hiding place. Aimée brought up the rear in case her sister might need her for any reason. She couldn't help staring at Georges Teverant, trying to read his expression, wondering what emotions stirred in his heart.

The young man declared that he would take care of Honorine, and so they were sent into a tiny recess on the third floor behind a half door under the stairway. Inside was a ladder that led down to a small room that projected over the street. Once they'd descended, St. Briac dragged trunks over to seal off the ladder and then closed and bolted the little door.

"I hope Chauvergé gets here before we all go mad closed up this way," he muttered.

Little golden-haired Thérèse went first as the remaining quartet climbed up to the large studio that occupied most of the fourth floor. Paints, canvases, and spattered rags were strewn everywhere. Light from enormous windows bathed the room.

"Pardon Michel's mess," Nicole apologized with a smile. "He's impossible."

A barely perceptible door was built into one of the paneled walls. Nicole found the groove that would open it and then led the way through a dark, cramped passageway that ran above the courtyard. It smelled of must, heat, and, Aimée thought, mouse droppings. At the other end was the attic. It was filled with boxes and trunks of all sizes plus various pieces of broken furniture, all piled helter-skelter.

"I would be very surprised if he can find the door that leads in here to begin with," Nicole observed, "but you probably should stack some things at this end of the passage just to be safe."

"Mille mercis, ma soeur." St. Briac smiled. He gave her a hug and lifted her off the ground for a moment. Nicole's delighted expression told Aimée that this was a very old ritual, dating back to their childhood.

"Will we have time to talk later?" Nicole wondered.

"Not very much. But we'll make plans for other visits. You must come home soon, you know."

Little Thérèse tugged at Aimée's skirt. "Can I stay with you, Tante Aimée?"

The child's immediate acceptance of her as part of the family brought tears to Aimée's eyes. "I wish you could, *chérie*, but I don't think so." She bent down and gathered her close all the same.

St. Briac spared her by playing the villain. "You'll have to wait to spend more time with Tante Aimée," he told Thérèse in a firm voice. "Now you must go with your mother."

Nicole smiled and dragged her daughter from the attic; then St. Briac set about stacking trunks and pieces of old furniture in front of the panel that led to the passageway. When he was done, he and Aimée pushed open a window and settled down in front of it to wait. St. Briac had removed his wig and jerkin upon entering the house, but he looked down at his shirt with distaste.

"I'd give anything for a bath," he remarked.

Smiling, she brushed the powder from his beard and leaned up for a long, slow kiss. "You look wonderful. Very heroic."

"Do I?" St. Briac grinned and pulled his wife onto his lap. For a moment, gazing at his beloved face that was the center of her world, Aimée was nearly overcome by emotion. His arms were hard yet warm about her; his blue-green eyes were filled with warmth and pride and the ever-present spark of humor. At moments like these she could scarcely believe she could be so fortunate as to be his wife. The thought of life without St. Briac was no longer bearable. Their hearts, souls, and bodies were one now. Together they had discovered the fulfillment each had yearned for alone.

"You were quite heroic yourself today, *miette,*" he told her in a low voice.

"You aren't sorry that I followed you to Paris?"

"What a question! If I say yes, you'll never obey me again." Lowering his head, he captured Aimée's mouth and kissed her deeply. His arms held her so tightly that she was breathless, yet she felt blissful as her husband spoke to her with his body. At length St. Briac traced her cheekbone with his lips and then whispered, "Of course I'm not sorry. Without your help, Teverant might not be free at this moment."

"Thank you for saying so," she murmured, feeling two hot tears slip from her eyes.

St. Briac knew why she was weeping. There were moments when he experienced the same urge, times when he asked himself what his life would be without Aimée. It was a thought too awful to bear. He looked back on his initial rejection of her with a mixture of amusement and horror. What if Aimée had believed him when he said he wanted to see her no more? Of course, such acceptance of him at his word was not in her character, thank God. St. Briac knew he could never control her, and that thought filled him with delight. Aimée was the most captivating woman alive.

He gently kissed away her tears, smiled, and said tenderly, "How precious you are to me, *miette.*"

The moment was right. "Thomas, I have something to tell you."

"Hmm." He'd begun to eye the lush curves of her breasts

displayed by the gaudy red gown. Even time locked in an attic might be pleasurable.

"Listen to me!" St. Briac's expression made her want to laugh. He was gazing at her, pretending to be contrite as a little boy. "I'm not joking now, Thomas."

"No? I suppose you have another plan to unveil. Oddly enough, I have one, too, but I can show it to you rather than waste time in conversation."

His long, tanned fingers caressed Aimée's throat and then slid downward. She nearly gave in and delayed her announcement again, but instinct insisted that this was the time. "We're going to have a baby."

St. Briac froze in the act of cupping her breast. He stared, straightened his back and blinked. "We're going to...*what*?"

"Have a baby," she repeated merrily, amused by his reaction. "It often happens when two people engage in love-making as often as we do."

He made a choking sound. "A baby!"

"Is the word unfamiliar to you?"

Putting a hand over his face, St. Briac peered at her around his tapered fingers. "No! That is, I just hadn't thought..." He closed his eyes and then opened them again. "When?"

"In early to mid-April, I would guess. Thomas, you are pleased, aren't you?"

"Of course I'm pleased! I'm just astonished! A baby!"

"You keep saying that."

"*Our* baby." He smiled at her now, and then he kissed her to communicate all the emotions he could not yet put into words. Aimée responded ardently, but St. Briac found his thoughts wandering from her news and warm body to the very subject Aimée had hoped would not occur to him.

"Wait a minute," he said suddenly, holding her away from him so that he could stare into her spring-green eyes. "What the devil is going on? If you are with child, why are you here in Paris? How could you have ridden so hard to catch me at Illiers in that condition? And today! When I think of the danger you were in today! I would never have allowed you to come to Paris, let alone—"

"I don't suppose you would believe me if I told you that I just learned about the child a few moments ago?"

"Absolutely not. I've heard you spin that tale about having visions before. Aimée, how could you do this? Why didn't you tell me? I could strangle you." Tendons stood out in his neck, but even as he raged at her, there was love in his voice.

"If I'd told you, I wouldn't be here now, and Georges Teverant might be on the block in the Place de la Grève even as we speak. I couldn't tell you until I knew for certain what all the subterfuge between you and Gaspard was about. I love you too much to stand by, stupidly obedient, if there's even a slight chance I can help."

"But what about the baby?"

"The baby is fine. I'll wager that he or she has been highly enjoying this entire escapade."

St. Briac put a hand to his head and shook it hopelessly. "I can't stand it. A man ought to at least be able to win arguments with his own wife."

Aimée burst out laughing and wrapped her arms about his broad shoulders. "How silly you are. Don't you know that I am so devoted to you that I would even act docile if I thought it would make you happy?"

A knock sounded at the door. "Thomas? Aimée? It's Nicole. The chevalier de Chauvergé has come and gone, so there's nothing to worry about now. You two must be ravenous. Come down for *déjeuner*."

St. Briac's turquoise eyes never left his wife's face as he replied, "*Merci, ma soeur*. We are ravenous, but it might be a few minutes before we join you downstairs."

Nicole's laughter was knowing. "*Eh bien*. Don't hurry."

CHAPTER 35

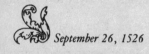 *September 26, 1526*

Stars still shone in a velvety black sky as St. Briac and Aimée prepared to leave Paris. They were finishing plates of eggs and apricot tarts in Nicole's candlelit kitchen, when Gaspard came in from the stables.

"The horses are ready, monseigneur," the manservant announced.

"And you?"

"I am always ready, as well you know. However, I do not like the idea of riding on without you and madame. I really do think—"

"Don't think."

"But, don't you worry that—"

"*Non*. I'm not worried about a thing." St. Briac laughed. "Just once, windbag, I would be grateful if you would obey my orders without an argument. Between you and my incorrigible wife, I shall lose my mind."

Aimée laughed and winked at Gaspard. "He'd be desolate without us, *n'est-ce pas?*"

The little man had to return her smile; it was irresistible. "I'm sure you're right, madame."

"Stop plotting against me, both of you," exclaimed St. Briac in mock horror. "I can see that I shall have to contrive to keep you apart in the future if I am ever to know any peace."

Leaning up to wrap an arm around her husband's neck, Aimée said teasingly, "Obviously you don't really want any peace, Thomas, since you chose Gaspard and me."

"Did I? Strangely enough, I've been under the impression that it was the other way around."

Everyone, including Nicole and her husband, laughed at this. Gaspard said his good-byes and went to fetch the Joubert carriage, which he would use to convey Honorine to Fontainebleau. For all his outspokenness, the little manservant never would have dreamed of disobeying any order given by St. Briac. For years he had trusted the younger man implicitly, even with his life, and had yet to fault his judgment.

"Finish your eggs, *miette*. We must be away soon as well." Thomas could not stop thinking about the fact that she was with child. Would it be safe for her to ride? During the night, he'd made her vow that she would tell him instantly if she experienced even a moment's discomfort. As it was, he was determined to keep their pace slow. Fontainebleau was not far. They would rest there with the court for a few days and then continue on to Chateau du Soleil by carriage.

"I wonder what's keeping Honorine?" Aimée said. "She won't have time to eat a bite."

At that moment her sister appeared, crisply immaculate as usual except for a soft lilac bruise on one side of her face. Only a step behind was Georges Teverant. He wore an expression that St. Briac and Aimée recognized instantly. The couple sat down on the long bench and smiled at each other.

"Georges has almost succeeded in persuading me to return to Brittany with him," Honorine announced.

"Oh, really?" Aimée replied carefully.

"I love your sister," Teverant exclaimed. "Since she has dreamed of visiting the royal court for so long, I agree that she should go, but I will find a way to come to her. I'll clear my name with the king somehow."

"Isn't this a little sudden?" Aimée murmured.

Honorine and Georges merely beamed in response; Aimée noticed how such ardent male attention made her sister glow. She would be showered with it at court, but it was always possible that Teverant, in his sincerity, might win out in the end.

St. Briac chuckled softly beside her. "This is not the time for romance. The sun will be rising soon and we must all be on our way before then. Come on. Time for *adieux*."

He and Aimée were to ride away before Teverant made his final escape. Pierre had served as a decoy in case Chauvergé might still be lurking about, and it was St. Briac's hope that by the time Teverant emerged from the stables, Chauvergé would be gone.

Kisses and hugs were exchanged all around. Tears flicked from Aimée's starry lashes as she embraced her lovely sister-in-law. Just a few weeks ago she had felt like an only child, and now it was as if she had two sisters. Everyone was very excited about the news that there would be a new St. Briac baby in the spring. Nicole, Michel, and their children already were making plans to travel west for the occasion.

Georges Teverant kissed Aimée and then turned to Thomas and unashamedly embraced his friend for a long moment. His voice full of emotion, he murmured, "I owe you my life, *mon ami*. If not for your courage, I would be dead."

"There was nothing else to be done." St. Briac smiled. "You are my friend."

Teverant took Honorine outside for their farewell. In minutes she and Gaspard started off toward Fontainebleau, and Georges waited astride his horse, also borrowed from the Jouberts. Finally, St. Briac was giving his wife a leg up onto Mignonne in the dark, chilly stables. Aimée shivered in her velvet doublet and then leaned forward to wrap her arms around her horse's neck and give her a good morning kiss. Sébastien, with St. Briac astride his powerful back, did a brief caracole to show off and then nudged at Aimée with his wet muzzle.

"Oh, for God's sake, grow up, Sébastien!" His master laughed softly. "You're as bad as Christophe."

The stallion whinnied and nodded in agreement and then nudged Aimée again until she giggled and reached out to stroke him. *"Bonjour, mon ange,"* she crooned.

"This is too much!" Shaking his head, St. Briac led the way into the courtyard. After a last wave to the waiting Teverant, they gained the street. Most of Paris was asleep at this hour; all was quiet. He'd hoped that Chauvergé would not have the patience to wait outside all day and night, and that appeared to be the case. They were alone as they cantered through the narrow lanes, across the Seine, and followed the twisting maze of passages that took them through the Left Bank to the gates of Paris.

Once they were outside the city's walls, Aimée's mood soared. The autumn air, though cold, was fresh and dewy as dawn approached. A sprinkling of stars like tiny diamonds still glittered overhead, but in the east the sky had begun to soften. It gradually changed from violet to mauve and then flushed hot pink and apricot as they galloped easily southward toward Fontainebleau. The road they traveled was the only paved thoroughfare in France. Known as the King's Highway, it connected Paris with Orleans via the hunting lodge at Fontainebleau. For a long time the land was flat, but still St. Briac brought Sébastien more than once near enough to reach out for Mignonne's bridle and slow her pace. Aimée would wrinkle her nose at him, but his ocean-crisp eyes told her that he would brook no rebellion. The baby was ever on St. Briac's mind. Too many chances had been taken already.

It was still early morning when they drew up outside a tidy-looking auberge in the hamlet of Barbizon, on the edge of the forest of Fontainebleau. Aimée protested that she was neither tired nor hungry, but St. Briac insisted on stopping. He lifted her down, turned the horses over to a groom to be watered, and joined Aimée at the entrance to the auberge, looking exceptionally pleased in a wicked sort of way.

"I'm certain that Chauvergé stopped here for the night," he whispered, devils dancing in his eyes. "I recognized his horse."

"We shouldn't go in, then."

"There's nothing he can do to us. I've a suspicion that he's bound for Fontainebleau to whine to the king about my part in Teverant's escape."

"Thomas!"

"Never fear, *miette*. I can deal with Chauvergé." He walked away in search of the innkeeper but threw her a rakish smile over one broad shoulder and added, "Starting now."

Aimée listened as her husband inquired about the chevalier. Yes, the man was here. He'd arrived late last night, past midnight, and was still asleep. St. Briac nodded at this news and then casually made arrangements with the innkeeper to make certain that Chauvergé was detained for an hour or two in some way that would cause him as much irritation as possible. He then led Aimée to a table near the fireplace and insisted that she drink a mug of hot mulled cider and eat some cheese and apple. All the while she glanced toward the stairway, panicked at the thought that Chauvergé might appear. When they left, St. Briac gave the innkeeper five *livres* more than he owed along with a knowing wink.

The sun was dazzling and golden overhead as they rode into the forest of Fontainebleau. Luminous beams of light slanted through the canopies of crimson, yellow, and orange leaves that fluttered in the breeze. It was a glorious day, cool and clear. To Aimée, the sky had never seemed bluer. She glanced over at St. Briac, who sat easily erect astride Sébastien as the horse trotted almost soundlessly over the carpet of leaves. Her heart skipped happily. How splendid a man was her husband! His chiseled profile was one that would warm the breast of any maiden, yet there was so much more to St. Briac's appeal than his handsome face and form. He exuded strength, wit, and a confidence that did not embrace vanity. All these were his effortlessly, as well as a seemingly charmed ability to make the best of any situation and emerge not only unscathed but smiling. No wonder Chauvergé hates him so, Aimée reflected.

"I am so very happy," she said aloud.

St. Briac glanced at her and smiled. "As am I, *miette*. I'm the most fortunate man alive."

When he nudged Sébastien with his knees and came alongside to reach for her hand and press it to his mouth, a wave of almost unbearable joy rushed over Aimée's body.

They rode on in silence, sharing a contentment that was all the richer because it did not need to be put into words. The forest was more beautiful than any Aimée had ever seen. Red stags that would soon turn gray for winter could be seen vaulting away from them, and a variety of birds sang and fluttered in the treetops.

When St. Briac spied the towers of Fontainebleau in the distance, he led the horses into a grove of yellow-leaved birch where Aimée could change from her boy's garb into a more appropriate gown. This was accomplished amid much laughter. Finally St. Briac made love to her tenderly in a soft bed of leaves. Aimée clung to him afterward, almost frightened by the force of her happiness.

"How can we go on this way forever?" she whispered, blinking back tears. "It's not possible!"

"Ah, *miette*, why indulge in such foolish worries when there is no reason?" Thomas bent to kiss her belly, now aware of its slight hardness, then her breasts, throat, and finally her eyes. "No doubt we will have moments that are less perfect than this, but one thing will never change as long as I live: my love for you. Never doubt that."

Aimée pulled him down and kissed him fervently, hungrily. They rolled to one side, and when she felt St. Briac hardening again, she pressed herself against him eagerly. His thigh hooked over Aimée's legs, holding her fast even as he drew his head away and smiled at her.

"We're both much too greedy. Let's finish this matter with François and Chauvergé and then indulge ourselves."

She made a moue and reached down toward his manhood, but St. Briac dodged gracefully. In the next instant he was pulling her to her feet, laughing. "Get dressed, Aimée. You would use me without mercy if I allowed it."

Pausing in the middle of donning her chemise, Aimée giggled. "You're a rogue."

"And you are a vixen. That's why we deal so well together."

St. Briac, helpless to resist her charm, took her in his arms and kissed her, but moments later he was helping her into her gown of soft peach velvet. He took the pins from Aimée's hair and combed it down into lustrous, swirling curls and then lifted her onto Mignonne's back before she could touch him again.

It was past eleven o'clock when they finally rode into the cobbled courtyard of Fontainebleau. The oval castle, with flanking towers and a square keep, had been constructed during the twelfth century. Aimée was struck immediately by its modest appearance, particularly compared with Chambord.

Pierre ran from the stables to meet them, informing them that Gaspard and Honorine had arrived safely more than an hour before. St. Briac was lifting Aimée down and turning over the horses to the boy when the king called out to them.

"Thomas, Aimée! How wonderful it is to see you." Garbed in dark red velvet and a jewel-encrusted jerkin of blue satin and fur, François strode toward them with an unidentified companion trailing behind. "Aimée, your beautiful sister is here. How thoughtful of you to bestow Honorine on the court since you have removed yourself from our touch." His eyes twinkled merrily. "Now tell me, my friends, how is married life?"

"Blissful," St. Briac informed him succinctly. He arched a thick, curving brow and smiled in a way that made Aimée blush.

"We're going to have a baby," she announced as she and the king embraced. "Sire, you are looking very well. We've missed you."

"Well, I'm glad to learn that you've found ways to pass the time in my absence," he said. After hugging his old friend, François gestured toward his guest. "Allow me to present Gilles le Breton, a master mason from Paris. We were just discussing the alterations and additions I have in mind for Fontainebleau. Picture this if you will." He swept out an arm. "Within a few short years, we will have a new entrance to the courtyard, a magnificent gallery that will run behind the keep, and two short blocks that will link the new entrance to the keep. I'd like a grand new courtyard as well and a huge *appartement des bains* where we will be able to bathe and sweat after a long day's hunting. Eventually there will be a ballroom, and I'm determined that the very best painters will be searched out and employed to create frescoes in the newest styles. I'll raid Italy of its finest talents."

"I'm speechless." St. Briac's tone was more than a little wry.

The king looked sharply at his friend, whose trim doublet of dull gold velvet reminded François of the restraint St. Briac tended to exercise in all material matters. "Is this indulgence on too grand a scale? I know you thought I'd lost my senses with Chambord."

St. Briac laughed fondly as the sun struck sparks on his dark chestnut hair. "Sire, I think that your plans for Fontainebleau are inspired."

"It's only that I want the best, the most glorious. Not for myself so much as for France."

"Future generations will thank you for that," Thomas assured him, and then asked that he and Aimée be excused so that they might wash away the dust from their travels before the midday meal. As they walked across the courtyard, he glanced back at François, who was gesturing animatedly to the awestruck Gilles le Breton. "So much for our monarch's *crise de foi.* His nature is too optimistic to let minor things like a lost battle and a year's imprisonment dampen his spirits for long. He may not be able to conquer Charles V at the moment, but he's discovered that there are other challenges to be met."

It was a wonderful feeling to be surrounded by the court again. Aimée hadn't realized how much she had missed all of them, especially Marguerite, and even her new friend Ghislaine Pepin. Happily flanked by St. Briac and a radiantly beautiful Honorine, she ate her *matelote de la Loire*, a fish stew crowded with eel and flavored with mushrooms, cream, and Vouvray wine.

Aimée had borrowed a gown and some jewels from Marguerite for her sister to wear, and Honorine, resplendent in sky-blue velvet, sapphires, and diamonds, was dazzling Bonnivet, who sat to her left. It was enough for Aimée to sense Honorine's happiness. She looked forward to all they now could share as sisters since each had found her niche. Aimée knew that Honorine needed to play for a while, to bask in the splendor of the court, but a part of her hoped that some day she would marry Teverant and discover a truer, more adult happiness.

Down the table, the king had just embarked on a long tale about the previous afternoon's hunt, when the doors flew open and a crazed-looking Chauvergé burst into the hall, followed by two harried guards.

"*Aha*," he shouted, pointing at St. Briac. "I knew it! I knew that this criminal would be brazen enough to appear at court. Guards! Arrest the seigneur de St. Briac immediately!"

The king held up his hand and said mildly, "*Pardonnez-moi*, chevalier, but if anyone is going to be arrested, it will be you. I have told you what fate would befall you if you dared to show your face at my court again. Aside from that, I am not charmed by such rude interruptions."

"Sire, you must hear me out. I would never have come if I did not bear news of the utmost urgency."

Louise de Savoy leaned over to place a hand on her son's arm. "Perhaps you should at least listen to what he has to say, *mon fils*. It may be important."

"Georges Teverant was rescued from his cell in the Conciergerie yesterday," Chauvergé announced. "The execution did not take place."

"I've already heard," François replied in a bored voice that was belied by the anger in his hazel eyes. "If that is all—"

"But it was your friend St. Briac who committed this act of treason. And he was aided by his wife. I saw them!"

The king laughed as though Chauvergé had made a particularly amusing joke. "St. Briac and Aimée? How silly. Everyone knows that Thomas cares nothing for the affairs of state. He'd be the last one to risk his neck for such a cause, and the thought of madame taking part in such a scheme is even more ridiculous. She is in a very delicate condition; her husband would not put her in such danger." He paused to sip his wine. "Before you begin ranting again, let me add that even if such slander were true, I would not be disposed to punish St. Briac. I never felt that Teverant deserved to die. If I could have shown mercy without giving the impression of weakness, I would have done so. I'm glad the man's been freed."

Louise gasped, the rest of the court stared, and Chauvergé looked as if he might be physically ill. Aimée felt a wild urge to laugh. St. Briac's mouth twitched as they held hands under the table.

"I've a feeling Teverant will be back at court after all," he whispered to his wife.

"Take this man away," François told the guards. "Perhaps some time in prison will teach him about mercy. I'll consider his fate at my leisure."

Later, Aimée was in the midst of peeling a plover's egg and laughing at one of St. Briac's witty remarks when he surprised her by suddenly lifting her onto his lap.

"Thomas, you forget yourself!" she pretended to scold.

"I think not, madame." Ignoring the affectionate glances of those around them, he pulled her close and kissed her soundly and sensuously. "One thing is certain; I can never forget you."

"You're certain that your eye won't wander when the next innocent virgin finds her way into François's court?" Aimée demanded, her green eyes dancing.

St. Briac reached for her left hand, which had stolen around his neck. "I had this ring made so that neither of us would forget." He bent his dark, handsome head and kissed the golden band. "*Tu et nul autre*. Forever, *miette!*"

ABOUT THE AUTHOR

Hailed by her loyal fans as the "successor to Kathleen Woodiwiss," author Cynthia Challed Wright wrote four bestselling historical romance novels before she turned thirty.

In the past 12 years, the Wright family, including husband Richard, a naval officer on a Trident submarine, and their ten-year-old daughter, Jenna, has moved 8 times. Still recuperating from yet another demanding cross-country move, the author confides that her work on the *sequel* to YOU, AND NO OTHER is progressing splendidly. "The peaceful environs of my new hilltop Washington home, designed with a custom built study and outfitted with skylights and word processor, are the perfect place to create," the author commented.

Ms. Wright loves to correspond with her faithful fans, and invites all interested readers to write to her care of her publisher.

One of the most beloved historical romance writers...

CYNTHIA WRIGHT

...casts her magic spell.